SHATTERING DREAMS

THE BEING OF DREAMS BOOK 1

CATHERINE M WALKER

ALSO BY CATHERINE M WALKER

Shattering Dreams

Path Of The Broken

Elder Born - Coming Soon

———————

Newsletter

If you'd like updates of my progress, promotions and advance notice of when the next book comes out drop by my website and join my newsletter.

You'll receive a copy of the character chart that I created while I was writing the Shattering Dreams and a few other extras as well.

Visit my website to get started!

Catherine M Walker

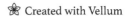

To Pam and John Walker (aka Mum & Dad) you always believed in me told me I could achieve anything. Thank you for teaching me that dreams are possible.

PROLOGUE

The small boy giggled gleefully as he ran scrambling over a fallen tree trunk, ducking around trees. Little legs pumping, he glanced back at the person pursuing him. She laughed too.

Mother had abandoned her traditional formality to play with him. Those moments were rare, and he cherished them.

He burst into the clearing, running toward a large boulder beside the stream. Hands grabbed him and hoisted him into the air as his mother caught up to him, holding him close, spinning him around.

He wrapped his arms about Mother's neck as she climbed the sloping rock at the edge of the river. They sat on a large boulder overlooking the stream, the dense forest continuing on the distant bank, comfortable with each other's company. Near to where they sat, Mother's people set up rugs and cushions, laying out food and drink in the centre with two places. As the servants stood back to admire their work from a discreet distance, Mother took his hand and they moved to the rug and pillows. The ever-present servants walked forward showing one dish at a time, pulling covers off once he and his mother had settled on the blanket.

He smiled, seeing his favourites set before him: a mug of water, nutty bread with tangy cheese (which he had only enjoyed eating when he realised it was his mother's favourite) and a mixture of berries he loved. Lessons on etiquette from his nanny running through his brain, he looked at his mother with contained impatience as she laughed and took a small bite out of her sandwich. His mother taking that first morsel signalled that he could start his meal. The boy grabbed his food using both hands, not wanting his cheese to fall off onto the ground as it had last time they'd gone on an excursion. Nanny warned him if he wanted to eat with his mother and father along with his brother and sister in the big hall, Mother had to see him showing his best manners—proving he was a grownup.

He took a mouthful, taking a moment to enjoy the taste he was familiar with, grinning at his mother after he'd swallowed. Mother liked it too, he could tell. Mirroring her moves, spilling nothing, he placed his bread on the plate; grabbing his mug, he gulped the water it held. With equal care, he settled the mug on the picnic blanket then smiled, thanking the servant who filled up his cup.

His meal progressed in much the same fashion, sitting there in quiet companionship with his mother, mirroring everything she did. He caught her smile of approval as he managed his whole lunch, spilling none of it, although he missed the amused glances of the servants and guards.

His mother rose, signalling the end of their meal, holding her hand out to him as he stood, helping him to his feet. She laughed again as they picked their course off the rock, careful not to lose their footing, across the clearing and toward the horses. He knew what that indicated. It meant their day out was ending. Still, he didn't voice his disappointment. For Mother to trust him outside of the nursery more, his tutors had advised him he needed to show he could behave.

A faint whistling noise followed by a pained grunt drew his attention and he looked over toward the sound. A guard fell to the ground, his half-drawn blade slipping from the sheath. He lay in a crumpled heap. Another guard, unmoving, slumped over as if he was sleeping; he had never, in the times he'd been out with his mother, seen any of the guards do that. Bewildered, the boy spun around, wide-eyed as more of the escort fell.

His mother's gasp caused him to look back up. He stumbled as she thrust him backwards.

"Run, hide ..."

She stopped, frozen for a moment. The boy recognised fear on her face as a tall, dark figure loomed over her. Her head wrenched to one side, then he saw a large hunting blade slice across her throat. The man screamed and shoved his mother aside. She crumpled, reminding him of his sister's rag dolls— dropped, left broken and forgotten by her attackers on the ground.

The boy remembered his lessons; he'd overheard guards talking often enough, knew they watched out for them. He knew, even though this was the first time he'd seen one, that the dark, looming figure was one of the Sundered.

He struggled as strong hands picked him up and he heard the cruel laughter of his captor. "Foolish child. Do you think you can escape me? You'll join your mother before long."

Then the figure stopped and looked at him, before throwing his head back. A harsh bark of laughter erupted from him. The boy fell to the ground as the Sundered dropped him.

"Live for now, boy. You'll join our ranks soon enough, brother."

The Sundered faded from sight, causing the boy to wonder if the monster had even been there. The boy realised he was alone in the glade with the fallen. His lips trembled as he scrambled over to his mother. Grabbing her shoulder, he shook her, trying to get her to wake, not understanding why she didn't. As darkness fell, he looked around. He sobbed, muffling the sound by pressing the fabric of his vest against his mouth in case the Sundered came back. Curled near his mother's side, not knowing what else to do, he finally fell asleep.

He woke to the noise of horses and bright, glaring light, in the strong arms of a man he recognised as one his father's guards. He clung to the guard, not willing to let go.

"It's ok, Alex. We'll take you home," the guard choked.

Guards slipped a blanket over his mother's unmoving form and the boy saw, with shock, a tear trail from the eye of the normally impassive guard.

1

REBELLION

A lex smiled. Outwardly, he appeared relaxed, accepting the compliments and praise, basking in the adoration of his peers. He swallowed the last of his wine, not even noticing as a hovering servant refilled his glass. Alex let his eyes roam over the ballroom, settling for a moment on the dais where the King sat on his throne, presiding over the proceedings attended by William, playing the dutiful Crown Prince.

Prince William looked in his direction and frowned, as he did whenever he looked away from his conversation with the King long enough to peer at him. Alex raised his glass to the perfect one in the court, the noble Prince—the King's favourite child— and drank the contents of his glass, laughing as William sighed and turned away.

Alex let his eyes rake over his contemporaries, the younger sons and daughters of the court's high lords and ladies as they fought for a position near him. He smiled bitterly and wondered if the sycophants would still try to gain his favour if they knew one of his father's closest guarded secrets. That if he'd been born to a typical family instead of a ruling family, it would have seen him killed at birth or as soon as the healers confirmed he bore the Taint. Alex laughed, his presence a ticking time bomb in the court, surrounded by the Elite in the Realm, waiting for the moment his father's guards deemed it prudent to end his life. Still, that possibility was a future concern.

Alex wished not for the first time that he lived in that long ago era where, so legend had it, being able to wield the power of the veil wasn't a bad thing. Those with the power where highly regarded and valued. Thinking of the folklore regarding the use of the veil in those days nearly made him laugh. Vaunted fighters, augmenting their strength and normal abilities, able to travel great distances, being able to control the very elements ... immortals. Until his Great Uncle Edward's day. Something had started going wrong. Those with access to the veil had started turning, going mad and killing people. Ordinary people who couldn't defend themselves, events that begun the Sundered War.

Alex caught himself before he slipped and rolled his eyes, drawn out of his introspection. He noticed Lord Minor Rathan Cartwright trying to insinuate himself into the group surrounding Lady Jessalan. Rathan was an irritating little Lordling who kept trying to gain not only his attention, but that of his friends. The only one who didn't realise he didn't have a chance was Rathan himself.

Alex caught Jess's eye. *You've got incoming.*

It was times like this being Tainted was handy. He may not be immortal or be able to control the elements but he could communicate with others who bore the Taint—Lady Jessalan Elena Barraclough was one of them. She was one of his closest friends, even though she was the daughter of a low-ranking lord who attained his rank due to the King's favour rather than through hereditary lines. She came to the Royal Court as a small girl, placed in the care of her Aunt and Uncle. Her Aunt had been a beauty in her time; she even overcame the challenge of her low birth to marry the second most powerful lord in the Realm.

They had been firm friends since childhood. Jess had grown up, and was now regarded as one of the most desired and beautiful ladies of the court. Her blonde hair was held in an intricate design by combs and pins, with a trail of hair running down one side as if it had wilfully escaped its bindings. With pale skin, startling green eyes and a slim waist, Jess appeared to be, on the surface, almost delicate.

Appearances can deceive. Alex knew she was athletic and an incredible swordsman. Well-known as one of the best hunters in the court and comfortable not only in wielding blades, but knives, bows—any weapon that came to hand. Jess rode with the royal party in the Royal Hunt, and when Elizabeth, William's twin, ventured from the palace, Jess was always in her entourage. Unknown to anyone else, Jess was one of the last forms of defence should anyone try to harm the Princess. The only reason most lords of their set let her be—other than light courting—was her association with Alex and Kyle. That is, other than Rathan, who had been trying to gain her attention of late, it seemed.

He chuckled as Jess rolled her eyes, her voice replying in kind in his mind. *Oh, save me. Is anyone in this court more irritating?*

Oh, I don't know. His sister, Janice, is right up there. Kyle's exasperated mind-voice filtered across to them both.

Alex glanced across at his friend, Lord Kyle Xavier Strafford who looked as if he was devoting his entire attention to Lady Minor Janice Cartwright. As the son of the most influential and the richest lord in the Realm, Kyle was a favourite amongst the ladies of the court. Just as their fathers had been from childhood, Alex and Kyle had been friends from the nursery, since they were often thrown together while their fathers talked matters of state. Kyle had a well-earned reputation as a ladies' man. Rumour had it he had been working his way through the ladies of the court—young and old—since he'd reached his majority. Kyle was tall with an athletic build, with black hair, olive skin and deep brown eyes that almost seemed black depending on his mood.

He was also one of the best swordsmen in the Realm, having been trained by the best since he'd been old enough to hold a sword. Most of the courtiers were unaware of that. Still, some were catching on. They had been giving him a clear path; if they thought he was ill-tempered.

Shall we stage an exit from this party? I'm bored anyway.

Alex smiled, receiving their replies, and excused himself from the group surrounding him. He made his way across the ballroom toward Jessalan with a trail of people following behind.

Alex's eyes scanned the ballroom as he walked, his eyes narrowing as he caught sight of Lady Amelia, Kyle's sister, her smile fixed as she deflected the attentions of one of the lords in her circle of admirers. Alex diverted, making his way across the crowded room to join her circle. Amelia's lips parted in a smile when she saw him and Alex took her hand and brushed his lips in a light kiss on her fingers.

"Amelia, you look lovely tonight."

Alex kept his eyes firmly on hers but knew that others in the court had tracked his movement and were watching the byplay avidly. He also knew that the King had noticed and had halted his conversation with Lord Strafford, Amelia's father. The minor lord that Amelia had discouraged paled, realising he had made a mistake.

Amelia blushed, glancing down before looking back up into his eyes. "Thank you, Alex."

"I trust there won't be any trouble tonight?" Alex let his eyes track across the men surrounding Amelia.

The miscreant that Amelia had pushed aside paled and took a step back subconsciously, trying to put some distance between him and Alex. Alex smiled at the hasty denials from all the men, realising that his hand had strayed to his sword hilt. Then, pulling Amelia closer, he kissed her on her forehead in a brotherly fashion.

"Have a good evening, Amelia. If you need anything, approach the guard; I'm sure they will be happy to help." Alex's eyes flicked up to the nearby guardsman on duty who nodded discreetly before transferring his attention to the Lordling, who by this stage looked like he was about to faint.

"I'll withdraw, with your permission My Lady?" Alex gave a half bow, grinning at Amelia impudently as he backed up; she laughed and flipped her hands at him.

With one final glare toward the men surrounding Amelia, he turned and made his way across the crowded ballroom, which magically cleared in front of him as he walked toward Jessalan. He moved through the group surrounding Jess; they moved aside good-naturedly as soon as they realised it was him. Slipping in next to Jess, he slid his arm around her waist. He kissed her on the cheek and in one practised motion he slipped his empty glass to a passing servant. Alex laughed outright as Jess placed her hand on the back of his head and pulled him closer to kiss him on the lips.

Come on, let's get out of here. There must be a party more entertaining than this courtroom somewhere in this kingdom!

Alex wrapped one arm around Lady Jessalan's slender waist, throwing his other arm around the shoulders of Kyle, who had divested himself of his followers and arrived at Alex's other side.

CATHERINE M WALKER

Alex dragged them toward the doors, oblivious to the obvious consternation of the courtiers in the ballroom, since the King had not left the hall yet.

Kyle exchanged glances with Jessalan, who sighed as Alex turned and hauled them both toward the doors. Kyle risked a glance over his shoulder toward the dais, catching the discreet nod from the Crowned Prince just as they exited the ballroom.

Alex knew that behind the scenes there was mad scrambling—runners heading off to alert guards they were on the move, looking likely to leave the palace. He threw back his head and laughed, knowing the mandatory entourage would swear and run to get ready. They hated it when he ran off and much preferred advance notice so they could get ready to go with him in a more orderly manner. Alex, however, much preferred to leave the guards behind. There were times when the press of people became stifling. He and his friends had much more fun relaxing away from the ever-prying eyes of the assorted lords, ladies, guards and servants, away from the stifling confines of the palace.

Still, despite the suddenness of his decision to leave, the palace servants would scramble, their horses saddled, waiting in the courtyard with attentive grooms holding them. Palace servants were, by now, well used to his ways. He wouldn't be surprised if they saddled his and his friends' horses every night, just in case. He hadn't been left standing impatiently on the stairs in the minor courtyard of the Royal Palace waiting for his horse for quite some time.

The three of them sped up their pace. Jess, hiking up her skirts, kept pace until they reached the large double doors to the courtyard. Alex always marvelled at how Jess' servants managed the transformation; somehow, they swarmed around her, taking her to a small room off the side of the hallway. He didn't know the room's original purpose, but now it was a small private dressing room. Alex and Kyle continued out the doors that swung open ahead of them and their own servants appeared with cloaks and blades. Both of them divested of their court weapons, their ceremonial vests peeled off them and replaced with vests that were, while still well-made and expensive, far more suitable for the night's entertainment—it would take trained eyes to spot them.

They continued down into the courtyard with a barely noticeable pause to change. Alex traded glances with Kyle, laughing. He'd been right. The servants had brought their saddled mounts out to the courtyard ahead of them. Both swung up onto their mounts with a practised ease, then turned as, only moments after, Jess came running down the stairs. Taking them two at a time, no longer attired in her gown and expensive jewellery, she wore attire much like their own, more suited to leaving the palace. Without pause, Jess mounted with an ease that spoke of someone well used to riding.

Seeing they were all ready, Alex laughed, spurring his horse into a gallop across the small courtyard. The guards on duty at the main gate to the palace complex struggled with the doors, only getting them open at the last minute. He shared glances with Kyle and Jessalan riding on either side of him and, in a manner that spoke of long association, the three of them guided their horses off the main road. They rode to one side, down a narrow path through the forest that was a shortcut into town, the guards left behind, cursing, still trying to mount in the courtyard.

Familiar with the small winding trail (they had ridden this path too many times to count), Alex slowed down as they approached the small gate that would allow them to gain access from the Royal Forest into the town. Alex smiled as the guards on the gate jumped up from their position resting against a nearby tree to sprint to the gate, staring in their direction as they cleared the tree line. Alex looked to Kyle and gestured with his head toward the gate and guards.

Kyle spurred his horse forward. Without comment, he threw back the hood to his cloak as he approached the guards and, when close enough, spoke calmly.

"Open the gates."

Alex didn't even bother to slow down the pace of his mount as he approached the gate. He saw the junior guardsman's eyes widen as he recognised Kyle. He and his fellow guard hauled the chains to open the portal to the outskirts of the town. Alex chuckled. Kyle had a growing reputation, well known not only to the lords and ladies of the court but also the guards.

As they passed through the gates, Alex, Kyle and Jess slowed their horses to a walk. The gates closed behind them with a soft thump. Alex grinned. The portal had been well kept since the first time they had used it—on that occasion, creaks and groans from the gate could be heard halfway across the residential section of town, announcing to all that a member of the court had passed from the palace grounds to the city proper.

Alex noted that Kyle drew the hood of his cloak up to obscure his face again and, without thought, spurred his horse up to a ground-devouring trot. They made their way through the town, drawing little attention as people went about their business without pause. The group moved from the more wealthy sections of town and crossed through the areas belonging to the middle class. Here was the domain of the tradesmen, merchants and stall owners—all of them still at work, plying their trades. Alex smiled and relaxed, the bustle of people going about their daily lives obscuring their movement through the streets effectively.

Slowing his horse to a walk, Alex led them down a side alley that opened out into a series of gated yards and stables. Alex slid from his horse as Kyle took the lead once more, passing coins to the stable keeper, who was eyeing off their mounts with an appreciative eye.

"We'll be back later to pick them up." Kyle passed his horse's reins to the man, commenting in a dry tone, "I expect them to still be here."

That provoked laughter from the portly stable keeper. "My Lord. I wouldn't dream of selling off your horses. I have a funny feeling you'd take it personally, which would be detrimental to my health." The man turned and bellowed toward the scruffy boy filling up a trough with water.

"Eddie, get your lazy rear end over here and help bed down these horses."

Alex passed over his reins without comment, noting that Jess had done the same. He turned and led them from the stockyards, down winding alleys, toward the rougher parts of the old town. During the day, it was sleepy and almost deserted. At night, as the markets and businesses closed, the old town moved from sluggishness, waking up to heave with activity. Strains of music filtered to the streets, flowing from bars with lights burning brightly from their windows.

The pleasure houses were open for business. Lower-end houses had their men and women out the front, calling out to the people passing, inviting them to come in and spend a night of pleasure with them. Unlike the lower-end houses, the better places were discreet. They didn't need to put their people out the front; their patronage knew where to find them and knew they were open for business—the lights burning from the front parlour of their premises gave that away.

It looked like a wild night already, with patrons stumbling from bars, or some being thrown out. One unlucky drunk came out of a bar and stumbled into Jess. She pushed him and, drawing her dagger, hit him on the side of the head. The man, who by the state of him had probably been drinking all day, slumped to the ground, unconscious, as Jess looked down at him disdainfully and stepped over his unmoving form.

She smiled. "Looks like a fun night."

All three of them laughed as they approached one of their favourite haunts—a three-storey establishment, a wooden sign hung just above the double doors with a frothing tankard burned into it, the image and plain script above proclaiming it *The Tankard*. It was a bustling bar on the lower floor, with rooms for hire above. Not that any of them stayed here. At least, not if they could help it. Alex pushed the doors open and the three of them walked inside.

2

THE KILLIAM ORDER'S RECRUIT

S cholar Clements stood looking out the windows over the serene mountains. The sprawling old fort and village, protected by stone walls that surrounded Yalleska, had stood undefeated for hundreds of years. This fort and village were the stronghold of the Killiam Order, which had been granted autonomy from the Crown generations ago.

A scream of pain rang through the citadel. At the anguished pleading, a cold smile spread across the Scholar's lips. It was always a pleasure when they had a victory over the monsters. The knowledge they gained, the endemic perversion of the healer ranks, caused great concern amongst the Order. Learning that the filth hiding in the healer ranks could be controlled with the medication gave them renewed hope.

If they survived under the medication's influence, they used their healer's gifts to gain a mental hold of their own kind. It had been a long laborious process of trial and error. In the early days, when they first discovered the medication, they thought they would win. Most of the monsters they dosed died, yet a few survived. Those that did, with mental manipulation from the healers, were being used to build a fighting force to use against the darkness. For the first time since the Order came into inception, they might just be on the brink of winning this war. How better to fight against the monsters than to pit their own kind against them?

He didn't have long to wait—once the pleading started they never lasted long. He grinned as the door opened behind him.

"So, how is our latest recruit going?"

"You heard, I take it?"

There wasn't a hint of emotion in Kevin's voice or expression; he'd been one of their first success stories.

Clements nodded, his satisfaction evident. "She's finally taking the medication willingly?"

"Yes. She is young and not resistant to the drug at all. As I predicted, she is an ideal candidate to enter the program." Kevin smiled. "Even though she is a little older than we prefer to start treatment, she doesn't possess the will to resist."

Clements turned his head to look at Kevin as he stood next to him, looking out the large windows. Kevin had come to him, to the Order, almost fifteen years earlier, a broken man. A healer, he'd returned to his home after his rounds in the village, only to discover his young family dead. They were lying on the ground in the backyard to his small property. Broken, discarded, slaughtered by a monster. Kevin knew about the Killiam Order, revealing, after he turned to them, that the healers had been keeping track of their presence. It was Kevin who had admitted that the healing order had been protecting and hiding the monsters in society, that many healers used the Taint. He'd been their first success story, helping them to distil and perfect the medication.

Clements had felt no need at all to mention that the monster that had killed Kevin's family had been one of the Order's failed experiments.

"Will she be ready for her task?"

He saw a smile spread on the face of the man who, against all odds, had become his friend. "She will be; she is skilled and her target will be drawn to her. With my guidance, she will be powerful enough to control his mind."

Scholar Clements laughed, clapping Kevin on the back. "Well done. I wish we had the time to instruct and train her properly. But we cannot wait, with these targets. We need to take them soon. Our friends will hopefully have achieved the first stage of the task before we get there."

The two men lapsed into silence, watching the sun set across the mountains. The sky was lit with orange and a baleful deep red, with shadows casting darkness as the sun sank. The screams and cries of agony from the medication cells beyond were oddly soothing.

3

A NIGHT AT THE TANKARD

lex laughed as the serving maid slipped from his grasp, winding her way through the crowded tavern back toward the bar.

Kyle's eyes flicked up to the door and tracked someone as they entered, causing Alex to smile. Without looking, he recognised from that brief look and the fact that his friend had relaxed that the guards had caught up with them. He shook his head. Their keepers should realise if the three of them meant to lose them, they certainly would not have come to The Tankard for their night of entertainment. Since this was one of their favourite haunts, their guards always checked here first.

Alex raised his goblet in silent salute and caught his friends' eyes. *Tainted we might be, but let's live this life while we have it.*

Hearing the musicians strike up his favourite song, Alex grinned. A mischievous expression on his face, he looked at Kyle and Jess and threw back the rest of his drink. He saw more than heard them groan. They knew what that meant before they followed suit. Alex stood and, catching sight of a familiar figure to one side of the bar, groaned himself.

What the hell is he doing here? Jess, watch out, your paramour has tracked us down.

Alex snorted as Jess looked up and spotted Rathan Cartwright standing awkwardly at the bar. If looks could kill, Lord Minor would be dead.

The idiot didn't even change out of his court clothes. As much as I like this place, we should find a new establishment for our night's entertainment if that fool can track us here.

Jess looked up as a serving maid refilled her goblet. She held up her hand to ask the maid to wait and threw back the contents before holding it out once more. Another benefit of being Tainted —they could wash away the sometimes-negative effects of alcohol if they chose to, negating the hangover regular people often suffered from. Still, tonight it seemed they were all determined to feel the after effects. At least, for now. The morning might be a different story entirely.

I'll speak to the guard. If they must follow us everywhere, they can be useful and dissuade unwanted attention. Alex's lips quirked in a half smile. *I'm sure his Royal Highness, Prince William, would be most displeased if he found out you have a stalker who goes to these lengths.*

Alex grinned at Jess, then turned and made his way through the packed bar toward the small island of space before the musicians. A blonde attached herself to him and before too much longer was joined by a redhead and a brunette. Alex threw back his head and laughed, moving rhythmically with the women in time to the music. The blonde ran her palm up his chest, biting her lip she looked down, feigning shyness before grinning and raising a bottle to his mouth.

He raised one hand, pushing the wine away, and turned to the redhead, who was demanding his attention most directly. He kissed her, causing the blonde to pout, drawing her busy hands away from his pants and up to his chest. He almost groaned as the brunette started in, then Kyle was there, peeling the brunette from him. At some stage, amidst the jostling, the bottle of wine the blonde had been trying to get him to drink smashed on the floor. The woman looked down, appearing way more upset than she should be over a smashed bottle of wine.

"Come on Alex, you can't show the proper attention to all three lovely ladies!" Kyle looked down at the smashed bottle of wine on the ground and winced. "Sorry, here, it's okay have this one, I appropriated it from a table on the way."

Kyle clamped his mouth on the brunette's, sliding his tongue through her parted lips. He pulled her away, thrusting a bottle of wine he'd swiped off a table into Alex's empty hand.

Alex glimpsed several unhappy looking men at the edge of the dance floor with their knuckles going white from gripping their belt knives. He dismissed the men, turning to the ladies as he saw familiar guards moving across the bar toward them. They would sort the men out.

Alex tossed his head back, laughing, and took a long swallow from the bottle of wine before returning his attention to the serving maid, pulling her into his body, not noticing as yet another of his female companions was dragged off him by Kyle.

Alex didn't care. His world had narrowed, and revolved entirely around him and the blonde serving maid.

J ess laughed, watching Kyle and Alex on the dance floor, and contemplated joining them. She glanced around the bar; there were several likely candidates that she felt she could persuade to get up and dance with her. That, or she could throw a pretend tantrum and haul the women off Alex and Kyle. The thought amused her for a moment, then she discarded it. They were determined to forget the world existed—she didn't want to spoil their fun. Scanning the room once more, she noticed that Lord Rathan Cartwright had stood up from his seat at the bar. He stood, tugging at his tunic, before walking in her direction, his intent clear.

"Oh, hell no." Jess muttered under her breath.

Jess stood, determined to head toward the dance floor. Creating a scene was more desirable than being stuck with Rathan. When she turned, she found herself face to face with the brightest blue eyes she had ever seen.

"I'd be honoured if you'd have a drink with me." He held a drink out to her.

Jess couldn't help but smile back and, nodding her thanks, accepted the goblet. "Why, thank you. Care to take a seat? I don't imagine my friends will need one for some time." Jess nodded toward the dance floor, where both Alex and Kyle remained otherwise entertained.

"I noticed they look distracted at the moment, so I thought it couldn't hurt, seeing if I could tempt you. I'm Damien." Damien grinned at her and held out his hand.

Jess hesitated for a moment then held out her hand. Damien grasped it and kissed her on the fingers, a simple act which caused Jess to blush. She sat back down at the table, breathing a sigh of relief as she saw Rathan. He stood, frozen, halfway between the bar and her, his confusion obvious. Briefly catching her eye, he retreated to his corner in the bar.

"Nice to meet you, Damien. Thanks for the drink. I'm Jess." She added, "It's not common for someone to behave like a gentleman here." Jess probed for information, suspecting that Damien was not a commoner, although she didn't recognise him at all.

Damien laughed and nodded his head, conceding that she made a point.

"The Royal Court begins the progress to the Summer Palace soon. Everyone who is anyone is here, so accommodation options are limited. I'm not sure I am anyone important, but I can hunt well. That many court-bound aristocrats riding together in one group, they need fresh food along the way—or, at the very least, we need to make sure the Royal Family don't get stinted. The rest can look after themselves." Damien grinned at her as she laughed.

"Ah, so you work for a living, unlike the self-entitled idiots who clutter the court with egos bigger than they are."

Jess took a sip of her wine and raised her eyebrow at her companion. She glanced at the goblet, swirling the deep red liquid in the glass as she closed her eyes and breathed in the aroma of the wine. She took another sip and decided the wine was as good as the company. He'd obviously splurged on one of the better quality wines The Tankard offered, rather than just the house wine. Still, the family that ran the establishment owned several bars in Vallantia and Callenhain, the location of the Summer Palace, a few of them catering to the more well-to-do clientele, as well as others, like this one, for the working class.

"Their egos find people like me useful during this time of the

CATHERINE M WALKER

year and for the hunts that follow, that is about it." Damien
shrugged, grinning to show he wasn't concerned at all. "Tell me,
what do you think of the wine, Jess?"

"The wine is excellent, I don't believe I've drunk it before. Which
one is it?"

Jess took another sip, savouring the flavour; it was more than
good. Jess was certain her companion didn't realise it was strange
she hadn't encountered it before, given that she lived in the
palace and mixed with the Royal Family.

"A small shipment came from the Heights. There is a delegation
visiting at the moment—they brought trade samples with them.
This was one of them. The owners have an agreement with them.
I'm surprised they are stocking it here though." Damien nodded
toward the bar absently, savouring the last of the wine.

Jess grinned. Seeing that he'd finished his, she swallowed the last
mouthful of her own wine. She stood, grabbed his hand and
hauled him toward the dance floor, winding through the tables,
pushing aside patrons who laughed as the pair made their way
past.

Damien laughed along with her and gathered her in his arms to
dance. Jess decided there were worse ways to spend her night.

Jess groaned, pulling a pillow over her head, trying to drown
out the insistent pounding at the door. Growling
inarticulately, she pulled the pillow off her head, knowing
they wouldn't go away. She also knew that if she didn't answer
shortly they would come in, regardless. She looked at Damien,
who suddenly woke up due to the pounding on the door, and sat

24

bolt upright. Before she could stop him, he'd rolled out of the bed stark naked, grabbing his long hunting knife and turning toward the door as it opened.

"No, Damien don't ..."

Jess groaned, sinking back onto the bed, one hand over her eyes as the guards entered the room. Damien was disarmed and taken to the ground as even more guards entered, cluttering the small room.

"My Lady? Is everything alright?"

"Yes, Megan, I'm fine, or I was until you all barged in here. Please let Damien up, he's not a threat. Damien calm down, I'm sorry, they won't hurt you."

Jess hauled herself out of the bed dragging the sheets with her since she didn't have any more clothes on than Damien did—not that it bothered her much, having grown up living in the palace, surrounded by and tended to by servants. She guessed from experience that Damien, like any other man, would be more likely to calm down if she wasn't standing there naked in front of men he perceived as a threat.

"Damien, calm down and they will let you up."

Her face impassive, Megan picked up Jess's shirt and handed it to her, then moved to shield her from the view of the male guards, although they were all studiously not looking at her. Jess smiled and thanked the guard despite herself. Pulling the shirt on, she then reached for her pants, passing the sheet to Damien, who was finally standing, under the watchful eye of the guards.

Jess looked at Megan and frowned. "I suppose it is useless asking you guys to wait outside?"

"Sorry, My Lady, he had a weapon."

Jess noticed that Megan didn't look at all sorry. Still, she couldn't be angry; the guard was only doing her job and if anything happened to her while the guards had their backs turned it would likely cost them their job.

"In case you hadn't noticed, so do I." Jess shook her head, knowing the futility of arguing with any of them.

She ran her hand though her hair, which wasn't tied up in its usual braid or a sophisticated pile on her head held in place with an assortment of pins and combs. Left to its own devices, her hair was thick and fell halfway down her back. She pushed it back in annoyance as she crossed the short distance between her and Damien.

Jess paused, her eyes narrowing as the guards tried to put themselves between her and Damien. "Move. Now. If Damien intended any harm, then he's had plenty of opportunity to do it." Jess tried to suppress her irritation and flicked her gaze across to Megan, knowing she was the senior ranking guard among them.

"Megan, you can stay in the room, but don't test my patience."

Megan looked at the other guards and jerked her head toward the door. One of them opened his mouth, intending to protest, but closed it again without a word, filing out the door as Megan's gaze turned deadly. The guard then moved her position—not so incidentally—giving her a straight line to Damien if she needed it. Jess noticed that the positioning wasn't lost on Damien, who seemed to be trying to regain some of his usual humour.

"Mad husband?" Damien smiled a little and shook his head.

Jess bit her lip and closed the distance between them. She raised one hand and ran her fingers down his cheek, pulling him down to kiss him on the lips.

"Not quite. I'm sorry, it's a little complicated. They've come to drag my friends back, I'm nobody important but from the point of view of the guards, it's a package deal."

Hearing a snort of laughter that was quickly suppressed behind her, Jess turned to glance at Megan, her eyebrow raised.

"Sorry, My Lady."

Unfortunately, the guard didn't look all at that sorry.

Jess sighed and turned back to Damien. Pulling his head down, she kissed him. "Thank you for an enjoyable night, Damien, I'm sure we will run into each other again."

Jess backed away, a little reluctant for the night to be over, then turned and walked out the door, sighing again as she walked into the hallway. She grinned, seeing both Alex and Kyle leaning against the wall at the end of the hallway near the stairs.

"Well, at least father can't complain about the guard hauling us out of one of the pleasure houses this time." Alex grinned at them all and trotted down the stairs, with Kyle and Jess following.

Kyle chuckled. "I'm not sure he'll find the upper rooms here at The Tankard much better."

Jess followed them across the deserted common room of the bar to the door being held open for them by a sleepy looking barkeep.

"Thanks." Jess smiled as he nodded acknowledgement and let them out on the street.

It wasn't the first time the guard had hauled the three of them out of the establishment in the early hours of the morning. Seeing their horses waiting for them in the cobbled street outside the bar, held by more guardsmen, she shared a grin with Alex and Kyle. At least the guards were useful for something. Mounting their horses, they walked them through the empty streets of the early dawn back toward the palace.

4

THE SUNDERED, KIN AND ELDER

Alex's last conscious thought as he merged between the waking world and blissful sleep was a jumble of confusion. He half hoped that he would sleep the night through this time, as he'd heard others did regularly. The other part of him hoped that he would return to his other self, the self that was competent and capable of being the hero he wished he would be. He slipped into a deep, restless sleep.

Alex groaned, trying to ignore the constant shaking and pretend he was still asleep. Unfortunately, the person doing the constant shaking had other ideas.

"Come on, boy. Get your lazy carcass out of bed."

The voice was familiar. A curious mix of refinement that spoke volumes, as if the speaker was brought up in the King's Court— yet there was an unusual roughness, as if the owner of the voice had known tough times. Alex groaned again. He was familiar with that voice.

"Great Uncle, please. I need to sleep just this once. Please?" Alex was astounded by the hint of pleading in his voice.

He cracked open one eye and looked up at his great uncle—not the rotting corpse he knew his great uncle must be by now, but the dashing figure from the family portrait. The later one, after he'd made his name and saved the Kingdom. Not the earlier, callow youth he'd been before the war had struck. Alex had seen that portrait too, even though he was never meant to. It had been hidden away in the attic, but he'd found it anyway. That picture revealed way too much about what his great uncle's peers had thought of him.

"I'm sorry, son. I wish I could let you sleep, but you don't have time." Great Uncle Edward Rathadon smiled slightly. "Get up. It's time to train."

Alex groaned again and hauled himself out of bed. His eyes swept across the empty bottle of wine on the floor, and he spared a moment to glare at his uncle. He wondered, not for the first time, why his great uncle was favouring him and not either of his brothers, who were much more capable for the task at hand, or his sister. When it came down to it, even Elizabeth was stronger. Then he snorted. He needed to wake up. His siblings didn't possess as much of the Taint as he did.

"So you keep saying, Uncle. Yet the world I live in does not change. I am still the useless fourth child: I stagger from one drunken party to another and get dragged out of some of the most disreputable establishments. The other half of my time I spend waiting to see if I'm going to go mad and kill everyone." Alex heard the bitterness in his own voice. The self-pity.

Alex hauled himself out of bed, noting that while he felt exhausted, he felt it draining away as he pulled in power, almost automatically, to wash away his fatigue. If he had to name one of the positives of being Tainted, one was certainly that he did not have to suffer through the hangover he knew he should have after the night's depravity and excess.

"Ok, Uncle. I'm sorry. I'll stop whining now. It's been months since you've paid a visit."

Alex caught a perplexed look flash across his uncle's face and smiled. Not expecting an answer, he looked around and saw his boots, flung off to the side of the room, right where he knew Kyle had left them. From what he remembered of the night before, he was in no state to take off his boots when he collapsed into bed, let alone fling them across the room. While it was hard for the three of them to get drunk, dedicated practise had made it possible. They had learned it was a matter of volume. Picking up his boots, he pulled them on, then walked to his weapons rack, arming himself before turning back to Edward.

"So, Uncle, what do you have prepared for tonight?"

Alex smiled and followed his uncle, the cold assaulting him as he merged between this world and the next—that place that all Tainted who were strong enough could access. A part of the real world, yet not a part of it; and time, as far as he could work out, moved differently. His sessions under his uncle's tender mercies seemed to go on for way longer than he was away from his bed.

Feeling the power vibrate and swirl around him, he knew another approached. Grinning, he turned and watched as Kyle appeared, walking toward them with Lady Leanna Katrina Shaddin, another figure from legend who, like his uncle, was reduced to so much dust in her tomb. He'd stopped asking exactly what they were now since they all routinely avoided answering.

My Lady, it's nice to see you again. Alex nodded to her. While she was always polite to him, she had a fierce legend surrounding her exploits.

Ah, always polite, Alex, it's refreshing. Kat grinned at him and nodded a greeting to his uncle.

They weren't waiting too long before Jess joined them with the taciturn Lord Callum Barraclough—yet another figure of legend; although, unlike his uncle and Kat, Lord Barraclough had retreated back out to his remote country estate not long after the end of the war. It was said he became a hermit, withdrawing from the court and society, dying on his county estate. Still, given they could all travel around readily using the veiled paths, where they actually resided had less meaning than most people today figured.

Now that we're all here, let's go. Edward tilted his head to one side, as if listening to something. *There is something you must all see and understand. You will not engage. That is not why I am taking you to see this.* Edward turned his gaze to each of them in turn until they nodded compliance.

Alex, Jess and Kyle traded glances as they followed Edward down the veiled paths. Before too long, they stood looking out from the veil toward a small farm house. He felt the strong surge of the Taint and the madness of one overwhelmed by the power. Alex felt himself restrained by his uncle as he automatically lunged to help those in trouble.

No, Alex, it's too late, just watch and learn. Alex glared at his uncle, but subsided and watched the scene unfold at the small remote farmhouse.

———

Smoke rose in plumbs from the farmhouse, a red glow coming from inside as it burned. Three bodies were still visible in the fading light, lying broken on the ground in the yard —telling all who might come by later on that whatever tragedy occurred was not an accident.

Devon Connor stood at the forest edge looking back at the

farmhouse he had called home his entire life, at the dead bodies of his mother, father and sister. He was calm, dispassionate, despite the horror in front of him, that even a week ago would have horrified and sickened him. Then the dispassion faded. Confusion came; the overwhelming pain Devon realised he should feel, yet somehow multiplied, worse. Devon threw back his head and screamed his pain out into the void—that place with the whispering voices, the voices that made him think for the longest time he was going mad.

In a small part of his brain, right back in its depths, he realised he was mad from the Taint, even though he'd tried his best to hide and push down. The treatments he'd been given by the healer hadn't worked. Overwhelmed by the emotions that ran through him, as if he could no longer tolerate them the way he used to, power surged through him which he didn't understand how to control, causing more pain. Causing inexplicable things to occur that he had no explanation for—except that even if he didn't understand how he'd done it, he knew that he had. The world around him would fade in and out; he would end up in places that he hadn't even known existed, with no notion of how he'd got there. Then home again, just as inexplicably. He'd suffered from blackouts, with time gone. Blood on his hands with only flashes of memory, which suggested he'd killed people he didn't recognise.

Confused, in pain, Devon retreated into the forest, leaving behind the only family he'd ever known. The family he had once loved. He had killed his family in agony, in a rage-filled frenzy. He didn't even comprehend why—just that, from the flashes of memory that came back to him and the evidence of blood on his hands, clothes and hunting knife, he had slaughtered them all.

Devon perceived the Taint surge through him. The fatigue disappeared, as it always did, and he picked up his pace, running through the forest. He didn't know where he was running to, except that it was toward the place where the whispering voices seemed stronger, toward the throb of energy that seemed like his own; it called him, leading him, like a beacon, toward his goal. He paused briefly, turning, sensing another like him nearby, watching. Devon dismissed them. Whoever it was wasn't a threat or of any interest to him right now. He turned and continued back on his path.

As he moved unerringly toward his goal, driven, he killed anyone he encountered. They were humans, so killing them appeased an ugly part of him. It fed the anger that bubbled inside and never truly went away.

A lex sensed the other's power, his pain and rage. He knew that the newly Sundered one's name was Devon, Devon Conner. He'd been the child of a farmer who bore the Taint as they all did, until today, when the Taint had consumed him.

Alex saw what was once a man cut down the three members of his own family before setting the farmhouse alight. He'd paused and looked in their direction. Alex realised that Devon sensed their presence, yet after what seemed only a moment, Devon dismissed them and continued on his way.

Uncle, I could have helped that family. They might still be alive if you'd let me intervene. Alex tried to push against his uncle's restraint, to no avail.

While Edward might be a shade from the past, he was still stronger than Alex was right now, or perhaps just had more knowledge of the Taint and how to use it. As Alex's anger drained, to be replaced by futility and loss, he felt the pressure which had kept him at bay release him.

Alex closed his eyes, the fragmented memory of the slaughter of his mother playing over in his mind. He took a shuddering breath and pushed the memory of that childhood trauma aside. Alex emerged from the Veiled World followed by Jess and Kyle, who looked just as shaken, and walked toward the bodies sprawled on the ground, cut to pieces moments before.

"No, Alex, you couldn't have. He was killing them as we arrived, they were already dead."

Kat's voice was soft, and he felt her hand on his shoulder. His uncle and Cal stood not far away, looking over the destruction at the small remote farm with haunted looks in their eyes. Alex understood they all would have seen such things and worse during the Sundered War.

Kyle paused his pacing around the small farmyard, closing his eyes and taking a deep breath. "He knew we were here. He sensed us. Why didn't he try to kill us?"

Cal's mood was grim, assessing him before answering. "The Sundered are not truly mad—well, some of them are; they die early on, killed off by their kind—but they sense others with the Taint, even from the first moment they are born into their new life."

Jess contemplated what Cal told them and, as the implication sunk in, she looked, horrified, from Alex to Kyle, then back to the slaughtered family. She shook her head in disbelief and took an inadvertent step back. She looked around at the dead people and the burning house.

"Will we become like him? Will I do this, Uncle?" Jess heard the catch in her voice but, for once, didn't care. She was genuinely horrified by what she'd seen.

"Not necessarily like him, Jess, but you are in transition; you grow stronger in your powers every day that goes by. You have nothing to fear—Edward, Kat and I all went through transition. I doubt that you will break entirely and become one of the Sundered." Cal's tone was calm and even.

Alex watched as Jess shook her head, not comprehending what she was being told—or rather, trying not to understand it.

"It is a carefully guarded and kept secret in this day and age. All of us had access to the power of the veiled world and, as with our people, we went through the transition, although not as that poor man did. We were just as capable of killing everyone around us. We found another target, though. Some of our kin were trying to destroy the human world, or so we thought. While you've been told details of the Sundered War, there is much of it you do not understand."

Jess turned and took a few steps away, her face in her hands as she fought off tears.

"I don't understand, Uncle. I don't want to understand." Even as she said the words, she realised it was a lie. Unfortunately, she knew and believed every word her uncle had uttered.

Alex continued to walk toward the butchered bodies on the ground; while he did not doubt they were dead, he felt compelled to check on them before they left, a part of his mind noticing that Jess and Kyle were doing the same.

Jess traded a worried glance with Kyle. Alex had withdrawn and barely said a word since the incident at the farm. He walked along a grey pathway of the veil on automatic, lost in his own world. She knew he was thinking of his mother—seeing the slaughtered family would have reminded him of the circumstances of her death, she was sure of it.

Jess saw a flicker of anger on Kyle's face as he turned his gaze from Alex to their mentors.

So was there a point to all this? Trust me when I tell you we are all very aware that we could end up being overwhelmed by the Taint, our minds breaking under the onslaught and going mad.

Kyle stopped, frowning. Then, grabbing Alex's shoulder, he transitioned them both back to the real world. Jess felt her eyes widen. She glanced at her uncle, Kat and Edward, then shrugged and followed Kyle. Following his path with her mind, she could see the faintly glowing trail they had taken, with Kyle's signature all over it. She didn't quite know how to explain it but they all left different patterns in the veil as they manipulated it to their will.

Jess walked from the mist, making her way down a cobbled street a few paces behind Kyle and Alex. Glancing around, she didn't recognise where they were. It was a small village, likely on one of the trade routes since the village, although small, still had a bar. Pulling up her hood in a move that mirrored Kyle's, she watched Alex do the same, with a little prompting, as they walked into a bar, *Trail's Rest*.

Taking only a moment to assess the dim interior of the bar, she wasn't surprised to see a few people inside—traders breaking their fast early before heading out onto the road to continue their journey. Places like this were open late, only to reopen early to cater to those who lived much of their lives on the road. After a brief pause, Jess followed Kyle to the back of the room, where he took a corner booth. Before long, two serving boys deposited standard morning fare on their table: steaming bowls of oats, mugs of coffee, bread, cheese and some mixed berries. She slid onto the bench, picked up her mug and sipped the steaming contents. She didn't have to wait long. Edward, Kat and Cal walked into the establishment and took their place in the booth opposite them.

"We didn't show you that to upset you all."

Cal was the first to speak, looking troubled, and traded glances with both Kat and Edward. He sighed and, catching the eye of the serving boy, indicated that they wanted three more servings. The breakfast platters were delivered with such promptness that Jess gathered they were already set up in the kitchen.

Cal paused and turned to look at her, his expression bland and unreadable. He waited until the serving boys left before he spoke, his voice calm, unconcerned, but with obvious censure.

"Tell me what you know of the Sundered ones."

Jess's eyes widened at the request, and she looked up from her coffee to glance at her uncle, who revealed nothing to her. His face was carefully guarded against giving away what he was thinking. It was unusual for anyone today to talk about the Sundered, although she knew that in her uncle's day it had been a common topic. She had no doubt he knew much more than she did. How could he not? He had been one of the pivotal people involved in the Sundered War.

Still, Jess considered his question, then spoke, her voice low. "They are spawned from those who have too much of the veil running through them—or Taint, as people call it today." Jess licked her lips nervously; this was not a topic she liked considering all that much.

Kyle took over.

"Healers say when a person controls too much of the Taint, it drives that person to madness. The madness consumes them, and they break, becoming the Sundered. They feel no common bonds with anyone around them. They kill—without thought or compassion—anyone or anything in their path." Kyle's voice was low so as not to carry to the surrounding tables. "You, Prince Edward and Lord Callum led the then-Kingsmen against the hordes of Sundered who had descended on the Realm, killing them all and saving the Realm."

Jess saw Edward nod as he contemplated their words. He smiled. "In a way that is correct, although those with the veil running through their blood were not considered the Tainted in our day. All humans who can manipulate the veil, like us, go through a transition period." Edward paused, trading a glance with Cal and Kat. "As they come into their power, some of those unfortunate souls' minds break; they descend into madness and become what you know as the Sundered. Not all those with power were killed off in the Sundered War—many of them weren't even Sundered. Some were bad, not mad. They still continue to exist. Not all Sundered are what you think them to be. You are not what you think you are."

Edward paused, but Jess could tell that he was not finished, there was more information he wanted to pass onto them. He was letting them process what he had already said.

Jess took a deep breath and asked the next question she knew he was waiting for. "What do you mean? What are the Sundered? What are we?"

"Tell me what you know of the Kin and the Elder." She felt more than saw Kat's smile.

Jess almost laughed, both from surprise at the question and because it was standard for Cal, Kat and Edward to answer a question with a probing question to see what they already knew. Trading incredulous looks with Kyle, she answered as best she could, trying to take the question seriously.

"Ancient beings of power, never to be crossed. Depending on which legends you follow, they are unpredictable—pranksters, powerful. They could just as easily take your life as save it." Jess glanced at her uncle but could get nothing from his expression, so she continued, knowing she would not get any more information from him or the others until she had finished answering. "Some legends state that the Kin were the offspring of a liaison between the Elder and a human, so half-breeds. Some even say this is where the Taint has come from in family lines. Kin blood corrupting the human blood, which isn't capable of handling the Taint, turning those with the power into the Sundered."

The silence stretched between them for such a long time that Jess became uncomfortable. She gathered her thoughts, about to say more, when Kat responded.

"The Elder are real; they have been real for a long time—longer, perhaps, than any but the Elder know. They have great power in this world. Some humans who can access the Taint, as you call it, who survive transition, become the Kin. The Kin, if they survive long enough, are powerful enough to become the Elder. The Sundered, Kin, the Elder—they are the same people."

Jess felt her mind spinning in disbelief as she listened to everything their three mentors passed onto them. The Taint, Kin, Elder—all real, all linked—yet she struggled to believe them. She'd known about the Taint; how could she not, since she bore it and the risk of becoming one of the Sundered? She'd heard stories about the Kin and the Elder when she was a little girl. Those folks out in the villages away from the Royal Court were a superstitious lot and held to the old beliefs.

Her introspection was shattered by Alex's harsh bark of laughter.

"Seriously? That is the fable you are all spinning? We're all going to become mad, kill everyone around us, but it's okay because somehow we'll turn into the fabled Elder?"

Alex laughed again, shook his head and stood, heading toward the door without saying another word. Jess watched as Kyle stood to follow Alex, throwing money on the bar from his belt pouch for their unfinished breakfast before heading out.

Jess shook her head and stood. "I'm not sure I believe you, although I don't know why you'd make it up. I'll speak with them when we are all a little calmer. Stuff like the slaughter of a family always unsettles Alex; you should know that by now." Jess then turned and followed in the wake of her friends, knowing without having to think about it that they were heading back to their beds at the palace. All of them had had enough for the night.

———

E d sighed, watching the three leave the bar, and shook his head as he felt the surge of them entering the veil. He didn't have to follow their power trail long to know they were returning to the palace. Done for the night. He looked across the table at his lifelong friends and companions.

"I'm not sure how we could have gotten our message across to them better, yet I know we should have been able to."

"They have grown up in a different world to the one we knew, Ed." Cal shook his head, looking troubled.

"Until they come into their powers fully it will be hard for them to understand."

Ed looked at Kat and had to concede the point—both hers and Cal's. In their day, those with power had been commonplace. However, where there was great power there was also corruption and betrayal. Ed stirred and shook his head.

"We need to keep a closer eye on them. Alex commented that it had been six months since he'd seen me." Ed smiled depreciatingly. "I hadn't realised that much time had passed."

Kat's eyes widened as she looked at them. "No, surely it hasn't been that long?"

"What is time to us?" Cal's eyebrow disappeared in his hairline as he laughed at his shocked friends, who finally began to laugh with him.

"You have a point. Should we come clean and tell them everything?"

"Ed, we just tried that. They didn't believe us." Kat shook her head and looked at Cal for support.

"They won't believe us until they transition. They can barely sense the power right now, let alone control it. We wait. Wait until they transition, until they can wield their powers better and sense the world around them." A frown creased Cal's forehead.

Ed softly groaned. "I don't like this. So much could go wrong, like us thinking a couple of days has passed where in their world it's been a year."

Kat's mouth firmed, her eyes narrowing. "We'll just have to be more conscientious. We used to understand how humans accounted time."

Ed couldn't help himself; he laughed at her consternation.

———

Alex collapsed onto his bed, one hand reaching for the sheets before he lapsed back down into an exhausted, restless slumber, plagued by nightmares. Seeing his mother's death repeatedly, the harsh voice of her killer calling him a brother and letting him live. It was a nightmare he'd had since he was a child.

Edward appeared in the room, less substantial than during the training sessions now that Alex was asleep. He looked down at Alex, a tear welling in his eyes.

"I'm sorry, my nephew. I wish I could spare you the pain. You must learn control or you will become what you fear."

Edward sighed and dissipated, his job for the night done.

5

A PLOT CONTINUES

Lord Creswell Vannen stepped out of his carriage, looking around the courtyard of the palace before walking up the stairs and into the large sprawling complex, paying no attention to any of the surrounding servants. He could hear his own people rushing after him and smiled. They needed to learn to keep up and anticipate his movements. It wasn't like this one should be a surprise.

Lord Vannen spoke, knowing his manservant was at his shoulder.

"You've arranged for the room as I requested? I don't have time to mess around."

"Yes, My Lord, it's your usual day room while you are here at the palace—it's not far My Lord." Mark scuttled up closer and took the lead. "This way, My Lord." Mark swallowed, knowing having to use day rooms when he came to the palace always irritated the Lord.

Lord Vannen sighed and followed the otherwise competent servant. He'd been pushing for permanent rooms here at the palace for years now, yet somehow the answer was always the same. There were none available. Still, he knew this meeting wouldn't take long.

He had time to settle in a chair in the dayroom before his guest arrived. Lord Vannen frowned as the man, Baine, stepped into his day room with a cursory glance around.

"I wasn't expecting you. I understood your master would come." Lord Vannen was irritated and let it show in his tone. He couldn't abide dealing with underlings, particularly those who believed they were better than they were.

Baine sneered at him. "My master has better things to occupy his time right now. It's a risk, me even being here. What do you want, Lord Vannen?"

Lord Vannen's back stiffened at the tone Baine used, outraged. "Your master may outrank me but you don't, Baine. You forget yourself."

Lord Vannen cringed back, his eyes widening as Baine stepped forward, his body language menacing.

"Neither I nor My Lord care what you think. I repeat: what do you want, Vannen?"

Lord Vannen swallowed. He noticed that Baine had dropped his title but thought better of mentioning it.

"Your master didn't make the last meeting of the Order. I wanted to advise him that everything is in place again. My girls and boys have been briefed; we worked out what went wrong, the poison was salvaged. We need the Prince and his friends to show up again." Lord Vannen licked his lips and glanced around the room. "Perhaps your master can help with that?"

Baine closed his eyes and muttered a curse. "We realise everything is set up Vannen—I helped set it up. I also know the plan has been reset. Just be ready; it won't be long now, we can't force it, otherwise it might draw attention to my master."

Lord Vannen swallowed once more and wished he had a glass of wine to dampen his dry throat.

"You must appreciate that we can't allow Sundered filth to live, even if they have parents with high birth. It's our duty to remedy this."

Baine shook his head. "My master well knows of this Vannen, his aims align with your precious Killiam Order, for now. Do not make the mistake of coming here again and trying to summon my master. It will mean your death and that of your Order—take word back to them. Now, get out of the palace before you draw more attention than you already have with this foolishness."

With that, Baine spun around and left the room without a backward glance at the now sweating Lord Vannen.

6

THE STRAFFORD'S DANCE

Kyle observed his opponent. James was good, excellent in fact, as he would expect from a member of the King's Elite. Kyle grinned hearing his opponents breath starting to labour from the exertion of their bout, his response starting to lag as Kyle lunged forcing James to retreat, as he hastily blocked the blade. Kyle grinned as sweat trailed down the side of James' face, the guard ignored it slowing to take a deep breath before trading a flurry of blows back at Kyle. He blocked James' efforts easily, yet slowed his own response enough to let James think he was gaining the advantage.

Kyle retreated a few steps, drawing James forward. James fought with one blade while Kyle fought with two blades. It was his preference—one blade long, the other short, both crafted for him by the master bladesman when he was first declared a blade master. They bore his family crest and that of a master. Kyle had not only received training from the best blade masters his whole life, he had trained in the veiled world with Kat, learning the assassin's skills. He had also traded blows with Edward and even hunted with Cal occasionally.

None of them had disclosed to the King that they even trained in the veiled world, let alone that they trained with their long-dead ancestors; it was confusing, even to them. The legend surrounding the Fourth and his Companions was just that: a legend. They all knew it, yet somehow parts of it were true.

Kyle parried his opponent's blade before raising his short blade to the man's throat, freezing as a quick halt was called by the weapons master. He felt the cool wash of the veil flow away as he stepped back.

His opponent stepped back too, shaking his head. "This is a good, if somewhat humiliating, practice for me My Lord, but I'm uncertain how much good it's doing you." James shook his head; despite his words, he had an amused look on his face.

Kyle laughed. "Oh, come on, James. You beat His Highness from one end of the practice ring to the other." He nodded toward Alex, who'd been watching from the sidelines. "I can't let you win every bout today or let His Highness's honour go unavenged now, can I?"

"That's not quite accurate Kyle," Alex almost spluttered in indignation as Kyle laughed.

Kyle thanked James and walked over to Alex, slumping on the bench next to him and slapping him on the back. He noted the dark circles under his friend's eyes, which gave away how little actual sleep Alex had had the night before.

"Bad night?" Kyle squeezed Alex's shoulder.

Alex never talked about his nightmares, yet both Kyle and Jess knew very well that he had them. Particularly at this time of year, as it drew closer to the anniversary of his mother's death. The first time they had all ended up in that place where the Taint dwells, Alex hadn't been sleeping well. Out of frustration, they had begun to re-enact what they'd done in the practice ring that day. This continued for a while. At first, it was just an escape from the palace and the pressure of always being watched because of the Taint. Then their trainers had made an appearance. They had all been astounded, but decided that their nightly excursions and contact with their new trainers was best kept to themselves. His eyes wandered across the practice yard to Jessalan, who sparred with a thin, wiry man. Although her style and sword were much different to his own or Kyle's, she was no less deadly.

"You did all right, Alex. In any other training arena you'd shine, I'm sure!" Kyle's grin broadened as Alex threw him a filthy look and Marcus, lurking nearby, choked back a laugh at their banter. Alex was an expert swordsman and everyone here knew it, even if those within the palace doubted his ability.

Kyle let his gaze slide around the training ring, watching the other practice bouts. Everyone training here excelled, as you'd expect from the King's Guard; however, it wasn't a fair example for his friend since he was only half joking. This private training ground was the inner training ring for the elite of the King's Guard, the ones who guarded the life of the King and his family. Kyle grimaced as he noticed that the man training opposite Jessalan was holding back and the Lady in question had noticed. He could feel her anger building, even if no one else could.

"Excuse me, My Prince. I think I should rescue the poor unfortunate sparring with Jessalan before she forgets it's only practise and skewers him!"

Pushing himself off the bench, Kyle drew his swords in a smooth, practised manner as he walked across the ring, noting that they were both wearing protective gear. Kyle was only remotely aware that others in the training ring had broken off their session and turned to watch as a heightened awareness of the veil washed over him.

Kyle flicked his glance over to the weapons master, then, at his nod, launched himself into the fight in a blur of motion. The wiry little man, whom Kyle didn't recognise, stumbled back. Not expecting the assault from a second attacker, he lost his feet and fell to the ground. Jessalan recovered quicker and launched her attack against Kyle with a grin. Kyle parried her first attack and smiled as he heard the weapons master bellow at the poor unfortunate he'd knocked out of the way.

"Get your lazy arse off the ground and get back into the fight." Weapons Master Gareth glared at his latest recruit, the poor unfortunate Matthew Webb, as he fumbled for his blade, almost wailing. Gareth tried not to laugh.

"But Weapons Master, h-he has no protective armour and she— well she's a lady." Matthew gulped, looking back at the deadly whirling blades of the unexpected attacker.

Gareth walked forward and leaned over Webb, glowering.

"Matthew, that's alright; you are wearing protective armour, we'll patch you up if you're lucky enough to survive. Get back in there. Now!" Gareth bellowed and tried not to laugh as the boy who would shine against any other opponent except him scrambled for his weapon before launching himself at Kyle.

Gareth winced as Kyle shunted Lady Jessalan aside and, in a blur of blades, landed one blow after another onto the boy. As Lady Jessalan rallied herself and launched back into the fight, Marcus stepped forward from his customary place at Alex's shoulder, sword in hand. Receiving a nod from Prince Alex, he drew his sword and gained the weapons master's attention.

"Let's try to even this up, shall we?"

Marcus grinned at Gareth and took a moment to assess the fight. While he could see that Jessalan and Kyle were enjoying their exchange, it was clear that Kyle's demeanour changed every time he crossed blades with Matthew. Seeing that all other bouts in the arena had now ceased, Marcus rolled his shoulders, raised his sword and launched into his assault on Kyle.

Kyle could hear the whispering, unescapable voices through the veil. Although, at first, he struggled to resist their pull, he found himself drawn. Power submerged him—thrummed and pulsed through him—neither here nor there, lost. Except for the fight, his world had slowed down around him as he dealt with the assault on three fronts. The veil enhanced his natural abilities, making him stronger, faster, and heightening his perception of the movement and threat he faced.

One was easy: the boy. Oh, he was good, he knew it. Just not as good as he thought. At least not yet.

Then there was Jessalan. She was good, brilliant even. If she hadn't been born a Lady of the Realm, she would have made the King's Guard, even the Elite in her right, and been numbered as one of the best of them.

As for Marcus, the last to join their little training exercise, he was the best in the King's Elite.

Everyone always wondered why Marcus was assigned to Alex and not the King. Everyone except Kyle, that was. Marcus believed, against all the odds, in the Legend of the Fourth. Alex was the Fourth Son; as a result, Marcus was his. Heart, blood and soul, he belonged to the Companions of the Fourth.

Marcus was also one of the Tainted, just like them, although he didn't wield as much of the power as they did. Even if no one else recognised it yet, Kyle did. He could feel and see the veil swirling, not only around himself, but around Jessalan, Marcus and the boy.

P rincess Elizabeth stood high in the palace looking down
onto the training grounds below, wincing as the new boy
was again sprawled on the floor of the ring, stunned after a brief
exchange with Kyle. She bit her lip, watching, as the remaining
three continued their fight in the training ring: Jessalan, Marcus
and Kyle.

She would know the figure that launched into the fight below
anywhere with his dark hair and athletic build she knew well.
Elizabeth bit her lip, not even trying to hide the grin. He was tall,
broad shouldered and had a back many ladies would scratch
each other's eyes out over. That and his dark smouldering eyes
and... Elizabeth cut off her train of thought with a breathy
chuckle as she realised she was mentally stripping him of his
customary black fighting leathers that fit him like a glove. Kyle,
his sword a blur of motion, his second blade appearing in his off
hand as he whirled and battled on three fronts. A master
swordsman doing what he did best.

She broke her gaze, turning away from the scene below, and
spoke to Daniel, who stood next to her.

"He's excellent with a blade, always has been, but when did he
become this good with a sword?"

Daniel glanced at her before flicking his attention back to the
fight below. "Don't know. He always seems to improve in leaps
and bounds; it's Jessalan who is amazing me. It has been a while
since I've seen her fight, but while she's not in Kyle's league, she's
definitely good." Daniel winced as Kyle's attack made her
stumble. "If I didn't think he'd skewer me in the attempt I'd cross
blades with Kyle myself for that."

Elizabeth turned her attention back to the training grounds

below. One of the few women present in the private training ground, Jessalan's small petite form was easy to spot. Plastered down the side of her face, a strand of her blonde hair had escaped the practical braid she had her long thick hair restrained in. A smile graced her lips as she parried a series of strikes from Kyle, her focus not wavering from her opponent. Her skill and confidence with the long thin blade she wielded was obvious to see.

Right now, Jess wore long pants, utilitarian black boots, a brown leather vest over a green shirt with leather vambraces on her forearms and a sword belt at her waist that was obviously her own. Elizabeth couldn't help the smile. She knew the eminently capable swordswoman below would be transformed tonight, her hair piled up in an intricate design, impeccably dressed for court. The Lady Jessalan would, as always, captivate the eye of every male in the court. Including her own brothers.

Elizabeth laughed, "Please don't. You irritate me, but I'd rather not lose a brother. If he didn't swat you away, Jessalan would for interfering with her fight. Or did you miss why Kyle jumped into the fight in the first place?"

Daniel shook his head, and they both fell into a comfortable silence watching the fight below. Elizabeth gazed at Daniel out of the corner of her eye for a moment before speaking up.

"Did William talk with you about Kyle and Alex?" Elizabeth slid her eyes back down to the practice yard.

"You mean about Kyle and speculation of him being the Shadow?" Daniel snorted, his disdain clear. "The expectation on Alex of all three of them to be what they're not because of that damn legend? Alex just needs to grow up before he gets someone killed."

Elizabeth frowned at Daniel. "You are too hard on him Daniel.

Alex has been through a lot, more than he ever should have had to."

Daniel grimaced. "We all lost Mother, Elizabeth—not just Alex. You don't see me being dragged out of the most disreputable establishments in the Kingdom regularly."

Elizabeth sighed, having had this argument with Daniel before. Her eyes tracked across to Alex where he sat on the sidelines, intently watching the fight. Alex had fought earlier and was obviously in his element right now. He was never this relaxed in court. Not that anyone who didn't know him would pick up that he was the youngest son of the King right now.

He was wearing a set of his nondescript fighting leathers, similar to those worn by Kyle. Alex leaned against the wall with one of his booted feet on the bench next to him, one arm resting on his knee. Alex pushed his hair out of his eyes, turning to the man next to him and obviously made an observation about the fight as both men laughed. Although she was too far away to see them, Elizabeth knew that Alex's eyes were a startling deep blue and his chocolate brown hair, although much shorter, was a mirror of her own. Alex wasn't as well built as Kyle but she could see why the ladies of the court favoured him. Alex, like William, would draw the attention of ladies far and wide, even if he wasn't the King's son.

"Yes, we all lost Mother, but the rest of us didn't watch her, the guards and servants get slaughtered. We don't have nightmares to this day about it. None of us bear enough of the Taint to cause an issue." Elizabeth's eyes flicked from the scene below to Daniel's set face momentarily before moving back to track the action below. "We don't have to contend with that damn legend. The bond between all three of them is clear. It always has been, because of the burden they all share. If nothing else, at least they have each other. I wish Alex could stay our irresponsible, party-boy brother, live his life free of the Taint." Elizabeth heard the sadness in her voice at the last observation, watching her little brother down below.

Daniel frowned at his sister; his expression hardened. "I don't know why you all insist on ignoring that our dear brother and his friends are dangerous. They will break—all of their kind do— and then we will all be at risk."

Elizabeth sighed, wishing she'd never brought up the Taint. Daniel was unreasonable about the subject; he had been since he was a young child. Nothing had ever seemed to shake him from that standpoint. She opened her mouth to reprimand him, but the training ground below caught her attention. She stiffened and raised a hand to her mouth, her eyes wide with astonishment. Daniel swung his attention back to the practice yard below and was equally speechless.

A petite woman had entered the training ground, her black hair restrained in a tight braid similar to the way Jess wore her own hair. She pushed herself off the wall that she'd been leaning on and strode across the training ground, drawing her sword from the scabbard at her side with practised ease.

"I didn't know Amelia attended the sword practice." Elizabeth's eyes widened, her hand pressed to her mouth.

"I didn't even know Amelia could use a blade more dangerous than a butter knife. Although, since Kyle is her brother, I guess we shouldn't be surprised."

Daniel was shocked. In all these years, he'd never once seen Amelia train with a sword, although her appearance suggested otherwise, since the blade strapped to her waist was obviously her own and the attire she was wearing resembled the training gear that her brother wore, although in green and brown tones rather than black. They did not look new.

"Well, I guess that might be why Father suggested that she would be perfect to be in my inner circle now she is of age."

Elizabeth frowned, and both she and Daniel kept their eyes on the training grounds below.

"Hold!"

The bellowed command from the weapons master rang out across the now silent practice field.

Kyle grinned tightly and removed his sword from the weak spot in the safety armour that the boy was wearing. He took a breath, shaking off the veiled world, and stepped back. Looking at his other two opponents, Kyle grinned and sheathed his swords. He looked down at the boy, who lay at his feet sucking in air.

"I don't think we've met, guardsman."

Kyle, faintly amused despite himself, felt his usual good humour starting to return. He felt a little sorry for the hapless guard. His eyebrow raised slightly; the boy didn't get up or answer, instead solidly ignoring him in his pursuit of breathing. Kyle glanced up at the weapons master and cocked his head to one side. He'd never seen the weapons master turn that shade of red before.

Weapons Master Gareth strode forward.

"Get your sorry arse off the ground, Webb. Practice is over, and in case that thick brain of yours hasn't caught on, that was Lord Kyle's polite way of enquiring after your sorry-arse name!"

Kyle didn't think it was possible for the lad's face to go any paler, but he managed it as he staggered to his feet. Kyle watched patiently as the boy continued to say nothing in response, his eyebrow raising even further.

Gareth muttered under his breath. "Powers preserve me. Your name, or did Lord Kyle manage to snuff out what little brainpower you possessed before the last bout?"

The lad gulped, looking wide-eyed at the weapons master, and shook his head. "No, Weapons Master, um ... sorry My Lord. I'm Guardsman Webb—Matthew Webb—from Lord Grumman's estate out west." He stumbled to a halt, aware he'd gone from being mute to almost babbling.

"Sorry to intrude on your session with Lady Jessalan, but you were holding back, and honestly you didn't need to. Her life might depend on the training she has here one day. It's not a game." Kyle nodded at the weapons master before walking over to join the others.

"Good fight, Marcus. You nearly had me a time or two." Kyle grinned at both Marcus and Jessalan, who sported smiles as wide as his own. "I think the pair of you have given me a new set of bruises."

Marcus finished stripping off the arm and chest guards he'd worn for training and chuckled as Alex joined them.

"I think I will have more than a few, My Lord Kyle. Good fight. I'd feel better about the compliment if you hadn't been fighting three of us at once. You too, My Lady Jessalan. You've come a long way from the little girl who tagged along with these two reprobates demanding to be taught swordplay right alongside them."

Kyle spun around when he saw Alex's stunned expression and tracked his gaze to see Amelia leaning against the wall, dressed for swordplay. Despite his mother being horrified by the idea, his father had had no intention of allowing his little girl to grow up unable to protect herself. An incident had occurred years ago in the ballroom, when a drunken Lord Minor tried to take advantage of her; this had only solidified his determination.

Still, to appease her mother, Amelia's practice sessions had been done privately, so the rest of the Realm likely didn't know how capable she was, much like Princess Elizabeth's practice sessions —done in the strictest confidence.

A melia chuckled, pushing herself off the wall, and drew her blade. Cocking her head to one side, she moved to the centre of the ring, not bothering with the protective training gear any more than Kyle had earlier. Amelia paused, and her gaze shifted over to the weapons master.

"With your permission, Weapons Master Gareth?"

Gareth looked startled, and his gaze slid over to Kyle, who chuckled and nodded.

"As you will, My Lady." Gareth gestured to the training ring. Most of the blade work around the arena halted once more as they noticed Amelia's presence and drew closer to watch.

Amelia drew her sword in a smooth, practised motion with an economy of movement that had the attention of all in the ring. Startled glances were traded by all the guards present. Amelia dismissed them as a distraction, her gaze sliding back to her brother. She gestured toward Kyle, beckoning him to come into the ring.

"Come, brother, enough with the play. Let's show them how the Straffords dance."

Kyle drew his blade, raising it in salute to his sister, smiling as she mirrored his movement. It was a courtesy of one Blade Master to another. He barely knew of the whispers that ran around the training ring. It got their attention. All activity in the training grounds stopped; the members present didn't even try to pretend they were not watching.

Without further pause, Kyle attacked, drawing his second blade, grinning. Amelia did the same. He could feel her use of the veil; her power was growing, although not to the same level as Jess. Still, Amelia was several years younger. Kyle forgot himself in his delight at the dance between their blades; they both moved with what was, to others, astonishing speed and skill. Their worlds narrowed to this moment, the power of the veil swirling through them both—as though they were opposite sides of the same coin, they mirrored each other perfectly.

Amelia looked just as delighted as he did, lost in the complexity of their lethal dance. Neither of them were aware of the time passing as they moved with deadly grace around the practice ring.

The weapons master bellowed, commanding them to hold.

Long practise and skill stilled both their blades as they straightened and withdrew. They flipped their blades up in salute to each other before sheathing them. Kyle was startled when the applause rang out around the practice ring. He looked at Amelia, laughing, and held his hand out to her. Amelia's laughter burst out from her lips as she took his hand and they both bowed to their appreciative audience.

"Amelia, I've missed trading blows with you. Mother will be beside herself when she finds out." Kyle chuckled as Amelia poked her tongue out at him in a very unladylike fashion.

"I'm sure our Lady Mother will get over it. Besides, our Lord Father will approve. It's his fault; after all, he's the one who insisted that I learn to defend myself." Amelia smiled. Her gaze turned to Jess and Alex as they joined them on the side of the training ring.

Weapons Master Gareth walked up to both, an appreciative smile on his face.

"My Lord, My Lady, thank you for that. I don't think I've ever seen a finer display of swordsmanship. My Lady, you are welcome on my training grounds any time."

Amelia smiled at the compliment. "Thank you, Weapons Master Gareth. The offer is appreciated."

Kyle laughed outright at the stunned look on Alex's face. "What, taken by surprise brother?"

Kyle could see Alex—the Alex he met in the veil for training. Not his drunken, party-boy alter ego that he generally displayed to the world. Kyle was aware enough that the real Alex showed up more often than not when Amelia was around. It was a subtle difference that most wouldn't pick, the calm competent Alex versus his wild, don't-give-a-damn mask.

Alex swallowed. Tearing his attention away from Amelia, he grinned briefly at Kyle before his eyes tracked back to his sister.

"You were amazing, Amelia. I knew you could fight, but I didn't realise you were that good. You are comparable to Kyle, and he is one of the best swordsmen in the Realm." Alex sighed and his smile turned self-depreciating. "If only I could display even half that skill with a sword."

Alex cleared his throat, turning his gaze back to Kyle. "Now, I believe we all have a state dinner to get ready for since Joshua has just shown up looking flustered and he never comes here unless I'm late for something. You'll be attending tonight, Marcus?"

"That I will be, Your Highness, along with James, so we'll take our leave to go and get ready, with your permission?"

Alex nodded his approval and Marcus bowed. He and James

dashed off, only waiting long enough to make sure Alex's security detail was trailing along behind the Prince as he and his companions made their way back to their rooms. Kyle grinned, noticing that Amelia and Jess had turned to each other and were in an animated discussion about fighting styles as they all walked to the exit of the training ground.

7

A SEPARATION

J essalan sat, her own green eyes staring back at her calmly as she inspected her appearance in the mirror. Laura, her maid, put the finishing touches on her hair. It always amazed her that Laura and the other girls she commanded, when the occasion warranted it, succeeded in transforming her from a 'wild hellion', as some would called her, to a 'Lady' in such a short space of time.

In a strange twist, it was the women born to the middle ranks in society who seemed to have more choice in what they did or wore —even their profession, if they chose to have one. There were even women in the King's Guard; granted, not too many, but they were shown the same respect as their male counterparts. Jessalan grinned. She knew that was, in part, because the guards in question were capable of beating common sense into anyone who thought otherwise.

As a Lady of the Realm, however, Jessalan knew that while people knew by birth she would have skill with a blade, many expected that she would have guards and a Lord husband to do all the dirty work for her. The fact that she trained in swordsmanship with Alex and Kyle, rather than in needlework with Elizabeth, was well known and frowned upon in the court. One of the ladies of the court had muttered to her current conquest how 'unseemly' Jessalan was.

However, she was given a wide berth by most, due to her association with the Royal Family—in particular Alex and Kyle. Alex may be the youngest of the King's children, but his word was still treated as law, with only the King or his eldest brother, Crown Prince William, able to countermand his will. That, and the court was becoming aware that Kyle was proficient at combat. While people muttered 'unseemly' or 'hellion' when she walked past, these days people stepped back to give room when Kyle walked past them. Kyle was a Lord. He could more or less do as he pleased.

But Jessalan knew that they called him one thing when they were sure he wasn't close enough to hear it: 'The Shadow'. The more perceptive or knowledgeable in the court were right: Kyle was death on two feet if he chose to be, a real descendent of the legend, the original Shadow of the Fourth. Kyle was always at his prince's side, his best friend and likely to be the blade in the darkness that would kill for Alex if necessary.

Of course, the original Shadow of the Fourth, Lady Leanna Katrina Shaddin, had been a street urchin, thief and assassin in training. That was before she'd taken to following Prince Edward around and became known as his 'shadow'. A legend grew around the pair, a legend that persisted to this day. Kyle may not have grown up on the streets as his ancestor had, but he was developing the same hard edge coupled with a sense of duty and friendship.

Jessalan heard a familiar voice in her outer rooms before her door unceremoniously opened, and her Aunt Elena sailed in with a satisfied smile, appraising Jessalan's dark green dress threaded with silver, hair, makeup and the necklace that Laura was just placing around her neck, which matched her earrings and bracelet. Laura closed the clasp then stepped back and sank into a graceful curtsey.

"My Lady." Laura rose at a gesture from Jessalan.

"Thank you, Laura, you've outdone yourself. That will be all until after tonight's festivities. I'll ring for you when I'm done." Jessalan waited until Laura withdrew, then rose gracefully and kissed her Aunt Elena on the cheek.

"You look so grim, Aunt Elena. I've been good the last couple of days, so unless the court is gossiping about my training session today, I cannot think what I've done."

Jessalan smiled at her aunt, knowing that the other reason she was left alone was that her estimable aunt was a lady in her right, married to Lord Thomas Hopkins' close friend, and advisor to the King.

Lady Elena sighed, "I thought I should warn you, dear, your parents have shown up at court intending to join in the progression this year and will be at the dinner tonight. I do not imagine that your father will be any trouble, but your mother … well you know her, dear. The gossips in court have been beating her door down to tell her about you, and I'm afraid she will try to drag you back to your father's estate." Elena hugged her for a moment before pulling back again. "I've kept her off our table since we are hosting some higher ranking Heights Protectorate Delegation members that couldn't fit on the High Table, but after the dinner, all bets are off. Please try not to get into a fight with her in the great hall." She paused. "Not even I could brush away you killing your mother in the grand hall in front of everyone." The last, Lady Elena delivered with a smile, though she was only half joking. She well knew that Jessalan and her mother did not get on.

Jessalan groaned. "Ah, powers, aunt. Couldn't we say I'm sick and have the physicians say no one is allowed near me till after they are gone?" Only long years of training at being a 'Lady' stopped Jessalan from slumping with defeat as her aunt shook her head.

"I'm sorry, dear. You must attend. Your absence will be noticed by the court if you do not. Now, come along. It's time we all took our places. It wouldn't do for us to arrive after the Royal Family." Lady Elena gave Jessalan a quick hug of support.

"Aunt Elena, does my mother know about the Taint?"

Jess had always wondered what her mother suspected. She knew her father knew of it and it was one of the many reasons he'd agreed for her to be sent here to court as a small child.

Aunt Elena smiled a little sadly. "I'm not sure what your mother is aware of, Jess. Neither your father nor I want to know what she'd do if she found out. That was one reason I persuaded Colin to let you come here, where you would at least have companions of similar ability, access to the best healers and the safety of the Royal Family. Now come, or we'll be late."

Elena turned, walking them both to the outer rooms to meet up with Uncle Thomas to attend the banquet.

———

Jessalan smiled, lifting her glass in salute toward Alex, who was a wonder of wonders sitting with his family at the High Table, every inch of him the prince. Alex grinned at her and raised his glass, dipping his head in acknowledgement before taking a sip in time with her own. Kyle, who sat at the next table, caught the exchange, shook his head and, grinning, took a sip.

This end of the great hall contained the most influential members of the court. Jessalan knew her mother must be simmering, thinking she'd been slighted. Her mother, who sat at one of the last tables toward the rear of the hall, had been glaring at her most of the evening, but protocol dictated that she stay at her assigned table.

Jessalan's attention was brought back to the table with a discreet clearing of the throat from her dining companion.

"So, is it accurate what people say, My Lady Jessalan, are you acquainted with the King's youngest child, Prince Alexander?"

Jessalan looked toward Lord Bennett Waterhouse and saw nothing but polite interest in his expression, although she realised he was digging for information, as he had been all night. Abruptly, she felt her smile freeze as she caught a surge she associated with those who bore the Taint or the Sundered, reinforcing her own mental barriers just before the probe cut off. This was more controlled than she'd ever known the Sundered ones to be.

Jess threw back her drink, pausing as a hovering waiter filled it for her, and she caught an amused glance from her uncle. He had caught the exchange and thought her action was due to Lord Waterhouse pestering her. Jess looked across at the lord and smiled. Her gaze scanned the dining room, trying to find the source of the surge, yet as quickly as she'd sensed it, it had cut off again. She turned her attention back to the heights delegate and his probing questions.

"Lord Waterhouse, of course I know Prince Alexander. I've spent most of my life here in the palace staying with my aunt and uncle. How could I fail to have met Alex in all this time?"

Jessalan caught herself before she could let her manners slip again and drained the contents of her glass. Instead, she sipped it, as she was supposed to. Jess wished the King would finish his last mouthful and signal that they could all retire to the grand ballroom. At least there she could escape the attention of her dining partner.

She saw Lord Waterhouse muster himself and smile at her deflection but was saved from further conversation as the King and members of the High Table stood, bringing an end to the banquet, and led the way to the ballroom.

Jessalan's stomach clenched; she hoped her mother's common sense would prevail and that she would keep her distance. At least for the evening. Standing as the server pulled her chair clear, Jess swept along with the courtiers to the ballroom in the King's wake, putting others between her and Lord Waterhouse as she exited the dining room.

J ess breathed a sigh as the usual throng of courtiers attempted to gain her attention. Looking around, she tried to see where her parents had ended up, having lost sight of them during the exit from the dining hall. Jessalan's back stiffened as her mother's unmistakable voice came from behind her.

"We're leaving now Jessalan, so get ready. You're coming with us."

Jessalan could see the astounded look on the faces of the courtiers that stood near her as she stumbled when her mother grabbed her arm and hauled her around to face her. Jessalan froze, shocked that her mother had dared to use violence in the grand ballroom. The King may have gone into conference with the leaders of the Heights Delegation, but until he departed, violence against a member of the court could mean a death sentence.

Her mother shook her. "Did you understand me, girl? You're coming with us."

Jessalan took a breath, taking stock of the approaching guards and worse, both Alex and Kyle making their way across the room in her direction. Jessalan wrenched her arm free of her mother's grasp and straightened, eyeing her mother coolly.

"Calm yourself, mother. This is not the place for this discussion. The King has guests and is still present at the ball." Jessalan winced at her mother's outraged expression.

"Do you think I haven't heard all about your gallivanting around? I sent you to the palace to turn you into a lady, not a common harlot." The volume of her mother's voice rose as she spoke.

Her mother raised her hand to slap her face, but Jessalan blocked reflexively before attempting to turn away, outraged that her mother would dare not only to grab her but to strike her.

To Jessalan's dismay, her mother grabbed her arm again, trying to shake her. When that failed, she once more drew her hand back to slap her. But before she could, she let out a gasp. The ballroom fell silent. The rustle of clothing, of people curtseying and bowing gave way to perfect silence, as all stopped to watch the figure who had walked up behind her.

"Lady Barraclough, assault a lady of this court in my presence, and you will find yourself in the deepest dungeon I can find to throw you in, no matter who your husband is. Even if the lady in question is your daughter." The King's voice was cold as he gazed at the now frozen scene in front of him.

She paled, looking guiltily at her raised hand. She dropped Jessalan's arm before sinking into a curtsey. Silence held until her mother finally realised that the King was waiting for an answer.

"Your Majesty. I was just ..."

Jessalan curtsied gracefully and moved to stand with Alex and Kyle at a gesture from the King, who cut her mother off.

"Enough. I could hear your screeching from the conference room. Lord Barraclough, your lady is overwhelmed by her visit to the court. You have my permission to return her to your estate. I'm not sure it would be prudent for her health for her to visit again without my permission. Ease your mind. Lady Jessalan is under my protection. Any who seek to harm her will be dealt with in the same fashion as they would were they to hurt my own child."

The King didn't wait for the quick thanks before addressing his next comments to the ever-present Karl, hovering in the background.

"Assist Lady Jessalan to move to one of the suites in the family wing and make sure some elite are assigned to her security details."

The King turned then stopped with a sigh. Looking at Kyle, he added, "Move, Lord Kyle as well. We might as well have all three of them in the same place to make things easier on us all."

With that, the King turned, a slight smile lingering on his lips at the stunned looks on the face of his youngest child and his two childhood friends. He walked past them, back toward the conference room

Jessalan watched as her mother and father were escorted out of the ballroom, recognising the moment that had just passed was a crossroad in her life. She felt a tremble wash through her and realised that the entire court was still frozen, watching. Out of the corner of her eye, she saw Lord Waterhouse shake himself free and move forward to offer sympathy. Suppressing a groan, she lay a hand on Alex's chest, stepping into his arms.

To her relief, Alex was not only sober but willing to play the game. He pulled her into his arms, his lips brushing against her forehead as he pulled her close, apparently unaware of the surrounding courtiers. Yet she felt the veil surge as he scanned the people around them.

"It's all right, My Lady. You are safe. I would lay waste to an entire kingdom to protect you."

His whisper, although seemingly just to her, was loud enough to carry across the ballroom. Unerringly, his eyes lifted and held those of the now frozen Lord Waterhouse, who swallowed before allowing some of his companions to pull him back into their midst.

Jessalan felt another hand on her shoulder and looked up to see William, who looked concerned, although she could see the amusement in his eyes.

William addressed her, his voice soft, "The Heights Delegate cannot be that boorish?"

Jessalan suppressed a laugh. "You do not understand, William. He's been very persistent and trying to pump me for information all night."

William's own expression hardened as he turned and saw the lord, who blanched at the combined death stares in his direction from Alex, Kyle and now William. William's gaze moved back, flicked to Alex, noting the dark rings under his eyes. Kyle looked like he wanted to skewer someone and Jess was clearly upset about her mother's actions but trying to hide it.

"Go, take the night off, I'll explain to father. Just try not to get into too much trouble."

William straightened. Turning to walk back to the conference room, he paused on the way, talking to the guards. His voice was low enough that she couldn't hear what he said, yet his glance back at them made it obvious that he was giving instructions. Jess laughed despite herself. It was rare for William to give them all a leave pass to head into town and party, particularly since he was the one who was woken first if they got into trouble.

Jess looked at William as his face closed down to his polite, formal mask. Jess tracked his gaze over toward his brother, Daniel, who was standing talking to an old man wearing a scholar's robe.

"What's wrong, William, who is that man?" Jess took the couple of steps to William's side, placing her hand lightly on his arm.

Jess frowned; she'd been at court long enough to recognise most who attended the court on sight. Both Alex and Kyle closed the small gap between them and looked past her toward Daniel and the scholar, yet neither showed any recognition.

William shook his head. "No one. It's been a long time since I've seen him and I'm surprised he would show up here at court." William paused and seemed to choose his words carefully. "He was one of our tutors; he was dismissed from service a long time ago. His beliefs were not in accordance with the crown, yet he still tried to indoctrinate them into us. I doubt you would remember him, Alex. All of you go, get out of here before I change my mind."

Daniel caught his brother's attention just before he entered the conference room. He took William's arm and they moved a couple of steps away from the group surrounding Daniel. The brothers talked briefly. William looked irritated at the interruption and his chin jerked in their direction as he and Daniel spoke, so Jess gathered they were the subject of the conversation. William broke away from Daniel and, noticing that she was watching, he smiled and gestured at the three of them, a little flicking motion with his hands before William turned and entered the conference room, the door closing behind him.

Daniel continued to stare in their direction for a moment, lost in thought. Then, suddenly aware that he was being watched, he raised his glass in salute, made a brief comment to the guards and returned his attention to the old scholar. Jess turned, looking from Alex to Kyle.

"Well, we have permission, which is rare. I need out of here. Join me?"

The only answer she received was their grins as they looped their arms through hers and guided her out of the ballroom.

8

KIDNAP

K yle looked around The Tankard and raised his eyebrow. "Not that I'm complaining and all, but this place is ... a little quieter than usual."

Interrupted by a chuckle, they looked up to see the barkeeper, Tim, who refilled their mugs from a jug.

"Well, it normally is quiet for a few days after the guards have been through to haul you three out." He grinned at them before heading back to the bar.

Alex shook his head. "Remind me to dig out some of that allowance from Father and give Tim a bonus for his troubles. Well, I guess things being quiet tonight may not be such a bad thing since William put himself out to give us some time out. Particularly since the King just ordered protection details on the both of you."

Kyle spluttered, looking between Jess and Alex.

"Both of us? Wait, the King only ordered guards to follow Jessalan around everywhere. Not me."

Jess chuckled and sipped her wine, frowning at the slight aftertaste.

"I think you need to review that whole incident. The King included you in the whole deal."

Kyle buried his face in his hands and groaned, much to Alex's amusement.

"You know I'm a better swordsman than your guards, right?"

Alex just shook his head, grinning at Kyle's misery. While he knew his friend was correct, an order from the King was an order the guards would not refuse. He picked up his goblet, his eyes glancing around the bar, picking out the guards scattered throughout the regular patrons. Still, while it was a little more constraining than he'd prefer, he appreciated William acknowledging that they might need time away from the court and didn't want to cause him any more issues than he already had. Alex pushed back into the corner, his back against the wall behind him feeling the coolness of the rough stone wall through his shirt and vest. Resting one booted foot on the wooden bench he glanced around the dimly lit bar. As always, there were musicians in the corner, although tonight, given the absence of the usual crowds, they played only quietly in the background.

Movement at the door caught his attention, as two women accompanied by a tall, athletic man walked in. After glancing around, the three moved to the bar, speaking to the red-haired barmaid that had served them when they had first come into the bar. He saw the three glance in his direction, then the barmaid busied herself behind the bar before handing them a jug and a platter.

"Wait, isn't that the blonde and brunette from the other night? Although it looks like they have company tonight, or is that the guy you entertained from the other night Jess?" Alex looked toward Jess, raising his eyebrow in enquiry.

Jess smiled and tilted her head to get a better look toward the bar.

"Those are the women you two had plastered all over you but no, that isn't Damien." Jess grinned at Alex and Kyle, detecting the hint of regret in her own voice.

"Oh, Jess, really? Are we going to track the mysterious Damien for you?" Kyle teased, his eyes sparkling. He laughed outright as she shoved him.

"He should be easy to find, he's a hunter. Said he'd come to Vallantia to help with the court's progress to the Summer Palace, I think I'll run into him again soon enough."

Jess grinned, taking the teasing of both Alex and Kyle with good humour. After the evening she'd had it was refreshing to have a little piece of normal.

"Well look who we found. Could we tempt you three to fun tonight?" The blonde smiled and held up a fresh jug she'd just purchased from the bar. The brunette slid a platter of food onto the table and moving around the side sat on the bench, giggling as Kyle grabbed her around the waist and pulled her close, kissing her.

Alex held out his hand to the blonde, who placed the jug onto the table before allowing him to draw her into his arms, settling contentedly against his chest. Tilting her head back, Alex laughed and kissed her.

The male placed a couple more mugs he'd brought with him on the table and refilled Alex and Kyle's goblets before turning to Jess, smiling at her.

"Refill?" He tilted his head, eyebrow raised, not refilling her glass until she nodded consent.

Jess turned her glance from him to the two girls then back to the male, who she had to admit was doing his best to be charming. She smiled, guessing they were likely all from one of the pleasure houses, out for the night. He finished one jug they had brought over then poured the two girls and himself a drink from the second.

"May I?" He gestured to the empty place on the high-backed bench chair next to Jess and grinned as she nodded assent. "I'm Oliver." He stretched his arm out around the back of the chair and, when she didn't object to his hand resting on her shoulder, began to trace idle patterns on her with his finger.

"Pleased to meet you, Oliver. I'm Jess." Jess turned and looked into the dark eyes of the man she was certain charged for this kind of attention. Thinking of her mother's horrified reaction if she were to find out which bar she was in and in which part of town—and that she was in the arms of a man of pleasure—Jess grinned. "What the hell."

Jess reached up, twining her fingers in his thick black hair and pulled him down until their lips met. As she'd suspected, he was agreeable to the notion and kissed her back, wasting no time at all in sliding onto the chair next to her.

J ess shook her head, trying to make sense of what was happening and where she was, immediately regretting it as the world began to spin around her. She closed her eyes and took a deep breath before opening them again to see Damien leaning over her, looking concerned. His lips moved, but the words were as indistinct as the blurry room around her. He gathered her in his arms and picked her up. Jess swallowed, trying not to be sick as she pressed her face into his shoulder.

She knew she must have blacked out for some time because the next time she became aware she was in the forest, although not moving; Damien was still holding her. He smiled, brushing the hair back from her face and kissed her on the forehead. Jess struggled to sit up, but he stopped her.

"Shh, rest Jess. You were drugged; that man meant you harm. You're safe now, although as much as I hate to say it, you need the care of a healer." Damien looked just as good as she remembered and she lost herself in his deep blue eyes.

"Wait, what about Alex and Kyle?" Even the idea she had been drugged alarmed her since it meant that her friends were likely in trouble.

Jess reached for the power of the veil and stopped, stunned, as she realised she couldn't sense it, let alone channel its power. This was an experience that had never occurred before, one that she didn't know was possible. If anything, it made her panic even more. As a wave of nausea washed over her, Jess turned to one side, supported by Damien's strong arms as she heaved up the contents of her stomach.

"I'll get you to safety then I will try to help your friends. Try not to move too much—it will make the effects of the drug worse. Don't use the power, you won't be able to channel it, but struggling to reach it will also make you worse." Damien held her close then stood, walking through the forest.

"Palace, take me to the palace, to William."

Jess closed her eyes, not waiting to see if Damien conceded with her request, his words not sinking in or making any sense, except for the *try not to move* part. She could feel steady movement and even that made her sick. She held her eyes closed to help with the effect.

"I hope you have enough clout to get us into the palace, Jess. Otherwise it will cause a fuss if I do it my way." Damien's voice was low. "We're approaching the main gate now and I don't think the guards look happy to see me."

Jess opened her eyes again, realising that she must have fallen asleep, since there was no way they could have covered the distance between the town and the palace in the time in which her rather foggy brain insisted they had. She pushed this concern aside, focusing on the guards, who were demanding that Damien identify himself and state his business.

"Guardsmen, get out of the way." Jess was appalled by how weak her voice sounded.

"Now listen here, miss ..."

Jess' eyes snapped open. "Guardsman, if I wasn't so sick and sure I'd fall flat on my face I'd skewer you for that. Alert Captain Jackson, now. I need to speak to William."

The guards' confusion caused her to groan and close her eyes again, although she heard booted feet running so she guessed someone was running for help. Getting in and out of the palace was so much easier in the company of Alex and Kyle. Then again, it was also much easier when she wasn't feeling so ill.

Jess wrenched herself back from darkness, hearing a commotion. Lamps flared, men were yelling and running.

She opened her eyes and realised with relief that she recognised the guard doing the yelling as Guardsman James. So while he wasn't Captain Jackson he was, in some ways, better. He recognised her, which explained the yelling for the guard to be turned out and healers summoned to attend the Lady. It took her drug fogged mind a few moments to realise she was the Lady he was demanding healers for. She was sure he'd been bellowing more orders as they walked across the courtyard into the palace but she hadn't caught them all.

Jess recognised the passages they were taking her down. They were taking her back to her rooms and from the direction the running servant was going, they were heading toward the healers.

"Take me to William."

Jess, surprised at how soft her voice sounded, raised one hand, slapping it on the guardsman's arm to gain his attention. His concerned face swam into her view.

"Relax, My Lady, we will get you to your rooms, and the healers are on their way." His eyes and tone expressed concern rather than judgement, although she could see by his glance that the senior guardsman reserved his judgement of Damien.

"No. Take me to William. You know I have access, any time of day or night. I must speak with him. Damien rescued me, he's not a threat."

Jess tried to sound commanding but her voice was anything but and she decided that moving her head around too much was ill advised. It made her head spin and darkness encroached on her vision, threatening to plunge her into unconsciousness again.

Guardsman James nodded abruptly and without a pause in his stride took another hallway that led further into the heart of the palace. The drumming of the booted feet as they made their way through the seemingly unending hallways lulled her back into darkness, despite the urgent need to pass on to William what had happened.

J ess came to again, hearing rather insistent voices. Yelling in the Royal Wing wasn't recommended. She thought about insisting she could stand, then considering how sick she was, decided that her dignity could be damned—being carried was fine.

Jess opened her eyes as Damien settled her on a couch, only to see his face replaced by William's.

"Jess, what's wrong? You need treatment by the healers. I'm sure this can wait." William's concerned face kept fading from her vision. Trying to concentrate, she opened her eyes as his hand touched her shoulder.

"We were all drugged, William. They've got Alex and Kyle." Jess' vision faded and she wasn't certain if she had said the last part aloud or not.

"The guards are already out Jess; I'm sure they will be all right." William's face showed no concern at all except for her. He turned from her briefly, barking a demand for the healers to attend to her.

"No William. You don't understand. We were at The Tankard, then things got confusing—I don't know what happened. I can't draw the power, I've never felt like this before. Damien found me, he can guide the guards back to wherever it was." Jess sank into the darkness once more. "Something is wrong, William. The boys are in trouble."

Jess continued to struggle until she heard his precise orders to the guards. Then William took her in his arms and settled her in a soft, comfortable bed. She let herself sink into unconsciousness, the healer's cool hands on her forehead.

You'll be fine My Lady. Relax, let me help you. Jess allowed the blackness to claim her, sinking into nothingness.

9

KYLE DEFENDS ALEX

K yle woke up groggy, his head pounding disproportionately to the amount of alcohol he remembered consuming. He groaned, realising that not only did he not have any clothes on, neither did the brunette lying unconscious next to him. Kyle leaned over the side of the pallet and his stomach heaved, emptying its contents onto the floor. He lay back in the bed covered in sweat, breathing deeply for a moment, trying to gather his thoughts about where he was and what had happened.

Through the fog that his last memories seemed to be, Kyle remembered being in the ballroom of the palace; it had been an official function. He then remembered that they had left after an incident involving Jess and her mother ... hooked up with the women—who were undoubtedly ladies of pleasure—which would explain where he was. This wasn't a room at The Tankard. Groaning, he realised it was likely he would have to endure yet another lecture from his mother about family responsibility.

Kyle reached for the power to settle his queasiness and the general fog over his mind, and froze. He couldn't touch it at all. It was there, he could still see the power flows and feel it, but every time he tried to grasp it, nothing happened. Panic rose, threatening to overwhelm him. His instinctive reaction was to fight against whatever barrier was standing between him and the veil. Kyle closed his eyes and took a deep, steadying breath. Something had happened, he needed to know what.

Trying to prod his sluggish mind, he replayed the last things he remembered: the palace, leaving the ballroom. Kyle frowned, and the glimpse of a small track lined by trees flashed in his mind. He knew that was their path into town, one that Jess had found years ago; the entrance wasn't recognisable unless you knew what you were looking at from the main road. It was a shortcut that always ensured they arrived at the minor portal to the town well before the guards that likely trailed behind them.

The next series of images flashed through his mind in quick succession. Kyle let them flow one after the other without trying to grasp them. He knew now where they had been. The Tankard, one of their favourite haunts, the girls from the other night showing up with the company for Jess, the three of them being plied with alcohol and food.

That was all normal—blacking out and ending up somewhere he didn't remember getting to was not. Kyle opened his eyes and looked at the sleeping brunette next to him. Neither was waking up naked next to a woman he had no recollection of sleeping with; that wasn't his style.

The next flash of memory sent Kyle sitting bolt upright with an overwhelming sense of wrongness. He took a long, slow breath then pushed against that barrier that stood between him and the veil.

Trembling with exhaustion, Kyle stopped trying to wield power, fighting down the fear that rose when he realised that he couldn't clear his body and head of any of the sickness he was feeling. Taking a few deep breaths, he concentrated on trying to calm himself—thankfully, not all his skills were due to being one of the Tainted. He may be cut off from the power, but he was hardly powerless.

Suddenly, the brunette's words flashed into his memory.

"Relax, My Lord Kyle. Jana will look after His Highness and Oliver is more than competent to take care of Lady Jessalan."

Then she had poured more of whatever was in the bottle down his throat, and that was the last he had known. They had known who he and Jess were, who Alex was. He was certain that was something none of them had revealed. And the guards who had come to drag them back to the palace had not worn uniform bearing the Royal Sigil. Oh, the regulars knew they were of some rank, but other than the publican, he doubted they knew or cared exactly who they were.

Kyle dragged himself out of the bed, breathing deeply and swallowing as his stomach heaved again. He glanced over at the woman, who had begun to stir. While he didn't fully understand what had happened but he had no doubt that she had been involved. Kyle picked up the heavy candlestick holder on the crate next to the bed and turning, rapped her on the temple as her eyes started to open. Kyle tossed his improvised weapon aside as the woman lapsed into enforced unconsciousness once more.

Kyle glanced around the room and saw his clothing, which had been tossed in the corner. Easing himself to his feet, he was unable to stop the groan that escaped his mouth as dizziness and sickness assaulted him. Thinking of Jess and Alex, he bit his lip,

CATHERINE M WALKER

concentrating, and instinctively tried to pull in the power of the Veiled World, only to fail again.

Kyle took some steadying breaths, pushing down the panic that threatened to overwhelm him. He opened his eyes and turned. Leaning against the wall, he reached down for his clothes. Of all the consequences of using the power, the healers had never warned him of anything that could block him. Only of the risk of overusing it. Pulling on the last of his clothes he registered that his weapons were missing. A small smile touched Kyle's lips; if any of their assailants had seen it, it would have chilled them to the bone.

"As if that will save them." Kyle turned back to the brunette in the bed. "Now for you."

Grabbing what he presumed was her shirt, he ripped it into strips then carefully bound her hands and feet before stuffing a wad of cloth in her mouth and securing it in place. Satisfied, he turned and concentrated on what he was doing rather than the desire to just curl up in the bed and wait for the guard to find him. Something was unaccountably very wrong.

Kyle was almost relieved to hear the whispering voices through the veil flickering in and out of his head; he didn't have the capability to block them out. He paused, wondering if this was what it was like for the Sundered. They were driven mad by the whispering voices in their heads that they couldn't explain and didn't have the training to block out. Casting the idea aside for another time, he pushed away from the wall.

Silently moving toward the door, ignoring the sense of wrongness and queasiness, Kyle knew without even thinking that there was a guard in the hall outside the room. Opening the door, he moved as quickly as he could, focusing unerringly on the one guard to the right of his door. Kyle slammed his knuckles into the man's throat, causing him to gag for breath. He stepped in behind the man, quickly wrapping one arm around his throat and putting him into a chokehold. The guard struggled briefly his hands, clawing at Kyle's arm before he slumped, unconscious. Kyle snapped the man's neck without a second thought. Kyle eased the dead guard gently to the floor, knowing that there were more people in the house. He relieved the former guard of the sword and knife hanging from his belt and walked smoothly across the hall, opening the door on the other side just as he heard the commotion from the front of the house. Smiling, he knew that Marcus had found them.

Surveying the room, he saw the blonde from The Tankard. Unlike the brunette in his own room, she was very much awake and plunging a sharp knife toward Alex's chest. Without pausing, Kyle dropped the weapons as he crossed the room, grabbing her head and snapping it in a smooth, practised motion.

He let her slump to the bed, half on top of the still-sleeping Alex. He spun around, hearing a noise behind him, only to relax when he recognised Marcus. The tall muscular guard's sharp eyes scanned the room for any remaining threat. Kyle almost groaned when he recognised that this time Marcus was in full uniform with the sigil of the King's Elite blazoned on the left of his vest. Any who saw him would have no doubt at all that he was on the King's business. Kyle guessed if Marcus was in full uniform that meant it was likely that the whole guard had been called out. There was no way they would be able to keep this incident, unlike previous ones, quiet. Kyle put one hand on the wall next to him in what he hoped looked like a casual manner, taking a deep breath as darkness at the sudden motion threatened to overwhelm him.

Marcus looked on calmly. "Well done, My Lord. Sorry it took us so long to find you."

"How long have we been taken Marcus, and where is *here*? Have you found Jess? Is she all right? I know it's not The Tankard, which is the last place I remember." Kyle moved around the bed and shook Alex, trying to wake him up.

"This place is in the Quarter, my Lord, and it's two hours before dawn. Jessalan is back at the palace; she was assisted by that hunter from the other night." Marcus looked briefly outside and indicated to his men to finish securing the house. "Are you sure you are well, My Lord? I received word that the healers are treating Lady Jessalan. As far as we can determine, your assailants drugged the three of you at The Tankard."

Kyle felt a sudden flash of concern. "Is Jess all right?"

"I believe so, My Lord. She is in the hands of the healers." Marcus continued to stare at him as though he wasn't quite sure he wasn't about to collapse.

"I'll be okay, Marcus. I think they gave me too much of whatever it was. I threw up the contents of my stomach in the other room." Putting on a show of confidence he didn't feel, Kyle turned and helped Alex locate his clothes to dress, although Alex seemed to want to continue partying.

"Not now, Alex. Come on, we've got to get back to the palace, it's near dawn." Kyle manoeuvred Alex out of the door, distracting him from the now-dead blonde in the bed and the dead guard in the hallway.

Alex blinked, noticing all the guards lining the hallway, turning over every room in the small house and the men they had bound up in the corner of the main room. Shrugging, he helped himself to a bottle of wine and glass from the table. Uncorking it with practised ease, he poured some carefully from the bottle into the glass before taking a sip and offering some to Kyle.

"We must have had a good night if Father's sent the guard out to haul us home. Pity I don't remember much of it."

He sighed as Kyle refused a drink; his friend was obviously serious about calling it a night. He staggered outside, blinking as he began to recognise the rather dilapidated neighbourhood, and wondered how they'd ended up in the Quarter, of all places. There were even more guards outside blocking all the side entrances. The Quarter was a disreputable rabbit warren of interlaced, tight alleyways with one small box-like house on top of the other. Some of the most disreputable and poorest of the Realm called this place home.

Alex politely offered the bottle to Marcus, who had trailed along behind them, but was not surprised when the guard refused, instead directing them into an enclosed carriage.

Alex staggered down the hallway, an empty wine glass clutched in one hand and the half empty bottle in the other. Pausing, he carefully aligned the bottle above his empty glass and poured, cursing as the wine splashed over the rim of the glass and onto the floor. Alex glared, casting frustrated glances between the bottle and his still-empty glass. After a moment of intense concentration, he shrugged and raised the bottle to his mouth. Swallowing quickly as the liquid rushed into his mouth and down his throat, he turned, thrusting the empty glass into the hands of the person behind him, then continued on his way down the corridor to his rooms.

Alex reached out to open the door and staggered to one side as he missed the handle. Strong arms caught him as he fell and held him more or less upright, bracing him against the wall. Alex turned, blinking at Kyle, and grinned.

"Thanks, forgot you were there." Alex laughed then raised the bottle to his lips only to discover that there was nothing in it. "It's empty!"

"Shush Alex, you'll wake up the King and everyone else. Besides, you've had enough for one night." Frowning, Kyle looked over to the impassive guard standing nearby. "Just get the door open, will you? I'll take care of the rest."

The guard stepped forward without saying a word or changing his expression and opened Alex's door. Kyle grimaced, staggering as Alex slumped against him.

"Come on, Alex, just a little further. I need you to help me a little here, all right? Just a few more steps and you'll be in your room."

Kyle passed the empty wine glass that Alex had thrust at him to the guard then braced himself before taking most of Alex's weight and steering him through the doorway of his rooms.

Kyle half dragged Alex through the public rooms and into Alex's bedroom, where he gave him a shove. Alex collapsed onto his bed, the empty wine bottle falling from his fingers to the floor with a dull thud, slipping into unconsciousness as his head hit his pillow. Kyle sighed. Frowning, he pulled off Alex's boots.

"Sorry, Alex, but that will have to do. I'm sure your servants will discover you before too long and tuck you into bed."

Kyle muttered under his breath before retracing his way out of the rooms. Closing the door quietly behind him he slumped against the door, closing his eyes slightly and letting out a deep breath.

"Are you all right, My Lord? Will you need help to get to your rooms?" The once impassive guardsman had a slight smile on his lips as he regarded the exhausted lord.

"Huge night. Thanks, Marcus, but I'll be fine."

Kyle smiled at Marcus before forcing the exhaustion back and pushing himself off the door. He had to get to his own rooms, then he could collapse and let go of the strict control he'd been holding over himself. He made his way down the hallway, hoping that whatever he'd ingested would wear off while he slept the day away.

10

KYLE FALLS SICK

Kyle opened one eye to look up at his tormentor. He noted his room had a bright—disgustingly bright— light streaming through the window. Kyle thought about punching his harasser for the inconsiderate act of pulling back the curtains that kept his room dark enough for him to sleep. Repressing a groan as he rolled over and throwing one arm up to shield his eyes, he knew by the crushing weight of exhaustion that he had slept nowhere near long enough.

"Forgive me if I do not get up, Your Highness. To what do I owe the pleasure of your exalted company?" Kyle winced at the tone of his voice.

William smiled. "Sorry, Kyle. I know you only got in a few hours ago. Still, Father already wants more details than the guards can supply. What happened last night?"

William grabbed the pitcher of water and refilled Kyle's empty water glass before passing it to him. William walked across and relaxed back in a chair near the window while Kyle tried to collect his scattered wits and shrug off his exhaustion.

"To put it simply, we were drugged."

Kyle sipped his water, watching William, knowing there would be a lot more questions he knew he would not be capable of answering in his current state.

William's eyes narrowed as he took in Kyle's statement, putting it together with what he already knew from the accounts of the hunter Damien—who he'd questioned at length—the guards and the brief conversation with Jess before she lost consciousness. William sighed, closing his eyes. While he had had more sleep than Kyle it was only a matter of a few hours. The first thing Lady Jessalan had done on her return to the palace was wake him. Her immediate collapse had meant that he had slept in the chair beside his bed while healers tended to her.

"We had pieced that together from the accounts of Damien, Jess and the guards. What I need to know is what happened—what you remember—from your perspective." William opened his eyes and tried to push his fatigue aside.

Kyle continued to sip at his water, watching William over the rim of the glass as he tried to collect his thoughts. Then he frowned.

"Wait, Damien, the hunter? I don't remember him being there." Kyle frowned then sighed. "I guess that isn't surprising. When the women and the male, Oliver I think his name was, joined us I thought nothing of it." He smiled cynically. "It so happens that to that point it was routine." Kyle paused, trying to collect his scattered memories of the night while William sat waiting for the rest of the story.

"I think whatever the drug was it was in the drink, or perhaps the food they brought over. The night seemed to go like most nights before it; I have a patchy memory of us going to some upper room in The Tankard. I seem to remember us feeling guilty because it gets quiet for a few days in there after the guards have hauled us out. That's when the room tilted and my memory is shot. I don't know how we ended up where we did. She knew me by name, William, she knew who Alex was, and Jess. I take it Marcus got Jessalan out?" Now he remembered the night he was concerned about Jess.

"Marcus didn't have to; her hunter friend from the other night accomplished that, took out the male and got Jess back here."

William tried not to let his concern show that Kyle wasn't tracking the conversation or remembering information he'd already been told. That was unlike him. He also refrained from saying that he knew about the drug because Jessalan had collapsed, falling into unconsciousness after she had told him she thought Alex and Kyle were in trouble.

"The rest is a blur until I woke up and heaved the contents of my stomach on the floor of a room I did not recognise with the woman I remember holding the mug. I disabled the brunette when I remembered what had happened. Don't know how long I was out or what occurred during the intervening time. I found Alex in the room across the hall. Disabled the blonde and dragged Alex out of the house and back here. Somehow the guard was there and helped us back to the palace. Why is it I think you know more than me?"

William smiled. "You could say that."

William rose, picking up the pitcher, and refilled Kyle's glass before replacing it on the bedside table, taking his seat once more.

"From all accounts, it appears to be a rather badly thought out plan for extortion. How Marcus and the rest of the guard found you is no mystery. The whole of the Quarter was locked down and that rather useful hunter Damien guided the guard to where you were being held." William raised his hand as Kyle groaned. "You and Jessalan have averted incidents like this from occurring many more times than I can count. Don't beat yourself up. We knew it was bound to happen. If it's any consolation, they didn't seem to think this through at all, seeming to assume they could keep you, Alex and Jess occupied while they got money out of the King for your return."

Despite himself, Kyle choked on his water. "They thought the King would just pay them whatever they wanted and then let them get away with kidnapping and drugging his son?"

William smiled, though there was no warmth at all in his face or eyes. "Not only did they think the King would excuse the drugging of his youngest son but they thought His Majesty would absolve them of the drugging of a lord and lady of the court."

Kyle sat up suddenly in alarm before groaning and sinking back into his pillows, the glass falling from his fingers as a wave of nausea hit him. He gulped for air before struggling to turn to the edge of the bed, trying not to vomit. Kyle felt a set of arms assist him, and a bowl appeared as if by magic at just the right moment.

William supported Kyle while he threw up to the point where his body still shuddered and heaved but nothing came out. He waited patiently until the heaving subsided before assisting Kyle to lie back in bed. William placed the bowl on the floor and pulled the bell for a servant. He pulled the linen cloth off the bed stand and soaked it in the pitcher of water, using it to bathe Kyle's sweating face, watching with concern as the young lord continued to shudder.

A manservant bustled into the room before stopping dead halfway across the room, his eyes wide.

"Your Highness, I'm sorry, I didn't realise." He swept down low in a bow.

William frowned. "Enough. Take the bowl out to the washroom, clean it out then bring it back here. We might need it. Then run and get the physician." William turned back as Kyle attempted to sit upright, placing a hand on his shoulder, concerned that it was the only restraint he needed to stop him. Kyle threw him around the practice ring both with a sword and in unarmed combat on a daily basis.

William turned back and snapped at the still immobile servant. "Now, man!"

The servant snapped into attention, moving forward grabbing up the bowl. "Yes, Your Highness."

Bowing again, he walked across the room, placing the bowl to one side in the bathing room just in case the physician needed to examine the contents. He grabbed another bowl from the cupboard and hurried back into the room, placing it within reach of the bed. He bowed then left the room at a run when he hit the hallway.

William breathed a sigh of relief as the physician walked into the room with an air of confidence, his assistants in a trail behind him, closely followed by the breathless servant.

"How is my brother, Aaron?" William made room for Aaron and his aids, moving over to the couch, and sat down.

"Prince Alex will be all right, Your Highness, he seems to be one of the few who is immune to the effects of the drug. I've left Gavin with him as a precaution in case things change and before you ask, Jessalan is responding well to treatment and Jocelyn is with her. They will deal with anything that may arise. If they cannot deal with it, they will send for one of the other masters or me."

Aaron muttered as he examined Kyle, sending his assistants scurrying to mix up the medications he required.

"Now, My Lord Kyle, I need you to drink this. I know you do not feel like it, but it will help soothe your stomach and allow you to rest while your body fights to flush the poison."

Aaron assisted Kyle to drink the medicine then nodded to one of his assistants to take his place in supporting the young lord.

"Your Highness, I think I will stay here a while. Lord Kyle, given how much he has already expelled, has either been given more of the drug than Prince Alex or Lady Jessalan, or is having an adverse reaction to the drug they used. His condition is not good. I should have checked on him sooner." Aaron frowned and glanced back toward his patient.

"Will he be all right, Aaron?" William looked toward the bed, concerned, then back toward the physician, not reassured at all by what he saw in the old man's face.

"It is too early to tell, Your Highness. Go, I will send someone to you if Lord Kyle's condition changes."

William went to leave before turning back to the healer. "I thought the Taint, the ability to utilise the power of the veil, healed him of things like this?"

Aaron smiled. "Yes, your Highness. It usually assists. There are some herbs that, when combined, form a toxin for those with the Taint. It can inhibit the Tainted from reaching the veil. We've experimented with some Tainted, but while it is effective in inhibiting their ability to control the power, it can also kill them if ingested in large quantities." Aaron hesitated, as if choosing his words with care. "If taken long term, it becomes addictive, and we have seen it turn those with access to the veil mad."

William looked alarmed. "He's had enough of that to kill him? Alex? Jess?"

Aaron shook his head. "Relax, William. Alex and Jess will be okay; neither of them ingested enough of the poison to kill them. Kyle has been at a guess by his reaction, but he has expelled a great deal of it. Thankfully, his severe reaction to the poison may be what saves his life."

11

WILLIAM BRIEFS THE KING

W illiam nodded at the guards stationed at the entrance to his father's study as he passed through the open doors, motioning with one hand for his guards to remain outside. Unnecessary as it was, it was a habit.

The doors closed behind him as he walked across the room. Ignoring the irritated look of the lord who was in conference with his father, he crossed the room and slumped in a comfortable chair to one side of the chamber. Sighing, he relaxed back into the cushions, closing his eyes, content to wait. After the night's events, the lord could be irritated at knowing his audience with the King was being cut short even though he'd been waiting months for the appointment for all William cared.

He listened to the drone of conversation between his father and the Lord Kessalan, trying to stay at least semiconscious until his father dismissed the lord and was ready to speak to him. He smiled as he recognised the whining, protesting note in Lord Kessalan's voice as his father's aide herded the unfortunate man out of the office. William waited until his father sat down in the chair next to him and heard the distinctive noise of the breakfast tray settling onto the coffee table.

A hand touched his shoulder and he opened his eyes to see his father holding out a steaming mug of coffee to him.

"Thank you, Father. I hope your business with Lord Kessalan wasn't too important."

William took the cup being handed to him and took a small sip, smiling as his father snorted in response. While the lord was from an old family that had money, they were not influential enough to have their permanent suite here in the palace. They had a house in town and reserved day rooms if the need brought them to the palace long enough to require a space of their own. Those were always at a premium and booked months in advance. William shook his head and pulled his scattered wits back to more important issues than the Lord Kessalan.

"Lord Kessalan has his own concerns with the rise of attacks from the Sundered on villagers and farmers on his lands. He slipped in a petition for me to give the Killiam Order legitimacy as a guild, which I refused. He is old and quarrelsome but will require watching." The King looked irritated but not alarmed by his last meeting.

"Ah, well that might explain why he invited Scholar Clements to the palace." William frowned, concerned. "We're getting a lot of reports of the Sundered of late, Father. There has always been a few, but we seem to get reports every other day about it."

"Yes, it's unusual. We will investigate the claims. Not that I think they will find much, except some destroyed lives." The King sighed, realising the futility of the actions he could take. "I'll discuss our options in council; we at least need to be seen to be protecting our people."

William hesitated. "This is right up Alex's area of interest Father; it's one of the few things he has ever studied other than the sword. He reads every report on the Sundered attacks. If anyone can track down and sort out the problem of the Sundered, legitimate or otherwise, it's Alex. I have no doubt that will also involve Kyle and Jess."

The King shook his head. "I don't doubt you, William, it's just not the right time to involve him. What with the kidnap attempt and this time of the year, he always struggles around the time of your mother's death. I'll consider bringing him in later when things have calmed down. Now, how are they all?"

William nodded, agreeing to his father's will. "Alex is resting, and according to Aaron, he will be just fine, as he always seems to." William frowned slightly and sipped his coffee. "Jessalan is in the hands of the healer Jocelyn, who reports she is responding well to treatment and will be as good as new in a few days." William paused, taking another sip of the steaming liquid as his eyes flashed up to meet his father's eyes.

"Alex is, no matter how we may despair, one of the Tainted. To the uneducated and some so-called educated, he's the product of legend, the Fourth Child. The record keepers have been at great pains to assure me that despite all appearances he will not sicken and that he is a lot stronger than he appears. I doubt they would be as enthusiastic if they knew the truth. What of Kyle?" The King picked up the coffee pot from the tray and refilled his son's mug.

William smiled grimly at the understatement. No one would envy Alex if they knew he was one of the Tainted, with the power of the veil running through him. The Royal Archives told them that there was a time before the Sundered War where those who used the veil were greatly valued for the power they possessed. Then some sickness spread and more often than not, those that possessed the power of the Veiled World went mad. They became the Sundered, sinking into madness and killing all those who stood in their way. People now would kill any they even suspected of having the ability to channel the power, even children. Superstition ran deep, even amongst the educated, dating back to the tales of the Sundered War. Thousands died during the Sundered War to protect the Realm from the incursion of the others, the Sundered ones—or Tainted, as the people called them today.

They revered the original Fourth Child, the Great—many times Great—Uncle Edward Rathadon, the man legend said had all but single-handedly saved them all from the Sundered. What history didn't tell them was that his Royal Highness Edward Rathadon, fourth son of the then King, had also possessed the power of the Veiled World. So did his closest companions and the men and women who surrounded him. It was one of the Royal Family's closest guarded secrets in this day, that the ability to possess the power of the veil, the Taint, ran through the royal line. Although it had been a long time for any of them to be as powerful as Alex appeared to be. It was even more unfortunate that he also happened to be the fourth child of the king, just like Edward. What people had long forgotten was that those who could wield the veil had once been held with high regard not just in high society but in the guard and throughout the Realm. Back in Edward's day, they were not referred to as the 'Tainted'. The known events from that time in history had warped into legend and Alex and his friends lived with all the expectations one would expect with a product of legend.

William shook his head and sipped the coffee that his father had poured him. "Thank you, Father, it's already been a long day. Kyle is not doing well. Given his reputation, I'd guess they poured more of the drug into him than either Jessalan or Alex." William matched his father's frown, lost in thought.

Young as Kyle was, he was already well known as the 'Shadow' to some, the one who was always one step behind Alex. It was whispered in certain circles that he was a deadly fighter, an assassin trained with uncanny abilities. They were close to the truth.

"It's what I would do if I were inclined to kidnap Alex and those around him. Reports suggest that rumours are already circulating outside of the palace and guard that Kyle is not the young drunken lord he appears to be. He's pulled Alex out of trouble too many times and he has done it rather too well."

The King sighed, wishing, not for the first time, that his son's blood didn't run so with the Taint of the veil, that he'd never had a fourth child. It hurt; he knew the whole legend of the Fourth had sprung from a lie. Edward hadn't been born 'normal' as they insisted today. He'd been born wielding the veil. When the Realm was threatened by those of his own warped kind, Edward and his friends stood between those with the warped power, infected with madness and the commoners, he'd fought for them all. It was just unfortunate that as far back as the known records traced, a fourth child was only born to the royal line when the Kingdom was threatened. Given that the fourth son of a King in those circumstances was the most expendable, he was thrown at the pointy end of any conflict. Thus, a legend was born that seemed to need managing.

No one looking at Alex now would ever think he could be competent at anything except drinking and partying. Few would imagine that he might be a threat. But under the surface, he was just that. Masked and hidden, trained in the Veiled World (so the record keepers said) by his dead relatives—the former 'Fourth Child'.

Alex was his fourth child, but was also a drunken, irresponsible party-boy Prince. Driven to wild excesses through a combination of childhood trauma, being the fourth son, and the hard reality of being one of the Tainted seemed to have eluded everyone. Thankfully.

Alex's closest friends were also wrapped up in the whole Legend of the Fourth just because they were Alex's friends. If it weren't such a headache to manage he'd be inclined to laugh; while records of the Fourth Child and his general attributes abounded, less was known about the Fourth Child's friends, the Companions. Details of the Companions were elusive, but they were always there with the Fourth Son, so the record keepers and ordinary people alike just ran ahead of the actual truth and made it up. It was incredible how they could fit the smallest detail into their legend and make it fit.

As a result, Kyle bore the tag of the fighter; allegedly, he was just as deadly as the Fourth Child, sometimes more so, called the Shadow of the Fourth. Everyday people today referred to those who were assassin-trained as 'Shadows', although they had lost the knowledge of where the term originated.

How the Companions prepared was never agreed upon—that helped the average person and historians interpret what they knew any way they wanted. Legend had it, the Shadow's skill became clear well before trouble started, unlike the Fourth Child, who remained masked until trouble stirred. All of it was built on a lie. The Fourth Child and his Companions, both historically and now, all bore the Taint, which gave them their remarkable abilities. It remained hidden until push came to shove and circumstances made them use those skills more overtly.

It didn't help that Kyle was an excellent swordsman, a master—not that many knew—trained as an assassin. Being as close as he was to Alex and the Royal Family, he was regarded as a worst case scenario defence. If all else failed, they'd have to get through Kyle first to get to Alex or any member of the Royal Family since he mixed in their inner circles.

The King stirred, realising they were both lost in their thoughts.

"He's not had much choice in that. Kyle is one of Alex's companions, and it's becoming well known he is one of the best swordsmen in the Realm; is it any wonder the ignorant label him as the Shadow?"

The King watched his eldest son's face for his reaction and, as he had thought, William showed no surprise at all.

William nodded. "I agree, I haven't been able to get past his guard, either armed or unarmed, in training for the last year, for all I'm older and have been training longer than he has. He is developing a hard edge that is unmistakable, though he keeps it hidden." He paused for a moment. "Or at least, he did until the other night. He dispatched one kidnapper when she threatened Alex with an efficiency that surprised even Marcus."

The King frowned, sipping more of his coffee before asking, "Jess?"

William shook his head. "Yes, they are wrapping her up into this foolishness. The three of them match known details of our ancestor and his best friends a little too much. Lord Callum Barraclough is Jess' ever-so-great Uncle. One of the few things known about him was his ability to hunt. An ability that Jess has in common—that, and being in Alex's inner circle of close friends."

William considered his next words with care. "Aaron said they were all given a poison that inhibits their contact with the veil, which is why they all got so sick. Kyle ingested enough to kill him, but Aaron thinks he has brought up enough of the drug that he will live."

His father looked at him, startled. "There's a drug that will stop them using the power of the veil? Why haven't the healers mentioned it before? Could it prevent them from becoming Sundered?"

William grimaced and relayed the rest of his conversation with Aaron and the consequences that the healers had found with the drug. William paused, noting his father looked a little disappointed but not surprised by the information. He carefully brought up his next concern although he had no doubt that it was something his father had already considered.

"It does raise the spectre that this was a deliberate attempt on Alex's life. Although thankfully it appears that Alex is somewhat resistant to the drug."

The King shook his head and was about to reply when his harried looking assistant came in, bowing.

"I'm sorry, Your Majesty, Your Highness, but Your Majesty you have the meeting with the security council." Karl waited for his master's reply.

"Yes, Karl, I haven't forgotten. All right, William, get some rest. It will be a long night with the Heights Protectorate Delegation here. Keep me updated on Kyle's condition; I know that Nathaniel is worried and would appreciate any extra help we can give to his son." The King moved toward the boardroom off to one side of his office with Karl following in his wake. He paused. "We leave for the Summer Palace next week after the Protectorate Delegation returns to the Heights; plan for the Complex of the Fourth to be opened. Alex, Kyle and Jess can move in there. In the meantime, arrange for extra guards to be placed on all three of them."

William felt his eyes widen. "Father, you know Alex doesn't want the rank, he never has."

"He doesn't want it but it is his, regardless. I don't see it will put any extra pressure on him he doesn't already have. It will, however, give the three of them a little privacy and extra protection, which is one reason the Fourth's Complex was built. Make sure all the associated arrangements are made."

With that last order, the King turned and walked into his office.

Karl followed the King, stopping at the door. "Leave those arrangements with me, Your Highness. I'll see things are done, and brief you with the details when you wake to see if there is anything else you think needs doing."

William acknowledged this offer with a brief nod of his head and Karl closed the door to the office, disappearing into the King's inner sanctum.

William sighed then went off to find his brother Daniel—another issue that made him groan. Daniel would not be pleased that his irresponsible little brother would be elevated and recognised as The Fourth, with the title, responsibilities and powers it inferred. William shook his head; he would have to cope with it. He figured Daniel could keep tabs on everyone while he got some sleep and then when he woke he'd have to break the news to Alex.

12

CONSEQUENCES

Alex stretched out on his bed, feeling better than he knew he should if his rather vague memories of the night before were accurate. He had a rather hazy memory of being seen by the healers but gave up trying to tease the details from his memory. Opening his eyes, he sighed as he saw his brother Daniel lounging in the chair next to him, his feet propped up on the bed.

"So, back in the land of the living, are you?" While Alex could only hear polite enquiry in Daniel's tone, he knew he'd be a fool to believe it. His usually reticent brother was angry with him.

"Yes, Daniel, I'm awake. What's wrong now? Did I miss some important breakfast this morning or something?" Alex knew he'd said the wrong thing when he saw the flash of anger in his brother's face.

"You will have to grow up some time, Alex. You put not only your own life but both Kyle's and Jessalan's in danger last night." Daniel watched Alex's face, seeing that his words weren't having much of an impact.

"Oh, come on, Daniel. You're a little overdramatic, aren't you? It was fun." Alex stopped, startled as his brother sprung forward and grabbed him by the shoulders, cutting off his train of thought.

"The drugs given to Jessalan last night could have killed her, Alex. She's lucky that her hunter friend got her out of the establishment in the Quarter and back here where the healers got to her early. Kyle wasn't as lucky as you; given his reputation, they gave him a lot more of the stuff. Aaron has been tending to him all day. Kyle killed for you last night, you fool!" Daniel glared at his brother, wondering how he got through so many scrapes unscathed. His dear brother should have been dead by now, yet here he was, behaving like he'd just had a night out on the town, seemingly with no ill effects at all.

Alex struggled upright, lurching out of bed and scrambling for some clothes.

"What? I don't remember ... what happened last night?"

Alex ran to his bathroom and performed hasty ablutions before pulling on clothes that had been laid out for him, all the while searching his memory of the previous evening, but he had only a vague recollection of a blonde, then being hustled out of a house just before dawn and brought back to the palace. There were healers in the mix somewhere as well, which gave him pause. He walked toward the door before Daniel stopped him.

"It's not common knowledge yet. I'm sure William will fill you in when he wakes. Some fools tried to kidnap you last night and demand ransom off our father for your safe return. They gave toxins to all three of you. Kyle more than the two of you—they were scared of his reaction—but they took him and Jess right along with you. Jessalan got out first with the aid of some hunter. Kyle regained consciousness somehow; he killed a guard who was keeping watch in the hallway between the rooms they kept you in then snapped the neck of the blonde you were with just before she was about to plunge a dagger into your chest. He collapsed when he got back here. Aaron said all the activity caused too much of the poison to run through his system. He nearly died today, Alex."

Daniel saw that Alex was concerned but did not relent or show any sympathy toward him. Instead, he followed behind as his brother spun, opened his door and ran down the hallway past startled guards. Daniel walked out and closed the door; he called after the guards as they pelted after Alex.

"It's all right; he's not going far, just going to Lord Kyle's rooms." Daniel shook his head. Once more, his little brother had the guards chasing after him. He breathed deeply, trying to suppress a burst of irritation. He seemed to be the nursemaid today. He continued in the other direction toward his older brother's rooms. It was time for him to stir.

A lex burst into Kyle's rooms, passing through the receiving room and into the bedroom, skidding to a halt as his sister Elizabeth glared at him. He saw Kyle, looking pale and shaken, propped up in his bed by pillows with Aaron sitting on the other side, still monitoring his patient. He barely noticed as Elizabeth let go of Kyle's hand. He walked up to the bed, propping himself on its edge.

"Kyle, I'm sorry, it's all my fault. Daniel told me what happened." Alex watched Kyle's face as he smiled.

"It's all right, Alex. I think it might have been the kidnappers' fault, not yours. Maybe we've been to The Tankard too much— they were well prepared for us, it seems." Kyle was trying to look alert and well, but failed. He sank back into his pillows, and within moments of closing his eyes, he was asleep.

"Aaron, Kyle—he will be all right, won't he?" Alex transferred his concerned gaze from his friend to the royal physician.

"I think the worst is over, Your Highness, and he needs rest now. You can stay if you wish but only if you are quiet and let him get the sleep he needs." Aaron fixed the Prince with a stern gaze until he nodded.

Alex eased off the edge of the bed and sank into the chair next to his sister.

"If you thought he was alright, you wouldn't still be here, Aaron. He doesn't look good."

Aaron sighed. "Your Highness, Lord Kyle has been sick, and will be for a while. But when I tell you the worst is over, I mean it. I would not lie to you or my patient. Still, his condition has been severe enough to monitor him for a little while longer and perhaps through the night." Aaron paused looking at Alex severely. "One of the other physicians, Cameron, will be here shortly to relieve me. It is at the King's request that we treat him as if he were a member of the Royal Family. Which means, as I am sure you are aware, a full physician must care for him, not one of our assistants."

Alex nodded and settled miserably onto the couch. He felt lost, panicked almost. Kyle and Jessalan had been constant companions as far back as he could remember; it felt like a part of his soul was being torn apart. He felt Elizabeth's arm around his shoulder as she relented and hugged him. He sank into her shoulder.

"Kyle will be okay, Alex. He needs rest for a while. I wish I could stay here with you both, but I must go. It's late, and I must prepare for the dinner tonight. The Heights Protectorate Delegation is still here and will think us remiss if some of us do not show up for dinner. You need not attend if you do not feel up to socialising. Father has officially announced last night's incident as an attempted kidnapping and assassination attempt. Even the Protectorate Delegates will understand your absence." With that, Elizabeth stood, looking down at him.

"Thank you, Elizabeth. I'll stay away from the dinner tonight. Thank Father for me."

He sank further into the couch to wait. As his sister left the room, he heard her murmuring to someone at the door. He jumped as someone dropped onto the sofa next to him and flung her arms around him with the sob.

"Jessalan, you look pale, are you all right? You should still be in bed." He held Jessalan as she shook and whispered to him, her head buried in his shoulder.

"I thought you were both going to die, Alex—between that poison and the concoction the healers gave me I kept losing contact with the veil and sight of you both. I wanted to come and help, but I didn't have enough control of the power." Jessalan held back a sob as Alex held her. She looked at Kyle, feeling cold, and she shivered. "I never thought I'd say this, but I hope I never lose the ability to control the Taint again. Without its power I was helpless."

Alex looked over toward the door where the healer, Jocelyn, hovered.

"Kyle will be okay, Jessalan, even Aaron says so. And as you can see, so am I, thanks to both you and Kyle. I'm sorry I caused harm to happen to you Jessalan. If Damien hadn't found you and got you clear..." Alex couldn't continue along with that train of thought, so he stopped. "Oh yes, I'm the epitome of the heroic

Fourth Child. So heroic I could have got you all killed." Alex laughed bitterly and just held her until she calmed.

Alex looked up and nodded his thanks as Jocelyn draped a blanket around Jessalan to keep her warm; summer might be upon them soon but while the days were warmer, the evenings were still cold. They sat together and watched Kyle.

Jocelyn walked over to Aaron and spoke. "Go get some rest, Aaron. You've been up longer than I have. Since my patient is here, I can keep watch until Cameron comes."

"Thank you, Jocelyn, I appreciate your courtesy. Have me called if I am needed." He smiled then stood slowly and walked across in the direction of the door before pausing and looking at the pair on the couch. "Your Highness, Lady Jessalan, you are both to rest tonight. You'll go to bed when Jocelyn so orders it, and she'll give you both sleeping draughts to make sure you sleep the night. That's a direction as your healer, and I do not want to hear either of you has disobeyed it. Understood?"

He waited until they both nodded, somewhat surprised that neither of them argued with his instructions, before leaving the room, closing the door gently behind him so as not to disturb his patient.

Alex slipped into Kyle's room trying to be quiet, noting the healer Jocelyn was curled up asleep on the long couch to one side of the chamber. A quick look at his friend showed that he was sleeping. Alex felt a little depressed at that. Every day he came, hoping his friend, the man closer to him than his brothers, would sit up, all but ready to burst out of his bed and out on another adventure.

Alex walked around the high-backed couch drawn up to the side of the bed and sat down, jumping out of his skin as he heard a muffled gasp coming from the other end of the couch. Alex turned his hand going for his dagger before he recognised that the gasp had come from Lady Amelia, Kyle's little sister, although Alex had to admit that she wasn't so 'little' anymore, and had been making her way through the various lords in the court, following in her big brother's footsteps. She was due to be presented at the court as a lady.

Alex looked into her brown eyes, her black hair falling in waves around her shoulders, and was stunned. It was almost like the first time he'd seen her. Her hand was raised up to her mouth, and her eyes were wide, a tear tracing its way down her cheek. Alex realised he'd startled her. Moving across the couch, he gathered her into his arms without thinking about it, one arm stretching around her slim waist while his other reached up, brushing the tear from her cheek before pulling her, unresisting, against his shoulder.

"Shhh, My Lady Amelia. I'm sorry, I didn't see you sitting there. The physicians all assure me that Kyle will be all right, he will heal."

Alex gently tilted her head up to him and, leaning slightly forward, went to kiss her on the cheek. At least, that was what he had intended to do; his body had other intentions. He hoped she hadn't noticed.

Alex stiffened as Amelia tilted her head further and he found that he was kissing her on the lips. He saw her eyes slide up to his, and her hand somehow slipped under his shirt, running up his chest.

"Please, Alex ..." Amelia locked her lips on his again, and it was obvious what she wanted.

Alex had a moment during which he battled with himself—given her brother, his best friend, was unconscious on the bed in the same room—then, with a soft groan, he gave in, lifting her to sit on his lap and kissing her back. With a sigh, he pulled back, and she settled, resting her head against his chest muffling her chuckling against his shirt.

"I know this is inappropriate, but I don't think you have any idea how long I've wanted you to see me."

"You're my best friend's baby sister, and in case it has escaped your attention, he is very good with a sword." Alex couldn't help but snort. "He will not like this if we go further, not to mention, your father will have a fit." Alex stopped as Amelia reached up, placing a finger against his lips.

"Let me worry about Kyle and my father. I think the moment I realised you were more than what people whispered was that time of my first presentation at court. Do you remember?" Amelia shifted slightly looking up into his eyes.

Alex frowned and his mood darkened as he felt that burning anger again as if he was right back there. It was the first time he remembered feeling that way. Amelia had only been presented as a minor in the court a few weeks before, and her father had been called away, to a conference with his father. He and Kyle had been late, something Kyle still kicked himself over even though on that occasion it had been unavoidable. He'd walked into the ballroom to hear Amelia cry out.

He'd known it was her, they'd known each other almost as long as he and Kyle had been inseparable friends. His eyes had tracked across the room and saw Amelia struggling, trying to push away from a drunken lord minor who was trying to take advantage of the situation. His blood had boiled at that point. A deep burning anger settled into him.

Before he'd known it, he was across the room with his sword out, pulling Amelia from the drunken lord's grasp and placing himself between her and her attacker. Alex couldn't quite remember how it had happened, but the drunken lord minor had ended up dead on the floor with a pool of blood spreading around him. The stunned silence had settled on the court as Alex had pulled Amelia to him and shielded her from their sight, guiding her toward the safety of the Royal Enclosure. He'd paused and pulled the dress cloak from his shoulder, wrapping it around her small frame, hiding the ripped sleeve and bodice of her dress from prying eyes.

He'd turned and run his eyes over the stunned court, demanding, just as the doors to the conference room opened and his father and Amelia's along with other assorted lords spilt out, "Does anyone else here feel the need to break the King's peace?"

Alex smiled a little grimly as he remembered that the only thing that had stopped his father from having the offending lord killed was that he was already dead. That was also the first time he saw a hint of respect in his father's eyes.

Alex pushed the memory aside and pulled Amelia closer, kissing the top of her head.

"I remember."

Amelia chuckled and raised a hand up behind his head, lacing her fingers at the back, through his hair. She pulled his head down and once more her lips met his and this time he kissed her without hesitation.

"You were, at that moment, my hero. Of all the people who stood and watched, laughing, none helped but you." Amelia smiled once more, content to lay in his arms. Her soft voice reached his ears. "That was the moment I determined that you would be mine. I hadn't realised it would take this long." Amelia pushed back and looked at him, her expression fierce. "You're not going to pretend you don't have feelings for me and run for the hills. Are you?" Amelia's gaze, which had been soft and loving moments before, was now hard and determined.

Alex chuckled and pulled her back against him. "I wouldn't dream of it. However, it might be best, for your sake more than anything, to keep this low-key for now. The court will go berserk when they find out, and you never know, you might just end up hating me when you spend more time with me."

Amelia smiled. "I can't ever imagine hating you, Alex. Anyway, you might end up hating me." She looked up at him, biting her lip. "It's not like I've been chaste. Even my Lady Mother has given up scolding me."

"I'm hardly one to judge, Amelia. You have heard all that gossip about me being hauled out of most of the least respectable establishments in the Quarter, along with the pleasure houses, right?" Alex looked down at her, and if he was honest with himself, he was concerned about what she would say.

"Alex, of course I've heard. My brother was right there with you hauled out at the same time. I'm not likely to judge when I've hardly been virtuous myself. As long as you don't sneak out of my bed to go sleep with one of your harlots." Amelia looked up at him at that point. Alex knew he was blushing, and it was likely going to his hairline.

"Well, we haven't quite got to the sex part yet, Amelia." Alex felt compelled to point it out although he did not doubt the direction in which this liaison was heading.

Even though a part of him knew this was a bad idea, he liked Amelia. He liked her way more than he should for someone of his birth and station. He may be insulated from marriage for the good of the Realm, unlike William and Elizabeth due to being the

Fourth Child, but he knew his father would use him in that fashion if he had to, just the same as he would use his brothers and sister.

"Don't worry so much about the sex thing, Alex, we'll get to that part. It's not appropriate here in my brother's room, though. Still, being low-key, or as much as we can, is a good idea. It will give us more time for, well, us."

Amelia grinned at Alex impudently and kissed him once more, leaving him with no doubt at all what her plans were for the evening.

13

THE SHADOW HUNTS

K yle felt the veil closing in on him, insistent and determined to pull him into that Realm that lay on the other side. The part of the world that few people could access. Still, it was a world he was familiar with, a place in which he was comfortable. More than he was with the intrigue of his peers in the palace. After endless days of feeling sick and disconnected with himself he was relieved, when he felt the cold wash of power as he started to transition between the worlds.

Even when he wasn't within the veil, he spent lots of time, even in his waking hours of late, treading that path between the two worlds. It was within the grips of the veil that his trainers found him. It was here that he had learned control to block the whispering voices of others from his mind, to use the veil to travel from one place to another. He was instructed to not only to refine his fighting skills but the shadow arts. He had learned to be an assassin.

Kyle smiled grimly. He was uncertain what his Lord Father would say; it was a conversation that never seemed to happen. Although

CATHERINE M WALKER

he knew his father guessed by now who and what he was, since he had snapped the neck of the girl in Alex's defence.

He felt the electrifying pulse of the veil wash over him, as it always did when he thought of his first real kills. He felt no remorse. Not in any way. The guard was a threat and in his way. The girl had intended to kill Alex. Why she had intended to kill Alex, that was the part that made little sense to him. Still, it was a moot point—Alex was the fourth son of the King. Why the girl had been intent on killing Prince Alexander didn't matter. His duty to his Prince, his friend, had been clear.

Finally releasing his hold on the waking world, Kyle sighed and rolled over, slipping into a deep sleep.

Well done, Kyle, although it was a close call. The voice was deadly, and if Kyle hadn't already known who it was, he would have found it menacing.

Kyle's eyes slid open and he smiled at his trainer, the first ever Shadow. The woman that the entire legend of the Shadow had grown up around. Lady Leanna Katrina Shaddin. A former child thief who had diverted from her trade as a child when her masters had discovered her skill with the dagger. From that point, she had been apprenticed and trained as an assassin.

Kat, as she'd been then, and no Lady, had chosen the youngest son of the King as her mark, sure he carried a fat purse. She'd thought her luck was with her when the boy had slipped away from his bodyguards and adult supervision, between stalls and down a dark alley.

Instead, she found the boy fighting with two men. Kat had said she didn't know what had motivated her at that moment to help the boy she'd intended to rob, but she'd thrown herself into the melee. With her small dirk clutched in her fist that moments before she'd planned to use to slit the purse strings of the boy,

128

she'd launched herself at one attacker, slashing it across the startled thug's neck. She was already far enough along in her training as an assassin that she knew by the spurt of blood, the man would die. The thug stumbled back, clutching at his neck. Slumping against the nearby wall, he stood for a moment, shock on his face, before sliding down the wall and collapsing to the ground, unconscious.

Kat had dismissed the man as not being a threat and swung back around to see the boy, sword in hand, disposing of his remaining attacker. The boy turned to face her, sword still grasped in a firm, practised grip, a smile on his lips.

Kat had said they became friends at that moment, despite all the odds against a street urchin and a prince becoming friends. An inconceivable friendship that ended up saving the Realm had been born. It wasn't until much later that she became Lady Leanna Katrina Strafford.

Kyle stood in the Veiled World, dressed in his customary black and brown leathers, and a long black cloak with his hood thrown back. He had his sword belt on and an assortment of other weapons besides the dagger in plain sight on his belt. Kyle could never work out if he was physically in the veil or if it was just his dream state and his body was still back in his bed. Kat was no help in that regard, shrugging and telling him that sometimes he was there and sometimes not.

Kyle pushed the thought aside; none of the servants had ever noticed him missing or remarked on it. He guessed if he was here in the veil he must somehow dress and arm himself without being aware of it.

Thanks, Kat. It's been a while since we've trained. Kyle assessed his trainer's mood and was relieved that she seemed to be in good spirits. *Although I misjudged the situation at The Tankard.*

Kyle couldn't help but think he should have somehow known that the women had intended to harm Alex. Although for the life of him he couldn't reasonably work out how he could have known in advance. Still, common sense didn't have much to do with it.

Kat shook her head. *You couldn't have known, Kyle, and by the time you did the poison was already racing through your system. At that point, there was nothing you could do. Come, enough of this. You're here to train, though since it's your first session back, it's an easy one. Let's walk the paths between the veil and the real world. You need the practise, and I have something to show you.*

Kyle grinned in anticipation; of all his lessons these were the ones he loved. Roaming the streets and rooftops of the Royal Capital or villages and cities he'd never seen in real life—neither in the Veiled World or the real one. It was a part of his assassin training, walking through the world unseen, unnoticed by others, at least until he killed them. That thought gave him a moment's pause. He'd always thought his kills had been simulated somehow here in the veil. That no one had really died until the woman who had tried to kill Alex. Now he wondered if they had been real.

Kyle didn't feel the shock or loathing he felt he should, that an average person would. Then again, he guessed he was not normal. How many others had been trained since they were a small child with the woman who had been The Shadow? As he was wondering about the kills, he caught the voice of his trainer whispering in his head through the veil.

Yes, the kills were real Kyle—all of them. You know they deserved their fate. You followed them, assessed them, knew what they were into and what they were doing. Most were guilty of treason against the crown. For that alone, as a Lord of the Realm, it was your duty to take action. The girl was just the first kill that anyone could attribute to your name.

Kat turned and looked back at him; reassured by what she saw, she nodded before continuing to lead the way on the pathways.

Kyle considered the information that Kat had given him and realised that he still felt no remorse. He hadn't just killed a man and woman in defence of the Realm. By his count he'd killed hundreds. He wasn't just a master swordsman, he was an assassin. Kyle considered his options and spoke back to his trainer in the same fashion.

The King needs to know. Alex needs to know.

Kyle didn't look at his trainer as they came out from the veiled paths, settling on the roof of a tavern in what appeared to be a small village.

Alex isn't ready to know yet, although when the time is right, I think you might find he is already aware. It's likely the King already knows, Prince William as well. They both guess who you are already, Kyle. Kat gained his attention and gestured toward two men who had spilt out into the street from the tavern.

Kyle frowned, and then his eyes narrowed as he recognised the men; both had been in The Tankard the night both he and Alex had been drugged and kidnapped. They had disappeared after their removal from the tavern, and no amount of searching by the Elite had discovered their whereabouts. Kyle stilled, pulling the veil closer to him almost by instinct, watching as the men staggered down the road. Standing, he moved from rooftop to rooftop, careful to keep to the shadows on the roof, always with his sight on the men.

At first, he thought the men were drunk, but as they turned the corner out of sight of the tavern, after a furtive glance behind them, they straightened and quickened their pace, heading toward one of the last houses in the street. Kyle turned to ask Kat how she'd found them only to discover that she'd slipped away, as she often did once she'd pointed him in the direction she wanted. Snorting, he realised he was on his own. So much for an easy start.

Kyle drew even more of the veil in and leapt from rooftop to rooftop until he was crouching on the roof of the house opposite the men. The house they were at was nondescript. It looked neither run down nor wealthy. It was just one house in a row of modest homes. As the door opened, Kyle drew a sharp breath only just stopping himself from swearing from a force of habit. Kyle recognised the man. He was Lord Minor Rathan Cartwright. He sometimes frequented the court, although his station was not high enough to have a suite at the palace. Rathan was also a snivelling little man who had been pestering Jess. Kyle remembered that he had also been at The Tankard the first night they met the girls who'd ended up trying to kidnap them.

Kyle watched as Rathan looked down the street then ushered the men into the house. Kyle ran to the edge of the roof he was on and jumped to the ground below, using the power from the veil to soften his landing. He paused in the shadows, assessing the street, then pulling up the hood of his cloak and kept to the shadows he drew in even more of the veil. He used the power to mask him as he walked across the street to the house where the men had disappeared.

Being careful not to make a noise as he took one careful step after another, Kyle walked around the home until he found an unsecured window. Smiling, he pulled the shutters open and climbed inside. Hearing muffled voices, Kyle paused before pulling the door open and glancing out into the empty hallway. He moved from room to room and was relieved that they were empty except for some baggage in the last room. Moving quickly but quietly, he walked down the hallway toward the voices, pausing outside an open door that from what he could see was a sitting room. Rathan sat in a chair while two men stood; none of them looked happy, and from his vantage point he could hear their conversation with perfect clarity.

"How could you be so sloppy? Now we've got nothing to show for all our efforts. How the hell did those drunken fools escape?" Rathan's voice was high pitched and angry with a hint of panic.

"We don't know how they did it, Rathan. The girls gave them the drug you supplied. It didn't work. The guards found the house and both the Prince and Lord Kyle, according to all reports, walked out. Lady Jessalan wasn't seen leaving, but she wasn't there and Oliver was located dead. Jana is dead as well, her neck snapped. We guess it was one of the Elite and Kelly was taken in by them, to all reports alive when she was taken but executed by the King for treason. We have to get out of Vallantia. I can't believe the King's men didn't pump her for all the information she had before they killed her." It was the bigger of the two men who spoke; his voice was low, but he sounded panicked.

The second man, a little shorter than his companion and stockier, with dark greasy hair, spoke in a gravelly voice.

"We've got a death sentence over our heads for this if the guard ever catches up with us. Rathan, you told us it would be easy, the King would pay up and that he hated his youngest son who was a drunken embarrassment to the throne. Well, it seems the King didn't quite see it the same way." The man looked around before turning his attention back to Rathan, although he looked like he wanted to bolt for the door.

"Well don't look for any more money, I don't have it. That was the idea behind taking the Prince to embarrass the King so he'd pay us to keep quiet about Prince Alexander's exploits." Rathan licked his lips and looked from one man to the other. "You need to lie low and stay out of sight for now. The King is likely to forget soon enough. Before you go, where are you staying?"

Both men opened their mouths then closed them, looking at each other, seeming to agree. The taller man reached out and poked Rathan in the chest, underscoring his words, his tone contemptuous.

"I suggest you find the money, Lord Minor Rathan, or your father will find another heir. You've got two days, get the money to us at the Crown and Kestrel down the road. It's a dive, but they had rooms for the right price."

Rathan stumbled back, a look of alarm crossing his face as the men turned and headed toward the door. Kyle stepped back down the hallway away from the main door, pressing himself into the dark corner near a cupboard. Neither man noticed him as they stormed out, slamming the door behind them.

Kyle grinned, although it wasn't the kind of smile anyone would want to see. It was the expression where if you had any sense and you saw it directed at you, you'd run in the other direction.

Kyle waited a moment to give the men time to walk to the end of the road and out of earshot in case the Lord Minor called them for help, although Kyle judged that was unlikely to happen.

Hearing movement in the room, Kyle walked toward the doorway where he'd stood moments before and saw that Rathan had slumped into a chair, cradling a drink in his hand with a panicked look on his face.

Kyle walked into the room. Rathan stood in alarm, his glass falling from his nerveless fingers as Kyle grabbed him and slammed him against the wall, his dagger moving to the now quivering Lord's throat.

Rathan spoke, his voice high-pitched. "You can't kill me, I'm a Lord. The King will come after you for this."

Rathan tried to straighten imperiously but failed miserably.

Kyle laughed, low and menacing. "I know well who you are, Rathan, and the King will not come after me; you gave up your life when you involved yourself in a plot to kidnap the Prince." Kyle threw back his hood and smiled as the man's eyes widened in recognition.

"Please, Lord Kyle, I can explain, I needed money, no harm would ever come to you or the Prince ..."

Rathan stopped talking as Kyle's blade pressed firmer into the skin against his throat, enough that the sharp blade cut into the skin. A thin trail of blood trickled down Rathan's throat.

"You're lying, Rathan. I was there. The blonde one was about to plunge a dagger into Alex's chest right before I came in and snapped her little neck. Tell me who is controlling you, Rathan, who suggested this little enterprise?" Kyle hauled the quivering Rathan forward and shoved him back into his seat. Seeing Rathan's eyes flick toward the exit, Kyle laughed.

"I wouldn't if I were you. You'll be dead before you reach the door. Now talk." Kyle's eyes bore down into the hapless lordling, who squirmed.

Rathan licked his lips. He looked up at Kyle, unable to look away.

"You will kill me anyway, won't you?"

Kyle felt nothing but contempt for the man but saw no point in denying the likely result of this encounter.

"You are guilty of treason, and I am the Shadow that protects the Fourth; it's my duty." Kyle saw no reason he couldn't use the damn legend to his advantage. "Still, there are easy ways to die and hard ways. Which way it ends for you is in your hands. Either way, before you die, you will tell me what I want to know."

Kyle once again marvelled at his cold detachment, knowing every word he spoke was true. He watched Rathan as he continued to squirm in his chair before slumping.

"I don't know. I don't know. It came up in conversation when I was at a bar in Vallantia. Everyone was laughing and drinking. I was telling my friends I was running out of money and my father refused to give me more. Jon and Caleb—I presume you were here while they were. Well, I owe their boss money." Rathan licked his lips again, his chin quivering, looking for all the world like he was about to cry.

Kyle said nothing. He continued to stare at the man. Waiting, patient, knowing he would continue. His type always did.

"I was at The Tankard waiting for you and the Prince to show up. I knew you both frequented the place, hoped I'd run into you both and we'd become friends. Then Jon and Caleb's boss wouldn't dare to touch me if I was a friend of the Prince."

Rathan's words had been tumbling out of his mouth one after the other, to the point that Kyle had to concentrate to make out what the man was babbling about. He also wondered where the story was going.

With a quick glance at Kyle for permission, or at least a sign he would not kill him, he reached over to the nearby table and pulled a bottle of cheap-looking alcohol toward him and a fresh glass, pouring the dark liqueur to the brim. He took a long gulp and sat there for a moment, lost in his thoughts.

"There was a man. I didn't recognise him, but he laughed when he heard of my troubles and suggested I abduct the Prince and Lady Jessalan—and you. Well I think he suggested you and Lady Jessalan because you're always with the Prince." Rathan contemplated his drink once more, taking another swallow of the cheap but potent brew.

Then he laughed. "He said 'the girl shouldn't be a problem'. Yet she somehow killed Oliver and escaped. He suggested the drug that could contain all of you, and Jana, Kelly and Oliver from The Leaf and Feather could help keep the three of you entertained until the King paid the ransom. The first night it all went wrong. You, you intervened and the bottle with the drug in it smashed on the floor. Lady Jessalan ended up with that other man. I was relieved. I thought it was over."

Kyle watched and waited; he knew Rathan wasn't finished.

"Then you all showed up again—they knew you would. They had to scramble but the plan rolled out, this time it was working. He said I'd only have to keep you all in the house for a few days and I'd be rich beyond what I could imagine, that I'd never need my father's money again." Rathan's voice shook; his voice trembled as he spoke, seemingly lost in memory. "I don't know what came over me, what the man said just kept playing on my mind. Then it was all in motion; you, Jess and the Prince showed up. It was going so well, then it all went wrong. I was ordered to keep you both there for two days; instead it was only a night." Rathan sobbed, biting his lip hard enough he drew his blood, before taking another drink.

Kyle contemplated the man, trying to make sense of his rambling story.

"Did the man say the King would pay a ransom or just that you

CATHERINE M WALKER

would be paid well for abducting and drugging us, for keeping us at the house?"

Rathan looked up at him, confusion written all over his face.

"Well, he didn't mention the King but who else would pay?"

Kyle gritted his teeth, willing patience. "How were you to get the money?"

Rathan blinked, took a quick drink before replying. "Baine, the man, called himself Baine, he said he'd get the money for me. That I'd be rich."

Kyle wanted to curse but restrained himself. "How did Jon and Caleb come into this whole affair, what was their part?"

"Jon and Caleb tracked me down. Their boss wanted his money, but they heard the conversation and wanted in on the whole thing, said they would help, be the muscle. Said I'd get my cut of the money, they'd take theirs and give a portion to their boss to pay off my debt. It sounded like a good deal, so I agreed. I don't know why I did, but I did. Then I left. Jon and Caleb stayed at the tavern talking to Baine." Rathan slumped back into his chair; he looked defeated.

"The man, Baine. Have you ever seen him at court?"

Kyle's mind was racing, trying to work out who Baine was, but he didn't hold much hope that Rathan knew anything else and, as he expected, Rathan just shook his head.

"How was he dressed? Rich, commoner, merchant, sell sword?" Kyle knew from what Rathan said the man he needed was Baine. He was the part of the thread—if he got the end and pulled, he could unravel this whole thing.

"Baine? He was well dressed, not a commoner or merchant but no lord either, otherwise I would have recognised him. Dark hair shaved close to the skull, a tattoo down his right arm, a trail of skulls from his neck to his knife hand. Oh, and a scar. He had a bad scar trailing down the line of his left jawbone." Rathan took another swig of his drink, emptying the glass, then poured himself another.

Kyle took a deep breath, pushing down his anger through sheer willpower. He didn't want to kill the man. Yet. The man Rathan had just described, Baine, with the shaved head and skull tattoos trailing down his right arm, belonged to the League of Skulls. Assassins, thieves, blades for hire. There was nothing they wouldn't do if the price were right. Still, they rarely went after members of the Royal Family; that ended in all-out warfare with the Crown—history showed that didn't pay so well.

Kyle thought for a moment more and asked one final question. "Who was the man you lost all your father's money to?"

Rathan was almost insensible now with the amount of arak he'd had but took a moment from drinking to look up at him.

"Lord Creswell Vannen. He owns half the illegal gambling houses in Vallantia."

Kyle paced two steps forward to Lord Minor Rathan, his face blank, calm. "Sleep well, Lord Minor Rathan. May the veil grant you rest and return to this world to redeem the life you failed."

With those words he moved behind the insensible Lord, wrapping his arm around his throat and cutting off his air supply until he slumped, unconscious. Satisfied, Kyle pulled his head back, extending his neck, and sliced his dagger across the man's throat before letting him go. The former Lord Minor slid forward out of the chair, crumpling in a lifeless heap on the floor, blood pooling around him. Kyle walked around his crumpled victim toward the door, his face calm, almost dispassionate, and he left without looking back.

K yle examined the house, but other than the travel bags from the late Lord Minor Rathan, there was nothing of interest. Exiting the home, he gathered the veil around him, using it to assist in hiding him from casual observers. Still he kept to the pools of shadow as he walked down the street, backtracking to the Crown and Kestrel.

Kyle paused on the opposite side of the road and watched the main doors from the sad and rather run-down looking pub. Even though from what he could see the clientele were not the 'who's who' of society, Kyle knew he'd be remarked on and remembered. Especially when the publican found two dead bodies in his rooms when he checked them after the men failed to pay for their room. Kyle grinned to himself. Then again, if the thugs had paid up for a few days, then it was likely the publican or his cleaning girls wouldn't check the rooms until the men failed to leave. Then they would go to the chamber to either get more money or kick them out.

Moving at a steady pace, Kyle walked to the side of the building, scanning his surroundings as he went. Once in the shadows out of direct sight from the road, Kyle jumped, catching a ledge on the second floor, hauling himself up with a graceful ease.

One glance through the window assured him that while the room was occupied, no one was in there right now. He guessed they were down in the tap room—lucky for them, at this point. Kyle assessed the room and, as he guessed, it belonged to the publican, cluttered with possessions that no itinerant traveller would have with them, and it had a private washroom. That was unlikely in most rooms in a pub as run-down and small as this one. He listened at the door to the chamber before easing out into the empty hallway. He could hear the noise from the tap room below and was satisfied that it would mask any indiscreet noise that might be made by the men.

Kyle looked down the dark, narrow wooden hallway, lit by one lamp halfway down. There were only six other doors besides the one he'd come out from. He dismissed the smaller one down the end of the hall as likely being the communal washroom for the other guests that the pub might house; he'd leave that to last. Besides, if either of his targets was in the washroom, killing them there was not the best option, since they'd be found quicker.

Working smoothly, he systematically checked the rooms; three of the five rooms had occupants; however, the room down the hall near the washroom had two small narrow beds with bags at their feet. The other two had single occupants, one of which was a woman, if the clothing was any testament, who had an impressive assortment of fine weapons. What she was doing here was an intriguing mystery. If he weren't already occupied, he'd take the time to find out who she was and what she was up to. It was a sign that he would have to show caution, if the mystery woman was even half as good as the weapons indicated she was.

Kyle picked the room with the two beds as being the room that his targets had rented off the publican. Leaving the woman's room after one last glance at the weapons, he moved back and re-entered the room he wanted. A quick glance around it revealed that there were no suitable hiding places; however, there was a small, grimy window that, with effort, Kyle could unlatch and open. There was a handy ledge running around the outside of the building from which he could either drop to the ground or access the rooftops, depending on which route he took or needed if he had to exit.

Coming back to the room, Kyle went through the contents of the first bag at the foot of the closest bed; he wrinkled his nose a little at the smell wafting up from the bag. The man could afford to part with a few coins and get his clothes cleaned more frequently. Grateful for his gloves, he picked through the contents, finding little of interest, except a vest with Lord Raymond Kessalan's family crest on it. Looking at the crest, his eyes narrowed; he would, no doubt, have to visit Lord Kessalan, although not tonight. Kyle put the contents of the bag back how he found it, although he suspected the men were the type who would not notice anyway.

Kyle walked over to the second bag, and he noticed this man was a little more methodical in his packing. His spare set of clothes, while still not clean by any stretch of the imagination, at least did not smell rancid. Still, the contents didn't give up anything of interest either, save the same vest with Lord Kessalan's crest stitched onto it.

Thugs they might be, but not stupid ones. If they had anything in writing it was likely on their person, not left in their baggage in their room. Kyle grimaced; that was a pity. Hearing movement down the hallway and a drunken argument between two men, Kyle closed the bag he'd been looking through. He looked around then moved over to the darkest corner of the room out of the line of sight from the doorway. He concentrated, pulling the shadows around him. He knew from experience it would assist in hiding his presence from the men. Kyle didn't plunge fully into the veil, so if they walked into him, they would end up bumping into something they couldn't see, although the likelihood of them walking into him while he was standing right in the corner of the room was remote—unless, of course, they stumbled into him, which was a distinct possibility given they seemed to be drunk.

The door opened with the two men staggering into the room, one of them tripping over the bag and landing heavily on the floor. He swore and blinked in confusion at the bag, glaring at it as if thinking it had moved on purpose. The short, squat man rolled over to his knees and went to stand up. Or at least he tried, but ended up back on his rear on the ground. Kyle had to stifle a laugh. The man gave up on walking and proceeded with a wobbly drunken crawl over to the bed and after he contemplated the distance between his position and the bed he hauled himself onto it and fell asleep.

The taller man, no more sober than his fellow thug but still upright, even if it was with the help of the wall, gave a bark of laughter.

"Huh, you can't hold your drink!"

The man's slurred words rumbled from his throat. He pushed off from the wall and made his stumbling path to the bed, taking a few more steps than he should need to. He managed to collapse on the bed without ending up on the floor.

Kyle's eyes widened, and he gathered even more of the shadow to him as the drunken man, perplexed, squinted in his direction from his newly gained position on the bed. Kyle felt a small tug on the veil and nearly breathed a sigh of relief. While he could touch the Taint and draw on it a small amount, he had nowhere near the power to unravel Kyle's hiding spot.

The man shook himself, muttering. "Drunk too much. Imagining ghosts now."

He laughed to himself as he hauled his boots off with a great display of effort that nearly sent him tumbling off the bed. He then placed them neatly near the edge of the bed, or as neatly as he was capable of with his level of intoxication, and attempted to unbuckle his vest. That was a trial. He pulled it off and, folding it haphazardly, placed it on the small table near the head of the bed after contemplating his bag and deciding that was too hard to get to in his current state.

The man lay back on his bed and after a short space of time slipped into a drunken slumber. Kyle waited a few moments more to make sure both of the men were asleep then paced over to them. Contemplating both men, he went over to the small table near the bed of the more fastidious of the two and, after a quick glance at the sleeping men, checked the vest. It was well-worn leather with some metal plates that looked like they had been stitched on by the wearer, but inside an inner pocket he found what he was looking for: a small black book. Placing the vest back where he found it, he flicked through the pages and saw notes within, including dates, places and times.

Kyle's head snapped around as he heard a faint noise from the window. Taking the diary, he wrapped the darkness around himself and moved back to the corner of the room, just this side of the veil. His eyes widened in shock as a woman wearing all black clothing slipped into the chamber. She wasted no time or effort but made quick work of dispatching both men. Quietly, without fuss or noise. She checked their belongings, frustrated, not finding what she was after. Kyle thought at her.

Too late, assassin, I have the diary already.

Kyle nearly swore in alarm as the woman's head snapped up and she spun around, seeking him. She raised her blade and dropped into a crouch, drawing on the veil and scanning the room.

Kyle made a quick decision and ran, diving out of the open window, his cloak billowing around him as he somersaulted and landed on the ground in the small courtyard below. He straightened from his crouch and glanced back toward the window he'd jumped from, seeing the shimmering dark movement along the ledge. He heard more than saw the throwing knife heading in his direction and, shimmering between this world and the next, he stepped to one side, swaying out of the way. At the last second, he snapped his hand out with perfect timing and plucked the blade from its flight, looking up.

Not this day, assassin. I don't have time for you. We'll dance another day.

While Kyle knew he shouldn't taunt the woman, he couldn't help himself. He was intrigued by her and if he hadn't been intent on getting back to the King with what he'd learned, he would have stayed to cross blades with her.

He heard her soft words float back to him; she was not as strong as he was in the gift, but her mind's voice was clear enough.

You interfere in the Skull Lord's business. He doesn't tolerate independents. Report to him before he tasks me with tracking you down.

As Kyle walked, merging from the real world into the Veiled World, he felt her shock before he cut their connection. She was a member of the Order of the Skull. That they had an assassin in their number who had talent and could use the power of the veil was a shock and something to be even wary of. That this was important enough for them to send out someone who was one of their best to 'clean up' for them was of even greater concern.

<hr>

Kyle moved down the pathways of the veil, those paths that only a few could tread; his pace was unhurried. It had been a long night by his estimation, but time moved at a different pace here in the Veiled World than it did in reality. Still, it gave him a chance to think.

He knew he would have to report the night's activities; doing so before he slept most of the morning away would be preferable. Still, appearing in the King's private bedchamber unannounced was probably not a good idea, even for him. Ultimately, though, it was the King who had to know what he had found out and the fact that his Kingdom was less one lord minor.

Making a decision, he altered his path and appeared back in his room, still shrouded by the veil. He could only use the veiled ways to go places he'd already been. William always invaded his domain when he wanted something; he had never been in William's rooms, but that didn't pose much of a problem since he knew where they were and how to get there from his chambers.

Walking over to his bedroom windows, he unbarred them and pushed the shutters open. He then stepped out onto the narrow ledge beyond them. The King's recent announcement meant that he had a new suite of rooms in the Royal wing, giving him even better access to William's rooms than he used to have.

Kyle carefully braced himself against the wall then pulled his shutters closed. Taking a moment to assess the courtyard and his surroundings, he noted that the guards on the wall and gate were not paying the slightest bit of attention, at least not to the palace. If he moved along the ledge, he doubted anyone would notice. Counting windows and suites, he finally made it to William's. Again, he checked on the guards and noticed that there were signs of movement down in the courtyard. He didn't have long before the palace would be active. He needed to pass on his message and slip back into his bed before the servants started to busy themselves in the Royal Wing.

Kyle grinned, observing that William's bedroom window was ajar, and eased himself inside. Scanning the room, he noticed it was still dark, with the drapes drawn and William asleep in the large canopied bed. Kyle breathed a soft sigh of relief, noting that tonight William had gone to bed alone. Crossing over to a chair off to one side, he dragged it over to the bed and sat, propping his feet up on the bed. He waited, knowing it wouldn't be long before William stirred.

Finally, William sighed and opened his eyes. It took a moment before he registered what he was seeing and he gasped, sitting bolt upright in bed. Kyle laughed softly and raised one gloved hand and pulled his hood back to reveal his face.

"Relax, William. It's just me. You'll not die in your bed this day, but consider closing and barring your bedroom windows." Kyle contemplated the Crown Prince as relief and anger played across his features. Relief won as William slumped back against his pillows, groaning.

"What the hell, Kyle? You scared the life out of me." William closed his eyes then cracked them open again, glaring at him.

Kyle smiled. "Sorry, William. Thought I should report before I crash and sleep most of the morning away. The King needs to know what I've been up to and found out tonight but I thought it was better to appear in your room than the King's."

Levering himself up from the chair while William gathered himself, he went over to the side table to see the offerings of the small service area. Water, wine, liquor and a pot of steaming coffee that had obviously just been put there by the servants prior to his arrival. William's servants knew him well. He wasn't the only one to bother the Crown Prince at all hours of the day and night with things that the King needed to know. Kyle stared toward the open window and the glowing light on the horizon and poured William a black coffee. It would be a long day for the Crown Prince, and he didn't have the power of the veil to draw from, or at least not as much of it.

Kyle returned and passed the steaming mug to William, who was now propped up in bed, having hauled the many pillows scattered on his bed together.

"Do the healers know about your night activities yet? I know they haven't cleared you for normal duty yet, I get a report every day." William was watching him steadily without a hint of censure in his voice, although there was a trace of concern.

"No, not yet. I'm fine, William, they are just being overly cautious." Kyle sat and closed his eyes briefly while William drank some of his coffee. He could feel the weight of the night's activities weighing down on him. He needed to sleep, and soon.

"The attempted abduction of Alex, Jess and me wasn't just a money-making tactic by some stupid people." Kyle kept his eyes closed, thinking through all he'd learned and getting his train of thought in order. He sensed that William was suddenly paying more attention.

"The King is now short one Lord Minor, Rathan Cartwright. He was cut off by his father but had gambling debts to Lord Creswell Vannen—he controls most of the brothels and gambling houses in Vallantia. His two thugs who also thought to capitalise on the abduction have paid with their lives, although not by my blade. There is another player."

Kyle felt his thoughts scatter for a space of time but fought off sleep, knowing he had to finish passing on the rest of what he'd learned.

"The man who instigated the attempted abduction was a man called Baine. His description places him as a member of the Order of the Skull, yet it's an unusual move from them that makes me wonder if they were set up. I'm sorry, William, there is more, I know there is, but the weight of my activities in the veil is pressing in on me, and I need to sleep." Kyle felt himself fading and passed on one final message: "For the love of the Realm, bar your windows. If I can get in, so can a disciple of the Skull; they have a gifted assassin, female—cute—although I don't think she'd be your type. Do not take any women you do not know to your bed until I can get a better notion of who exactly she is. This was all I could retrieve from the thugs before the woman showed up and killed them."

With that last advice, Kyle dropped the black diary on William's nightstand and faded, disappearing into the place between the worlds, making his way back to his bed, finally, to sleep the morning away.

14

A MEETING OF LORDS

K yle knew he had a visitor even before he cracked his eyes open. He even knew who it was without much effort.

"You know, Your Highness, sneaking into my room while we've got a gifted Skulls Assassin potentially after me is probably not the best notion. To what do I owe the pleasure of this visit?" Kyle opened his eyes to see William bringing him a steaming cup of coffee in one hand and a familiar black notebook in the other. "I take it this is not just payback for the other day—what task do you and the King have for me? I'm thinking that there is one."

Kyle hauled himself up in bed and glanced toward the open drapes that William habitually drew wide whenever he paid him one of his visits. Kyle sighed and accepted the coffee from William; at least this time it looked to be after midday.

William sunk into a nearby chair and grinned at him. "Well, you know the easy way to stop these visits is for you to tell your guards I'm not allowed to just walk in."

Kyle sipped his coffee and flicked his eyes to the Prince over the rim and saw that he at least appeared relaxed. Kyle snorted.

"Oh, and I can see that going down well. Just because I could, it doesn't mean I should. Besides, it's the most private place we can talk without other ears." Kyle took another sip of his coffee and eyed the black notebook that William was slapping into his palm.

"Regardless, you can. It's one reason Father had you all moved. We know times are coming where you might need that extra space. Promise me if you require the time to yourself you will let your guards know to refuse all visitors." William looked at him without any hint of arrogance.

Kyle closed his eyes and nodded. "I will, William, but regardless you will always be welcome. The needs of the Crown will always come first." Kyle smiled cynically. "Even if I take a few days to get to it. Someone in power should know I'm going off the rails."

William stared at him for the longest time before nodding acceptance. He looked toward the window, gathering his thoughts before returning his attention to the small black book. He turned to regard Kyle once more.

"The healers assure me you are fit for duty and need not ride in a carriage for the move to the Summer Palace." William grinned at the look of horror on Kyle's face at the thought of being cooped up in a carriage. His smile faded as he contemplated the book once more. "This was an interesting read and a good find, Kyle. While neither Father nor myself believe Lord Creswell Vannen is involved with the League of the Skulls, we believe his associations are closer than those of any Lord Major of this Realm should be. If he wants to remain alive and doesn't want the King to have him killed for treason, he will never be found to be connected in any action against the Crown again. If he is, his whole line will cease to exist." William still appeared to be calm and flipped the little black notebook to Kyle, who caught it without spilling so much as a single drop of coffee.

Kyle waited for a heartbeat then smiled. "Ah, so now that Lord Kyle has been officially moved into the Royal Wing, the King ordered the Fourth's Wing be made ready at the Summer Palace and new clothes appear in my wardrobe with the Fourth's Crest. The King would like Lord Kyle, the Fourth's Blade, to pay a visit to said Lord?"

William chuckled at Kyle's bland tone. "See, I knew you'd catch on quick. If you could find somewhere safe, out of the way of prying eyes for that, it would be appreciated. Wear something appropriate from your new wardrobe and report the results to the King tonight at the ball." William stood and handed him a slip of paper that had a list of businesses on it.

One quick scan of it told him they were all gambling institutions and pleasure houses. All of them owned by Lord Vannen.

"The King would like you to suggest to Lord Vannen that he may wish to distance himself from the listed establishments before they get raided by the guard. Don't kill him, Kyle. We want to see how he reacts, who he goes to, just in case." William smiled tightly as Kyle whistled.

"That will cause consternation in certain circles." Kyle grinned and nodded, then spoke up with a small note of alarm in his voice, causing William to turn back to him.

"Wait, have you had to send the guard to get Alex, Jess and myself out of any of these places?" Kyle's grin widened even further as William burst out laughing.

"Just one: The Harlot. I believe Father was most insistent that the establishment was to be closed down." William shook his head before turning and walking toward the door, throwing one more parting shot back at Kyle. "Oh, and that doesn't mean you three have to go out on a wild party spree and visit every pleasure house on that list. It would not go down well if you three were taken in by the guard when they are raided."

"William, wait." Kyle frowned as William turned back to him, his eyebrow raised. "How has Alex taken the King's acknowledgement of his title as the Fourth Child?"

William shook his head. "We've had several conversations about it while you were sick; even Alex noticed the new clothing that appeared in his wardrobe. As you'd imagine, he is not happy, but is taking it better than I expected. He hasn't had a yelling match with Father over the decision. Yet."

Kyle grimaced at William's response, knowing Alex not being happy was an understatement. "You will speak to him about this, right? I can't report to you and the King tonight as the Fourth's Blade and blindside Alex that way."

William nodded. "Yes, I will speak with him now. He'll be wearing his new clothes, displaying his rank. Father felt it best, rather than an official announcement; Alex always has been the Fourth and doesn't need the King's acknowledgement before he can assume the role."

———

Kyle walked into his massive wardrobe and stared at the racks upon racks of clothing. The contents of his closet had been multiplying as the new formal clothing with the Crest of the Fourth was being added. Walking out, somewhat frustrated, he pulled a small rope he knew rang a bell in the servants' waiting area.

His door opened with a promptness that startled him, and

Bennett walked in with a tray containing a selection of baked items, fruits, cheeses and sliced meats from the kitchen and placed it on the table.

"Afternoon, My Lord, I prepared a tray for you. With His Highness' visit, I guessed you'd be calling. Is there anything else you need, My Lord? Should I prepare your bath while you eat?"

Bennett was an active, wiry man; his servant since, it seemed, forever, although he was not much older than he was. He was by all reports a cousin's illegitimate son who had begged service off his Lady Mother. His mother had not only granted his request but seen that Bennet's mother was taken care of with a nice cottage of her own and regular deliveries of supplies. She was not wealthy by any stretch of the imagination, but she didn't want for anything, which lent weight to the rumour regarding his parentage. Bennett was good with a blade and more than capable of seeing to Kyle's household with expanding responsibilities.

"Thanks, Bennett. I need to pay an official visit today to Lord Vannen. Could you pull out a set of my court clothes—the new ones with the Crest of the Fourth on them? Seems I will wear them sooner than I thought." Kyle saw no surprise from Bennett, who only nodded and walked through the wardrobe and dressing rooms into the bathroom beyond.

What seemed like hours later, Kyle was looking in the mirror, tugging at his tunic while the ever-present and capable Bennett fussed and made sure he looked perfect. Standing back, he assessed his handy work with a small satisfied smile and a nod before heading back to the weapons rack, which had its own place, taking up one whole section of his wardrobe. Bennett came back with his hands and arms full of an assortment of blades. The ones that would be on ceremonial display caught Kyle's eye; they were new.

As Bennett dumped the weapons on a nearby table and assisted him in arming up, Kyle plucked one of the new daggers up and assessed its weight. Despite the glossy new Fourth's Crest embossed on the hilt and the sigil of the Shadow, as well as the Fourth's Blade etched into the blade itself, it was finely balanced. Kyle flicked his eyes to Bennett in the mirror and raised an eyebrow in enquiry.

"His Majesty and your father commissioned and paid for them, My Lord. I believe they bickered about who would pay for your wardrobe and outfitting, and settled on a compromise." Bennett's lips twitched, although his tone had been bland.

That Bennett was admiring the appearance of his lord was not lost on Kyle. He well knew that Bennett slept with men, not women. His servant also knew his master was into women— Bennett had walked in on Kyle with partners in the morning often enough. He had helped more than one lady discreetly to her own rooms. He'd never put a foot out of line with Kyle or any other man, to Kyle's knowledge. Kyle had even set his servant up a few times, making recommendations on bedmates not only in the servant's ranks but in the ranks of the lords.

If any had thought they could pump Bennett for information about his lord, they soon discovered the error of their ways. Bennett was loyal not only to the Strafford family but to Kyle, in particular. Bennett was discreet and few knew his inclinations. He'd left more than one lady who'd been trying to extract information about his Lord, confused as to why their wiles hadn't worked.

"So will I pass muster?" Kyle kept his tone light and bantering.

Bennett took the question seriously and appraised him openly, a slight smile tugging at the edges of his lips.

"Yes, My Lord, you do. The ladies are a mystery but I have noticed a, shall we say, similarity in their tastes. Cool, competent, powerful—the sigil of the Shadow. You mix civilised and refinement with dangerous. The ladies will fall all over you if you let them. Lord Vannen will be terrified if that is your intent."

Kyle saw his own eyes narrow.

"Good. A terrified lord major would be my intent. If he's smart, he will understand the message I have to deliver and, given who it is from, take heed. Thank you, Bennett, you might as well take the night off, if you choose. I have orders and, dressed like this, will be palace-bound this evening." His servant bowed and walked toward the door before Kyle added as an afterthought, "I don't think you'll have to usher any ladies out of my bed in the morning. At least, I'm not planning it."

He grinned as he surprised a laugh out of Bennett. "You never do, My Lord. I will check anyway. Still, it will be easy for a lady to get back to her rooms unnoticed should she spend the night with you here, unlike in the case of your previous suite." With that last parting shot, Bennett departed his Lord's rooms, intent on his own pursuits.

Kyle knew precisely which wing Lord Raymond Vannen was housed in when he was at the palace. While he was a lord major—and wealthy—at least now he knew where the wealth came from. He was in one of the more remote wings of the palace since he wasn't particularly influential. Or at least on the surface, he had never appeared to be. Now, given what he'd found out, he wondered if Lord Major Vannen had more influence on some lords than he'd known of.

Kyle approached the door and observed the household guards, without weapons, outside the door, surveying with some alarm the approach of an armed lord with Elite in tow. Kyle didn't pause as he approached the door, giving a flat stare to the guards, who looked likely to object.

"I wouldn't if I were you."

Kyle didn't wait for an answer; he simply walked past them, opening the door and indicating that James and Matthew could remain outside. Both men acknowledged his order and took the wall opposite the household guards, who looked panicked to be facing off against the Fourth's Elite.

Kyle entered the small reception room without ceremony only to see a house girl who squeaked in alarm and dropped the glass of wine she'd been carrying, its red liquid spreading all over the floor.

Kyle smiled at the symmetry of the spreading wine and the likelihood of blood spilling if the lord didn't like the message he received. Assessing the room, he moved and sat in what he determined was the most comfortable chair and the one that Lord Vannen had claimed as his own.

"Tell Lord Vannen his presence is required."

Kyle kept his gaze flat, his tone commanding. The hapless serving girl looked at him wide-eyed, mumbled something that sounded like "of course, My Lord" and almost ran inside the inner doors to the bedroom.

There was some loud commotion in the bedroom, then Lord Vannen came strutting out with a hunting blade strapped to his waist. It didn't match his dress and wasn't something he should be seen wearing in the court, given it would be deemed treason. The lords and their guards had to hand in their weapons to the armoury on their arrival at the palace. Only certain lords had the permission of the Crown to bear arms in the Royal Palace. Lord Vannen wasn't one of them. Kyle smiled humourlessly.

"James!" Kyle's voice was just loud enough to carry through the doors to the guards beyond.

James entered the room with what sounded like a slight scuffle outside. Kyle glimpsed Matthew through the door holding a blade to the throat of one guard before the doors closed; by the sound of booted feet drumming down the hallway, extra guards were on their way. Kyle smiled; his guard knew him well enough already, it seemed. Then the doors closed, with the competent Elite Guardsman James Caldwell on his side of the doorway.

"My Lord?"

While James addressed Kyle, his eyes were on Lord Vannen and the knife he carried at his waist.

"James, I think the Lord forgot to declare weapons he might have. If you could be so good as to seize the dagger and alert the King's Guard. They may want to consider a search of the Lord's rooms, goods and people for other contraband."

Kyle appeared relaxed, but he was watching the lord for any sign he might do something stupid, like attack James rather than hand over his weapons. While he knew and trusted James' skill with both hand-to-hand combat and the blade, he still stood ready to intervene.

James turned his attention to the lord, who swallowed nervously, having not thought out his course of action.

"By the command of the Fourth's Blade, you'll draw your blade, slowly, and drop it on the ground, Lord Vannen." James was all business, not taking his eyes away from the lord as he slowly drew his knife and dropped it as instructed on the floor. "Now take two steps backwards, turn slowly and place your hands where I can see them on the wall." James watched calmly as the terrified lord followed instructions. "Stay still Lord Vannen, I will retrieve the knife. If you move I will kill you, I don't want to do that. So please just stay put until you're given permission to do otherwise."

James moved forward when the lord complied with his instructions. Without taking his eyes off the lord, he retrieved the dagger from the floor.

James backed up and passed the blade through the door to the guards beyond then, with a determined glare, shut the door, staying inside. Kyle almost groaned out loud before indicating for James to move to the far side of the room. James looked determined but complied; however, he withdrew his sword from its hilt.

"Sit down, Lord Vannen." Kyle's voice did not betray even a hint of emotion.

The shaken lord pushed himself off the wall and turned. He paused, looking at Kyle, his eyes occasionally darting up to focus on the King's Elite in the corner of the room. He licked his lips and stepped forward, perching on the edge of the nearest chair facing Kyle. Kyle let the silence last, watching as the unnerved lord cringed.

"The King is most displeased, Creswell. You know having any connection at all to a plot to abduct a Prince of the Royal Blood is treason. Right?" Kyle kept his voice calm without even the slightest edge of emotion, his eyes on the lord.

"I-I don't know what you mean, My Lord, I haven't committed treason. Um, I don't think." Lord Vannen looked so befuddled and confused that only strict control stopped Kyle from laughing outright.

Kyle appraised the quivering lord and handed over the list that William had given him.

"You deny owning these premises?"

The lord edged forward and reached across the intervening gap, his hand shaking as he took the list from Kyle. Raymond's eyes scanned down the list of local houses of pleasure and gambling dens. As he read down the list, he went even paler than Kyle thought was possible.

"Yes, they belong to my family. They have for generations. I have little to do with them, my house staff administer them. It's a legacy from my Lord Grandfather's day." Lord Vannen looked like he was almost pleading for understanding.

"It matters not, Creswell, you will quit your interest in those businesses. You have been found to be closer than the King cares for in the plot to abduct Prince Alexander. The two women who drugged the Prince and myself and the male who drugged Lady Jessalan have proven to come from one of your houses of pleasure with connections to the League of Skulls. If you do not comply, your whole family will be found to have committed treason. As a family line, you will cease to exist."

Kyle didn't wait for an answer, taking the written note from the shaken lord's fingers. He walked from the apartment, James following behind him, not bothering to close the door. The King's Guard, who were waiting outside, allowed Kyle to get clear before entering the room to begin their search without being told. Kyle walked down the hall without giving it a second thought, both James and Mathew falling in behind him.

Kyle vowed to never wear the Fourth's court gear again unless he was ordered to, then grimaced as he realised that wouldn't be possible. While he usually could pass through the courtiers without hindrance, this evening he found himself in the middle of a gaggle of ladies and lords who seemed to be with him no matter where he moved. His only consolation was that Alex, up on the main Dias for once near the King and his brother, the Crown Prince, looked equally miserable, although he doubted any but he or Jess could tell.

Jess looked calm but was dealing, it seemed, with a never-ending supply of lordlings who seemed to think that with Alex out of the way, stationed by the King, and Kyle being contained by his followers, they could partition the lady for her favour with no hindrance.

Kyle paused briefly on his way across the courtroom; if he hadn't been surrounded by a gaggle of ladies trying to gain his attention, he would have smacked his forehead as he suddenly understood that together the three of them seemed way too formidable to go near. It looked like the courtiers felt they stood a chance only while they were alone. All of them had noticed the Fourth's Crest, and he'd been deflecting or just plain ignoring questions from his peers about it and Alex all evening. Kyle realised that he was out of practice since the healers had exempted him from official duties while he had been sick.

Fed up with being polite, Kyle excused himself and waded his way through the crowded ballroom toward the King. Reaching the stairs, the King's Elite parted to let him through, leaving the unwanted entourage behind. Kyle could almost feel the guards' amusement; they had just observed everything and likely been warned of the events in the hapless Lord Vannen's apartments just before the dinner.

Kyle pushed aside his irritation as he approached the King. He drew his blade and bowed his head, placing the hand containing the dagger against his heart, dropping to one knee.

"Your Blade reports."

Kyle said the honorific words so only those on the dais could hear, but knew the whole court was whispering, watching, taking in every detail.

"Report to our King, Fourth's Blade," Alex replied, as was customary, which caused even more whispers.

Knowing his face was not visible to any of the court behind him, he grinned at the King. "My liege, you have a very shaken lord major. I think he will divest himself of any interest in the businesses you stipulated. He claims it was his grandfather who had the primary association with the businesses in question and that his staff were the ones maintaining them. He will bear watching though. I don't believe him. As pathetic as he may seem, he came out armed to meet me. He didn't draw on me. Otherwise, you'd be down one lord to a major house."

Kyle saw the King, William and Alex stiffen at that last piece of information and all their gazes tracked across the ballroom to the location where Kyle was sure the Lord Vannen was standing.

"He's still alive." William's eyes were wide as he looked at the lord.

Kyle couldn't help but grin at the incredulous tone in William's voice. "Well you told me not to kill him. I took that as an order from His Majesty."

Kyle didn't turn to look at Vannen but was sure that there were Elite Guard near him, called in by his own guard after the discovery of one of the lords bearing arms without the King's prior approval, in a severe breach of protocol. Kyle grinned again and drew the attention of the three back to him.

"Let me guess, when the three of you looked from me over to him he nearly collapsed in a dead faint?" Kyle was feeling amused despite the circumstances.

"You would be correct, Kyle. What on earth did you do to the man or is he that spineless?" William looked back to the Lord then back at Kyle.

Keeping his voice low so only those on the Dias were party to the conversation, Kyle couldn't help the chuckle that escaped his lips.

"That's just it. I didn't do much except inform him you knew about his involvement. James disarmed him, Matthew held his guards at bay. I think there is a fair amount of posturing in him. Still, I think he was shaken to have his interests uncovered."

"You must appease your Lady Mother, she looks a little distressed. While the rumours about you being The Shadow have been circulating in the court for years, it seems this official public acknowledgement of your status has upset her." The King looked concerned, and Kyle had to force himself not to break protocol to turn around and look.

"Yes, Your Majesty. I still don't quite get why everyone is so shocked. I've been permitted to carry my blades in the court for years." Kyle looked a little perplexed, and the King laughed.

"Perhaps they hoped it was just my favour due to your friendship with my children? Although in Gwen's case, I think your mother is more upset about the acknowledgement of your title. You know 'The Shadow', 'Fourth's Blade'—the assassin thing. You may have been trained in blade work since you were old enough to hold a dagger, yet it is still a shock to a parent." The King's tone was dry.

Alex gave his friend a tight smile as he continued to scan the room. "So, do you think your assassin friend will work out who you are now?"

"Ah, watching my back for me, Alex? Appreciated. I think she'd check me out, regardless. The court has been whispering about me being 'The Shadow' behind my back for years." Kyle realised his genuine interest in the assassin was clear.

Alex looked at him and shook his head. "Kyle, tracking down a gifted female assassin who wants to kill you because you think she's cute isn't recommended." Alex threw a disgusted look at his father and brother. "You think I'm the trouble in our group? I know that look. He will end up sleeping with her. Or killing her. Maybe both."

Kyle found himself under the real gaze of the King, Crown Prince and the Fourth, and had to try very hard not to squirm. He smiled back at the three of them.

"There's more than one way to take out an enemy, but I have a feeling I'll have no choice but to dance with the Skulls Assassin. Still, I have to track her down—she's dangerous, but so am I."

Kyle looked back at them, drawing on the power of the veil, entirely in the persona of the Shadow, as he stood and sheathed his blade.

A lex looked across the ballroom as the tempo of the music picked up. There were two distinct sets. Older and more formal couples moved together in the traditional stylised dance moves. Then the younger, more daring, paired up in a version that was similar yet more intimate, which had caused the musicians to up the beat to accommodate them. At this time of the evening, now that the King had officially left, the crowds had thinned out. Alex grinned at Kyle; it seemed that the party tonight might just be here at the palace since their contemporaries had decided to play.

Alex caught sight of Amelia being dragged into a dance by one of the lordlings and his eyes narrowed. The lord was trying to pretend he was contemporary and failing miserably. He grinned over at his brother and Kyle.

"If you will excuse me, I think I will go rescue Amelia from that clod with two left feet." Alex barely paused to catch William's wave of approval before he trotted down the stairs, making his way through the court toward the dance floor.

Paying Lord Castings no mind at all, Alex adroitly caught Amelia in his arms as her dance partner lost control of a spin, nearly dumping her on the floor. Amelia grinned at him as he brought her upright, moving in close so their bodies were pressed together. Alex moved them around the dance floor, knowing they were the object of attention. Still, given the laughter at Lord Castings' expense when he had intervened, Alex doubted anyone guessed he had any real interest in Amelia.

"Jealous, Alex?" Amelia whispered in his ear, her arms around his neck moving in sync with him as if they had done this hundreds of times before.

"Couldn't resist the opportunity. Besides, would you rather have hit the floor?" Alex grinned, keeping his voice low, grateful that the dance style was perfect for whispering in her ear and wouldn't draw undue attention.

"No, definitely not." Amelia's dark eyes sparkled in amusement.

Alex noticed that Kyle had dragged Elizabeth up to dance and Jess had co-opted William for a dance partner. Although he had a sneaking suspicion that Jess was leading, since William tended to opt for the more traditional dance forms.

Alex spun Amelia expertly back into his arms as the music changed into a slower dance. She laughed, a little breathless.

"Looks like the party is about to split and start to move elsewhere." Alex looked down at her small petite form, loath to let her go. "Join me tonight? When all this breaks up? It would be remarked on if you suddenly started mixing with our set."

He was rewarded as a grin spread onto her lips. "Of course."

As the music ended, they reluctantly parted, then Kyle was on one side and Jess the other, drawing him away in the direction of the doors to wherever it was that the others had decided to party. He had a sneaking suspicion they were headed to the minor stateroom with doors leading to the courtyard and gardens.

"Come on, Alex, let's go!" Kyle clapped Alex on the back as he herded him out of the ballroom.

Alex caught Amelia's eyes as she moved off in Elizabeth's wake and rolled his eyes. He was rewarded by her grin and chuckle, as well as a dry look from William who caught the exchange. That almost made him groan; he knew that look. William somehow seemed to find out everything. If William knew about his liaison with Amelia, then their father knew too. Still, the fact that he hadn't intervened at all meant a tacit approval, which was a first.

Alex felt his eyebrows raise and traded a glance with Kyle as William obviously decided to have one of his rare nights off and join them. His arms snaking around Jess' waist, it was obvious how he intended the night to go.

15

THE ORDER RECONSIDERS

Lord Vannen paced in the study of his old run-down family home near the docks in Vallantia. The area had once known better times but had long fallen into disrepute. He was agitated and the fact that everyone else appeared to be calm infuriated him; then again, they were not the ones who'd had their lives threatened by Lord Kyle.

"What are we going to do now? How did everything go so wrong? I thought the drug stopped them from being able to do their tricks and either killed them or brought them under your control." He glared around at the men and women in the room.

Baine shook his head, his disgust clear. "Calm down, Vannen, panic will not help. I hope you all have something else up your sleeve. My master reminds you that the court is about to leave the Winter Palace for the Summer Palace—things are a little more relaxed on the road than they are in the palace itself."

Vannen turned and glared at Baine. "I notice your master is missing again, what is his excuse this time?"

Baine chuckled. "Careful, Vannen, you wouldn't want me to think you are a threat to my master. It should be evident that the King is a little unsettled by the attack; until things calm down, any movement my master makes from the palace would be noted."

Scholar Clements snorted, and all eyes turned to him. "Yes, I'm thinking it would be noticed. Baine is correct, Lord Vannen, calm down. You survived the encounter with Lord Kyle; if he knew your full involvement you'd be dead. We have an asset in contact who is, shall we say, talented. It needs time to play out." Scholar Clements smiled. "We also have a group that can take action when the court is on the road, given the habit of the Prince and his friends have of riding separately from the party of the King and court."

Baine nodded at the old man. "I'll pass that on to my master, Scholar Clements. By the way, he sends his regards. I must go, even my absence will be noticed if I stay away from my duties for too long."

With that, Baine dipped his head to the old man, the only one in the group he had any regard for, and left, with Vannen's indigent spluttering behind him. Baine was grateful that this new approach didn't have him painting himself up to look like one of the Skulls' Mercenaries. The League of Skulls took people impersonating their ranks a little personally. He had no doubt that, regardless of his position in the court, if they ever worked out it had been him, he'd end up dead. That was a circumstance he'd rather avoid, no matter how much he owed his master.

16

RELOCATION TO THE SUMMER PALACE

"Damn it, Father, why wasn't I consulted about this?" Alex plucked at his vest with the crest of the Fourth emblazoned on it, a look of disgust on his face. "You know the whole Legend of the Fourth is based on a lie. Instead of ignoring all the rumours and muttering, you lend weight to the whole thing by acknowledging the title."

Alex stood and paced, running his right hand through his hair. Annoyance and frustration clear in every line of his body. It had been a tough couple of weeks for them all with the added attention thrown their way due to being acknowledged as the Fourth. It didn't help at all that Alex felt like a total fraud. It had also made his trysts with Amelia a lot more difficult to arrange.

"I'm no kind of hero or protector of the Realm. So I'm a wonder with a sword and superb at partying, drinking, and can give you an expert opinion of the various pleasure houses in Vallantia. I'm just one of the Tainted. One of the kind that the general population would kill if they knew. I'm one of the monsters that killed Mother." The bitterness was clear in his voice.

"Alex, you are not responsible for your mother's death. Tainted, yes, but not one of the Sundered ones."

The King rose and in a rare display of affection, he gathered his youngest child in his arms and hugged him. Alex let his father hold him for a moment as if he was a small child again, accepting the comfort it gave him.

Then, drawing away, surprising himself at how reluctant he was to do so, Alex smiled.

"Sorry, Father. I'm just feeling sorry for myself, I guess." Alex walked back to his chair and, pausing long enough for his father to take his own seat, slumped backed into his own.

"There would be even more talk if I didn't acknowledge you as the Fourth, complete with installing you in the Fourth's Complex when we get to the Summer Palace, Alex." The King sighed. "I was already fending off questions as to why that hadn't happened. Besides, along with the negative of all the extra attention, as a positive side effect you get a lot more freedom. I'm sorry, Alex, I couldn't delay anymore, it would have gained more attention if I had. Your elevation to Fourth was expected. It's your role by birth, just as it is William's role to be the heir to the throne. It's not a choice, I'm afraid."

Kyle watched as the tension drained out of Alex. He traded a quick look with Jess and William.

"I didn't mean to snap, or whine like a child. Just when I think I've grown out of that, I behave like I'm a three-year-old having a tantrum." Alex shook his head and sighed.

Kyle couldn't help but laugh. "I guess we are all a little guilty. It's not that much extra attention than we used to get. The court has always watched us all."

Jess smiled. "Can't complain about our new accommodation

either. At least the courtiers find it way harder to get at us in the Royal Wing—that will become even harder when we get to the Summer Palace I imagine. We can play this fiction of the Fourth and his Companions. After all, it is true, just not in the way some people imagine."

Alex smiled at his friends. "I'm sorry. You've all been saddled with this Legend of the Fourth crap because of me." Alex shook his head and sighed. "Although, if I'm being fair, you would both attract your fair share of attention all by yourselves anyhow."

They all turned to look at William, startled as he threw back his head and laughed, his whole body shaking. Alex, Kyle and Jess all looked at each other, smiling in response, then back at William, who was still laughing. Finally, he controlled himself, wiping tears of laughter from his eyes.

"The three of you were always destined for trouble, even without that damn legend to contend with. I'm not sure you see the power that moves in the court, the way the courtiers gravitate toward you. Alex, you are still the son of a King, I don't think you understand how many of the lords try to gain your favour—you seem oblivious to it."

"I'm not oblivious, I ignore them as it is obvious they only seek me out to get at you and Father." Alex frowned. It was yet another reason he was friends with Kyle and Jess. They liked him for himself, not because they sought favour with the King.

William nodded, acceding the point. He turned his gaze to his next target. "Kyle is the son of one of the most important and influential lords in the Realm; Blade Master and rumoured to be assassin-trained, they'd be calling Kyle 'The Shadow' even if he wasn't mixed up with you, Alex. You are an obvious connection to the King and your father."

Then William turned to Jess, smiling as he regarded her. She was dressed in her customary hunting clothes, of finer make than any hunter he'd ever met and with the crest of a Companion of the Fourth on the vest. Her booted feet were up on the table in a very unladylike pose. "Jess' own parentage may not be as high but if it wasn't for hanging around you two all the time she'd be fending all her suitors off with a stick, or rather her sword. She is not only regarded as one of the most beautiful women in court, she is well known as one of the best hunters as well, which terrifies most of the lords into behaving themselves. Add to that your close connection to the Royal Family and you are a real power in this court, without the need of a powerful family name."

Alex, Kyle and Jess all stared at each other wide-eyed, in shock at William's blunt assessment of them, not knowing how to respond. So Alex changed the subject, since Jess was wearing her hunting clothes as a subtle reminder. It was hunt season, her favourite time of the year, and if he was honest, it was his as well since that meant they were allowed out of the palace for a space of time and could get out and about around the countryside.

His father glanced at William, who nodded. "There is also the rising number of reports of the Sundered. I've kept you out of it due to recent events but you, all of you, are ideally placed to help us investigate and sort it out. It was the traditional role of the Fourth and his Companions before historic events turned into a legend."

Alex closed his eyes and nodded. "So tomorrow we head off, starting the progression to the Summer Palace. I'll behave, Father, although as has become customary for us, we'll leave a little later and join up with you all at the first camp." Alex didn't make it a request. He wasn't about to turn into the perfect son, meek and mild, agreeable. To his shock, his father laughed.

"I wouldn't expect anything else, Alex. I would ask that you at least keep your guards with you. With the implication of the

League of Skulls in the kidnapping attempt and all the recent reports of Sundered roaming the wild areas of the Kingdom in groups, I'd rather you err on the side of caution." The King's tone held no hint of a request either.

Alex knew a royal order when he heard one, even if it wasn't phrased as one, and nodded agreement. "As you wish, Father. I'll behave that much, I promise. I've been keeping track of the reports of the Sundered, despite your best efforts to shield me from them." Alex shrugged. "We'll keep our eyes open; with the three of us together I don't think we have as much to worry about with the Sundered ones as most would, but it would give away to everyone we are Tainted if we wield the veil blatantly in front of everyone. Or at least give it away to those that haven't guessed."

Alex knew his father, brother and council were becoming worried about the increased reports from all over the Kingdom regarding sightings of the Sundered. Alex wasn't worried since the Sundered could move around as the three of them could using the power of the veil. It was likely that there were not as many of them as his father feared. Probably just a small handful moving around causing mayhem wherever they appeared.

Between the three of them they had kept their own council regarding what they had learned about the Sundered and their own ancestors. Alex had the growing impression he wasn't quite being told the truth or at least being kept away from certain information. That Kyle had been searching for the Sundered Assassin most nights they had kept to themselves for now. What the King and William didn't know, they couldn't forbid them to do.

A lex grinned at his friends in anticipation, then he nodded to both Jess and Kyle before leading them to the door of the private courtyard off the Royal Wing.

In discussing their strategy with the King, William, Elizabeth and a few of the King's closest advisors, it was decided that Alex would continue to live it up and play the spoilt youngest son of the King—that is, taking advantage of his position to the hilt. Alex was astounded since they had all been on at him for years to grow up and remember that he was a Prince, responsibilities were his by birth. The list of various reasons his behaviour was inappropriate according to the various members of the court seemed to be unending. Except, for now, he was advised to stay the same. If he became conscientious in his duty they feared he would make a bigger target of himself for whoever had tried to arrange his kidnapping. Alex felt their logic was flawed but was more than willing to go on being himself, paying little consideration to what was proper behaviour for his rank.

Alex paused just outside the door, smiling at the milling guards, servants and gear. He chuckled to himself, trying to imagine engaging against any serious threat with the entourage in tow. Still, he knew it would only get worse when they joined up with the rest of the Royal Party as they journeyed around the countryside and engaged in the hunt season.

That the King and his court engaged in the hunt season and moved to the Summer Court every year seemed to be lost on many, since every year it caused much fuss and drama. Nevertheless, every year they went out to hunt, staying in camps around the Kingdom. It was less formal—a lot of fun was enjoyed by many of them. Not only did they hunt, it afforded the King and his court the opportunity to see some of his people and be seen by them. Occasionally, someone, even a farmer, rather than the lord he was beholden to, would approach for an audience with the King. It never ceased to astound Alex how many little issues and concerns were put on hold by all and sundry just so they could have the chance to petition the King themselves. Some forgot there was real business as well as the hunting.

Alex was assured that the Compound of the Fourth in the Royal camp would be made ready for his arrival. He shook his head, wondering what his new tent looked like; it might be a fancy tent, but it was still just a heap of canvas held up with posts.

Shaking himself out of his introspection, he trotted down the stairs toward his horse, noting that both Jess and Kyle were already mounted and waiting for him. Like him, they were all dressed in their new travel clothes. Or at least the more adorned version of them that let all know who they were. They'd been emblazoned with the new royal crest, the one that only the Fourth Child and his Companions could wear. Still, although their new travel clothes were a little more ostentatious than any of them would have liked, he knew they were far more practical than they showed. He also knew their plain, by comparison, hunting and evening wear were packed within their baggage should they choose to go into a village unannounced and remain as inconspicuous as they could.

Mounting his favourite horse, he spurred him forward, as was his usual fashion, with no warning to anyone. As always, these days both Kyle and Jess were in sync with him and spurred their own mounts, riding to either side of him as his guards and servants trailed behind. Although he noticed that since this was all scripted, their core guard unit were quickly forming up in their standard defensive formation around them. Alex appreciated the private entry and exit to the Royal Wing at the Winter Palace and guessed he would grow to appreciate it even more when they arrived at the Complex of the Fourth.

Seeing his own crest blazoned on his guard unit, horses and their equipment, still took getting used to. This was his first foray out into the Realm as the Fourth. He knew it would cause both fear and a sense of hope for the people. While they had known a fourth child had been born to the King for a long time, now they would know there was a *Fourth Child*. Even if they didn't realise it was all based on a lie. It had been impressed on him by Elizabeth that as the Fourth Child he gave the people hope that they were safe; he and his Companions would inspire a sense of safety and security. They would trust, even if the worst happened, that he and his friends would stand guard between them and the monsters in their midst.

As they rode through the town, he was aware of the citizens' responses to his passing. Some whispered, others ducked for cover; many pressed their hands to their heart then forehead, heads bowed as he passed. An obeisance shown to the Fourth as far back as their history, signalling that they gave their hearts, minds and lives to the cause of the Fourth.

Finally, they circled around the outside of the inner city and wound their way through the sprawling outer city. They wouldn't join the rest of the Royal Party until they were well out of the city limits.

A lex looked over and waved as Jess whistled at the hunters in their group. With a wave in his general direction, she spurred her horse ahead off the road toward the nearby forest. He chuckled as two of the Elite swore and took off after her.

"Oh, she will not like that. They'll scare off the game."

Kyle grinned back at him. "Well maybe they can be useful and hold the reins of her horse, or perhaps they'll make so much noise it'll flush a deer or something in her direction?"

Marcus, who was riding nearby, grinned. "I chose Lady Jessalan's primary guards with her habit of hunting and tracking in mind, Your Highness, My Lord. Those two might surprise you."

"I'll take your word for it, Marcus, but I'll lay odds Jess is better and she still won't be amused."

Alex threw his head back and laughed, thinking of Jess' response. Looking up, he saw the King's camp, set up and waiting for their arrival. He grinned and spurred his horse on in anticipation, slowing down as they entered the edge of the camp. Most of his guard detail peeled off as he and Kyle continued on with their own guards toward the centre of the camp, where he knew their tents would have been erected.

To say they were staying in tents was a little simplistic. While most of the entourage were staying in tents, they were staying in something that looked like a small cottage and was comfortable. Path finders, guards and palace staff had gone ahead of them to set up not only the King's Camp but, for the first time in generations, the Fourth's Compound, ahead of their arrival.

Alex could see from the flag flying above the largest of the royal pavilions that his father was already in camp, and saw his own flag rising up the pole outside his own. Alex dismounted and looked over to see his sister, Elizabeth, duck out of her tent with Amelia close behind. His heart nearly stopped at the sight of her.

As Alex walked forward, she curtseyed, placing her hands against her heart then forehead.

"Your Highness."

Alex, forgetting himself, found he was captivated. A slight smile touched his lips, and he closed the distance between them, capturing one of Amelia's hands as she rose out of her curtsey. He raised her hand to his lips and kissed her palm, watching as she blushed to her hairline.

"There is no need for such formality, Amelia; after all, we've all grown up together and this, well, it's the camping equivalent of the Royal Wing."

Alex couldn't believe he was flirting so outrageously with Amelia in front of everyone, but he couldn't seem to help himself. He smiled, losing track of time in that moment while they gazed at each other. Alex found himself lost, drinking in her long dark hair that fell in waves around her shoulders, drowning in her dark chocolate eyes that seemed to drill deep into his soul. He could feel the veil swirling around them both, forming a bond between them in that moment, just as Kyle cleared his throat.

"No greeting for your big brother, Amelia?" Kyle stepped forward and claimed Amelia in a hug, swinging her around like she was still a little girl. Amelia snapped out of her focus on Alex and laughed.

"Kyle, put me down!" Amelia laughed and swatted at her brother as Elizabeth smiled.

Alex shook his head and stepped forward again, this time leaning forward to brush his lips against his sister's cheeks.

"Sister, I hope the journey today was not too tiring for you." Alex raised an eyebrow at Elizabeth and hoped she realised he was trying to regain his composure, breathing a soft sigh as he saw her grin.

"It was a little tiresome, Alex, but more because Father insisted I ride in a carriage, as if I'm made out of glass. I'd much rather ride than be cooped up in the carriage. Still, we're out of the city now, perhaps I can persuade him to let me ride tomorrow. Now you should go wash up, little brother. I've heard already that Jess has gone to join the hunters, so that means we should eat well tonight!"

Elizabeth pushed Alex toward his own pavilion and gathered Amelia up in her wake. Both women walked toward the King's pavilion and disappeared into its depths.

Alex watched Amelia depart before he sighed and turned to see Kyle, his arms crossed, watching him.

"Come on, Alex, let's go to your pavilion to have a chat."

Alex was alarmed as his friend turned his back on him and stalked over to his pavilion, disappearing inside. Alex shook his head and, with one last look in the direction Amelia had gone, followed him inside, a rueful expression on his face.

A lex walked in and found Kyle sitting on one chair and accepting a drink from Miranda, looking troubled but not like he was about to stick a dagger into his best friend's heart.

Alex accepted a goblet from Miranda and thanked her, before sitting and relaxing back into his own chair. He wasn't certain how the crafters made the camp chairs and foot rests comfortable, but somehow they did. Alex kept his peace, knowing Kyle would let him know what was troubling him when he was ready.

Alex watched as Kyle ran a hand through his hair, taking one more sip from his goblet before looking at him.

"Amelia is my little baby sister, Alex. I'm not silly enough to believe she hasn't been breaking various lords' hearts throughout your father's court. Just promise me you won't hurt her."

Alex choked on his drink and picked up a napkin from a nearby table to wipe his mouth. He swallowed, looking at Kyle a little wide-eyed.

"Kyle, I would never harm Amelia. Ever. I know in the past I've been a little irresponsible, I have no excuse. I'm sorry, I dragged you out there with me, every single time, I'm sorry."

Kyle smiled. "I understand that. I'm not saying don't pursue Amelia, heck it wouldn't work even if you agreed. I know my little sister. Just, don't hurt her. She's not as strong as Jess. I don't think Amelia knows the world of hurt that will head in her direction by falling into your world—our world."

Alex took a breath and nodded. "I'm sorry, Kyle, I don't know what came over me. I must have seen Amelia a million times but just then, when she walked out of Elizabeth's tent, it was like the world stopped still. I would lay waste to entire nations to protect Amelia." Alex shook his head as Kyle looked at him, the silence stretching between them. "Who am I trying to kid, you know already don't you? How did you find out? We've been careful."

Kyle laughed, "Yes, you've both been careful until now. But after that little display out there it's likely already all over the camp. To answer your question, I've known since just after I recovered from being sick. I came down to see you and, as was normal practice, just walked in to wake you up. Imagine my surprise, to see you sound asleep with your arms wrapped around my little sister. Since then I've been careful to listen when your guards advise me you have company."

"Amelia came in to sit by your bedside while you were sick. We spent a lot of time sitting on that couch, Kyle. It was my fault you were so sick. It happened, Kyle, but I can't explain how much I adore Amelia." Alex couldn't help but smile when thinking of her.

Alex thanked Miranda as she walked over and filled up both his and Kyle's goblets. Then he looked at Kyle.

"If you'll accept my advice, become as overt in your relationship now as you were covert about it before. Hiding it before protected her from the court and others. Now? With the knowledge out there and spreading? It will hurt her. Hell, she spends every night in your bed, Alex. Have her move in if that is what you both wish, and be done with it. That way, if it's official, if Amelia is the Consort Elect of the Fourth, you can put the Elite on her."

Alex choked on his drink again and gave Kyle a horrified look.

"I think it could be a little early to be going down the Consort Elect path, Kyle." Alex wiped his mouth and considered the options. "However, I'll talk with Amelia. We can dispense with trying to be discreet. This road trip could be the perfect place to start; everything is less formal when the court is on the road. By the time we get to the Summer Palace, everyone will be used to the idea."

Kyle laughed. "You are deluding yourself, Alex. The ladies will be green with envy and looking daggers at Amelia—though I'm certain she can hold her own there. Just take the real ones off her for a while; she might be a little too direct in her response. Still, if she is with you most of the time then, by default, your guards are protecting her."

Alex groaned as he thought of the circus his relationship with Amelia was about to become.

"Well you and Elizabeth could make a spectacle of yourselves. That would draw heat."

This time it was Kyle who spluttered his drink, only just catching the liquid on his napkin. "Alex, Elizabeth and I, hell I know this sounds bad, but it's just a casual thing."

This time it was Alex who smirked. "Payback. Yes I know about you and Elizabeth. You two have been nowhere near as discreet. So do me a favour and be outrageous. The court will gossip about the pair of you instead of Amelia and me."

Kyle didn't know whether he should laugh or be indignant; he settled with laughing. "You mean they will go into overdrive. No, Alex, that wouldn't be fair to Elizabeth, besides it's a casual affair that has been on and off for years. Currently it's off."

Alex shook his head, smiling as he took a sip of his drink.

"You're supposed to be my best friend, Kyle. I guess if you reignite your passion for my sister it might hinder your ability to hunt down that assassin you are so fascinated by." Alex laughed, showing he didn't mind in the least that his friend was now interested in another. "I'll talk with Amelia and we'll see how things go. Sneaking around was fun in its own way but I guess not having to will be just as good."

17

ACKNOWLEDGING AMELIA

Alex walked into the dining tent with little fanfare. It was one highlight of being on the road rather than in the palace. The dinners were reduced to the family and a few of his father's closest advisors and friends. As a result, it was a lot more relaxed than normal. It was almost as good as dining in his own rooms, on the rare occasions he'd been permitted to since being acknowledged as a Prince of the Realm at his coming of age. It made Alex sad, since one of his biggest desires as a small child was to be present in court at the Royal Table with his mother, father, brothers and sister. Now he cherished the moments he dined alone.

The smell of the food being prepared had been floating over the camp for several hours, attesting to the success of the hunting trip. Alex glanced around and saw Amelia off to one side talking with his sister. He paused, smiling when she turned, her eyes tracking to his. She smiled in return. Her eyes widened as he walked to her and slipped an arm around her waist and kissed her on the lips. Alex lowered his gaze, staring into her deep dark eyes, and pulled her in close, whispering to her.

"Let's stop pretending. I'd prefer the whole court to know we are courting with the permission of your father and mine. Although if it's too soon for you, at least stop pretending around family. I'm advised they know anyhow."

Alex breathed a sigh of relief as he felt Amelia relax in his embrace and looked down to see her looking up at him, grinning.

"Well we were hardly subtle earlier. I don't know what came over me. I'm glad my brother didn't turn you into a pin cushion. I'm game if you are, Alex, though I'm thinking my father is looking a little stunned, even if yours isn't." Amelia glanced over toward her father and the King and tried not to laugh.

Alex swallowed. "I might as well get this part over with—wish me luck."

He grinned at Amelia as she stifled a chuckle with her palm and walked over toward his father and Lord Strafford, both of whom were looking at him. Alex paused the exact distance from the King required by protocol and bowed formally. This showed that he had a formal petition to put before the King.

The King indicated he could rise. "Yes, Prince Alexander, what petition do you have for me to consider?"

Alex was grateful that his father didn't tell him to wait until they returned to the court.

"My King, I seek permission as a son of Royal Blood to officially court Lady Amelia Joanna Strafford." Alex surprised himself; his voice sounded calm even though he was anything but.

His father glanced at Lord Strafford then back at Alex.

"Lady Amelia is a suitable match and I see no issue with you courting her or a union should you both be agreeable. Prince Alexander, you have my permission to court Lady Amelia." His father relaxed and grinned at him. Alex let go of a breath he hadn't known he was holding.

Next, Alex turned, and this time bowed to Lord Strafford in a show of respect since he didn't have to give their difference in rank. He could see by Lord Strafford's hint of a smile that he appreciated the gesture for what it was.

"My Lord Strafford, I'm sorry for this being a more public display than I would have wished. I was a little unwise when I arrived in showing my affection for Amelia; it was pointed out that while keeping my relationship with your daughter—with Amelia— low-key at the start to protect her was a good idea. Now that the word is spreading throughout the camp, that same discretion could cause her harm." Alex cleared his throat. "I'm sorry for that, My Lord; a part of my soul would die if anything happened to Amelia. My Lord, I seek your permission to court Lady Amelia."

Lord Strafford considered Alex for a moment; it seemed everyone in the tent held their breath. Lord Strafford stood and stepped closer to Alex. "Not that long ago I would have refused, Alex; however, you have grown up a great deal."

Lord Strafford looked over toward Amelia and beckoned her over to him, ignoring Alex and his request for a moment.

Alex turned and couldn't help but smile as Amelia, graceful as ever, moved over to stand beside him and took his hand.

"Amelia, do you wish this union?"

Amelia smiled then looked from her father up to Alex. "Yes, Father. I wish it with all my heart."

Lord Strafford bowed his head before looking back up. "Prince Alexander, you have my permission to court my daughter." Lord Strafford then took the last step forward and hugged them both, his manner relaxing. "I hope that one day I will get to call you my son."

Both Alex and Amelia withdrew, only to be surrounded by the rest of the family, with congratulations all round.

———

A melia eyed Alex, biting her lip, her eyes crinkling. "How did you survive Kyle? I saw him stalk away earlier today; I thought for sure any moment after you walked in after him your guards would have to try and split you two up."

Amelia twisted her head up and looked at Alex then transferred her gaze from him to William, who had begun to choke on his wine and reached for a napkin that the King, poker-faced, handed to him. Both gazed back at her, their expressions bland.

Alex bit his lip as she looked back up at him.

"Well, you know how we thought we were being clever and sneaky?" He stopped and looked up at William, observing that his father was also paying attention.

The King snorted. "Oh, don't look at me to explain it. It's not that bad, Alex. Here, I'll tell part of it. I already knew you two were seeing each other, so did William. It's hard to sneak in and out of the Royal Wing without me finding out about it."

Alex sighed, glancing around at his family staring at him. He pulled Amelia over to the far side of the tent. It wasn't far enough to truly have a private conversation but it could give the allusion of privacy. He snorted, just like the royal wing in the palace gave the perception of privacy, it wasn't real. Alex pulled Amelia close to him and kept his voice low, whispering to her.

"Amelia, it seems Kyle has known almost from the beginning. Or at least since the first day he got out of his sick bed." Alex waited, hoping Amelia would work it out without him having to explain, then sighed again. "It seems he came to see me the first morning he got out of bed. He kind of walked in and found us asleep in bed together."

Amelia's hand flew up to her mouth in astonishment and she blushed, burying her face into his shoulder, blocking out the sight of everyone pretending not to be looking intently at the exchange between.

Alex couldn't help the chuckle that escaped his lips and kissed her on the top of her head. He moved them slightly so that she was screened from view from the rest of their family, who were trying to pretend they weren't paying attention.

"Oh, that beast! Wait till I get my hands on him." Amelia's voice was muffled by his shirt as she kept her face pressed against his shoulder. Her cheeks flaming red as it occurred to her that the King and William had obviously been briefed on her relationship with Alex, a thought that made her groan in embarrassment.

Right at that moment, Kyle walked in and paused, glancing from Alex and Amelia to the others on the opposite side of the tent. He grinned, taking the couple of steps to them. He spoke first, not giving his sister a chance to get in before him.

"It wasn't my fault, Amelia. Besides, I'm certain we drove Mother to distraction for a time there, running stark naked down the corridors of the palace with our nursemaids in hot pursuit. You didn't seem to mind at all then." Kyle laughed and ducked sideways as Amelia attempted to punch his arm, catching her as she stumbled. "Now is that dignified, Amelia? Calm down, you were both covered!" Kyle grinned at her, unrepentant. "Seriously, congratulations little sister." Kyle laughed then kissed the top of her head as he hugged her.

Kyle released Amelia and took the few steps necessary to pull Alex into a hug.

"Congratulations, my friend, promise me you'll keep her safe." Stepping back, he smiled at his friend.

"Always, Kyle; Amelia has my heart in her keeping." Alex wrapped his arm around Amelia's waist again and couldn't help grinning.

"You have my promise I'll try very hard not to walk in on you both like that again." Kyle chuckled as Amelia glared at him, then nodded his thanks at Karl as he presented the drink tray.

Amelia's eyes narrowed. "You'll do more than try, Kyle. If you must speak with Alex, send a servant in to get him."

Amelia tried to maintain her glare but realised she was failing and gave up, letting a chuckle escape.

Kyle walked across the room and slumped into one chair as the King and William sat. He looked at William, holding his hand up to mask his lips, and spoke in an overly loud whisper, intending it to be heard.

"I don't get girls. I mean, she's embarrassed about her own brother walking in the bedroom but has no problems with the servants walking in and out?" He looked at William, all fake wide-eyed innocence.

"I know, it's a girl thing. I mean, Elizabeth and I shared a womb once, but she's insistent about me not entering her room ever again since I tipped her out of bed when we were fifteen." He traded glances with Kyle. "Sisters, they're impossible and make little sense."

The King watched Alex and Amelia. They seemed glued together. He looked at his long-time friend again to see he was gazing at the pair too. As though sensing he was being watched, Lord Strafford leaned over to the King.

"Michael, am I the only one who had no idea my daughter was seeing your son?"

The King laughed. "No, of course not. They kept things discreet, but it's hard to sneak in and out of the Royal Wing without me finding out about it." The king kept his gaze on the room and spoke in a low voice. "What are you thinking, Nath, are you okay with this union?"

Nath smiled and took a sip of his wine. "I never thought I'd say this, but yes. Alex has grown up of late."

The King nodded. "That kidnap attempt shook him up more than he cares to admit. This time of the year, with the anniversary of his mother's death approaching—I've never seen him so relaxed and happy."

Lord Strafford took another sip and his smile faded. "It can't have been easy, watching her die that way. I had hoped he was young enough he would forget, as children often do. Incidents like recent events are my only concern. Alex is the Fourth; it will be his duty to protect the Realm. He'll be at the pointy end of any conflict. If that occurs, they will see Amelia as the soft target to distract and hurt the Fourth, to hurt Alex."

The King sighed. "I know, my friend, and both Alex and Kyle are aware. Amelia was at risk from the first moment she and Alex started exploring the possibility of a relationship. Given the bond between them seems to be genuine, she would be at more risk without the status that being courted by a Prince of the Royal Blood grants her. Should she become Consort Elect—I have no doubt that is Alex's intent or he would not have made this official—that would put even more protection around her. At that stage, as you well know, she would be regarded as a member of the Royal Family."

"You're right. Call me selfish, but I had hoped one child would be safe from destiny's clutch. I hold nothing against Alex; I can see they are besotted with each other. I always wished, though, that if my little baby girl were to fall in love with a Prince that it would be Daniel—she'd be so much safer."

Nath swallowed the last of his wine and held his goblet out again to a servant who refilled it.

"What, my friend? Not William and the crown?" The King laughed as his friend glared at him.

"Not likely, Michael. We've been friends our whole lives. I know the weight of that crown. Besides, if conflict comes to the Realm again, Amelia would be almost as badly off being the Crown Prince's Consort." Nath looked up as Alex left Amelia chatting with Elizabeth and Kyle, walking over to sit beside them.

"I'm sorry, Lord Strafford." Alex glanced over at Amelia and couldn't help the soft smile that touched his lips. "I could wish we'd just spent time together, none the wiser, and gone our separate paths. It's what we agreed the smart thing would be early on. Yet somehow, despite our best intentions, that didn't happen. We talked about it but neither of us could bear it." Alex took a deep breath and held Lord Strafford's gaze.

Nath shook his head. "Don't be sorry, Alex. It's obvious that Amelia adores you and that it's mutual. I hope you will forgive a father's concern for his daughter."

Alex smiled. "I understand, My Lord. There is nothing to forgive."

Alex stood and excused himself, walking back and wrapping his arms around Amelia. He pulled her in close, resting his cheek on the top of her head. Closing his eyes, he felt the veil swirl around them, and he willed it to keep her safe from harm.

A melia glanced up at Alex and leaned into him with her head nestled into his shoulder. She couldn't believe the turn her life had taken since she'd entered Alex's world. When she was younger, she had idolised Alex and swore she would marry him one day. Yet as she grew and Alex didn't seem to see her in that way, not even after he'd killed for her, she'd given up on the daydream.

Yet now, somehow, they had ended up together. Even when they had first slept together, Amelia didn't believe they would get to this point. That she would be in Alex's arms in a gathering for dinner surrounded by their family and friends.

Amelia glanced up as William walked over from his father's side and extracted her from his brother's embrace to give her a hug himself.

"Come on, Alex, just because you two are all official now doesn't mean you get to hog Amelia to yourself all night. Congratulations, Amelia; you are too good for my little brother, you know that, right?" William smiled at his brother, who shook his head and laughed.

Amelia swatted William's arm but didn't step away. She was astounded but hoped none of them noticed. While she had always mixed in these circles, she had always been on the outside. Then she'd been placed in Elizabeth's inner circle, due to her sword skills. Others might have been astonished, but the King realised full well she was a weapons master in her own right. Her father had explained that she was another layer of defence, should it be required.

"Oh please, William. It's me, aiming out of my league." Amelia blushed at the looks of disbelief thrown her direction by not only William but Elizabeth and Daniel.

Daniel laughed and stepped forward, placing a hand on her forehead and frowning in mock concern. "Amelia, you must be unwell, otherwise there is no way you could think you are out of your league being courted by *that*." Daniel threw a teasing look at Alex and punched him on the arm.

Jess, who had been observing the byplay between them all, smiled at Amelia. "Amelia, how is it you saw past the front that Alex puts up?"

Amelia looked at Jess, wide-eyed at her bluntness. "Ah. It was that time in court, when that lord grabbed me and ripped my dress, but no one helped."

William hugged her in response to the small shiver that shook her as she spoke of the attack. He knew she never did. He was also aware it was that moment that had sparked her keen interest in taking up the sword and led to her becoming a weapons master. She looked up at him and smiled then looked at Alex and, as she had in that moment in the court, she felt calm.

"He kept grabbing at me and was trying to kiss me—none of the courtiers helped; they all stood there laughing, looking on like it was entertainment. Then Alex was there between me and that man, protecting me." Amelia was speaking, her voice calm and low as she looked at Alex. "It was like something was torn away and in place of the Alex that everyone else knew, I saw a different Alex. One who handled a blade as if he were born with it. Alex was there—really there. It was like I was seeing him for the first time." Amelia blushed. "In that moment, it didn't matter what anyone said, Alex was my protector when no one else cared, a hero. He's always made a habit of checking in on me when I'm at functions in court." Amelia frowned and then laughed. "Afterwards, others kept telling me how horrible it must have been since the Prince had slaughtered the lord in front of me. I didn't see it that way. Alex saved me from him."

Jess stepped forward and gathered Amelia in her arms and hugged her. "You have more than a little of the veil running through you. I'm sorry I didn't notice, we've all been a little preoccupied in our own worlds." Jess pulled back and caught Amelia in her gaze. "If anyone, and I mean *anyone*, hurts you like that again and you need help, come to me. I will help you track him down and hold him while you skewer him."

Amelia looked at Jess, startled, then glanced around the tent a little. Alex laughed and reclaimed her, hugging her close for a moment.

"Don't worry, it's the worst kept secret in these circles. We're all screwed in that department—all of us have more than a little of the veil running through our blood." Alex looked at Kyle and Jess, and they all shared a grin. "It's why Father likes to keep us all together, I guess. Easier to contain if we all go mad."

18

THE SUNDERED ATTACK

Kyle walked out of his tent, a mug of steaming coffee still in his hand, dressed in his dark brown and black riding leathers. Although they were embossed with the Fourth's Crest, they were comfortable and practical; the vest was studded with small metal plates, which would afford some protection against an attacker.

As usual, he had his sword and a knife strapped to his waist, along with other weapons in a variety of accessible locations on his person. He was, to the trained eye, a walking arsenal, if they knew what they were looking for. Even then, there were weapons he knew they would miss.

Looking around, he saw, as expected, that the bulk of the Royal Camp had packed up and moved on. They would catch up with the main party since, with the carriages, it moved much more slowly than they could themselves. Although this wasn't a pitch-your-tent kind of camp, it was semi-permanent, since the Royal Court went on this little expedition across the Kingdom every year. The route was well established and a wise Rathadon King way back at the founding of Vallantia had decreed that no favour would be shown to any lord when the Royal Court moved location.

Spotting Jess over to one side, he smiled and wandered over. Sitting down next to her, he leaned over and kissed her on the cheek.

"Morning, Jess. Alex and Amelia not up yet I take it?"

Jess smiled in response and shook her head. "I expect they'll make an appearance soon." Jess gave him an appraising look before continuing, "I must admit, Kyle, you're taking the news that your best friend is sleeping with your baby sister well."

Kyle took another sip from his steaming mug, smiling. "Probably because I've known they have been sleeping together for months. Besides, Amelia has always had her eye on Alex—ever since we were both children. Better Alex than the rest of the simpering lords she was mixing with."

Jess laughed, but was cut off. Her eyes widened and she groaned.

"What is my sister wearing and what is she still doing here? She should be in a carriage with the King's party."

Kyle looked over and saw Alison approaching and choked on his coffee. Alison was wearing what looked like a stylised version of hunting leathers. Except, unlike the version that Jess was wearing (similar to his own and affording considerable protection), the ones that Alison was wearing were anything but. She wore what looked like halfway between pants and a long flowing skirt, matched with a top that looked like a corset, bound at the middle with leather laces, and thin straps over the shoulders. Her ample chest and cleavage were on display, her arms bare. Up the sides of the corset, it looked like lace. Kyle swore as she approached them.

"See, sister dearest? No need to look like a commoner. You can wear practical hunting clothes without looking like a male. I'm sure Master Harrison could make you up more suitable clothes if you asked him." Alison seemed unaware of the reaction from not only her sister and Kyle, but of the guards. While Jess just stared at her sister, unable to retort, Kyle placed his mug on the bench before standing and walking back to his tent, muttering the whole way.

"Bennett! Bring me that horrible red jacket you tried to get me to wear, that my mother made you pack—the one I told you to leave behind. I have found a use for it." Kyle paced back and forth a little before his servant appeared with the offending jacket in hand.

"Here, My Lord." Bennett was too professional to swear but his eyes widened at the sight of Lady Alison. He couldn't help but whisper to Kyle, "I take it the Princess has decided to ride with us today, which would explain Lady Alison's presence, although I'm not sure anything explains what she's wearing, My Lord."

Kyle grinned at his small, wiry but competent, servant. "That's her version of 'hunting gear'. She thinks Jess should follow her style choices." Kyle took the jacket, too bright and glaring for his tastes, but it might serve a purpose.

Striding back to Alison, he grabbed her arm and slid the arm of the jacket on, ignoring Alison's indignant spluttering. He turned her, grabbing her other arm and shoving it in the remaining arm of the jacket. It was too big for her, but then again, it afforded better protection than her ridiculous clothing. He began doing up and tightening the front buckles, which ran all the way to the top.

"Alison, stop squirming. This thing is *bright red*—my mother chose it—but it has plates stitched into the back and the chest. Enough to keep you alive at least if we get attacked on the road.

Remind me to pay a visit to your dressmaker and explain to him the purpose of hunting clothes."

Having done what he could with the buckles, he grabbed her left arm and rolled up the sleeve so her hands weren't covered, before grabbing her other arm and doing the same.

"Kyle, this is most ungentlemanly of you. I'll have you know Master Harrison assures me it will be the height of fashion this season." She looked indignant, rounding on her sister when Jess burst out laughing.

"Hunting and riding gear is functional and designed to keep you more or less in one piece, offering protection from attack should the thing you are hunting hunts you instead. It's not a fashion show." Jess ignored her sister's spluttering and moved over to Elizabeth, who had walked up unnoticed while Kyle was dressing Alison.

"Your Highness, let me help with that. You've almost got it right, but you'll want the buckles on the sides done up tighter. In the long run, it will be more comfortable, not to mention safer." At Elizabeth's nod, Jess tightened the buckles in a practised fashion.

Elizabeth's clothing was mostly modelled on Jess' own hunting gear. Jess suspected her own maids had been talking with Elizabeth's. They were as practical as her own, other than the colour being a deep green with silver running through it and bearing the Royal Crest instead of the Fourth's Crest, as her own bore. After finishing with the straps, she gestured for Elizabeth to take a seat and undid her ponytail.

"If you braid your hair, it will keep it out of your face. Leaving it long like you had is fine for a gentle ride in the King's Party, but we'll be riding harder than you're used to. You also want your hair contained if we come under attack. Makes the fighting part easier if you don't have to keep brushing your hair out of your eyes to see." Elizabeth murmured her thanks and smiled at Jess when she was done.

"Thanks Jess. I appreciate the advice. You would know more about this than me." Elizabeth turned then blushed as Kyle took one of her hands in his own and kissed her palm.

He smiled at her. "Good morning, Your Highness. So you persuaded the King to let you ride with us today?"

"I did, My Lord Kyle. Father felt that since Amelia would ride with you all today that perhaps it would be safe enough. Besides, I kept pestering him till he agreed." Elizabeth grinned, tilting her head up to look at him.

Elizabeth had left unsaid that the King knew he would protect her. Kyle and Elizabeth had a long-term understanding, which the King knew of, even though both knew Elizabeth would marry for the good of the Realm to bring closer ties with one of the neighbouring kingdoms. They kept their relationship low-key, although they did not try to hide it.

Alex emerged, his fingers interlinked with Amelia's as they walked toward the main group. He took in the jacket that Alison was wearing and his eyes flicked to Kyle as he recognised it as one he hated. Mostly due to the bright red colour.

"Should I ask? Or don't I want to know?" Alex was relaxed and amused. "Ali, I'm not sure you want to be wearing that skirt thing. If it doesn't detach from the pants, let Kyle cut it off with one of his daggers. I take it what's under the jacket is even worse, since it's a little big on you and belongs to Kyle." Alex stood with a slight smile on his lips, his eyes drilling into Alison's, waiting for a response.

Alison went bright red, her fingers pressing against her lips in shock at Alex's blunt assessment. Alex, not waiting for a response, walked up to his sister and kissed her on the cheek. "Morning Eliza, so Father gave in to your pleading?" He gave her a quick hug then planted a kiss on Jess' forehead. "Morning, Jess."

Alex looked around, appraising Kyle's efforts with his knife as he cut off the skirt from Ali's pants with one of his blades. Ali mostly stood silent, somewhat mortified with the response she had received at her clothing choice. When Kyle was done, he tossed the fabric aside at one of the passing servants who disposed of it in the last of the carts as it pulled out of the camp and headed down the road. They had a fair bit of distance to cover and would reach the next camp much later than the rest of them. Still, they would change drivers and horses at the next campsite and the carts would leapfrog the camp and head toward the next to start the set-up in preparation for the King's arrival.

Nodding, Alex grinned at the others as their horses were led to them by the remaining guards.

"Sorry we kept you waiting. Let's go, shall we?"

At their murmured agreement, he took the reins of Amelia's horse while she mounted, waiting as the others followed suit before mounting his own.

"Let's ride." Alex spurred his horse forward, leading the party out of the camp.

Jess glanced back at her sister's miserable face, noticing that Elizabeth was also looking a little tired. She then checked on Amelia, although she needn't have worried on that score.

Not only was Amelia holding up well compared to the other two ladies, Alex was keeping a close eye on her fatigue levels.

Trying to hide her impatience at their slow pace (and not succeeding all that well), Jess captured Alex and Kyle's attention and drew their attention to a suitable spot to rest. Kyle looked as irritated as she felt but indicated agreement with a gesture that Alex mirrored. Jess sighed and spurred her horse into a gallop toward the forest edge; it was off their usual path but they didn't require as many regular breaks as they had been having. She could hear her guards, who'd followed her; they were getting used to her now. Jess glanced to either side and with some simple hand signs let them know she was checking out the site ahead.

Both guards acknowledged and passed the message back. Or Jess thought they must have, since more of the guards broke away from the main party and spurred their horses to catch up, or at least follow, in their wake.

Jess breathed a sigh of relief to get away from the main party—or rather, her sister. That Alison had joined them today instead of riding with the King's party was painful. Alison was everything their mother thought a lady should be and looked down on her little sister with disdain. Jess smiled; this was her element, not her sister's. She was more wild, along with both Kyle and Alex. They were even seen that way in the palace. Still, where everyone more or less gave her a wide berth due not only to her own reputation but because of her association with Kyle and Alex, Alison did not. There was the inner power circle. Then there was the three of them, both within that circle of power, yet separate.

As she approached the forest edge, Jess slowed her horse to a trot as she searched for a suitable glade close enough for ease of access but far enough in that the trees would screen them from view of the casual observer. She knew there was a small village nearby but the rules governing the moving of the Royal Court prevented them from utilising any of the facilities outside of an emergency, so the local tavern in the village was out of the question, which was a shame. Jess grinned at the memory of one occasion when the three of them had gone there despite the rules. That tavern made the best potpies and had a decent brew that the tavern owner and his wife made themselves. It turned out they were related to the owner of one of their favourite bars in Taverns Row: The Barrel in Callenhain. Grinning as she came to an idea, Jess drew in a small amount of the veil and reached out to Alex and Kyle.

The Sisters Barrel is in the village over the hill there. How about I take some guards, find a temporary camp and go get us some food packaged up and two skins of their best brew? We can take a longer break so your sister can rest a little and then still make it into camp before nightfall.

She felt Alex's immediate interest and even Kyle perked up at the thought. It was Kyle who responded. *That sounds like a good idea. Need a hand with the supplies?*

Jess considered her options and grinned. *Well I wasn't planning on walking or riding so yes, why not? It would be easier. I'll wait for you to get here and while the others are setting up the rough camp we'll disappear.*

Jess heard Alex's chuckle as he appreciated her quip. *Just make sure the others don't see you go.* Alex's frustration was clear in his tone. *I'd like to come but I'll keep your sister (and mine) distracted.*

Jess snorted at the likely reaction if everyone saw her disappear into the Veiled World. While the members of the Royal Family knew that the three of them had more of the veil running through their blood, she didn't think even they realised how much of what the three of them were capable of. Jess wasn't even aware of when they had kept that information to themselves or why they had thought it necessary.

As she waited, Jess frowned, glancing around, but could not work out what was making her uneasy. She'd found a small glade that looked suitable for their party and sent one of the hunter-trackers to guide the rest of the party to their location.

Jess rubbed the back of her neck and pulled in the veil, scanning her surroundings with not only her eyes but ranging out with her mind. The forest became overlaid with the grey strands that pulsed with power; with her vision augmented she could see the glowing, pulsing heartbeats of the small creatures in the forest, power seeping from the ground, trees and even the animals. Finding nothing but small game animals and birds, Jess shook off her unease, dismissing it as likely just due to the unknown location and having the responsibility of seeing to others' safety.

J ess sat on a fallen log, leaning back against the trunk of another tree that had fallen nearby with one booted foot up on the log while the other hung down the side of the trunk, her foot on the ground. Some of the hunters had gone off to see if they could collect small game to supplement the evening meal while they were here—saving time at the other end, since it was obvious they would be a little later than normal.

Jess looked up as the others arrived at the glade and noted her sister's pinched look of disapproval. Jess sighed and pushed her irritation aside. Alison was suited to many things, like sitting in a bower; however, being on the road was not one of them. Jess ignored her sister and looked toward Alex, seeing that Kyle was already sliding from his horse and extracting an empty leather bag from one of his saddlebags. Jess grinned. Kyle always seemed to be prepared for anything. She wouldn't be surprised if he'd figured that they would stop somewhere around here and had remembered The Sisters Barrel long before it had occurred to her.

As Kyle left his horse to the guards, he waved off his own pair of Elite that, as always, had turned to go with him.

"The path we will use is not one you can tread on."

His guards looked at each other then back at Marcus, who waved them back.

"Be careful, My Lord." With that sole admonishment, he turned and went about securing the temporary camp.

As Kyle drew near, Jess stood and joined in step with him as they left the glade. Her own Elite were waved off by Marcus before she had to do anything. When they were far enough from the encampment, they both pulled in the veil and, without breaking step, shifted to that grey place, neither in this world or the other. It allowed them to move from one place to another much quicker than they could in the normal world. Still, thinking about the how and why of the Veiled World and that place between both worlds made their heads hurt. Other than the rare occasions when they tried to make sense of it all, they ignored it. It worked, that was the main thing, and it was a path that few could use.

Both paused as the veil parted and revealed the village and tavern. It was a sleepy little village but big enough to support a number of taverns. Checking that no one was in the small alleyway behind The Barrel's Sister, they transitioned, and as they strode forward, the grey mist dropped from them. If someone had been watching at that moment it would be like the pair of them slowly materialised out of nowhere. Jess smirked as she remembered one time when an old drunk had seen the three of them appear in the Old Town. The experience had scared him sober; they'd heard he was sober to this day, thinking the drink had caused him to see things that weren't there.

Continuing to scan their surroundings, they wandered around the side of The Barrel's Sister into the main street. While the village might have been small, thanks to its proximity to the Royal Way, others who weren't constrained by the rules of the Royal Court could stop at the village. Thus, this acceptable tavern didn't look like it would have been out of place on Taverns Row in Vallantia or Callenhain. It did a bustling trade not just with locals but with all the through traffic. Well used to strangers wandering through their village, the locals paid them no more attention than they would anyone else who came through. Their travel clothes may have marked them as wealthy, but then again so were many of the merchant caravans that passed through. Their weapons wouldn't draw much attention unless they drew them with intent to use them. Just about everyone who passed through was armed and the merchant caravans used armed guards. Again, it was familiar. Jess pulled the hood of her cloak further down so it obscured her face within its depths and the cloak itself hid the sigils of the Fourth from casual observers. She didn't have to look to know Kyle had done the same.

They walked into the tavern through the large double wooden doors, pausing just inside by habit to scan the room for any threat. As they had expected, the tavern was bustling with an assortment of traders, guards and a handful of mercenaries, a few them professional enough to have noted their entrance and, by instinct, checked their own weapons.

Jess smiled within the confines of her hood, knowing those in the room couldn't see her face. They saw two well-armed, unknown individuals and were assessing them for a threat, just as she and Kyle were assessing them. Kyle, she knew, looked dangerous. Dressed in his usual dark, black tones, his every move was a combination of strength and grace. No one who saw him had any doubt at all he could handle himself. She also knew that most, seeing her dressed this way with the weapons she was carrying and in company with Kyle, pegged her as being just as dangerous.

Moving together, not needing to talk to coordinate their movement, they walked toward the bar, dismissing the assorted people as harmless. Getting involved in a bar room brawl was not their goal today. The tavern owner working behind the bar had noted their entrance and smiled at their approach.

"Welcome to The Barrel's Sister, travellers. What can I get for you?"

The man was well muscled and had scars that proclaimed he'd been a swordsman at one stage in his life, and the way he assessed their own weaponry gave away he'd been a good one. Or at least good enough to recognise good weaponry when he saw it.

"So formal, Evan? I know it's been some time since we've called in but I didn't think you'd forget me so soon." Jess smiled and drew back her hood as she settled on a stool.

The barman, Evan, looked startled and then grinned. "My, um, Jess, it's good to see you. I take it you aren't staying given the time of the year?"

Jess grinned; not only had Evan been a good swordsman, he was a smart one. Kyle chuckled and threw back his own hood, taking the drink that Evan slid toward him.

"Thank you, Evan. Yes we'd like nothing better than to stay but circumstances prevent it. Could we get trail lunch, whatever it is today, enough for a party of six, and some extras for, well let's just say, assorted others—use your own judgement there—and two skins of your fine brew?" Kyle passed the empty satchels both he and Jess had brought across the bar to Evan, who nodded with a grin and disappeared into the kitchen.

Jess knew from experience that it wouldn't take long so she

settled in and sipped her drink while they waited. She noted that most of the occupants of the bar, given the barman's reaction to them, had gone back to their own meals and discussions. She'd only just finished her drink when the barman reappeared and passed the full bags back to them.

"There's beef and wild mushroom pies today, fresh from the oven, and the usual bread, cheese, meat and some fruit, and two skins of our brew." Evan grinned at them as Jess slid coins across the bar, not failing to notice she'd paid him well for the food.

"Thank you Jess, Kyle, I hope you all come back when you have more time to stay overnight. We'll always have room for you all." Evan's smile faltered then he continued in a lower voice. "I'd show caution on the road, my friends. One of the farmers' lads went mad the other night, slaughtered the whole family. He's still out there somewhere—there's been rumours of a few attacks against caravans by the Sundered of late from the merchant caravans that pass through."

Kyle paused and nodded. "Thank you for the provisions and the information. We will keep our wits about us."

Jess swung the pack onto her back and pulled her hood up once more as they left the dark confines of the bar, walking purposefully back out into the main street then around the side to the back alleyway they'd arrived in. Without pause, they both drew in the veil and dissipated from view in a matter of four steps down the alleyway, making their way back to the small clearing where they had left the rest of their group.

A lex had deflected several questions about where Jess and Kyle had disappeared to, and ignored the rest. While Elizabeth wasn't too bad and took a hint, Jess' sister, Alison, was getting on his nerves. The only positive thing he could say about her coming on the ride with them was that he doubted she would ever ride with them again. He predicted she would be back in a carriage with the King's party the next day.

While he was happy perched on the log he'd seen Jess on earlier with the convenient tree as a backrest and Amelia next to him, that hadn't been good enough for Alison. She'd thrown a fit and insisted that a camping chair be unpacked. Her mood did not improve when Alex countermanded her order, much to the relief of their staff. So she sat on the other end of the same log with a pained and disapproving expression on her face.

Elizabeth looked happy and had shrugged and sat on the ground with her back against a log. One guard, seeing her sitting on the ground, smiled then untied a blanket from the back of his saddle and spread it on the ground next to her.

"Here, Your Highness, it's not much but you are welcome to it." The guardsman blushed when Elizabeth thanked him for his kindness and deposited herself on the blanket, lying down and looking up at the canopy above her.

"I can see why you escape the confines of the palace as much as you can, Alex, it's so peaceful out here." Elizabeth cocked her head to one side, looking up at Alex.

"It is—even more so when it's just Kyle, Jess and me. The entourage makes it a little less peaceful than it normally is." Alex laughed and then closed his eyes, feeling the power of the veil flow and pulse through him, around him, not trying to use or control anything; it was peaceful. Controlling and using the power took work; cutting off from the veil took even more, and was not as easy as the healers seemed to think it was. Alex smiled when he sensed that familiar surge, each of them had their own 'signature', and he knew Jess and Kyle were back with their booty from the tavern.

A few moments later, Jess and Kyle walked into the clearing with packs full to bursting point. They handed the bags to the servants, murmuring a few instructions. While they had been gone, the servants had placed down blankets on the ground with some mugs and napkins. Now, opening the backpacks, they pulled out the wrapped food. The second backpack that held bread, cheese, meat, fruits and even a few of the pies they handed off to the guards, who set about dividing the unexpected food with appreciation. It was much better than the trail fare they had been about to eat. Other than when their charges went off, leaving them behind, it was these thoughtful touches that made all of them vie to remain on duty with Alex, Kyle and Jess, even though others seemed to think the three were more trouble than they were worth. Then again, those of them who worked with the three weren't inclined to tell them otherwise.

Both Jess and Kyle wandered over, grinning, and Alex grinned back. "Successful shopping trip, I see."

Kyle nodded and sprawled on the rug next to Elizabeth while Jess regained her perch on the log near Alex and Amelia. They all murmured their thanks as the servants bustled around, handing them mugs of the ale they had poured from the skins. Elizabeth propped herself up and took a tentative sip of the brew and then looked up at Alex and across at Kyle. Her surprise clear, she took another sip.

"This is good. Wherever did you get it from? It's even still chilled!" Elizabeth grinned and took another sip.

Alex laughed. "There is a village just over the hill. It has a good tavern; the barman and his wife make the brew themselves and belong to the same family that brews the ale at The Barrel—that inn belongs to his father."

"They also make the best trail food. Wait until you eat the pies. Beef and wild mushroom today, Evan told me." Kyle licked his lips in anticipation, making Elizabeth laugh.

All of them thanked the servants, who had handed them napkins holding the still-warm pies. Alex placed his mug on the trunk next to him and bit into the pie, savouring the taste. The crisp flaky pastry and pie filling was just as good as he remembered; nice chunks of slow cooked beef, a selection of wild mushrooms and gravy. Alex couldn't help but notice that Alison was about to reject the offering and sighed. She was such hard work.

Jess, noticing, shook her head. "You should try them, Alison. Megan, the cook, is the daughter of the chef that works in the King's kitchen. She often gets called in to assist at the palace when some bigger functions are being held. Her food is divine."

Kyle shrugged and ignored Alison as she nibbled on the edge of the pie. He remembered the warning they'd received in town and gained Marcus' attention, indicating to him that he needed to have a word.

"Evan warned us before we left the tavern. One local succumbed to the madness and slaughtered his whole family the other night." Kyle continued to speak, his voice low. "He said there have been rumours of attacks in the area by groups of Sundered."

Marcus straightened and glanced around the clearing. "We shouldn't linger here too long then, My Lord. The King's party should also be warned, although given how many are in it I think it's unlikely that the Sundered will go anywhere near them."

Alex finished his pie and, licking his fingers, to all the world seeming unconcerned, glanced around the clearing. Kyle wasn't fooled. He perceived the surge as Alex drew in more of the power of the veil and searched; he and Jess were doing the same. The problem was, even if the Sundered were nearby it was unlikely that they would detect them until it was too late. Just as they could all mask themselves from detection if they willed it so, he knew the Sundered could do the same.

Marcus excused himself and went around alerting his own men and calling them in. Those not on guard duty packed up the few supplies that had been unpacked for the rest break. The servants finished cleaning up and Alex threw back the rest of his ale and handed the mug to one of them, murmuring his thanks as they collected it from him.

Elizabeth looked at them, wide-eyed, and glanced around the clearing as if expecting one of the Sundered to jump out at them. "Surely the Sundered is gone by now. He wouldn't still be in the area."

Alex was about to reply when he felt a surge nearby and spun his sword out before he even realised that he'd reached for it. He yelled, "Alison, run, now!"

Alex didn't wait for her to comply; he took the three steps to her and, grabbing her arm, flung the girl toward the guards. He spun, his sword rising in a defensive parry and caught the blade that had been sweeping to take off Alison's head. Alex sensed multiple surges and the movement around him; he knew that the guards were reacting and that both Kyle and Jessalan were near him with their own blades drawn, locked in their own battles. He took a breath and drew in more of the veil and pushed with it, catching the shimmering figure of the Sundered, once a man, now consumed by madness. Alex had a moment to be horrified that there was more than one of them before he was too busy fighting to be worried.

Even though the Sundered were stronger and more able to use the veil to their advantage, they hadn't spent their entire lives swinging a blade or fighting alongside weapons masters. Alex felt himself struck by a solid ball of power and grunted in pain. His eyes widened as he realised they were using the veil as a weapon; until that moment, he hadn't even thought of that application. Alex answered the feral grin of the Sundered that he faced off against with one of his own and, gathering the power, willing it into a hard ball, he hammered his opponent back with it.

His opponent staggered. Throwing his head back, he screamed— it was primal and angry. Alex was shocked; the scream was mental as well as verbal. Rage and pain beat against him. He shook his head. Putting up a mental barrier between him and the Sundered, Alex lunged again, thrusting his blade through the abdomen of the Sundered. He brought his second, smaller knife up, stabbing him up under the armpit. Alex shoved him away, pulling his blade free as the Sundered slumped to the ground. He felt the Sundered's attempts to use the power to heal himself. He could see the blood being held and the skin mending—the amount of power the Sundered was using was astounding. Alex's eyes widened in shock, realising that a strong Sundered could heal what should be a mortal wound. He plunged his dagger into the creature's heart.

Alex shook his head, his breathing ragged. He came back to himself and out of the veil-induced battle rage. He noted that Jess and Kyle had dispatched their own opponents.

Stab them in the hearts, they heal otherwise. Alex warned his friends before he spun around. His eyes tracked back and caught sight of Amelia and Elizabeth, blades drawn, standing in front of Alison, who was crumpled on the ground, sobbing, with Bennett, blade drawn, fighting on the other side. His eyes widened as he saw she was defending herself against one of the Sundered and he ran to her aid.

Alex screamed, his own fury boiling to the surface to see her being attacked. Two of the elite lay unmoving and bloodied on the ground. A third was pressing a cloth he was certain had been ripped from Amelia's own undershirt to a wound on his chest, showing he was in trouble but still alive. All of this Alex noted as he struck the Sundered who was about to attack Amelia and Elizabeth from behind. Kyle did the same, with Jess just a moment behind. The Sundered didn't stand a chance and, stumbling, fell to the ground, dead.

Once more, the world slowed down around him. Alex saw a few more of the guards and one servant were down or injured. Seeing that the clearing was free of attackers, he took a moment and, ignoring the blood, gathered Amelia to him, hugging her.

"You fought well. I would lose my mind if anything happened to you." Alex's voice was soft and only intended for her ears.

Amelia smiled up at Alex. "That was my first real fight." She made no move to pull herself from his embrace, content for a moment to rest her head on his shoulder. She was relieved that it was over although astonished that everything had seemed to happen so quickly. She was exhausted beyond what she thought she should have been for such a short fight.

Alex drew his wandering attention back and noted that Marcus was rounding up the rest of his men and they were applying hasty field dressings to those who needed them. He ordered everyone back on their horses.

"I'm sorry, My Lord, we must leave the dead for the animals, it's not safe. We need to get moving and get to the King's camp." Marcus looked down at the wailing Alison, not knowing quite what to do with her.

Jess turned and grabbed her sister's shoulders, shaking her. "Alison, snap out of it. We need to get out of here. Move!" Jess hauled her sister to her feet and herded her over to her horse, showing her no compassion at all. She knew they didn't have time.

The wounded were strapped to their horses with a lead rope tethering them to another guardsman's horse. With a final look around the clearing, they rode from camp without another backwards glance. Unlike the morning's ride, they rode hard, making no concessions for those unfamiliar with hard travel or the injured.

For the first time that day, there wasn't a single complaint from Alison. She clung onto her horse and the only thing they heard from her was the occasional sob.

19

PROTECTION AND RECOVERY

A lex kept their party going at a steady ground-devouring trot, with only a few short rest breaks to check on the injured and rest the horses. Alex kept a strong hold on the power of the veil, channelling more of it than he ever had, pulling it to him from every available source within his grasp. He pushed it out from himself, trying to obscure their path from anyone who might try to observe them, creating a shield around them at the same time. He didn't know how successful he was; it was something he'd only practised with Jess and Kyle for short periods of time. Alex knew, could feel, that both Kyle and Jess also drew power, although he couldn't spare the attention or strength to work out what they were doing. At a guess, he thought they probably quested ahead of their progress, checking for danger and turning small groups and individuals to another path. They'd discussed contingency plans before, even though they had never believed they would need them.

Despite the pace they set, it was dusk as they caught sight of the King's camp, with little light left. Still, Alex continued his efforts, not wanting to drop any protection he could offer too soon. The burden he would carry if they were attacked this close to camp and lost a life was not something he cared to contemplate. Alex gritted his teeth and drew in yet more power. He couldn't stop the groan that escaped his mouth as pain shot through his head, a sure sign he'd channelled too much of the veil already.

"Your Highness?" Marcus was riding close enough to hear the groan.

"I'll be fine, Marcus. I won't be worth much when we get to camp. Try to get me to my tent before I collapse. Brief the King." Alex didn't recognise his own voice. His tone was low and rough, the fatigue obvious.

Alex saw Marcus nod, then pass rapid hand signals to his men. He knew Marcus was far more aware of what was going on than anyone at court, outside of his family or Jess and Kyle; he had seen a lot and Alex suspected he'd also been briefed by William, if not his father himself. On this occasion, at least, Alex was glad that Marcus had pulled him out of trouble often enough and seen his near insensible charge to his rooms so many times he knew enough not to question.

Alex nearly cried with relief when he heard Marcus' voice, loud enough that he could hear, but he doubted others would.

"Whatever you are doing, Your Highness, you can stop. We don't want the archers to be startled and turn us into pincushions. Leave the rest to us."

Alex nodded and withdrew his compulsion and shield. It should, if he had managed it well enough, look like they had appeared out of the darkness, rather than just all at once. He heard his own trumpet blare a warning signal, and knew it was telling the camp they were approaching, that they were in trouble and the camp's guard should stand alert. Alex let go of the veil. As he let go of the power, he felt his head pounding and fatigue hit him like a hammer. In a litany running through his brain, he kept telling himself to stay conscious and on his horse.

Alex was aware, beyond the pain and the crushing fatigue, of the yelling, the movement of men and scrape of swords being pulled from scabbards, then the camp blurred as they passed. He vaguely knew that hands were supporting him, pulling him from his saddle. Voices he recognised as belonging to Marcus and James reassured him they were safe. The last thing he remembered was being carried before he lost his battle and sunk into unconsciousness.

A lex struggled to regain consciousness, aware enough to hear fragments of conversation, 'over extended' being the most common, only to be compelled back to sleep, a soothing voice in his head reassuring him he and his companions were safe. As gentle as the mental touch was, he winced away from it, sinking into the black depths, unaware for a space of time.

Alex became aware in stages and his fogged mind put together enough information to know he was rocking. A memory from his childhood told him he was in a carriage. Alex groaned as he noticed the pounding in his head, although it was not as bad as it had been. He felt hands support him and prop him up with extra pillows behind him so he was in a semi recline. He raised a hand and rubbed his temple before opening his eyes to see William on the bench next to him.

"Sorry, little brother. Aaron tells me you need to wake; it's not good for you to stay unconscious for so long." William's voice was soft and he looked concerned but not panicked.

That observation made Alex smile. He wasn't sure he'd ever seen

William panicked. Alex knew he wasn't all there, since the next thing that occurred to him was to be grateful that the light was filtered. He contemplated the information he wanted and decided what was most important to him right now.

"How is everyone?" Alex relaxed back into the pillows and was surprised that he wished he was lying flat again.

"Kyle and Jess are recovering, just as you are. We commandeered three carriages, so you'd each have your own. There are some very disgruntled lords and ladies, although their offspring are delighted. The healers assure me the guards who were injured will recover." William sat, relaxed, although Alex knew he was being assessed.

"How long?" Alex had a million things he wanted to ask but didn't think he'd be awake long enough to ask them all.

"You slept the night through and most of the day, some of it assisted and enforced by the healers. They said you overextended yourself. Alex, you know it isn't good for you." William wasn't critical, only concerned.

"I know, it was necessary. William, there were more Sundered than the ones we killed. I could sense them, I've never felt so many." As the memory of the Sundered assaulted him, Alex shuddered. "William, what if I become like them?" Alex felt a tear slide down his cheek. It was a fear he'd had since he was a small boy that seemed an increasing possibility the older he got.

William moved, sitting on the edge of his makeshift bed, gripping his shoulder. "Believe in yourself, Alex." Despite his calm words, Alex could see William was concerned. He also knew the healers and his father must have been as well. It's why William was here. Ever since he was a child, it was his big brother who had the uncanny ability to chase away the night demons from his dreams.

Alex couldn't help but chuckle. "You've always looked out for me, William; I know they are worried, otherwise you wouldn't be here."

William smiled and nodded in acknowledgment. "Of course everyone is worried, Alex. You collapsed after being attacked by the Sundered. Trust me, the court remembers, so none of them are second-guessing why. They all think after what happened when you were a child it must have been traumatising and are praising your brave actions in defending everyone. Your guards and the servants have been spreading word about how the three of you defended all of them."

Alex closed his eyes again, contemplating that the court was happy with his actions, the first time in his life he remembered that being the case. His eyes widened and he tried to sit upright, only to be restrained by William. In his current condition, he did not have the strength to fight him.

"Stop it, Alex; Amelia is fine if that has concerned you. She's riding in the carriage with Father, surrounded by almost half the guard contingent. No one, not even a Sundered, is getting anywhere near her." William kept pressure on his shoulders for a moment longer, then believing he wouldn't struggle anymore, sat back. "Just relax, we'll be in camp soon and we'll get you into your tent. Then you can sleep, assisted by the healers if you can't fall asleep yourself."

Alex knew that he was already drifting in and out of sleep, lulled by the rock of the carriage. He wasn't sure how long they had been stationary, only that he knew they were. He sighed; the pounding of his head was almost a common feature, so it at least let him know it hadn't been that long. William had been consulting with someone outside the door of the carriage, or rather, delivering firm orders to whoever was on the other side.

Hearing the commands for people to move back, Alex gathered that William had been giving orders to the guards.

"Joshua, we'll get him out of the carriage now and into his tent and bed. I trust everything is made up ready." The dim light of dusk flooded into the carriage and the rear was opened to allow easy access.

Alex cleared his throat and spoke as William turned. "I can walk, there's no need ..." Alex stopped as William cut him off.

"No, you won't. You will stay in the stretcher, you will be carried into your accommodation and you will be settled in bed. Before you think you can try anything, by Father's orders I'm staying with you tonight. It's not that he doesn't trust you, Alex. It's just that he knows you." William smiled, taking the sting off his comments. "We all know you well enough, little brother. Rest. You'll feel better for it tomorrow."

Alex had a moment where he contemplated arguing but then sighed and settled back against his pillows once more. In his current state, he knew he wouldn't win any argument he started. He wondered if he should be embarrassed to be carried into his tent on a stretcher but then decided that he was too fatigued, that it hurt too much to care.

There was a little jostling as several of the servants manoeuvred his stretcher out of the rear of the carriage and Alex vaguely knew of the row of guards with courtiers being held back by their line. Then he was within the confines of his tent and the healer's aids had him off the stretcher and settled in his bed. Even though he had done nothing to move himself, Alex was weary after the manoeuvring had been completed. He noticed that his brother hadn't been joking—a second bed had been made up in the tent. Alex snorted, amused despite the circumstances. Just as well it wasn't a traditional tent and was more like a small cabin, otherwise the second bed wouldn't have fit in at all.

Much to his irritation, Alex realised he must have drifted off again since the next thing he knew of was his brother talking with Aaron before they stopped, hearing his soft groan from the bed.

"Aaron, isn't there something you can give me to stop my head pounding?"

Alex had pushed himself too far before but it had never been this bad. Aaron was at his bedside and placed his cool, competent hands on his temples.

Relax Alex, let go of the veil, just let it wash through you.

Aaron's mind voice was cool, calm and familiar. Alex knew with those words the healer was compelling him to relax and using his own power to heal, but for once he didn't object, since the pounding in his head receded. Despite everything he wanted to do and ask, Alex felt himself drifting off again, hastened by the healer's firm compulsion for him to sleep.

A lex woke, still tired, yet the pounding in his head had at least receded. Knowing from experience that using any power right now would bring a return of the pain, he cracked his eyes open then sighed. He opened them when he saw his tent was dark. Still, it caused him to wonder if they'd helped keep the light out more than usual or if it was the middle of the night. Then his sleep-fogged mind caught up, processing a noise consistent with packing.

"Yes, it's morning, Your Highness. No, don't get up. You cannot

exert yourself too soon. You could have killed yourself, Alex."
Aaron's voice was calm, not even a hint of scolding or censure in
his tone.

"I didn't have a choice, Aaron. I couldn't stand by or flee and leave
everyone to die." Alex was sober, realising that his healer was
serious. After all the scraps he'd been through, he thought he was
impervious to being hurt.

Aaron smiled. "I know Alex and it speaks well of you, of the
person you are. Unlike many, I know you could have extracted
yourself with no harm to yourself. You need to understand the
restrictions I'm placing on you and follow them. You could
relapse if you don't do things my way. Veil sickness can be very
dangerous."

Alex frowned. "Veil sickness?"

"You drew that much power it burnt you out, both mind and
body. When you are hurt, you heal yourself with the power of the
veil—it's unconscious, mostly. Now you can't until you heal. If
you do, it is likely that you will relapse and you may not be as
lucky." Aaron beckoned to two of his assistants, off to one side.
Alex hadn't noticed their presence, which startled him since he
always knew when people were around.

"Help His Highness get cleaned up and ready for the day, then
help him to the table for breakfast." Aaron gave his patient a firm
glare then, reassured by what he saw, left him in the hands of the
aids.

They were competent at getting him bathed and redressed in
lounging clothes, much to his disgust. Still, given how firm Aaron
had been, he didn't argue with them; he'd only get them in
trouble. Alex wanted to wave off their help when he went to walk
to the outer room of the tent but had to admit he needed it, even
with the small distance between his bed and the outer section.

Alex found he was trembling, even with the help of the healer's aids, and they were taking the bulk of his weight by the time they eased him into a chair. He thanked the men as they stepped back to the edge of the tent. Alex didn't even have the energy to be embarrassed. He closed his eyes and took a slow deep breath, opening them and glancing across to the entrance as he heard the flap open. His brother walked in, which he was expecting, but his eyes widened when his father followed him into the tent.

"Father, I ..."

Alex made the mistake of trying to stand at the sight of his father. The sudden motion caused his vision to black out and the world spun. Alex grabbed the edge of the table then felt the competent hands of the healer's aid as they eased him back into his chair.

"Easy, Your Highness." The man steadied him until he was certain that his patient would not topple out of the chair before stepping back.

Alex opened his eyes again and saw that both his father and brother were seated opposite him, concerned.

"Alex, for once, please do as the healer's say." The King's voice was soft but firm.

"Yes, Father, I'm sorry. It's just when I saw you I forgot and tried to stand. I don't think I want to try that again."

Alex looked at the food on the table and guessed that explained why there was so much of it. He hoped his father and brother were hungry; even though he knew he should be, he wasn't sure he could bear the thought of eating.

William grinned at him, taking a bowl, spooning some cooked fruit into it and placing it in front of him.

"Here, and that mug has a concoction that Aaron said you have to drink."

Alex grinned at his brother then; grimacing at the mug, he picked it up and sipped it, cautious. Alex gagged as he swallowed and would have put it back down again except for his father's steady glance. He stopped halfway between his mouth and the table.

"Yes, Father, okay, I'll finish it." Closing his eyes, Alex threw the concoction back into his throat and swallowed, trying not to gag.

"Here, this might help chase away the taste." His father passed him a small glass of juice.

Alex grabbed it and took a mouthful, taking a second before placing the glass on the table.

"We've been discussing options and I've decided you will stay with the progression for now. With lords being implicated in the kidnapping attempt and packs of Sundered being abroad attacking a large, well-armed group, I'd rather you ride with us. Splitting the guard contingent right now isn't advisable. The healers advise me they would rather you be in a proper bed but as long as you follow instructions it shouldn't do you any harm." His father looked at him and Alex realised that he was waiting for a response.

"It makes sense, I guess, Father, and I'd be useless at defending myself right now, let alone others." Alex looked at his father before trying a spoonful of the stewed fruit.

His father looked at him for such a long time that Alex squirmed under his close regard, before his father returned to his meal. Much to Alex's astonishment, the breakfast passed in companionable silence—no scolding or lectures.

"I'm proud of you, Alex; by all the accounts of the fight and the rest of the journey to camp, you acquitted yourself well. Now let us take care of you while you heal."

Alex couldn't tell right now if it was the King or his father speaking to him, then settled with a mixture of both. He'd never quite seen him like this and guessed that Aaron had passed on the bit about killing himself this time. Alex ducked his head, a little self-conscious. While he never meant to cause his father concern, he always seemed to be very good at doing so.

"I'll do as I'm told, Father. To be frank, I don't think I could do anything else right now." Alex surprised himself with his honesty.

"Good, now it's time we got moving. William, if you could stay with your brother again today? Alex always rested easier when you were nearby. It seems it's a habit from his childhood he hasn't outgrown." At William's nod, the King turned and walked from the tent.

Alex looked at William, a little wide-eyed. He'd never seen his father like that before. "Father is worried for you, Alex. Aaron's brief to him didn't pull any punches."

Alex grimaced then rewound, remembering his father's words. "Packs of Sundered? There are reports of more than the ones we ran into?"

William closed his eyes, then seemed to choose his words with care. "Yes, Alex, Father has had reports not only from his court session here today, but from yesterday."

Alex closed his eyes and took a deep breath. "I must see the reports. I'll take care of it."

William looked shocked. "No, Alex, you'll rest and heal."

Alex smiled, touched that his brother cared so much. "I will rest and heal, William. Then I will go after the Sundered. After all, who else do we have who is likely to succeed and survive the task?" He shook his head and smiled. "I have the title, the friends and the guard, all of them bearing the Taint to varying degrees. After all, isn't this what being the Fourth is all about?"

"Promise me you won't do anything stupid and you will consult with me first." William was still concerned and not willing to concede the point.

Alex crooked his head on one side, looking at his big brother. "I'm the Fourth, the expendable one remember?" Alex held his hands up as William went to object. "It's alright, William, I won't just run off. I'll let you know first so you can have a sleepless night worrying about me."

Alex could see that William wasn't happy with the situation but was obviously willing to leave the arguing for another day. Alex had no doubt the subject would come up again. Likely after his brother had briefed their father. Still, he was right. He knew he was, there wasn't anyone else who had the ability to track down and kill the Sundered ones except for Jess, Kyle and himself.

***

Alex had taken a nap after breakfast while he was waiting for them to depart—well, he hadn't intended to nap, that had just happened because he thought he could relax for a few moments before going to the carriage. The next thing he knew, he was waking up in the carriage. Opening his eyes, he noticed that, as he expected and their father had ordered, William was riding in the carriage with him along with Aaron, who had been talking until they noticed he was awake. He knew they had been discussing him. Without thinking about it, Alex reached for the power of the veil. The pain was sharp and blinding, causing him to scream in agony. He felt hands restraining him as his body arched and spasmed.

"Listen, Alex, drop the power. You're not healed enough to wield it."

The voice was Aaron's. Then he felt a barrier go around him that was not his own and Alex collapsed back onto his pillows. Turning onto his side he curled up in a foetal position, hands cradling his head, which felt like it was about to explode.

Alex was aware enough to realise that the carriage had stopped, but he paid it no attention.

"Thank you, Aaron, sorry, it was a habit." Alex moaned in pain. "Please make it stop." The last was almost a whimper.

"Shh, Alex. Try to relax. The worst will be over soon. William, can you reach into my bag and take out the large green bottle and pour a full measure in the cup? You'll see it's marked on the side." Alex felt hands on him and knew others must have come into the carriage while they were stopped. "Come on, Alex, I need you to sit up a little so you can drink this. Don't worry, it doesn't taste that bad. It will help dull the pain. I can't use the healer's gift on you right now; it would hurt you too much."

As Aaron spoke, Alex felt other hands propping him up, a cup held to his lips. He swallowed as the liquid was poured into his mouth, relieved that it didn't taste as bad as the potion he'd taken that morning. Still, with the promise it would help relieve the pain, he would have drunk even that one. The cup was removed and the hands supporting him eased him back onto his pillows. Alex turned onto his side again, trying not to whimper, without succeeding.

For Alex, it seemed like an eternity, but the pain receded and he felt his body relax, the trembling stop. Still, he lay for a space of time, letting the drug-induced lethargy take over. He opened his eyes, looking across at Aaron and William. He licked his lips.

"I don't think I want to do that again in a hurry. Thank you." Alex smiled.

"I will withdraw my shield, Alex, I can't maintain it much longer." Aaron waited until Alex nodded then dropped the shield he'd been maintaining. "I'm sorry, Alex. If I could maintain it I would but you are way too strong, even hurt as you are."

Alex nodded his understanding. He didn't quite understand the difference between the healer's gift and the way he handled the power of the veil, but he knew he was a lot stronger than the healer, even if Aaron understood and wielded his own powers much better than Alex.

"The drug won't last long." It wasn't a question; he could feel his body burning through it. He shuddered despite himself.

"Easy, Alex, by the time the drug wears off you will be tired still. Your head may ache—I'll give you more pain medication to ease that, although not as much as you had." Aaron held up the half-empty bottle sitting on the bench next to him.

Alex thought about it and nodded; he trusted Aaron. "I think I need to sleep again."

"Sleep ,Alex, it's the best thing for you right now. Just don't touch the veil when you wake."

Alex smiled and let the last of the tension drain from his body. As he drifted off to sleep, he contemplated that all he'd done the past few days was sleep. In the past it was hard to drag him out of bed, yet now he was ordered to rest and all he wanted to do was get out and about.

S moke billowed in thick columns from the village, birds of prey circling high above as if sensing their time to feast was not long off. Flames licked up the side of the town hall in the centre of the village unabated. Screams of pain, mingled with sobbing and wailing, could be heard.

A woman was running from the village, cutting across the ploughed fields toward the road that led to a neighbouring village, the bundle of her baby clutch in her arms, a small leather backpack strapped to her back. She glanced back over her shoulder at the burning village before turning back, her pace picking up as she reached the road and safe footing.

Skidding to a halt, she fell backwards as she tried to turn, screaming, trying to shield her baby from the man who'd appeared in front of her. She scrambled to her feet, trying to flee back the way she'd come, only to be grabbed from behind. What was once a man roared, shaking her like she was a child's doll. In a desperate move to try and save her child, she flung the baby from her into the low bush at the edge of the field, her heart breaking as she heard his wail.

Hearing the shimmering noise in her brain and cold air wash over her, she moaned, knowing more with power had arrived. Her attacker froze, snarling over her shoulder at whoever had appeared. She felt herself tossed aside. She was momentarily stunned as the breath exploded from her lungs and she hit the ground.

She looked up as she felt the air shimmer and sizzle from the use of power around her; the look of relief almost palpable as she looked up at the newcomers.

"Now is that anyway to treat a lady?" The rough yet somehow cultured voice scolded the man who had terrorised her.

The woman looked on, shocked as the blade of the newcomer, sheathed in power, which crackled along its length, took off the head of the man as he was held, motionless, his feet dangling just above the ground by an unseen hand. The headless body then crumpled to the ground, lifeless.

The woman looked at the crumpled body on the ground, trembling as the man who'd saved her walked from the cluster of his people around him. He reached down with one hand and helped her to her feet.

She pressed a hand to her mouth, a tear welling in her eye as she curtseyed. "Thank you, Your Highness." She then looked at one of his companions, appearing to hold her breath as he walked over to her. Her baby bundled up in his arms, he smiled and passed the baby over to the trembling woman. She caught a sob, clutching her child to her chest. "Thank you, My Lord Callum."

The prince turned, looking at one of his men. "Simon, take the woman and her child to safety. Join us in the village to clean up when you are done."

Simon took a few steps forward, pushing the hood back from his face as the woman took an uncertain step back at the cowled figured that had walked up to her.

"Certainly, Edward, as you wish. Save some of the fun for me." His tone was lightly mocking yet his smile reassuring as he grasped the woman's shoulder and the veil wrapped around them until they disappeared from sight.

Alex woke, slowly becoming aware of his surroundings, and tried to shake off the very vivid dream he'd just had. Either that or his uncle's ghost was dreaming and somehow communicating it to him. He rolled over and saw his brother sitting in the chair next to his bed, looking at him intently.

William smiled. "So, dreaming again? Not your usual nightmare, though, I think."

The last was a statement more than a question. Alex knew William had seen him, woken him from enough nightmares to be able to tell the difference.

"Mmm, odd one. About Uncle Edward and his companions during the Sundered War, although why I'd dream about that I don't know."

William looked at him seriously. "The Sundered are on the rise again. You've just had your first real battle with some. It's probably not that odd."

Alex snorted, amused despite himself. "I guess, but why the heck did Great Uncle Edward have a flaming sword?"

William burst out laughing. "Sorry, Alex, no idea. We can ask the Master Swordsmith if he can make one for you if you like?"

Alex shook his head at the thought of the Master Swordsmith's reaction if anyone made a request like that and chuckled once more. It would be an interesting thing to see, as long as he wasn't the one making the ludicrous request.

A lex sat in the carriage, on a seat rather than a bed for once, one foot up on the seat opposite him, looking out the window. William sat, relaxed, on the next seat, looking out the window on his own side.

"You must be sick of babysitting me by now, William." Alex looked at his brother.

William snorted. "Well now that you're more or less better, to be honest, it's more peaceful. The lords can't get anywhere near you by the King's orders, which means they can't get near me while I'm looking after you. That means I don't have to listen to their various petitions." William looked at him and grinned.

Alex laughed. "Well, at least you got something worthwhile for your trouble." Alex watched the parade of lords, who seemed to find a reason to ride past his carriage on horseback, although the Elite maintained a cordon that made them all keep their distance. "You know, I swear I have never seen half of the lords we've seen today on horseback during the court migration ever before."

William's lips quirked and he shook his head. "You're right, and I doubt we will again. They are reassuring themselves that you are alive and well. There was a rumour there you were mortally wounded by the Sundered you'd fought and the King was hiding it from them."

Alex threw his head back and laughed. "That concerned them? I'm the scapegrace—the youngest, most irresponsible child of the King."

William shook his head. "Yes, you were, until you heroically defended the ladies—and even your own guards—from attack by the Sundered and suffered grave injury while doing so." William grinned. "Now they have forgotten all their previous misgivings and your many misdemeanours and you are their favourite."

Alex shook his head and went back to gazing out the window. His brain was picking away at information he'd gathered from the healers while under their care. Problem was, he didn't quite know yet what he was seeing. He wished he could compare notes with Jess and Kyle, but his father had been firm. No visitors at all until he got the all clear from the healers, which meant that he was isolated until Aaron said otherwise.

Healers wielded the power of the veil yet it was different to how he did. Aaron's simple instructions not to touch the veil were not as simple as he thought. While he was not using the veil, he knew it was running through him, regardless. He could feel the power all around him, flowing through him; he could see its muted brown, green and grey, flowing through the window of the carriage. It was why he'd had a headache for days, despite not channelling or using the power—it was flowing through him; a part of him, anyway. He'd pulled in so much raw power during the fight with the Sundered and then when trying to hide and shield the whole party during their flight to the safety of the King's Camp. He'd burnt the channels in his mind that wielded the power. Alex became aware he was rubbing his temples and stopped. Then he shook his head as he realised that it was too late and William had noticed anyway.

William handed him a small dose of the pain medication and Alex sighed, throwing the medicine back. Handing the cup back, he relaxed into his chair, pulling the lever on the side so he was half reclining. He'd learned that if he relaxed, the medication worked faster and better than if he fought against it. Aaron had warned him not to channel the power of the veil until he was no longer getting headaches. After that morning where he'd drawn power, the healer didn't need to emphasise his point. Alex was prepared to do this the healer's way, even if it was slow. Power went through him regardless of whether or not he willed it, which meant it was taking him longer to heal since even the low level of unconscious power hurt, although not as much as it had, giving him hope.

Healers were different in their use of the power, though; it was like they grasped hold of power external to them and twisted it to their own ends; however, they didn't channel it through their own bodies. They manipulated what was around them, which is why an injunction of *just don't use the power* was easy for a healer to follow. He shaped power from within him and drew more power into himself, manipulating it to his own will. The healers used their apprentices as well, from what he'd observed, to somehow bolster their own abilities.

Alex sighed as the medication took effect and settled in more comfortably.

"So, how's your head?" When Alex cracked his eyes open, he saw William was observing him.

"Not bad. It's more like what you'd describe as a mild hangover. You know, the one where you can function but you wish you weren't in court with Father all day? Not the you-want-to-stay-in-bed and die variety." Alex frowned as he observed his brother. That was the other side effect of burning his brain out—he could see the veil much more without having to concentrate like he used to. William had power flowing through him—not much, but he still had it.

"What? Did I grow horns or something?" William looked at him, perplexed, and even looked over his shoulder to check out the carriage window.

Alex smiled. "No, William, you use the veil, even if it's not much and it's unconscious on your part you have it running through you. That's not normal—well not normal for the average person, anyway."

William's eyes widened at that announcement and he swallowed. "Are you sure? Alex, you aren't meant to be drawing on the veil yet."

Alex shook his head. "I'm not, William. It's just a part of me, whether or not I will it. You, though... yes, I'm sure, I can see it winding around you, through you. Not much of it, but it's there."

Alex laughed as William raised his hand in front of his eyes and stared at it as if he'd never seen it before.

William opened his mouth, closed it again and looked back at his hand, concerned.

Alex sobered, realising that he'd caused William to worry. "You'll be fine, William. You're not like Jess, Kyle or me. Well, I can't see myself, but Jess and Kyle... well, they shine with energy, like it's bursting out of them. You, not so much."

A lex had spent most of the hunt progression healing, his recovery slow. While Aaron's manipulation of the power differed from his own, he trusted his judgement. He knew also that he would do irreparable damage to himself if he kept pushing himself. So while it wasn't in his nature to be patient, he tried his best. The person he felt more sorry for was William, since his father had been adamant: he was to have no visitors at all except the healers and William would stay with him to enforce that order until Alex received full clearance. Still, William had said that this was the most peace he'd had in years and didn't mind the duty in the slightest.

Alex had been taken aback that his father had been very serious —he hadn't even been able to see Amelia, which was the most time they had spent apart since they had been going out with each other. He knew she'd spent the rest of the journey so far either in his father's company or Elizabeth's, so in the heart of the royal progression. He knew she was as safe as she could be.

Alex relaxed back on his bed, waiting for Aaron to arrive. He let his mind idle, concentrating on his breathing, keeping it slow and controlled. He knew in the back of his mind he was feeling better. He could hear the whispering voices floating through his mind, although he didn't focus in on any of them. Then again, none of them were directed at him either. Without even thinking about it, he knew Kyle and Jess were nearby; their power drew his own.

There were others who felt similar to his own power but they were further off and he assessed they were not a direct threat. They were Sundered. He knew it should scare him how many he could feel, yet he knew they weren't close. Most were far afield from their current location—he assessed most were not in the Realm at all. Still, it was a difficult task to assess the Veiled World and he knew it wasn't wise for him to explore that right now. Although he had the sinking feeling he would, perhaps sooner than he wished.

He sensed Aaron come into his tent and grinned. The healer was disapproving. He knew his patient—while not quite breaching his injunction, he wasn't obeying it either.

"Good morning, Aaron. Yes, I know, I'm not doing anything except letting my mind wander. I've told you before that the veil works in a different way for me than it does for you. I don't have a headache at all, if that helps?" Alex opened his eyes and looked at the healer, seeing he was correct. The healer had a disapproving look.

Aaron shook his head and gave up with a faint smile. "Yes, I know, Alex." The healer walked over and placed his hands on his patient's temples and closed his eyes, concentrating.

Alex could feel the healer's power trailing over him, testing, but this time it caused him no pain at all. The healer withdrew and smiled.

"You're all clear, Alex. I'd prefer it if you would limit your use of the power for the next few weeks. Pushing yourself the way you have done, although many would have died without your intervention, it has done you irreparable harm. It has blasted your mind wide open to the power—it would have happened anyway, but it's much sooner than I would have liked." The healer looked at him in that way that healers had, making him want to squirm.

"I will do my best, Aaron. If I had to do it all over again, I would do the same thing, even knowing the pain it would cause me."

20

ALEX AND AMELIA

Alex breathed a sigh of relief walking through the forest. The healers had cleared him for light exercise, meaning he could go for a walk. One of the side effects of his father's determination to give him the time he needed to heal was the Elite preventing the hangers on of the royal progression from following him on his walk. They were camped on the outskirts of a larger settlement and would be here for a few days before moving on. This particular part of the Realm was beautiful and being excused from royal duties meant he had more time to enjoy it.

Even William had granted him some space; of course, that space had come with strict orders to the Elite. There were double the number that normally followed him around, although his own normal guard were the inner circle. With the extras being an extra ring of security further out. Of his own guard, only Marcus and James were in sight and even they were at a respectful distance. The guards had turned back several Lords and Ladies in their attempts to intercept him already; a circumstance that he found amusing. He was also aware that some of the best hunters and trackers had been turned out as well. Although this time their instructions had nothing to do with looking for game to feed the hoards.

He glanced across at Amelia; she was abnormally quiet, her gaze darting around at the guards. He knew that it had been hard for her, with their courtship being acknowledged. Then he was out of bounds due to the attack, and unable to shield her from some of the petty, small-minded members of the court.

Alex took a breath to calm his nerves. "It's not too late to back out of my world, Amelia. We could stage the most wonderful fight if you prefer."

Amelia turned and thumped him on the arm. "Alex, no! That's not what I'm thinking." Amelia's lent her head against his shoulder as they walked. "They told me you could have died, Alex."

Alex paused, tilting her face up to his and kissed her. "It's alright, I'm hard to kill." Lacing his fingers though hers, he continued to walk. "The healers are always on at me not to overextend myself, to limit my use of the taint. It isn't as easy as they think and none of us had a choice when the Sundered attacked. As the Fourth, it kind of goes with the job description, to put myself between the Sundered and those without the power to defend themselves."

Alex looked up and smiled; they were close to the little glade he wanted to show Amelia. He could hear the rush of the river and the waterfall. The trees around them were much bigger than those around the coast and the Winter Palace, although not comparable to those that surrounded the Summer Palace. The dappled light filtering through the forest canopy above and the slight breeze helped cool them both down. Still, a swim in the river would do so even more. He looked sideways at Amelia and grinned. Pulling her hand, he started to run toward the water.

"Come on, Amelia, the waterfall is close." She laughed, dropping his hand to pick up the skirts of her dress and run with him. It became a game as they dodged around trees in an impromptu game of catch with their laughter ringing out across the forest.

Finally, they burst through the trees, skidding to a halt as the rocks rose above, with the waterfall falling like a curtain down into a pool. Alex took a moment to catch his breath, please at the stunned expression on Amelia's face. Grinning at her, he gathered her up into his arms and started striding to the edge of the rocky outcrop with the pool below. Amelia's eyes widened and she laughed, battering his chest with her hands.

"Alex, don't you dare!"

Alex laughed and jumped. Amelia squealed in shock as she hit the water. They sunk under the cool surface before bursting back up. Alex laughed and grabbed Amelia's hands as she tried to dunk him under the water again in retaliation. He pulled her closer, moving them both to the edge so they could stand. He brushed a wet strand of her hair back, cupping her face with his hand, and kissed her. Amelia's voice was low and breathy as she pulled back enough to glance up at the banks around them.

"Alex, the guards—" A blush spread on her cheeks although there was a hint of regret in her voice.

Alex glanced up and, sure enough, the guards had spread out around the edge of the pool, with some wading their way across to the other bank. He smiled, his eyes flicking up to the curtain of the waterfall behind them. His eyes tracked back to hers as he moved them slowly back, kissing her as they passed under the waterfall, the spray of the water washing over them as they moved under it to the small clearing behind. He chuckled as she gasped and looked around at the moss-lined rocks, ferns and a sandy outcrop forming a small cave. He kissed her again and moved them back to the cavern. Amelia did not object as they sunk to the sandy floor, her hands busy undoing his trousers with the waterfall screening them from view.

21

HUNTING PARTIES

Alex had spent most of the last few days pouring over the reports from the villagers about the attacks of the Sundered Ones. Neither his father nor William was happy that he intended to go after them but had conceded when he pointed out that without others to care for and protect, he could remove himself from the situation if he chose. Due to the increased reports to the King, the progression was slow and in the camps near bigger settlements, the King's Court stayed an extra day just to gather more facts about what was happening in the region.

Alex had also been giving himself time to build up his strength and stamina again, exercising and training every day. He'd been surprised at how he'd bounced back once he had full access to the power again without it causing blinding, burning pain. One of the other side effects he'd noticed since was the colour. Before, the Taint appeared as wisps of energy, all different shades of grey that came from every living thing. He could grasp that power, bind it together and direct it as he willed. Now, he noticed that the Taint was coloured and the different colours came from different places. Some was still a silvery grey but even that seemed to have more depth to it now. There was also Taint in blue, green and red. He'd noticed that the colours ranged from pale to deep, which seemed to show the strength of the power— as far as he'd been able to work out, anyway. It was a development he wanted to check with Kyle and Jess to see if they had a similar after-effect from the veil sickness as him.

Alex slid the last of his weapons into their appropriate holsters and picked up his cloak, pausing as what passed as a door to his lodging in the camp opened. Jess and Kyle were standing there looking at him, their expressions bland. Both were dressed for hunting and equipped for a fight.

"You don't have to come with me. I won't find any of them anyway, given from what we saw last time, they move around like we can."

Any glimmer of hope he had that they would agree with him and stay behind in safety died when they both shook their heads.

"Alex, you will not hunt the Sundered ones in the Realm without us. It's too dangerous." Kyle's expression showed no hint he would back down.

Alex was about to reply, then hearing the doors open again, he paused, frowning as Marcus, James and Megan all crowded in behind Jess and Kyle. He groaned and looked at Marcus, his eyebrow raised in enquiry.

Marcus looked at James and Megan, who both nodded at him. "We'll come with you, My Lord. I know we may not be as powerful with the Taint as you three, but you know very well we all bear it, even if it's something we've never discussed. It's why we were placed in your service. We have enough that we can come with you; we can protect ourselves somewhat and you three can use our swords if you encounter any of the Sundered."

Alex, Jess and Kyle all looked at each other, startled, but it was Kyle who asked what they were all thinking.

"What do you mean, protect yourselves somewhat?"

"The Elite have training annuals, My Lord; even as old, as long ago as the last Fourth's Elite, they kept records. So we've been training in creating shields, strikes—none of us are strong enough to do much more but we can deflect attacks from the Sundered ones if they use the Taint as a weapon."

Jess looked as wide-eyed and shocked as Alex guessed he looked.

"Training records about how to use the Taint as a weapon?"

"Yes, My Lady. I'm sure it's nothing compared to what is kept in the Royal Library or even the Fourth's Library in the Compound of the Fourth, but the instructions were fairly clear. All the Fourth's Elite have proficiency but we are the most advanced and strongest." Megan was earnest as she looked at each of them.

Kyle chuckled. "I think none of us are inclined toward sitting in libraries—the Fourth's or otherwise—but remind us to go check it out when we get to the Summer Palace."

Alex shook his head, pushing the thought of un-looked-for training manuals in his own library to one side for now. Then again, it was only on arrival at the Summer Palace, moving into the Compound of the Fourth, that he would have his own library —or, rather, he trusted Megan's assertion that he had one since it hadn't occurred to him there would be one. Most of his training with his ancestor had been centred around staying in control and keeping his mental barriers up. He'd only discovered that he could use the power as a weapon to thrust at his opponent in his last fight with the Sundered. Still, he didn't think admitting that to their guards was advisable right now.

"There's more of us than I'd like, but still, I guess you are all going to insist. Can you all travel in the Veiled World or are you going to hitch a ride?" Alex was thinking that if they couldn't travel themselves that he would have to haul them along. He'd never done it, though, and only knew it could be done due to his ancestor dragging him along when he was younger.

"None of us can travel by the paths, Your Highness; we're not strong enough to do it ourselves." James chimed in, yet neither he nor Marcus and Megan had even the faintest look of concern on their faces, which seemed to suggest that the three guards all assumed it could be done.

Alex looked at Jess and Kyle, who both shrugged. Kyle raised his eyebrow at both then made one more test, this time with his mind. His forehead crinkled as he concentrated.

Can you hear me now? Can you speak with your mind voice? Kyle's mind voice was cool and smooth, yet Alex could tell he was putting a little more effort into it and focusing on the three guards.

If the expression on the guards' faces were anything to go by, Alex guessed that they could at least hear Kyle. Once more, the three guards looked at each other, wide-eyed with astonishment. It was Marcus who replied, his mind voice uncertain and weak compared to Jess and Kyle.

Yes, My Lord, sometimes we hear you, all of you, but it seems to come and go. Marcus had a look of deep concentration on his face; Alex turned his head to hide his smile.

Alex glanced at Jess and Kyle. "We must be a little more careful about broadcasting. If we will do this, then we should go, now. Marcus, you're with me. James, stay with Kyle—Megan, with Jess."

Then in a tight communication with both Jess and Kyle, he added for them alone, *Let's try not to lose them. I know that we can do this, just never done it before.*

Jess smiled and motioned for Megan to stand closer. *Well it should be interesting.*

I don't want to explain to your father how we lost his guards. Kyle chuckled and motioned for James to move closer.

Alex noted that Marcus had moved closer to him without having to be told, then with a glance at both Kyle and Jess, he took a deep breath. Concentrating, he pulled in the Taint, expanding his reach to include Marcus as he transitioned them into the Veiled World. Alex gasped as the familiar washed-out grey he knew was transformed. Lines of power from all the different colours he'd noticed were visible. Realising that he was holding his breath, he exhaled. He checked that Marcus was still with him and grinned at his guard's stunned expression. Glancing around, he saw both Jess and Kyle had also transitioned into the Veiled World with their charges in tow.

At a slight widening of their eyes, he gathered he wasn't alone in seeing the colourful power flows trailing all around them. Thinking about it, he watched, fascinated, as a path formed, with strands of the green energy but noticeable wisps of the silver-grey, blue and red intertwined.

I take it you both see the different colours now as well? Any ideas why everything is so colourful? Not that I'm complaining, the old look was a little depressing.

Alex concentrated to make sure he was talking to his friends only with that comment. He didn't want their guards to panic, thinking anything was wrong and that things weren't quite appearing as they normally did.

Jess looked relieved. *I'm glad it's not just me. The elements, maybe?*

Earth, Wind, Fire and Water? Why is it our dead ancestors never show up when we have pertinent questions for them?

Kyle nodded, thoughtful. *That makes a weird sense I guess. Aaron described the veil sickness as, what was it? Drawing more of the power than we should have, burning through the channels in our mind that manipulate the Taint?*

This time Alex nodded. *Yes, he said it was sooner than he'd like. So perhaps this would always happen, just circumstance caused it to happen sooner?*

Kyle grimaced. *Why is it I feel like everyone knows more than we do and they are keeping secrets from us?*

Because they are? Alex shook his head and broadened his focus. *Sorry to exclude you there, guys, we were discussing options. Stay close to us, I don't quite know what would happen if you got separated from us. I'd hate to think of you all wandering around here, lost with no ability to get home again.*

Yes, Your Highness.

Marcus moved a step closer, which made Alex smile and as the others' mind voices whispered their understanding, he turned and, keeping careful track of them all, walked down the trail that had spun out ahead of him. Noting that Kyle was trailing at the rear, he breathed a small sigh of relief. It was less likely that they would lose one of them with Kyle keeping an eye out from behind.

Alex grinned outright at the guards' palpable relief as they emerged from the Veiled World to the real world once more. He frowned and looked around what appeared to be a cluster of small farms on the edge of a small forest. Small it might be, but there had been several reports that the Sundered Ones had appeared here. While the reports indicated that the Sundered were in the area, they did not show that anyone had been killed. That had drawn Alex's interest in the first place; he wanted to know if it was an oversight in the report or if it was true. If true, it was odd in his experience, even if that experience was limited. He'd never heard of the Sundered coming into a habited area, encountering people and not killing them.

Alex resisted the urge to pull up his hood as he approached the farmhouse. This time he was here as the Fourth, his crest on display, stitched onto his vest. Kyle kept his own hood drawn up, but that was his normal practice when he was in places he didn't know. Jess followed his lead, although while her hood was on, it wasn't pulled forward so it didn't obscure her face. Both kept pace with him, one on either side, with the guards trailing behind them. He knew by the glow of light in the farmhouse that the farmer was still up. Frowning, Alex changed track and walked to the door and rapped on it.

The door cracked open. The first thing Alex saw was a machete held in the firm, competent grip of a middle-aged, stocky man. Alex held his hands up, gesturing for the guards to stay put. He knew their first thought was to disarm him and have him face-down on the ground. He didn't have to turn to see Kyle or Jess to know they had their hands on their own blades.

"Peace, Farmer Caine, we mean you no ill will. It is Farmer Caine, correct?" Alex spoke, his voice low, and willed the man to calm down.

"Yes. Who are you and what do you want, stranger?" The man was trying to seem strong yet his voice shook, unsettled to receive visitors at this time of night.

"Be civil, man, His Highness Prince Alexander just has questions for you, then we will be on our way." Marcus' gravelly voice spoke up from behind Alex, a hint of threat in his tone.

Farmer Caine's eyes grew wide with shock as he took in Alex's appearance with the Fourth's crest on his vest. His hand flew up, touching his forehead then resting on his heart. Bowing, his blade clattered as it hit the floor of his cabin.

"I'm sorry, Fourth, I didn't recognise you." The man seemed shaken to the core and kept his eyes on the ground.

Alex sighed and glanced back at Marcus before turning back to the Farmer. "Please, Farmer Caine, I didn't mean to startle you. I am just interested in a report you gave to the King regarding the Sundered you encountered. It's unusual to survive such encounters." Alex hoped his prompting would elicit answers and was regretting his impulse.

"Yes, Fourth. I know it's unusual, that's why I reported it. I don't know what else I can tell you. I heard my boy screaming, I looked up and saw him being held up by the thing. The Sundered threw his head back and screamed—started shaking my boy like he was a rag doll. I don't quite know what came over me. I ran at him, yelling at him to drop my boy." The man paused, his eyes flicking up to Alex's before casting back down to the ground again. "I got right up to him and hacked at his arm. The Sundered stumbled back, there was anger in his eyes and he threw my boy aside to concentrate on me. The monster took a step toward me then. I can't explain it, he stopped, seemed confused. Looked at his hands, then to my boy, back toward me. He said sorry, that he didn't know what he was doing, then he ran toward the forest and disappeared." The man's voice appeared both awed and shocked at that last point and he stood there silently, waiting.

"Your boy, is he here?" Kyle spoke up from Alex's shoulder. His voice was soothing and he seemed to feel empathy for the man.

Alex knew and Kyle likely did, too, before the man shook his head that the boy wasn't present in the house.

Farmer Caine's eyes darted up to Kyle, and he licked his lips. "No, My Lord, my wife took my boy and our youngest to Callenhain to stay with her parents. It's too dangerous with a Sundered around. I'll finish things here, lock the place down and join them; it will be safer in the city."

Alex nodded. "Thank you, Farmer Caine, you've been a great help. We'll have a look around but it is likely the Sundered is long gone. If it will give you peace of mind and you can be ready to travel tomorrow morning, you'd be welcome to travel in convoy with the progress; it will be a safer for you in company, although I admit a little slower."

The farmer looked up, forgetting himself for a moment for the first time since he had learned who Alex was.

"Thank you, Fourth. I appreciate the offer, I still have a few days' worth of work, though. There is a group of us heading for the city, so there will be safety in numbers."

Alex nodded his thanks and excused himself, thinking it best not to push the point that if a group of Sundered would attack a large armed group, then a small group of farmers wouldn't cause them to pause.

They walked away from the farmhouse toward the forest. The light shining in the window almost seemed lonely in the surrounding darkness. Alex hoped the brave farmer survived to see his family again. As they walked, Alex hauled them into the half world, neither in the Veiled World or a part of the real world. It was a transitional place between both. The others maintained their silence as he ranged out with his mind, looking and listening for the broken ones he knew must be around—even if the one that the farmer had described was curled up in a bed in his home, petrified at what he was becoming.

What the farmer had described was someone born with the Taint being overwhelmed by it. Still, there had been several reports from locals about attacks and those sounded like a group of Sundered had made their home nearby. If they followed the normal patterns, they would be in the forest somewhere. He felt both Kyle and Jess ranging out, conducting their own search of the area as well, so he concentrated on his own patch as they walked through the forest. The real world flickered as they walked, passing though trees and boulders like they weren't there. He could tell that their guards were astounded even though they kept their eyes on Alex and stayed close.

Jess paused. He could feel that her mind almost did a double take over an area again, then she turned, giving them a tight grin.

Found a group. I think. It's strange, they feel different. It's like they've even made a shelter for themselves.

Without further comment, Jess took the lead, pulling more power. Alex noted that it was more of the silvery grey colour as their pace increased, the flickering trees blurring as they moved through the forest to their destination. Then they paused on the outskirts of a makeshift camp. Alex could hear the whispering voices of the former men and women in the camp, disjointed, confused, suffering pain and anger. He almost groaned as the noise and feelings assaulted his brain before increasing his own shield on his mind and on Marcus. He trusted that Jess and Kyle were taking care of Megan and James since their pinched expressions had softened. Alex drew his sword, an action followed by both Kyle and Jess, mirroring him without having to think about it. Their guards drew their own swords with only a short pause, taking their lead from Alex, Jess and Kyle.

All right, get ready. I'll drop us in the camp, they will be alerted to our presence by the sudden pull of energy, so they are not likely to be surprised. There are eight of them here in the camp; I can sense that doesn't mean that there are not more of them here. If it gets too dangerous, I will pull us out. Be warned, if they are strong in the Taint they can heal even what would be a mortal wound. Pierce the heart, or take the head, don't just trust because they go down, they will die. They are no longer human.

Alex looked from one grim face to another, assured that they would follow his instructions. Then, taking one steadying breath, he pulled in power and drew all of them into the camp.

A lex raised his sword as they appeared in the midst of the camp. It was like the Tainted world took a breath and paused, watching, waiting for what seemed like an eternity, yet in reality was only moments. Then, as still as the world was in that split second, the world around them erupted. The Sundered appearing around them, soft popping noises as they released their hold on the Taint to drop them around their attackers, while others chose the more pedestrian mode of charging out of their makeshift shelters. There was no hint of sanity that Alex could hear in their mental voices or demeanours.

Alex drew his wandering attention back to the task at hand, although he noted that even if his mind had been wandering, his body hadn't been—he'd blocked the blade of the Sundered One who faced off against him. This one had armour and a sword, even if everything was a little worse for wear, giving testament that either he'd stolen the gear of one of his victims or he'd had training before he'd succumbed to the Taint. Alex felt his world narrow to just him and the one he faced, trusting that his companions had their own battles in hand. Even though his world narrowed, there was a small part of his brain that seemed to track their progress, so he knew Marcus was in his own fight nearby using the Taint as a shield. He thrust at his attacker with power and with his sword. He also knew Kyle engaged two of the Sundered, his blades whirling in what would be considered a graceful dance if it wasn't so deadly. Jess, in her part just as deadly, was taking down her opponent and wasting no time in heeding Alex's warning. She dropped, withdrawing her hunting knife from her belt and shoved it up from the man's abdomen, its long blade piercing his heart.

Alex battled his own opponent and settled on the fact he'd been trained, even if he wasn't trained all that well. Alex stepped to one side and parried, forcing the man's arm up as he stumbled. With a feral grin, Alex withdrew one of the small pointed long daggers that Kyle had insisted he carry and lunged in, thrusting it through the gap in the man's armour under his armpit. He withdrew it as his opponent stumbled back then, dropping the dagger, swung his sword two-handed, slicing through his neck, severing it from the body.

Turning toward where he could still hear battle going on, Alex ran toward Jess, seeing two of the Sundered coming at her from behind as she battled the one in front of her. Alex screamed a warning then gathered the Taint, drawing in the green and silver-grey. Then, on instinct, he also gathered in the rarer wispy red and, willing it into a solid thing, thrust it at the Sundered.

Despite himself, Alex froze for a moment as the Sundered staggered as if hit, then glowed. They opened their mouths and screamed in clear pain, frozen in agony. Alex didn't have time to analyse what had happened; he launched himself at them and thrust his blade up through the abdomen, much as Jess had earlier, and pierced the man's heart. Alex turned to tackle the second one but then paused as calm fell on the camp. Kyle had beaten him to it and Jess was dropping her own attacker.

The world slowed down to its normal pace. The murmuring of the Tainted had ceased—it was like the world had gone into shock. The Sundered, at least, were dead.

22

THE WATCHERS

E d watched the slaughter of the Sundered, shrouded by the veil, impressed at how well the group was working together. It had taken months and months of hard training for Kat, Cal and himself to form a tight fighting unit with their guards and that was in the days when those born with power didn't live with a death sentence—in the days where possessing the power of the veil and being able to wield it was seen as an asset. It was not referred to as the 'Taint' like it was in this day and age. Then something went wrong and those born with the veil running through them started going truly mad.

"They are doing well." Ed looked over at his companions, who observed the scene below.

Cal snorted. "So they should, they've spent enough time training together."

"Do you think they noticed that not all those in the camp they killed were Sundered?"

Kat turned from her observation of the six down in the clearing to regard her friends. Without waiting for a reply, Kat transitioned into the camp after Alex and his friends had left to return to their own camp.

Ed sighed and followed Kat, knowing Cal was following without having to check. Kat was always straight to the point; she was also correct, and he doubted they had noticed.

Ed used his other sight to make sure that all in the camp were dead. Not that he needed to; Kat had already done so, it was like breathing for her after all these years to check for any threats. They needn't have bothered, though; Alex and his crew had done a remarkable job for one of their first forays. Ed frowned, glancing around the creaky makeshift camp. This was a concern and out of character with all his experience with the broken ones. They did not make camps, makeshift or otherwise. They did not combine forces with those who were not of the broken.

"This is not right, Ed, this should not have been." Cal turned around, his arm sweeping, encompassing the dead bodies and the surrounding camp.

Kat was kneeling down, examining a dead body of one that had been human, sprawled on the ground.

"How did they commit this monstrosity? This new breed, they aren't just broken ones. They really are the monsters humans think of, the Sundered ones. Ed, we need to investigate." Kat stood looking at him.

"But the young ones, this is not good timing." Ed looked from Kat to Cal, thinking he'd get support, only to see his friend shake his head.

"No, my friend, Kat is right. We need to sort this out. There have been too many of our kind breaking, and this?" He glanced around the broken camp. "Mixing with whoever the hell these people were? That shouldn't have been possible; the broken ones should have killed the humans. We need to find out what is going on, something has changed. The children will be fine, they are doing alright on their own so far. It's time they stood on their own for a space of time. Let them grow and learn, they won't do that with us holding their hands and cleaning up for them."

Kat stood, nodding. "If things go wrong, we can help them pick themselves up and dust themselves off."

Cal grinned but there was little humour in him as he switched his gaze from one to the other of his lifelong friends.

"As harsh as it sounds, Ed, you know there isn't much we can do to help them until they start transition. This effort proves they are well able to defend themselves while we look into this."

Ed held his hands up, frustrated, yet conceding the point. "Alright, you are both right. We need to investigate and try to discover what is going on. The Broken sharing a camp with humans should not have been possible."

Ed took a breath and pulled the veil to him, disappearing into its folds, trusting that Cal and Kat would use their own methods to at least try to track down what had changed.

23

COMPOUND OF THE FOURTH

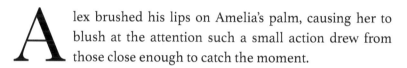lex brushed his lips on Amelia's palm, causing her to blush at the attention such a small action drew from those close enough to catch the moment.

"I'll see you again soon, my heart."

Alex let go of her hand and drew his horse away from the carriage she rode in with Elizabeth. Until their union was formalised, Amelia wasn't a part of his household, although in reality all those in the inner circle of the court at least knew it was just a matter of time. Amelia had dealt well with some negativity and sniping from some of her peers, though had been shocked at the assault and now moved, associating instead with the inner circle of the courtiers. While there had been some rather uncharitable reactions from that circle as well, they were at least a little more restrained. She had recognised that some of them had courted her favour, a situation she had been shocked at and had discussed with Alex. Alex smiled, remembering her reaction to it since she'd spent her life in such circles, although somewhat insulated from such behaviour until it became common knowledge that she was being courted by him.

He spurred his horse, raising one hand in farewell, not looking back even if he was tempted to. It was a temporary parting after all. His party broke off from the main group and headed off on a spur road that looked like it had been cleared and repaired. Alex chuckled, realising that it had been. It led through the trees around the side of the Summer Palace to the Compound of the Fourth. The Fourth's Wing at the Summer Palace had its own private entrance; he remembered exploring it when he was younger. It had shown signs of age and disuse, the courtyard overgrown with weeds growing wild up through the cracks in the cobbled courtyard. The compound had been closed for generations with only basic upkeep to stop it becoming a wreck. He'd been wondering what he and his friends would ride into, yet the state of the access road showed that perhaps his father had been planning this move for longer than he'd known.

The rest of the journey to the palace had passed without incident, except the hunting trips. Alex had been surprised by the addition of the three guards to their hunting parties, yet the successive hunting trips had helped forge them as a hunting party. The three guards had merged with them so they became a tight fighting unit. While not all of their hunting excursions had turned up results, they had at least helped to forge them. Alex still wished he'd been able to go off on his own rather than risk his friends but had to concede that some groups would have been too much for him to take on alone.

He'd also learned the healing trick, to heal small cuts and injuries rather than on an instinctive level as he realised he must have been doing so before. Another thing that had changed from his brush with veil sickness, it was hard to tell but Alex felt that he was stronger now than he had been before. Still, this gave him cause for concern, one he had not divulged to Kyle or Jess, or even his healer, Aaron. It brought the dark spectre of being overwhelmed by the Taint even closer. Shaking his head, he pushed his dark thoughts aside, knowing it did him no good to worry about it; whatever the future had in store would happen, regardless.

Through the trees, he could see the wall and the side gates of the little-used entrance to the palace. As they reached the tree line, a trumpet blared from his own ranks. Two of the guards spurred their horses to the lead, one on each side, each raising the banner of the Fourth, alerting those on the gate of their Prince approaching. His party clattered over the stonework laid in the outer courtyard as the large gates swung open without even a hint of disuse or neglect. Riding into the inner courtyard, Alex had time to notice the guard, his household guard lined up with his household staff, something that would take him time to get used to. The guard stood at attention while the captain of the household guard snapped a crisp salute, only relaxing as Alex passed him into the courtyard, before yelling for the gates to be secured.

Alex had no sooner dismounted than a stable boy, wearing his crest on his livery, ran forward to take the reins to his horse and led it away. Alex shook his head at the evidence that the Fourth's Compound even had its own stables.

Not even looking around, Alex knew his household staff would be stuck there in the courtyard until he entered, given what happened at the main entrance. He couldn't abide making them stand out for longer than they had to. Jess and Kyle fell into step with him as he clattered up the stone staircase to the large, ornate wooden doors embossed with the crest of the Fourth. The doors were pulled open by two attentive young household staff who were bursting with pride at being selected for this big task, today, of all days. Alex knew they were sons of his adult household staff co-opted into his service. He smiled and nodded his thanks as he passed inside the doors. The day the Fourth was installed in the Fourth's Compound for the first time in many generations.

Alex took a few steps into the reception room as the doors closed behind them, before gasping and stopping mid stride, looking around, wide-eyed even though he'd grown up and spent his entire life surround by luxury. The Fourth's Compound was even more stunning than the Royal Wing. Alex hadn't realised until that moment it wasn't just a wing—it was a compound, as its name suggested. It appeared to be a miniature palace. He traded a startled glance with Kyle.

"This can't be, I mean I've heard the Fourth's Compound was its own 'world', but this, it can't be—it's like a palace within the palace."

Alex continued gazing around the opulent entrance and they walked through the large open reception area before casting an incredulous glance at Kyle, who just grinned at him.

The ever-competent Joshua, who had come on ahead to supervise setting up his Prince's new accommodation, spoke up from where he'd been standing to the front of a line-up of the inner household staff.

Walking forward, he gestured further into the room and walked with Alex toward it. "It is, Your Highness. Inner and outer reception rooms, dining room, guards' rooms, a small kitchen, laundry and staff wing—well, it's all here. It even has its own walled gardens, courtyard, stables and exit. The actual Fourth's Wing is back here; this is the main entrance and reception area. Come, Your Highness. They've even put on breakfast for you, we knew you would have had an early start today and likely not had much besides your morning coffee."

Alex laughed and followed Joshua, with Kyle and Jess trailing behind looking around the rather ostentatious public reception room. They walked through yet another set of doors with a pair of the Elite on guard, who snapped to attention as they walked through.

Alex threw a glance over his shoulder and grinned. "It's okay, Marcus, I promise you I plan to find this comfortable inner sanctum and food and crash for the next few hours. Mess up the bed if it's made and get more sleep. I'll explore later. You should get rest before then yourself. You must have had way less sleep than I have." Alex laughed as Marcus let a rare chuckle escape.

"Yes, Your Highness. I'll brief the guards, and I might just do that after I've seen my men installed in their new barracks."

Marcus bowed as Alex, Kyle and Jess disappeared into the inner sanctum of the Fourth's Wing.

Alex looked around the sitting room they were led into, with its comfortable chairs of all different sizes arranged around a series of coffee tables. He slumped into the closest chair, groaning as he did so.

"Damn, we got up too early this morning, with all our nightly excursions. I need at least a few hours more sleep than what I've had. We all do, I'm sure." Alex slumped back in the chair, sighing as he sunk into the cushions. "This is comfortable. I could sleep in this chair."

Alex threw a glance at Jess, who laughed. "I know. Now you mention it, I could use more sleep myself. Still, can you believe all this, Alex?" Jess' hand made a little flitting gesture at their rather palatial surroundings as she sagged into a chair herself.

"No, not really. This place seems much bigger than what I was expecting. I had an image in my head of a wing tacked onto the end of the Royal Wing, only with its own entry and exit." He switched his gaze to the door as a servant came in and, without asking, poured him some coffee, placing it on a small coffee table within reach before going back to breakfast on offer, selecting a few pastries—his favourites—and placing them on the coffee table with a slight discreet bow.

Miranda then turned and served both Jess and Kyle, topping up their drinks and food plates then excusing herself with no fuss.

Kyle smiled. "I vote we all have this 'early morning snack', go get more sleep, then explore when we wake up. I don't have the energy to do much else right now."

All three looked at each other, then burst out laughing. Alex looked at his two closest friends in the world and closed his eyes. Memory flooding him, he winced. "I'm sorry for all the trouble I've caused you both. I know, I can be an obnoxious royal idiot. I don't understand how you've both put up with me."

The laughter died. Kyle and Jess smiled at each other, then back at him. Kyle chuckled again and shook his head. "No more than me, my brother. Besides. It's the Taint we all bear—we all act out because of it. It's better than hiding here in the palace moaning about our fate, though."

Jess shook her head. "You're not obnoxious, Alex, any more than I'm the 'harlot' my Lady Mother thinks I am." Jess closed her eyes and pushed the hurt that memory brought her, despite the trails of power from the Veiled World, reaching out its fingers to her, through her, almost willing her to forget.

"Now we're here, I think I should go back to trying to track down that assassin I ran into." Kyle swallowed the last of his coffee, then glared at the coffee pot sitting on the coffee table nearby, which was not close enough for him to reach without moving. He contemplated hauling himself out of his comfortable chair before the ever-competent Miranda bustled in and, without a world, filled up not only his mug but his plate and Jess' and Alex's as well.

Alex watched his friend over the rim of his coffee mug. "I still don't understand why the League of Skulls would embroil themselves in a plot to kidnap us. It's a move that just makes little sense." Alex stopped when he saw that Kyle's attention had wandered, then shook his head. "Do you think it's wise to track her down?"

Kyle brought himself back to the conversation with a visible effort, grinning at Alex.

"Might as well. I think we need to try at least to work out what is going on—the only avenues left are the League of Skulls and the assassin. Besides, I'm intrigued by the assassin; she is one of the Tainted, Alex, Jess—whoever she is, she is like us."

Jess chuckled. "I'd say your mysterious assassin is cute in a rough way, too." She shared a look with Alex, and they both laughed.

Alex cut Kyle some slack. "Just be careful. I know this is your thing, but if you are right, she is dangerous. The assassin didn't survive as one of the Tainted out there on the street by being incompetent at her chosen profession. If you need backup, let us know, and we'll come with you."

Jess looked at Alex and frowned. "No, Kyle, come and get me. Alex, it's likely you were the real target. Kyle and I were in the way and likely always would be no matter where they had tried to take you."

Alex opened his mouth, intending to object, but saw that his friends were of the same mind where this topic was concerned. He pushed it aside as an argument to have with them another day since it would take the pair time to track down the League of Skulls members.

Alex found himself diverted, his mind connecting to the servants, the guards.

"So how long do you think they have all been training for this moment, waiting for an excuse to move us in here? The Elite we've been training with, they're my Elite. The servants, everything." Alex threw his head back and laughed. "I even remember arguing with Father about the number of servants and guards we had."

Kyle and Jess looked at each other dumbfounded, then back at Alex before they both swore.

"Damn it. He planned to put guards on us all along. Your father was just waiting for the right moment. Why the hell didn't we see this before now?" Kyle was annoyed with himself for not picking up on the obvious before Alex did.

Jess looked at the outraged faces of both Kyle and Alex and laughed. "Of course they planned—they knew. They may have been protecting and hiding that we are Tainted but they know what it could mean and that time when we could become one of the Sundered; well, it could happen anytime. We are within that age now."

Alex and Kyle sobered at the thought, and Alex looked around at the surrounding opulence.

"Ah, well, I guess we have a little more privacy now, and the fallout can be contained a little if we all break. On that cheery thought, even though I want to explore, what I'm going to do is find a bed and sleep. I don't care if the bed is not made, I'll explore when I wake up." Alex gave them a self-depreciating smile. "If I'm back to being a self-indulgent twat feeling sorry for myself when I wake up, smack me over the head and tell me to get over it."

Alex hauled himself out of his chair and took a couple of steps, glancing at the nearby Miranda, who appeared as she always did.

"Please, I need a bed, or I'm just going to fall asleep on the lounge."

Miranda curtseyed. "Your Highness, follow me, your chambers are ready."

Alex felt his energy fading as he was led down more corridors, past more guards, then into yet another reception room before being led into a chamber with one of the largest, most comfortable beds he'd ever seen. He waved Miranda off and almost collapsed on the edge of the bed, pausing just long enough to pull off his boots before crawling up into the centre. He had almost fallen asleep when his door opened and Amelia slipped in, pushing sleep to the back burner for a space of time.

A lex stretched, rolled over and relaxed, feeling no immediate need to move. He realised the stillness seemed a little strange. The camps had been anything but quiet and still —even the Royal Wing in either the Summer or Winter Palaces weren't still. Oh, everyone tried to be quiet, but petitioners even made their way through the Royal Wing into the King's chambers on matters of 'great importance', arguing and talking through their case the entire way. It was quiet. Restful.

Alex felt the veil gather and, without thinking, slipped into its folds and found himself looking at his uncle sitting on the chair against the far wall of his bedroom.

"Uncle, it's been a while since you've graced me with your

presence." Alex grinned at his Uncle Rathadon, seeing a smile he was familiar with mirrored back at him.

"You seemed to have everything sorted, Alex. Besides. You should get time to enjoy your new home." Uncle Rathadon chuckled as he gestured around Alex's new luxurious surroundings.

"You know, I've contemplated letting Father or at least William know I've been chatting and training with you, but somehow I think I'd find myself subject to the healers and dosed up to my eyeballs with medications." Alex smiled as his uncle laughed at the idea.

"I'm not sure the timing is right for that yet, Alex. You are correct, though, I suspect you would find yourself in the hands of the healers. Still, you know you can burn off whatever medications they try to give you."

Alex watched as his uncle looked away, considering his next words.

"Spit it out, Uncle, what's wrong now?" Alex was too relaxed to be concerned with whatever it was.

"I'll be gone for a space of time, so will Kat and Cal. There are some ... circumstances we need to check out. You will all be on your own—try to stay out of trouble."

Alex didn't know if he should squirm or laugh. "I'll try my best, Uncle, although it seems trouble finds me."

Ed snorted at that, amused. "Enjoy your day. This palace was my sanctuary in my day, a place where Kat, Cal and I could escape the pressure, the looks and intrigue of the court. Oh, and I approve of your attachment, Alex, you show good taste, she will transition well I think." With those last cryptic comments his uncle dissipated and Alex, sighing, let go of the veil's folds.

Alex rolled over in bed and wrapped his arms around Amelia, kissing her on the lips, enjoying a moment of relative peace. Her arrival had delayed the whole rest thing and pushed it right out of his mind for some time.

Shaking the last of the mist of sleep from his mind, he slipped out of bed, drawing her with him. He helped her into a robe that was her size, which had been left on the dressing rack, before he slipped into a comfortable lounging robe himself.

"Your servants must be used to me, Alex. This is new." Amelia smiled and ran her hand down the smooth, silky fabric. "Not one of mine and I don't think it would fit you somehow."

Alex looked at Amelia, draped in the green silken robe made for her. With her head nestled into his shoulder, slim build—if he was honest, a fantastic figure—black hair and incredible eyes, Alex was stunned he hadn't noticed before she pushed the issue that she was all grown up.

"As soon as our relationship became common knowledge, you were doomed to have clothing start appearing in my rooms; the servants are very efficient." Alex shook his head and chuckled.

Amelia blushed, then rose on her toes, pulling his head down and kissing him. "Thank you, Alex, I think it is the first time you have called what we have a relationship."

Alex smiled and kissed Amelia back. Closing his eyes, he held her for a moment. Then, looking around, he became astounded as his surroundings registered. His current bedroom was larger than his entire suite in the Royal Wing. He reached back with one hand and, twining his fingers through hers, led her across the expanse of his room, which included his own sitting room. He walked to double doors and opened them, peering inside to see row upon row of clothes on one side. Empty racks and shelf space were on the other side, except for some rather new looking dresses that were intended for Amelia. At the far end, there was yet another door. Alex looked at Amelia wide-eyed, feeling like a child exploring a new world. She stifled her giggles with the palm of her free hand. Smiling as he walked through all the clothes, he realised, seeing them all like this, he was a clothes horse. He opened the next door and, as expected, saw the bathing room, containing the biggest bath he'd ever seen.

Alex laughed to see the bath was steaming as if it had been prepared just before he woke up. He dropped his robe and was delighted to see that Amelia had as well. He reclaimed her hand and dragged her into the bath, kissing her with a single-minded intent as they sunk into the hot steaming water.

Alex wasn't sure how long they spent in the luxury of the bath, except that it wasn't steaming by the time they stepped out, dried off and pulled on the clothes laid out for them on a nearby rack. His staff, it seemed, knew him and his regular sleeping patterns better than he thought.

Making their way back out through the closet, he paused before the floor-to-ceiling mirror and ran his fingers through his still-damp hair, before heading once more into his bedroom.

"So as much as I hate to admit it, I have a feeling I'm late for my appointment with the dressmaker. My mother is insistent that I have a new wardrobe, although Jessalan has had a hand in it so some of them are at least practical for fighting. Well, as practical as a dress can be." Amelia looked up at him with an impish grin at his sudden woeful expression. "You can be cute! I will see you later on. Try not to get into too much trouble." Her eyebrow arched and she laughed.

Alex concentrated, pulling in a little of the power. He grinned. He could feel both Kyle and Jess; they were in the next room, awake and waiting for him. He remembered that they had arranged to meet up and explore their new world when they woke up.

"Well I can try to not get into any trouble but I cannot guarantee it, as much as I'd like to. Trouble always seems to find me even when I don't seek it. As much as I hate to leave you, Kyle and Jess are waiting." Alex leaned in for one last kiss. "Until next time."

Keeping his fingers entwined with Amelia's, he opened the door, making his way through the inner sitting room into the outer rooms to find both Kyle and Jess waiting for him. Both looked up and smiled as they entered.

"About time, Alex. We've been waiting ever so patiently for you to get up and come join us so we can explore our new 'wing'." Jess laughed at his indignant expression

"Oh, like you've been up long. You rushed your bath and got out here sooner than I did!" Alex laughed and looked around the outer room, realising that they all shared a common reception area.

Kyle laughed outright and stood, kissing Amelia on the cheek and murmuring a greeting.

Jess grinned at Amelia. "Aren't you late for your dressmaker appointment? Don't let your mother bully you with the dress selection."

Amelia rolled her eyes and, with one last stolen kiss from Alex, she left at a hurried pace, hoping her mother hadn't had too much influence with the dressmaker while waiting for her to show up.

"Now if my memory of getting here is anything to go by, that door leads to the reception and dining area. I think." Alex paused, looking around. "Those would be the doors to your rooms. That leaves that one. Shall we explore?" Alex raised one eyebrow and grinned as his friends leapt from their respective lounge chairs.

"Thought you'd never get to the point, Alex. Let's go!" Kyle and Jess almost pushed him out of the way as they all made a direct line to the door that led into the unknown—they wanted to explore.

24

THE BALL

A melia couldn't help the small smile that seemed permanently on her lips, or the flutter of nerves that ran through her as a veritable horde of servants fussed around, getting her ready for her first formal appearance in the Royal Court with Alex.

She eyed her appearance as the maids fussed with her hair and applied the finishing touches to her makeup. They nodded and stepped back as she stood and went to examine herself in the full-length mirror nearby.

Her maids stepped forward to remove her dressing robe, then halted, startled, as Amelia flicked her eyes toward the reflection of the door in the mirror as it opened to reveal her brother, Kyle. He strode in, a simple hand gesture keeping his ever-present guards outside her dressing room, although they didn't look too thrilled to be ordered to stay put or that there would be a door between them and the lord they were bound to protect.

"Please, James. I think I'll be fine in my baby sister's dressing room, the hardest thing I'll face is likely the glares from her maids. I won't be long." He didn't even pause or check to see if he was obeyed. He was confident enough to know they would.

Amelia stifled a giggle as her maids formed a human barrier between her and the guards outside—and, she suspected, her own brother—since she stood there in her undergarments.

Kyle grinned at their protective barrier. "While I appreciate you protecting my younger sister's dignity, you should note we gave our mother, father and nursemaids severe stress as children, divesting ourselves of clothes every chance we got, including running into the great hall here at the palace while the King was holding a court session."

Kyle ignored the glares from the maids and placed the boxes he was carrying on a low table side by side, opening their catches with practised ease, paying no notice at all to the glaring maids. Satisfied, he turned and assessed the human barrier between him and his sister.

"Ladies, I suggest you move before I call the guards in and have you removed. Now." Kyle's gaze turned serious.

"Please, it's all right. I'm sure my brother has a reason for this intrusion. He's also right, you know, and while I'm not fully dressed, I'm not exactly standing here naked. In fact, I'm certain he is more adept at unfastening all of the clasps on the undergarments than I am." Amelia smiled at her big brother while several of her maids gasped in shock. She flicked her hands at them and they moved back to stand by the wall.

Kyle, satisfied, drew what Amelia recognised as a sheath, although with an intricate design and pattern. Amelia gasped and stepped forward, reaching out with one hand and tracing the sigils stitched into the leather. Her family's crest, the Royal Family's and the Crest of the Fourth. Her eyes tracked the sigils and her hand raised to her mouth as she gasped, startled, her eyes flicking wide-eyed up to her brother.

"Kyle, what, I ..." Amelia took an involuntary step back before stopping herself. Kyle chuckled and smiled.

"I'm not sure you understand the world you are entering, little sister. Until now you've been on the fringe, peeking in—that was a simpler world. You had the protection of being in the inner circle of the Royal Court with little of the cost. Alex is a son of the royal blood, the Fourth Child. When he petitioned the King and our Lord Father to acknowledge you, well let's just say, it's not just dating a random minor lord's son. It comes with baggage, a lot of baggage. You're not quite Alex's Consort Elect yet, but you are not that far off either, if I know Alex." Kyle threw his head back and laughed outright as a blush flamed up his sister's cheeks.

Amelia spun and flipped her hands once more at her maids. Their startled murmurs stopped as she gestured for silence. "Enough. I need to speak with my brother. Please wait in the sitting room with the guards until I need you."

Amelia waited while her startled maids exited the room. She watched them until the door closed, before meeting her brother's eyes in the mirror.

"I don't understand, Kyle, you've always mixed in the inner circle of the Royal Family and it's done you no harm. What could be negative about being Alex's Consort?" Amelia was puzzled at the thought.

Having pity on her, Kyle paced forward and kissed her on the forehead before he positioned the sheath for her and tightened the buckles. "Alex is a target, Amelia, just from being the son of the King, let alone the crap about the Fourth. He lives in a glass cage with everyone watching and judging his every move, as all the members of the Royal Family do. You are moving into the world, I'm sure you noticed that, even though we've been casual since your relationship with Alex was made public."

Kyle shook his head before picking up another of the sheathes and buckling them into place. The silence stretched between them as he positioned the rest of them before flipping the second case open to reveal an assortment of fine blades, all bearing the dual crests of her family and the Fourth.

"These blades are all ceremonial but functional. I left a set of everyday court weapons for you out in your main room." Kyle picked up one of the small blades and handed it to her, with one eyebrow raised.

Grinning, she grabbed the blade and slipped it into the breast sheath. All her concealed sheathes were new, concealed by her new court clothes. She'd been thinking her normal blades would have paled by comparison. She'd wondered at the time at the array of new sheathes and now guessed it was Kyle who had arranged for them to be made.

Kyle grabbed twin daggers and again just looked at her without saying a word. Amelia lifted the fabrics of her underskirts and, with an elegant pace forward, placed one foot up on a small footstool. Kyle placed one of the daggers in her palm and she slid it into the boot sheath, then repeated the process with the twin blade in the other boot.

The time passed in an almost companionable silence; Amelia had almost forgotten the tone of the conversation they had been having.

"Alex, Jess and I became friends not just through circumstance, Amelia. If we were not born to the parents we were, we all would have been killed in early childhood due to the risk we pose." Kyle paused, looking at Amelia to see her reaction.

Amelia gasped in shock at Kyle's blunt assessment, one small delicate hand raising to cover her mouth. "Kyle, no. Father would never consent to that."

"I have enough of the veil running through me, we all do, that I stand the chance of becoming one of the Sundered." Kyle's laugh was bitter with a hint of mockery. "Alex, Jess and I are no extra risk to each other. We all have the same risk. You, though—think about the position you are putting yourself in. If Alex breaks, you will still be in the gilded cage after tonight. There will be no going back."

Amelia looked at Kyle wide-eyed, unable to think of anything to say.

Kyle sighed. "I am close to Alex, he is like a brother. I know he loves you but that doesn't mean he's not conflicted about this. I also know Alex is not the first man you've slept with, although he is the one you vowed you would marry when he saved you from that disgrace of a lord on your first appearance at court." Kyle paused and looked Amelia in the eyes. "Don't hurt him, Amelia. He's not the carefree womaniser that most in the court think he is —he has enough pressure on him right now."

Amelia smothered laughter. "Isn't that speech meant to go the other way around?"

As he turned to leave, she reached out, grabbing his hand. "Kyle, wait." Amelia closed her eyes and took a steadying breath. "We never meant for this to happen. I was just an infatuated child back when Alex became my hero. Alex never saw me that way and I'd given up all hope he would. It's just, when you were sick, we spent a lot of time by your bedside and well, things just happened."

Amelia paused and chuckled as she thought back, her lips twitching into a smile. "I worked out that I somehow have more experience than Alex does in the bedroom. I'm aware of the risk you all face with becoming Sundered, Kyle. How could I not be? The healers say I'm borderline myself." Amelia turned to face Kyle, the smile slipping off her lips as she looked at her brother. "I would never hurt him, Kyle."

Kyle considered her for a moment before opening the door to her dressing room and waving her maids back into the room. They skirted around him to fuss over Amelia. Carissa, Amelia's head maid, rolled her eyes in Kyle's direction.

She took one look at the addition of the extra sheaths and weapons, assessing the addition before flicking her hands at the others and sending them running with a series of orders.

As the maids surrounded his sister in a flurry of activity, Kyle moved to one side and perched on the edge of the chair, watching as they finished dressing her. He'd gotten ready himself earlier, so he didn't need to sprint back to his own rooms.

At Amelia's nod, Carissa stepped forward with another maid, who held a jewellery box. Smiling, Carissa placed the necklace adorned with the green gemstones from her family's holdings around her neck, then the matching bracelet and earrings. The complete set had been commissioned by Amelia's mother and father for this moment.

Once again, her maids stepped back so she could see the full effect in the mirror. Her dress was a dark green of the deepest forest. It hugged her upper body, showing off her figure, flaring from her hips to drape down her full length. It also had the effect of concealing the blades they had just put in place moments earlier.

Amelia watched Kyle through the mirror as he inspected her and, with a smile, he gave her a half bow. "You look beautiful, Amelia."

Amelia lost all her newfound ladylike dignity and giggled, spinning around so that the skirt of the dress twirled around. "When Elizabeth introduced me to her dressmaker, I never would have believed the difference—you know, I can't believe the lady looking out of the mirror is me!"

Kyle took the remaining blade, an ornate silver hunting blade he'd been twirling in his hand and, with a grin, handed it to her. Amelia accepted the blade with due courtesy and slipped it into what she'd thought was a decorative silver chain and leather waist belt. The silver links sparkled with small emeralds across her slim waist and the weight of the blade made the whole belt drape perfectly.

A lex did his best to smile at those around him and pretend that he was happy to be at the ball. Yet, as always, he found it tedious with the only bright spark on his horizon being that when Amelia showed up, he would have the rather perfect excuse to give most of his attention to her rather than the sycophants in the court. Kyle wasn't in attendance yet either, still, he knew it was because he would escort Amelia from her rooms to the ball. He'd toyed with the idea of escorting her himself, yet his sister had informed him in no uncertain terms that this moment, appearing at the ball after the official announcements he was courting her, was Amelia's moment. Not his.

Alex felt his lips twitch at his sister's exasperation with him, pointing out to him that if he escorted her in it would all be about him. He didn't get why it was different but it was and even Jess backed up Elizabeth on that one. He trusted them both so he conceded to their judgement. Amelia was to have her entrance, then he'd claim her for himself.

Alex looked over, sensing that Jess had just made an appearance that had caused whispering among the ladies and some disgruntled looks from the lords. He spotted her from across the ballroom, incredible in a white and green dress with silver thread, glittering with the ballroom lights. Her hair was piled in an intricate design on her head, held in place with what was likely to be hundreds of pins. What he knew was that what looked like decorative combs in her hair were stilettos. Despite appearances to the contrary, she was a walking arsenal.

Alex choked on his wine and covered it by coughing. A hovering waiter handed him a napkin and he covered his mouth, blotting his lips while he was at it. Jess herself wasn't causing the chatter; well, not all of it, anyway. It was her companion, the mystery man on her arm, who was making the various lords very disgruntled —not that any of them ever stood a chance—and causing the ladies to speculate. Half of the ladies looked like they were wondering if they would stand a chance of stealing him off Jess.

What they didn't know or realise was that mystery man was Damien Harper. Jess' hunter friend who had rescued her from the kidnapping attempt and led the guards back to retrieve him and Kyle. He knew they had kept in contact during the progression between the Winter and Summer Palace, keeping a rather discreet liaison going. He knew the court had not picked up on it. He also knew Damien, for all his appearance right now, was a common hunter.

Evening, Jess, you look lovely. Does William know you brought Damien to the ball? If not, since he knows who he is, well, I want to see his reaction. Alex kept his tone light.

Yes, Alex, William knows and so does your father. He plans to reward Damien for his efforts in coming to our aid during the kidnap attempt. Jess' mind voice was threaded with amusement for not only his reaction but also the reaction and speculation of the courtiers.

While the kidnapping attempt was public knowledge due to the King's announcement and swift justice for those involved (at least those they could get their hands on), Damien's involvement had been kept under wraps. Until now.

Alex, in a rare show of behaviour, took her hand and kissed her fingertips. "My Lady, you look lovely tonight." Jess grinned at Alex and murmured her thanks as he turned to her friend. "Damien, it's good to see you again."

Damien smiled at Alex and bowed, causing Alex to wonder if Jess had been giving him lessons.

"Thank you, Your Highness, it's more than I ever expected." Damien's careful response showed that perhaps he wasn't a simple woodsman—he obviously knew that all eyes were on them and listening to every word.

Kyle walked through and acknowledged Damien's presence after greeting Jess and Alex. Damien bowed to Kyle, which caused him to grin.

"Heads up, Alex, my sister is about to make her appearance, her first time appearing in the ball from the private entrance and her first ball with everyone knowing you guys are seeing each other." Kyle grinned at Alex's response as he turned to watch the doors that led to the private waiting room only the Royal Family members and their closest advisers used.

There was a hush of expectation as the doors opened and Amelia stepped through. She stood, poised, on the edge of the doors, scanning the room until her eyes met Alex's. A smile bloomed on her lips and a blush coloured her cheeks as she noticed his regard. She had taken only two steps into the room before she was surrounded by a flock of her contemporaries, fussing at her and trying their hardest to gain her attention. Other than her eyes widening in shock at the reaction (in the past no one noticed when she walked into a room), she took it in her stride.

Alex shook his head and looked at Jess. "Should I rescue her from that gaggle of ladies?"

Jess laughed and shook her head. "No, let her get used to it. You'll be able to tell when she needs a break. It's the first time she's ever had more than cursory attention given to her at these functions; let her have the moment."

Alex opened his mouth to object, then thought better of it and closed his mouth again with a sigh. He was sure that right now while all the attention was a novelty, it wouldn't take Amelia long to realise that it was all fake. They were after her rank and the status they perceived they would gain by being in her inner circle, but right now it was all new and shiny for her.

Alex looked at the guards and gave a discreet hand signal for them to keep watch on her.

Jess, just an idle thought: do you think your Damien might have seen or could track down the mysterious Baine? I can't think how else we can find him since Kyle kind of killed everyone. At that last comment, he glanced over at Kyle.

He was rewarded as Kyle forgot himself and spluttered. Laughing, Alex handed his napkin across, grinning at his friend.

Alex, I did not kill our only leads. That was the female assassin. I would have at least gotten information out of them before I killed them. Kyle threw his friend an amused glance, knowing Alex well enough to realise he was joking.

Jess laughed and shook her head at them. *I haven't asked but I can when we end up somewhere a little more discreet than here.*

Well we can invite him back to the compound when we're done here tonight, if you don't have objections. Alex glanced across at Amelia and smiled. *That might be a little later than normal.*

Jess grinned. *I think I should be able to handle that invite.*

A lex walked from his rooms. It hadn't taken long for Amelia to fall into a deep, exhausted sleep. It had been a long day for her. Alex didn't notice anymore how exhausting the official balls could be, he'd attended them as a Prince of the Realm with all the associate attention that brought. However, as had been pointed out to him, Amelia was not used to the attention that being with him brought with it.

Damien had been rewarded by the King with a grant of lands, a title and a sum of money. They'd all been blown away by that announcement, even Damien. It wasn't much of a title or lands but it would be enough to keep him well, even if he chose not to live there but kept the current arrangements in place for running the estates, which for now seemed likely.

Walking out into the general sitting room, Alex collapsed into one of the large comfortable chairs and assessed Damien, who sat with his arms around Jess, comfortable in his surroundings. The man was confident.

"So, Damien, we have a little problem we hope you might help with." Alex watched the man, who didn't appear at all surprised.

"I wondered. You kept looking at me all night and having those half conversations... kind of like I was missing half of it." Damien smiled and waited, knowing there was more to come.

"Most of the people involved in the kidnap have been brought to justice already. We have information to suggest that a man named Baine arranged everything." Alex glanced at Kyle.

Kyle took up the account with the man's description, at least the information they had. "He was described as having dark hair, shaved close to the skull, a tattoo down his right arm, with a trail of skulls from his neck to his knife hand. The final piece of information was that he had a bad scar trailing down the line of his left jawbone."

Damien whistled. "I'm guessing you know he sounds like he's a member of the League of Skulls, right? A blade for hire?"

Alex smiled, although it didn't reach his eyes. "Yes, we know that part. It's just strange, though, the League has never meddled with the Royal Family before, it causes a terrible reaction from the Crown."

Kyle nodded. "He's a loose end we'd like to tie up. None of us like loose ends—I'm allergic to them, especially when those loose ends try to have us kidnapped."

Damien's eyes moved between Kyle and Alex before settling on Jess, one eyebrow raised, causing her to grin. "Well I thought it might be right up your alley. Alex is right, though, there is something a little clumsy about the whole thing for it to be arranged by the League."

Damien shook his head. "I saw no one matching that description the night of the kidnap. I can poke around, though; he sounds distinctive. If I find someone who matches I'll let you know."

Alex stood and nodded. "Thank you, we appreciate any help you can give. You seem accomplished but don't put yourself at any risk."

Alex waited until Damien acknowledged what amounted to an order before he excused himself and retreated to his rooms. He was tired but he knew he wouldn't get much rest tonight. At this time of the year, he never did. Even now, although he was awake, he could hear his mother's final words, screaming at him to run, replaying in his mind.

A lex moaned, his eyes flickering under his eyelids, tossing on the bed, his sheets twisting around him evidence of the restless night he was having. His head shook from side to side like he was trying to negate what he was seeing in his nightmare.

Guards and servants slumped to the ground around him, his mother telling him to run and hide just as her head was wrenched back, a large hunting knife slicing across her throat. Fear froze him to the spot as the large figure of the Sundered loomed over him.

Brother

You'll join our ranks soon enough.

One of us

You'll be a killer.

The menacing voices whispered to him as the forest darkened around him. Shadowy cloaked figures in the trees leering out at him, only retreating when the guards came.

Then out of the darkness the tomb, shadows thrown over it by the surrounding trees, guttering light thrown by the torches. The wind moaned, causing the trees to groan and thrash. Five cloaked figures stood outside the tomb; as the mist gathered around them, one figure turned its face up. A delicate arm and hand reaching up toward where his room was. He knew the figure was female but the hood hid her face in its depths.

"Alex, I'm sorry. Forgive me for leaving you. You'll be safer this way."

Alex sat bolt upright in bed, breathing rapidly, and he could feel the sweat prickling all over, tremors still wracking his body. He groaned and leaned forward, hiding his face in his hands. He took slow deep breaths trying to calm himself.

Looking over, he noticed that Amelia was still sleeping soundly. Alex levered himself carefully out of the bed, grabbing his robe and shrugging it on. He paused to pour himself a drink from the sideboard before retreating to the sitting room. He wasn't likely to get any more sleep and didn't want to wake Amelia.

25

AN ANNUAL EVENT

Alex found himself in the library, trying to distract himself from acknowledging what day it was and not succeeding well, although this one was his own library in the Fourth's Compound. It was smaller than the Royal Library but was big enough to qualify as a library rather than a room with a few bookshelves.

He gazed around the room, with floor to ceiling shelves filled with books, a few scattered chairs that looked like you could sink right into them and fall asleep, and a few others opposite that looked uncomfortable. Alex snorted, figuring they would at least keep him awake if he ever found anything worth studying. Noticing a small pile of books sitting on a low table next to a high-backed leather chair that looked halfway between falling asleep and running to the nearest bar, Alex walked over, picking up the book on top as he sank into the chair. Despite himself, a smile touched his lips as he sensed Joseph's hand in selecting the book and knew the other two had been left right there for him to discover.

He'd always been Joseph's despair when it came to the scholarly occupations, but he figured this time at least the book looked interesting. It was one of the old accounts of the era of his Uncle Edward, the former occupant of the Fourth's Wing. The time of the Sundered War, Vallantia's war and final triumph of humans against the Sundered.

Without realising what he was doing, Alex settled into the chair and flipped open the book, in his usual fashion flicking through the pages, scanning as he went. Smiling at the acerbic tone, which spoke volumes, he realised that he could hear his uncle in the words, even if it was a scholar who wrote the book. In the process of flipping over more of the pages, a description of the Sundered caught his attention; he shuddered and skipped the section.

Alex paused and flipped back a few pages, finding the start of the section that described the Kin. Tall, athletic, with an economy of movement. Intelligent yet remote, almost a calmness in nature no matter what was occurring around them, making them deadly opponents. Although fewer in numbers than humans, they were just as diverse; however, while they lacked in population they lived longer, which his Uncle believed was in part the reason for their uncanny abilities in the tasks they pursued. Living in the wild lands, as they did most of the time, no matter what other skill sets they had learned in their long lives, they were excellent with a blade and in the art of killing. Alex frowned, more than a little confused. That didn't sound like any of the Sundered he'd encountered. Calm, remote and intelligent were not words he'd ever think of using to describe them. Alex shrugged and moved on; it was a conversation to have with his ancestor next time he saw him.

At the next paragraph, Alex felt his eyes widen as his uncle described the broken ones—ruled by hatred for any but their own kind, sunken in madness. In contrast, ruled by their emotions. The rise in the numbers of the Broken was rapid and unexplained. No one. Not even the Kin could, or would, say what had happened to those Kin to cause them to descend into such madness. The passage went on to theorise that something had changed in the veil to cause more of their kind to sink into madness.

Alex froze. He reread the earlier passage then the one about the broken ones, his breath catching in his throat as he thought about the description of the Kin. He realised that the Kin, as his uncle had called them, were not quite the same as the broken ones. His eyes tracked back up the page once more and reread the passage again, the characteristics jumping out at him, triggering memories of his training sessions with Kyle and Jess. He stared at the book in his hands, whispering in the empty room.

"Athletic with an economy of movement." As he spoke the words, they triggered a memory of Kyle sparring in the practice ground, his blade whirling—graceful, dancing, deadly.

Alex's finger trailed down the page once more, words jumping out at him. "Calmness in nature..." The memory of the veil, the soothing calmness, the certainty that flooded him every time he was there, hit him. The image of Jess sighting down an arrow, her smooth draw, the certainty, the kill—all without even a flicker of emotion.

His eyes widened as the book fell from his fingers. "No, it can't be real."

Alex shook his head, considering what he'd learned so far. He felt his eyes widen as he considered the implications, his mind racing with events from his life flashing though his head in succession triggered by what he'd read, horrified at where his thoughts were going and what everything meant. Yet he shied away from any conclusion, his mind balking at the idea.

Alex wished he could erase what he'd learned, erase that moment in time where he walked into the library and picked up that book. Erase the moment where he read that passage about the Kin and the Broken Ones; when his mind made the sudden connection between what was written in those pages and its connection to him. Its connection to his friends.

Although he'd spent a long time trying to erase his mother's death from his memory, it was still etched there. Every moment. The confusion his child-self had felt, not understanding what was happening around him. Alex closed his eyes and took a deep, steadying breath.

He felt the veil shift around him as his unconscious mind allowed him to escape from the library where he didn't want to be. Alex didn't pay it much mind until he felt himself settle, although he knew where he'd ended up. Not the Veiled World. Alex opened his eyes to find himself on his knees in front of a large tomb. Four large statues of guards, one on each corner, with shields and swords, stood sentinel, guarding the resident of the tomb, even in the afterlife. Large and ornate, stamped with the Royal Crest, Alex knew it contained one casket. This was his mother's resting place, deep inside the protection of the palace in what had been her favourite garden.

Alex felt a tear slide down his face. "I'm sorry, Mother. If I could change this, if I had a choice, I would not be one of the very monsters who slaughtered you."

Alex didn't expect an answer but wasn't shocked when he got one. It had happened before, even if he didn't know who or what answered him. He knew it wasn't his mother, it couldn't be, since she was dead. Yet somehow he always associated it with her since it was the voice that soothed him as a child after his mother's death. He heard it in his head, through the veil, as he heard it when his uncle was speaking to him. Except this voice that whispered to him through the veil was female.

It's alright, Alex. Everything will be all right in time. You are who you have always been.

Alex could hear the sadness in the voice, knew there was more that was not being communicated to him. He could feel the veil, willing him to accept what—who—he was.

"Why, Mother? Why did I have to be Tainted?" Alex whispered the words out loud but knew he was throwing them out into the veil, to the other. To that person a part of his brain insisted was his mother.

Sorry, Alex, it is who you are. You should not beat yourself up every year over what happened. It was not your fault, you could not have done anything, you were a child. The words washed through him again, leaving a distinct feeling of sorrow.

Alex remembered the time in the glade, then after when his uncle and friends had tried to tell them about the Kin and the Elder.

The Sundered, the Kin, the Elder. Is there a connection? Alex threw the question out, not expecting a reply from his unexpected tutor.

The Sundered. The Kin. They are one, the same. Dual souls. The Kin have balanced their nature. The Sundered are at war with themselves. The Elder are the most powerful of their kind. Alex felt the presence remain, waiting.

Who are you? It had never occurred to Alex to ask before. Then again, before now he had thought this whole thing was a sign he was going mad.

This time there was no answer.

A lex took a deep settling breath and stood, making his way through the garden, trying to process what he'd guessed and learned. Trying to bury the growing horror he felt inside— that scared little boy sobbing at the death of his mother. Trying to ignore the flashing images that appeared in his head of the deaths that occurred so long ago.

Hearing a footfall, he looked up, unsurprised to see Kyle, who fell in beside him on his aimless pacing through the garden. Alex smiled to himself, appreciating that Kyle said nothing, just waited, knowing Alex would tell him what was up when he was ready.

"It's the anniversary of my mother's death. I'm the same as what killed my mother." Alex didn't have to look at Kyle to know he wore a stunned expression on his face.

"Alex, we are all Tainted. You know not all Tainted turn into the Sundered, not even all of them turn into the Sundered that killed the Queen, your mother." Kyle looked concerned but didn't press further.

Alex laughed, but it held nothing but pain. "You don't understand. I found a reference in an old diary of my uncle's in the library; I was trying to distract myself. That will teach me to think a library, of all places, as the place to do that. I had hope when our relatives told us about the existence of the Elder and the Kin that we'd be all right. That I'd be all right, we might be creatures of magic—the Kin, not the Sundered. Then I read passages in the diary; one described the Kin. It's uncanny how it fits us all. The next described what he referred to as the Broken Ones, that no one could explain it, not even the Kin." Alex looked at Kyle and saw his expression was still blank, not understanding. "The Broken Ones are the

Sundered, they are the Kin, or would be if their minds didn't break."

Alex stopped and waited while his friend processed the information he'd just been given. While Alex was sure Kyle felt as if he'd just been hit on the back of the head, nothing of the shock showed on his face or body language.

How do you know this, Alex? Kyle drew on the power of the veil and spoke through it so that not even the guards could hear the conversation.

Alex smiled and continued walking before he shared the memory of the conversation he'd just had, which was faster than repeating the conversation he'd had verbatim. It also had the bonus that Kyle would believe him straight away, being able to assess the memory itself.

Kyle's eyes widened in shock as Alex dumped the memory on him and it took time for him to process.

Alex, this is ... I don't know what to make of it. Even if whoever it was told the truth it doesn't mean you'll become Sundered. It doesn't mean any of us will. Look at Edward, look at all of our trainers. There is nothing in the records to suggest any of them descended into madness.

Alex could see Kyle looking at him, concern written all over his face. Alex shook his head and didn't reply, keeping what he was thinking at that point to himself. What he hadn't told his friends was that while they seemed at peace with their emerging nature, he was struggling. Sometimes he felt he was drowning, overwhelmed by all the conflicting emotions. Losing awareness of who he was. It was a relief when the calmness washed over him, but it never seemed to last for long.

Kyle was his best friend; they were closer than brothers but still, that was something he wasn't ready to share.

The other thing he'd never shared was the parting words of the Sundered who had killed his mother and all the guards, but who had left him alive. They were seared into his brain. *You will join our ranks soon enough, brother.* He had been too young back then to understand what had happened or how unusual it was for him to be alive, let alone to understand what the man had meant.

"I need a drink—several, actually. Let's head into town. At least it is easier from here and we don't have to sneak out." Alex glanced at Kyle and led the way from the garden.

Kyle knew a deflection when he heard it but for now was willing to let it go. He called out to Jess, letting her know they were heading into town. He wasn't surprised to know she was already in the courtyard waiting with the horses. It was this time of the year; they always ended up in a bar on the anniversary of Alex's mother's death.

"Let's try not to destroy the bar this time. Last year your father and mine had to rebuild the publican's bar for him." Kyle clapped a hand between Alex's shoulder blades as they both walked out of the garden and back into the Fourth's Compound, heading toward the main entrance and the courtyard where their horses waited.

Kyle's eyes flicked over to Marcus and he flipped a hand signal to the guards, letting them know that they were heading into town (although given how many years in a row this excursion had occurred, he knew the guards were ready for it). This was the one time of year they were never surprised. Alex always took the anniversary of his mother's death hard. Kyle knew there was something that his friend was keeping from him and this year he was determined to find out what it was.

He'd been just as determined in previous years, to no avail.

A lex thanked the barmaid for refilling his drink, not paying much attention to his surroundings. They had made their way to the Barrel. It was their favourite haunt to escape the Summer Palace; there wasn't as much competition in Callenhain as there was in Vallantia but the beer and wine they served was comparable to the best. While there was music and laughter in the dimly lit but packed bar, his mind kept going back over the moments of his mother's death he could remember from his childhood, as it always did on the anniversary of her death.

Still, there was something in that memory of the small boy he had been that was niggling at the back of his brain. It was causing him to review it over and over in his head, trying to work out what was causing him to be uneasy. It wasn't like there was anything new in that memory, yet he knew there was something wrong.

Jess nudged him with her foot under the table. "What's wrong, Alex? Other than the obvious, of course."

Alex looked up and smiled, taking another sip of his beer before he answered. "There is something about the memory of my mother's death that is bugging me, but I can't work out what it is. Something just makes very little sense."

He saw Kyle and Jess trade glances before Jess shrugged, took a drink and spoke so that both he and Kyle could hear. *Show me, Alex. Show us the memory. Maybe we can help you understand what is wrong and put this to rest.*

Kyle nodded and signalled to the barmaid to refill their mugs before replying in kind. *Yes, brother, show us. We are both more adept at killing than you—perhaps we can help puzzle out what it is about the memory, besides the obvious that is jarring with you.*

Alex took a deep breath, trying to settle his nerves, aware his hand shook as he placed his mug on the table. Alex nodded then concentrated on what he remembered from that day. Drawing both Kyle and Jess inside the barriers he kept between himself and the outside world, the images, sights and sounds from that day flicked through his mind. It had been the subject of his nightmares since he was five—only William had ever been able to wake him from them.

As the images flicked through his brain, he interpreted to his friends as best he could. *I was on a picnic with Mother. I was trying so very hard to impress her.* Alex smiled despite himself at the first part, the memory and images of his childish self, trying so hard to impress his mother, and he heard his friends chuckle at the images, which were backed up by his childish inner monologue.

Then Alex sobered, feeling a tear trace down his cheek, knowing what was coming. He'd seen the memory, the flashing images, the sounds, repeatedly since he was five years old, waking screaming from sleep. The whistling noise, the grunts and gasps of pain, the guards and servants crumpling to the ground. Stumbling back as his mother pushed him, her voice, the last thing she'd said to him. "Run, hide ..." echoing though his brain.

Looking up, confused, despite screaming at himself not to look, not to see her death this time. The fear on her face, the dark figure, her head being wrenched back, a large knife drawn across her throat. Warm blood splattering on him, her lifeless broken form crumpling to the ground. Then staring, terrified, into the face of the Sundered One, the sharp bark of laughter, the final words ringing through his head. *You'll join our ranks soon enough, brother.*

Alex only knew he'd caused a commotion in the bar, screaming and throwing the mug he was holding, when he saw his own guards holding back the Barrel's muscle that maintained position on the door.

Alex closed his eyes, taking a trembling breath, hearing Marcus' calm, confident voice assuring the barkeep all would be fine, that the King would compensate for any damages. Hearing muted voices around the bar mutter "Queen's death ...", he gathered the hood of his cloak had fallen back. It wasn't the first time he'd gotten out of control on the anniversary of his mother's death.

Alex allowed his friends to pull him back onto the bench he'd been sitting on. Slumping against the wall, he shook and held back the sob that wanted to escape. Hearing a thump on the table, he looked up to see the barkeep place new goblets on the table, pouring a double measure of an amber liquid in them. As Kyle went to offer the barkeep money, the man held up his hands, declining the offer.

"No, My Lord, it's unnecessary. My niece was a servant in the hunting party a few weeks back. She tells me she'd be dead if it wasn't for the bravery of you, Lady Jessalan and His Highness. She said the three of you protected them all against the Tainted ones, at the risk of your own lives. My family is in your debt; you are all welcome here anytime you need." With that, the barkeep placed the bottle on the table. "My family makes that, it's new. If you like it I'll get you more." The barkeep turned, making his way through the ring of guards and back to the bar. He gestured at the musicians in the corner, who started up playing again, and sent his barmaids around with full jugs of beer to fill up the mugs of his other patrons.

Alex took a steadying breath, wiping the tear from his cheek. He picked up his goblet, considering the amber liquid it contained for a moment, then raised it to his friends, who matched his gesture before throwing back the contents. Alex's eyes widened in shock as the fiery liquid spilled down his throat. Glancing at his friends, he knew the barman would have a hit as soon as everyone found out about the new product.

"Marcus, arrange for a shipment of this to go to the palace. Some for our own stocks and some for the King. I'm sure he will like it. Make sure the barman is paid well." Alex reached for the bottle and poured them all another measure of the liquid gold, placing the bottle onto the table before looking up at his friends. Not being able to put off the moment any longer, he ran his finger through his hair, looking up at them.

"Well, anything?"

Kyle and Jess looked at each other, seeming to come to a silent accord, although Alex knew they weren't talking since he'd know if they did. It was Kyle who spoke up first.

"The Sundered One killed your Lady Mother, but you knew that. He wasn't alone." Kyle took a sip of his drink and glanced at Jess.

Jess looked down, contemplating her drink, then took up the conversation. "There were arrows, Alex. The guards, servants— all of them were taken out by other people. The Sundered One killed your mother, but others assisted in the kill by taking out any who would protect her. That was the 'whistling' noise you remember, the flight of the arrows."

Alex caught another look between his friends before Kyle continued. *Your Lady Mother was Tainted, Alex. She pushed you, but not with her hands. She told you to run, but only you would have heard it. The order reverberates in your head because she ordered you with her mental voice to run. Your child self wasn't confused, I'd say you always communicated with her that way. I'd say it's why you are so good at it.*

Alex looked at his two friends, stunned, then turned his thoughts inwards, running through his memories again, trying to pay attention to all the details. Not that he needed to, he'd replayed that incident from his childhood repeatedly—more times than he could count. Alex took a steadying breath, this time to calm the burning anger that burst inside as he realised they were right. There were others there that fateful day. Others that had never been found or even looked for; everyone accepted the obvious: a Sundered had killed his mother, along with the guards and servants.

26

ASSASSINS HUNT

Thinking of the Skull's Assassin he'd encountered made Kyle smile in anticipation. He realised he was taking more time dressing and arming himself than normal. Kyle grinned at himself in the mirror as he tugged at the edge of his long black shirt. He caught sight of Bennett's grin in the mirror and his eyebrow rose.

"She'll take one look and ravish you, My Lord." Bennett laughed at his lord's look of astonishment. "Oh, come now. You've not had a single lady to your bed since you had that encounter with the female assassin and you've obsessed about her since. Now, go. Don't keep her waiting; I'm sure with your skill you'll be able to track her down."

With that last piece of advice, Bennett bowed to his lord and left the room. Kyle looked at Alex, who sat in the corner, through the mirror. His friend grinned at him but he could see he was concerned even before Alex spoke.

"I should come with you, Kyle. I'm not sure you continuing to chase after this gifted Skull Assassin by yourself is such a good idea." Alex was subdued, his concern clear.

Kyle turned and faced his lifelong friend, the man he considered a brother. "I'll be fine, Alex. I grant you she is dangerous but I need to find her before she finds me."

Alex shook his head. "I'm not sure you're thinking straight when it comes to this girl, Kyle. You're enamoured with her, she's all you can think of—and don't deny that you want to bed her. Despite what everyone seems to think of me, you've bedded more women than I have and don't go to bed alone!" Alex chuckled, taking the sting out of his words, amused despite his concern for his friend.

Kyle laughed and walked toward Alex, dragging him in for a quick hug. "I'll be fine, brother, cease your worrying. I'm more at risk from an angry lord discovering that his lady has been having an affair with me than I am from the mysterious assassin."

Kyle laughed outright as his friend snorted and threw him a filthy look. "Like any of those lords followed through after they found out you were the lord their lady was sleeping with."

"Alex, I don't know why, we only had that brief meeting, but I feel drawn to the assassin. I'd rather bed her than kill her. To be honest, she'd be an amazing source of information on the League of Skulls if I can sway her loyalty to our side. This dance is mine to make, Alex, although I appreciate the show of support." Kyle clapped his friend on the shoulder as he shook his head and headed toward the door.

"Just be careful, Kyle, and don't sire any illegitimate children by her. I'm not sure your mother would be so forgiving as to accept a Skull's Assassin into the family fold." With that last parting shot, Alex left Kyle's apartments to follow his own pursuits.

Despite his best intentions, he laughed in delight at his opponent, who grinned back at him. Gazing into her eyes, he reached forward and drew back her hood, revealing her face. Kyle's breath caught as he was captivated and almost lost in her dark brown eyes and delicate features.

Keeping his eyes on hers, he took one careful step after another until he was pressed up against her. He could feel her breath on his cheek as she turned her head to one side. Smiling, he raised one hand to her cheek, turning her head to him. He lost himself in her eyes again and brushed his lips against hers.

He felt the bloodlust and rage rush away to be replaced by simple lust and desire. He felt his breathing rate increase as his free hand sheathed his dagger and snaked around her tiny waist.

"My name's Kyle." Kyle licked his lips, realising his throat was dry.

Her delighted laughter rang out; it was light and carefree in that moment, causing him to smile.

"I know who you are, Lord Kyle. You're notorious in certain circles and your kill count is higher than mine. My name's Alyssa." This time Alyssa took the initiative and locked her lips onto his. He was aware when she sheathed her own blades then made short work of his shirt, which ended up in pieces on the floor of the abandoned warehouse.

Once again, Kyle was lost and Alyssa's name kept repeating in his brain like a litany as he pulled her shirt over her head, guiding her back toward a pile of discarded bales and cloths in the corner behind her.

Laughing, they both paused between kissing each other, their hands diverting from their mutual exploration to pull off their boots and trousers. Then they fell onto each other.

Lost in the lust, Kyle spared a moment to think perhaps this was yet another sign of his descent into the world of the Sundered— sudden inescapable, overwhelming emotion—before losing himself in Alyssa.

Kyle gasped and wrenched himself back, at the sudden sharp pain that seem to shoot through him, blinking at Alyssa, gasping as the pain ran through him, yet somehow unable to tear his eyes away from her.

"Alyssa, what——" Kyle shuddered and groaned as yet another sharp pain ran through him.

"You can't be a virgin, Kyle." A smile curved Alyssa's lips, then she raised one hand in dismay. "Oh, you've never had sex with the gifted before! I'm sorry, my love, if I'd known I would have warned you, instructed you."

Kyle looked at Alyssa, confusion, wariness and lust warring within him. Even though a part of him screamed caution, he gave into the lust and kissed her.

"No, I've never had sex with a gifted." Kyle had meant to say more and ask for clarification but lost himself again as Alyssa flipped him onto his back and reared up, moving her hips in a smooth rhythmic motion that took Kyle's breath away.

Alyssa's eyes bore into his own and a smile curved her lips as he groaned in pleasure. "Let me show you what it means to bed one of your own, my love." With that, he felt a burst of pleasure run through him. Kyle stiffened and screamed as the pleasure overran him, everything forgotten except this moment with Alyssa, then on the second burst of pure bliss his eyes rolled as his world dissolved into ecstasy, his vision darkening with spots of light dancing before his eyes.

Kyle groaned, waking gasping as the memory came back to him. His eyes flared open to find himself entangled with Alyssa. She smiled at him, her hand tracing absent patterns on his chest. "Welcome back, my love."

Kyle took her hand and turning her hand kissed her palm. "Thank you, my love, I've never been rendered unconscious like that before. What was that?"

Alyssa blushed and lay down on top of his chest with her head in the crook of his arm. "We're both gifted, so I forged a bond—it's what the gifted do and, well, that was the pain you felt, but then we can feel each other's pleasure. It multiplies. Did you like it?"

Kyle chuckled, still lost in his desire and lust for her. Propping himself up on one elbow, he rolled on top of Alyssa, getting lost in her eyes once more. Running his fingers lightly down the side of her face he brushed her hair back then lent toward her, kissing her before whispering in her ear, his voice low and husky.

"Show me what you did so I can return the favour?"

Alyssa chuckled breathlessly as he began kissing his way down her body, then she groaned, pushing him back, capturing his eyes with her own once more. "Yes, but that will happen another night. Dawn is on us and you have to get back to your Master's house, as I must get back to mine. Tonight? If you're not busy." Alyssa looked down and blushed as if she was embarrassed at being potentially too forward.

"Never too busy for you. Shall we meet here?" Kyle looked around and wrinkled his nose. "Although perhaps we can find somewhere better for our tryst." He sat up, dragging her to him, and kissed her, his voice deep and husky when he spoke. "Tonight might be too long. Are you sure you must go back? You could come with me." Kyle kissed her again and felt her melt into him.

"I wish I could, but the Skull Lord will notice my absence. Tonight. I'll meet you here tonight." With that, Alyssa rose, pulling on her discarded clothing. Kyle chuckled and did likewise, except for his shirt, which was in tatters.

Fully dressed, Alyssa faced him again and noticed his tattered shirt and the marks she'd left on his chest during their lovemaking. She blushed again and ran a hand up his chest, one small step taking her into his arms, where she sank into his kiss. "I'm sorry, I didn't mean to mark you up like that and I'm sure that shirt was expensive."

Kyle laughed. "It's okay, it's not the first shirt I've trashed."

Alyssa looked up at him, her eyes sharp, causing Kyle's heart to pause, and a thrill of fear ran though him. "I'll warn you, I know Lord Kyle Xavier Strafford's reputation. I'll not share you with anyone. Lady or otherwise."

Kyle breathed again and pulled her in for another kiss. "Truth be told, Alyssa, I've not bedded another woman since we first set eyes on each other and you threw that knife at me." He chuckled and then, as if an afterthought, pulled a dagger from his boot. "I believe this is yours."

Alyssa blushed again and took her knife back. She closed her eyes and kissed him one last time. "I must go. Tonight, I'll be here tonight." With that, she was gone. He could feel her pulling in the power of the veil as she shifted into the shadow paths to mask her on her flight back to her master.

Kyle smiled and transitioned into the Veiled World, treading the pathways she didn't have the strength to walk, although he vowed he'd show her.

As he collapsed into his own bed in the palace after cleaning up and dumping his shredded shirt in the corner, he marvelled that he was still not feeling the all-consuming rage in the back of his head that had been his world for months.

Instead, he slipped into sleep with a pair of brown eyes boring into his own and a soft voice whispering in his head, *Sleep in peace my love.* Kyle slipped into a dreamless, undisturbed sleep.

K yle woke, aware that both Alex and William were in his room. He groaned, although at least this time the drapes were drawn, which he was sure he owed to Alex's intervention.

"Let me guess, both of you were consumed by curiosity and just couldn't wait?" Kyle cracked his eyes open again and realised he was more tired, than perhaps he should be given he'd slept the morning away. It was unusual for Alex to be up and mobile before he was.

Alex laughed. "Come on, brother, we're dying to know what happened, although looking at how you're scratched up and the evidence of your tattered shirt there in the corner by the window, I guess your months-long celibacy is at an end. Congratulations! I think's it's the longest you've gone without sleeping with a woman." Alex grinned at him and ignored his glare, holding out a cup of steaming coffee in his direction.

Kyle gave in and hauled himself up, piling his pillows behind him. He sank back into them and accepted the coffee.

William waited for him to finish his first mouthful, a smile playing on his lips, then spoke up. "Okay, spill. How'd it go?"

Kyle choked on his coffee, finding himself glaring at his tormentors. "Yes, I tracked Alyssa." Kyle rolled his eyes as the princes looked at each other, grinning. Kyle tried to gather his scattered wits, knowing there were things about his activities he couldn't confess. "As you've mentioned, the night went well. We started off trying to kill each other again and then we kind of stopped trying to kill each other and—well, you've guess the rest. We've agreed to meet again tonight."

Alex laughed. "I'm guessing Alyssa is our mysterious female Skulls Assassin and another of your shirts will get shredded. Perhaps you should alert your tailor *and* you should get the healers to look at some of those scratches."

Kyle contemplated throwing his mug at Alex but decided in the long run it wasn't worth it. The coffee was too good.

"The scratches will heal and I have plenty of black shirts. Thanks for your concern, Alex." Kyle looked at his friend, which only seemed to increase his amusement; it didn't help that William was almost doubled up in laughter.

Kyle watched them and sipped his coffee, determined not to give them more to laugh about. William straightened and brushed a tear of laughter from his eyes.

"Sorry, Kyle. You are a little notorious with the ladies. I've seen your servant ushering them out of your bedroom on more than one occasion. Alex is right, you've been tracking this woman for months. I've never known you to be celibate for more than a few days at a time. You can't blame us for curiosity."

Alex grinned at him, unrepentant. "So, you were saying, you found her, you both tried to kill each other, then, well ..." Alex paused and racked his friend's appearance, his eyes flicking over to the shredded shirt. "It must have gotten way better from there."

Kyle couldn't help the smile that touched his lips, even with the memory of the kill he'd helped her with before they'd fallen on each other. Kyle decided that neither William nor Alex needed to know of the rather messy death of people whose names he didn't even know.

"Well, yes, all right. Alyssa and I slept together. Then we talked a little and agreed to meet up tonight. There isn't much else to tell." He glanced down at his scratched chest and a small chuckle escaped him. "As you'd expect, she's rather *active* in bed, and informs me she most certainly does not share. Given she's a gifted Skulls Assassin, I'll take the warning seriously."

William burst out laughing. "I'm sorry, Kyle, you know it's customary to talk to the lady before you throw her down and have your wicked way with her?" William raised his eyebrow at Kyle, who couldn't help but laugh.

"Yes, William, in the normal course of events I'm sure. We were just a little preoccupied with the killing thing to bother with the talking thing." Kyle only just covered up mentioning that he'd helped her in the kill and smiled, hoping neither William nor Alex caught his slip. "Then, well, after the kill—trying to kill each other—we were a little ... hot and bothered, to put it in simple terms, so we did the next best thing and had sex. It's an assassin thing; I don't think either of you would understand." Kyle blanched when he stumbled again, wishing that people wouldn't come into his bedroom when he'd just woken up and was trying to hide details.

Alex looked at William and spoke in a bland voice. "I don't know about you, but I'm still stuck on Kyle and Alyssa going from trying to kill each other to ripping each other's clothes off and falling into the sack together."

William smiled at his brother and replied in kind. "Yes, I don't get that part either. I hope you didn't mark Alyssa up as much as she marked you. I mean, I admire her passion, Kyle, but if you did that to her—well, if she's got a brother or father, I'm thinking he'd be after your blood."

At the mention of blood, Kyle's memory took him back to that moment when he'd discovered Alyssa. She had been in the middle of a hit; she'd taken down her mark when three city guards had stumbled onto the scene. She'd turned, raising her blade to block a strike from one of them when his bloodlust and rage had overwhelmed him. Kyle had thrown one of his daggers, taking out the man closest to her, before dropping to the floor from the rafters and joining her in battle against the other two. Kyle knew he should feel bad about killing members of the city guard, whose only mistake was to be there trying to do their job, but he lost himself yet again in the kill. He knew it should have sickened him that he and Alyssa had fallen on each other and had sex close to the cooling bodies of their kill, yet it didn't. Kyle shook himself and brought his attention back to the brothers, forcing himself to laugh.

"No, Alyssa doesn't have brothers and the closest person she'd have to a father is the Skull Lord. She's been with him since she was a small child. She's an assassin; I'm sure she's had more than a few bruises in her life."

William looked at Kyle with feigned wide-eyed shock. "Oh tell me you didn't hit her and leave her all bruised. From your past track record, you need not beat the ladies on the back of the head to drag them off to your bed."

Kyle couldn't help the chuckle that escaped his lips. "Well, no, but we were, well let's say we could have chosen a better place."

Alex grinned and shook his head, then turned serious. "So you think pursuing her further is a good idea?" He rolled his eyes as Kyle chuckled. "For information on the League of Skulls, Kyle."

Kyle grinned back at Alex and William, his tone amused. "Well that too, yes."

Alex shook his head. "Be careful, Kyle, the woman is an assassin." Alex was concerned. "Oh, and you might want to get cleaned up and wear something appropriate. I can guarantee there will be a dinner tonight."

"In case you haven't noticed, so am I—and good at it, too." Kyle's tone was impassive. "Wait, what do you mean? There is always dinner, Alex, what are you up to?

Alex shrugged and walked out of his room. "You'll find out soon enough." He laughed as Kyle threw one of his pillows at his departing back.

Kyle shook his head then, groaning, he hauled himself out of bed. He grimaced as pain ripped through his skull and he felt simmering rage in the back of his head. Kyle clutched his temples between his hands and sank to his knees, groaning, fighting the rage back, although not defeating it entirely.

Kyle knew his power had changed after the veil sickness. He also knew after conversations with healers that rage, anger and pain were signs he could become one of the Sundered. Signs he might descend into madness. Kyle contemplated sending for a healer—knew he should. They had made him promise he would. Shaking in response, he stood, continuing to the bathroom, pushing his duty to tell the healers of this new development aside.

27

THE CONSORT ELECT OF THE FOURTH

Alex tugged at the edge of his formal tunic then waved his guards off, walking into his father's outer office. He went in through the door opened for him by an attentive servant and into the outer receiving room. Looking around, he spotted Karl off to one side.

"Is Father busy, Karl? Does he have time to see me before the ball tonight?" Alex couldn't help the fluttering of nerves, second guessing what his father would say.

Karl smiled. "I will let His Majesty know you are here and seeking an audience, Your Highness."

Alex closed his eyes and took a deep, settling breath, trying to calm his nerves. His life had changed so much in the last couple of months from what it had been, and he felt like he was being hurled at an enemy he didn't yet understand or know. Hearing a noise behind him, he turned and saw not only his father, but his brother William enter. They had been in conference.

Alex bowed formally to show he was there to make an official request, catching his father and William exchange startled glances. Alex rose and waited for his father, for the King, to speak.

"What petition do you have for me to consider, Prince Alex?" The King gestured for Alex to take a seat and gestured to Karl to bring refreshments.

"Your Majesty—Father—I seek your approval to take a Consort Elect." Alex held his breath and, smiling, he let it out as his father gazed at him and his brother, outright grinned and relaxed back into his chair.

"Karl, could you bring me that package I asked you to get designed and made? So I take it the lady you would ask to be your Consort Elect, should she agree, is Lady Amelia?" The King gazed at his son, marvelling at the change in him over the last few months, and relaxed, letting a smile play across his lips. "Come, Alex, you asked formal permission to court her some time back. So unless there is another lady you've been seeing in secret, it would have to be Lady Amelia."

Alex chuckled and relaxed, only just noticing that Karl had placed a goblet of wine on the small table near him.

"Well, Father, I guess that would be a consideration, but I don't think Amelia would take it that well. I don't think Kyle would take it that well if I cheated on Amelia, given she is his baby sister." Alex bit his lip, thinking things through. "I know it's a risk, Father, but I can't live my whole life with everything on hold just in case I break."

Karl walked in and handed a small but ornate jewellery box to the King before bowing and leaving the room. Smiling, he opened the box to reveal the intricate necklace, circlet and bracelet of the Consort Elect, made of fine white gold with his heart-stone in place. The second set, the Consort of the Fourth, lay in the box, as yet without the adornment of the heart-stone.

Should Amelia agree to be his Consort Elect, the jewellery set proclaimed her rank. Should she then become the Consort of the Fourth, the second set would be adorned with her own heart-stone and the two sets would be woven together, symbolising their union.

"Yes, Prince Alexander, you have my permission to ask Lady Amelia to be your Consort Elect." The King stood and walked over, embracing Alex and handing him the box containing the jewellery.

William walked forward and gave his brother a brief hug. "Congratulations, little brother."

Alex breathed a sigh of relief and sagged down into the chair. He picked up the goblet and sipped the wine, smiling in appreciation. Karl had raided his father's wine cellar for a good bottle to celebrate the occasion.

Alex looked up to see both his father and brother appraising him before glancing at each other. Alex recognised the expressions on their faces and groaned, knowing he wouldn't like it.

"Come on, spit it out. What?"

The King cleared his throat and took a sip of his own wine before responding, choosing his words with care. "Alex, you know your brother doesn't have a consort, and neither does Elizabeth."

Alex smiled, having a sinking idea where the conversation was going. Duty. The duty of a son of the royal blood even if he was the Fourth.

"Yes, Father, that isn't likely a detail I would have failed to notice."

"I would rather keep the position of Consort a viable option for them both for a little longer. I also want Daniel to find his own suitable match if he can, rather than a state marriage." His father paused, taking another sip of his wine while William finished his own and waved at Karl to refill his goblet.

"Amelia will have official status as your Consort Elect tonight. Any child the pair of you conceive would be in line for the throne."

Alex swallowed his wine, trying not to choke. "Yes, Father, that child, if it existed, would. There are a few of us in-between that non-existent child and the throne, though."

At that retort, the King smiled. "Yes, Alex, I know. But since your brother, as yet, does not have an heir, any child of yours could stand in place to secure the throne until William takes a Consort of his own and has children."

"Amelia isn't even wearing the band of the Consort Elect, and we are talking about her getting pregnant to produce a potential heir already?"

Alex didn't know if he should be astounded or resigned. After all, he wasn't entirely sure he was surprised. The topic was bound to be raised eventually, he just wasn't expecting it to be this soon.

William looked embarrassed. "Sorry, Alex. It's unfair to you both to bring this up so early."

Alex sighed. "It's all right, William. Father, I'll discuss the issue with Amelia, although not, I think, tonight."

His father smiled. "I'm sure it won't be too onerous a chore for either of you." The King turned to Karl. "Send someone for Amelia. Let her know there is no rush. Alert the kitchen I think we will have a family affair tonight. The court can look after themselves for the evening. Depending on Lady Amelia's response, we'll plan a formal dinner and announcement tomorrow."

A lex fidgeted, and it didn't help having his father and brother chuckle at him as they noticed. Waiting for Amelia to arrive was testing his patience.

"How can the idea of skewering someone with a sword not phase me at all, but asking Amelia to be my Consort Elect makes me want to up and run for the forest?" Alex stood and paced.

"Alex, relax. She'll say yes and we will all have a fine dinner in celebration." William chuckled again as Alex threw a filthy look in his direction and kept pacing.

Hearing the door to his father's office open, Alex swung around to see Amelia walking in. She stopped, in shock to see Alex there, but training took over and she moved forward a few more paces, as protocol dictated, and curtseyed.

"Your Majesty, you sent for me?" Amelia's voice was low and calm, although Alex could tell she was nervous.

The King smiled. "Rise, Lady Amelia. It is Prince Alexander who has requested your presence at this audience. Prince Alexander?"

Alex gave a half bow to the King and saw Amelia's eyes widen in reaction to their formality before she regained control.

"My Lady Amelia, I cannot explain how I feel. I don't quite understand how this all happened, but know my world would crumble if you were not in it." Alex reached forward and, grabbing her hands, raised them and brushed his lips to her palms. His eyes never left hers. "Would you do me the honour of agreeing to be my Consort Elect?"

Alex held his breath again, waiting for her reply, and let it out as a smile graced her lips.

"My Prince, Alex, life without you in it would be meaningless. It would be my honour to be your Consort Elect."

Alex wanted to pick Amelia up kiss her and twirl her around. Instead, he followed protocol and took the necklace of the Consort Elect from its box, held by Karl and, placing it around her slim neck as she held her hair aside, he did up the clasp with a snap. He followed this with the circlet, placing it on her brow. Its deep green emeralds glittered like rain drops on her forehead. As Amelia held up her wrist, he did the clasp of the bracelet, smiling as it clicked and bonded. It would take the severing to unbind the symbols of their status as the clasps on both the bracelet and necklace, once locked, fused together, making their removal impossible without destroying them.

"Know I love you, Amelia. You are mine in this life, through the veil and into the next; I will always love you. I give my heart, mind and soul to your keeping." Alex wasn't sure where the words came from, except from beyond the veil itself; they were ancient.

"Heart, mind and soul, I am yours, Alex." Amelia reached a hand up to his cheek, rising on her toes to kiss him on the lips, only to laugh as he gave into his desire, picking her up and twirling her around.

"Alex, my heart stopped in shock, you could have given me some warning." She tried to glare at him but couldn't keep the smile from her lips. Amelia turned, resting her head on Alex's chest as the King and William approached.

"Welcome to the family, Amelia." The King's formality dropped as he grinned and planted a kiss on her cheek before making room for William who stepped forward and, swatting his little brother's hand aside, pulled her into his arm and gave her a hug.

"Welcome, Amelia, it's nice to have another little sister!" William grinned and kissed her before throwing a cheeky grin at his brother. "Although, why you would lower your standards to accept Alex is beyond me!" William laughed as Alex reclaimed Amelia and, in an adult manner, stuck his tongue out at his brother before dissolving into laughter.

K yle grinned as he walked from the doors that led from the Fourth's Compound to the Royal Wing, having a good idea what this summons from the King was about given Alex's parting comment earlier in the day. He already knew Alex had been closeted with his father and brother for some time. Kyle followed the servant who had come to fetch him, led to the private family dining room in the Royal Wing. It was rarely used since the King dined with the court most nights. Only on special occasions did he dine with the family alone.

Kyle thanked the servant as he was ushered into the room and grinned as he saw Amelia, adorned with the circlet that proclaimed her as the Consort Elect of the Fourth. Not wasting any time, he crossed the room and, pulling her from Alex's arms, hugged her before kissing her on the cheek.

"Congratulations, Amelia."

He then turned and hugged Alex. "Congratulations, Alex, I guess we really will be brothers now."

Alex grinned at Kyle and reclaimed Amelia. "Thanks, Kyle. I can't image you are all that surprised, though."

Kyle shook his head and laughed. "No. So the formal presentation is tomorrow, I take it?"

William, overhearing, grinned. "You would be correct. Tonight, however, we get to have our very own private celebration."

CATHERINE M WALKER

A helpful servant appeared at his elbow with a glass of wine, which he accepted. He raised his glass in salute to the couple and took a sip. Kyle nearly dropped his glass as a wave of pain, followed by anger, assaulted him. Only just managing to hide it, he took a sip and endured until the worst was over. As the pain washed over him, Kyle threw back his drink, not caring that it was likely superb wine brought up from the King's private cellar for the occasion. His glass wasn't empty long before it was topped up again by an attentive servant.

Kyle smiled at his friends, thankful that they had noticed nothing at all, and wondered how he would get through the evening under their scrutiny without giving away he had a problem. Kyle pushed aside the thought of confessing to them all. It wasn't appropriate since tonight was about Alex and Amelia, not about him.

28

ENCROACHING MADNESS

Kyle slipped through the shadow paths, grateful he'd held himself together long enough to slip away from the palace. It helped that everyone was distracted by Amelia and Alex right now. His desire to kill again rose almost as high as his desire to meet up with Alyssa; almost equal pulses of lust and rage were running through him, overpowering him. Only the thought that he would meet up with Alyssa soon kept him moving and stopped him from falling to his knees. He'd tried to suppress the sudden bloodlust and pulsing anger that assaulted his mind, then realised that trying to fight his conflicting emotions was what had caused him a great deal of pain. He wasn't consumed by it, but he felt he was losing more of himself as time passed. Kyle knew he would kill again this night —that would settle some bloodlust and rage he felt. Meeting up with Alyssa was sure to suppress the rest.

Kyle smiled as he saw Alyssa in an abandoned courtyard below and he almost moaned in pleasure just from the sight of her. Startled, Kyle nearly laughed as he realised she used that trick from last night, the bond she'd created that had blown his mind away with pleasure. Throwing off the shadows, he walked across the courtyard, gathering her, unresisting, into his arms.

"I don't know how you do what you do—you will have to show me how to do that bond thing so I can return the favour." Kyle bent his head, his hand rising to brush the strand of brown hair that had escaped from her hair tie and kissed her, feeling his lust rise.

"All in good time, Kyle. I'm sorry, but I have work to clear up first but I didn't want to leave you here waiting and wondering where I was. Do you want to come and help? It will go quicker than me doing the kills by myself." Alyssa ran her hand up his chest, her eyes staring into his own, causing Kyle to shudder, a soft moan escaping his lips as she sent him another small burst of pleasure.

"If you keep doing that, I'll be too distracted to kill anyone. Who's the mark and what has he done? Or don't I want to know the finer parts?" Kyle stepped back, somewhat reluctant, and grinned at her.

Alyssa smiled in return. "Oh, it's the last of the clean-up from that botched attempt to abduct the Prince so it's kind of right up your alley." Alyssa held out a hand to him and he grabbed it in his own, allowing her to lead him through the streets, both drawing the shadows to them to obscure their passage.

Kyle felt bloodlust rearing up inside him, bubbling just below the surface, and allowed it to wash over him. The rage was still in the background but he knew that once he starting killing that would rise too. Still, now he wasn't fighting against the lust and rage, he noted that the pain had receded.

Alyssa stopped and pointed to a small apothecary shop with the lights still on, testifying that someone was still inside. "Inside are the men who supplied the drugs used on you. My Master doesn't like loose ends."

Kyle nodded his understanding and realised he should have been relieved that the men he was about to kill had an involvement in the abduction attempt, for him it was a legal kill. He found he didn't care; he would have killed them anyway.

Kyle moved over to the window and glanced in, seeing two men inside the shop, which was filled with row upon row of bottles containing powders, liquids and herbs. He looked back at Alyssa and held up two fingers. She smiled at him and nodded. Cocking her head to one side, she walked toward the door.

Kyle raised his eyebrow at the rather straightforward approach, shrugged and followed her into the shop. While both men paused and looked up, neither of them looked all that surprised to see Alyssa. It was almost like they were expecting her. They were putting together what looked like an order.

"I'm not sure what he wants this time but if you write it down on the pad on the bench, we'll get to it. We've just got to finish up this order first." The man who spoke was a balding fat man, in counterpoint to his partner, who was tall and skinny and didn't even look at them.

Alyssa said nothing, simply circling as if she was heading for the bench, yet Kyle knew it was so she'd get a better angle on the fat man. Kyle circled around and placed himself in a position to take the tall skinny one. He waited just long enough for Alyssa to make her move, her knife darting forward and stabbing the man in the chest, who gaped at her, uncomprehending. Kyle moved forward as the tall skinny man looked up, struggling to comprehend what was happening. Grabbing him by the hair, he hauled his head back, exposing his neck. His long hunting knife ripped through the man's throat, his blood spurting. Kyle felt laughter well up inside of him. Hearing the door open and multiple bodies behind him, he span around. There were five men and, looking at the boxes, they were there to collect their order.

They stumbled into the room, not in that moment aware that the owners were slumped dead on the floor with their blood pooling out.

Kyle leapt on the first man, losing himself as rage, bloodlust and the thrill of the kill took over. A part of him knew that Alyssa fought next to him but they were outnumbered. These men, after their initial startled response, knew how to fight and Kyle's eyes widened as he felt them draw on the veil.

Kyle lost himself in the battle, aware of nothing except anger, rage and the kill.

He came back to himself to find Alyssa gripping his knife hand, staring into his eyes. "He is dead, my love. Come on, I know you're hurt; come back, we need to get out of here before someone else shows up."

Kyle struggled, realising that he was sitting on a dead man he'd stabbed multiple times in his rage. He was covered in blood. He looked at Alyssa, lost in confusion as the bloodlust and rage were still to the front, consuming him, threatening to overwhelm him again. He closed his eyes and tried to push it back, groaning.

"Alyssa, I'm too dangerous, it's too strong—you need to get away from me." Kyle found he was shaking with the effort. Then he felt her move closer, her hand on the side of his face.

"Look at me, my love, it's okay, I can help you. You lost yourself for some time there in the kill. Come on, trust me. I'll get you back and cleaned up." Kyle felt himself rise at her bidding. He stumbled as he stood and she wrapped her arm around him. He found, with her closeness, that the rage receded and he was retaining some of himself.

Kyle realised he must have lost time again, finding himself on the floor of his own bathroom. He'd been stripped down and Alyssa was cleaning the blood from his body with cloths.

Flashing images of the fight and what he'd done came back to Kyle. He groaned and bit back a sob. "How can you stand me, Alyssa, what have I done?"

Alyssa paused, drying him off, and he felt her lips brush his own. "Shh, it's okay Kyle, everything will be *okay*. You're cleaned up. Come on, let's get you to bed. I can help you." Alyssa stood, grabbing his hand, and helped him to stand. At her urging, he made it to his bed.

He rolled onto the bed on his side, covering his face, trying to muffle the sob that escaped his lips. Alyssa climbed up on the bed and over him. He felt her hands on him, stroking, soothing, her voice murmuring to him.

"It's all right, Kyle, this happens. I can help. I may not have as much of the Taint as you but I've seen this before. Trust me, Kyle, let me in." Under Alyssa's expert hands, Kyle felt his body respond, despite his inner turmoil.

Kyle moaned and pulled Alyssa to him, burying his head in her neck. "Powers, Alyssa, it hurts, help me, please ..." Kyle broke off in a moan as he felt a small burst of pleasure run through him. He felt her lips brush against his shoulder.

"Look at me, Kyle. It's okay—you're going to be okay." Alyssa's eyes bore into his own and he found he couldn't turn away from them. He didn't know whether to groan in agony or pleasure as Alyssa rolled him onto his back and straddled him, stoking him. "Just concentrate on me, Kyle, on the pleasure. Drop your bloodlust and just concentrate on me. I know you want me, Kyle, you desire me, I can feel it." Kyle found the bloodlust slipping away, replaced by his desire for Alyssa. Along with it, though, came pain.

"It hurts, Alyssa—powers, it hurts. The only time it doesn't is when I'm lost in the kill or lost in you." Kyle raised his hand, cupping her breast and massaging her, smiling as her own breathing came faster and her nipples hardened, realising he wasn't the only one lost in desire.

"Relax, my love, you're hurting. Let me do the work. Just look at me and feel your lust; lose yourself in it." Alyssa grabbed him and guided him into her, riding him, rocking with increasing intensity. Kyle moaned as she sent another burst of passion down the bonds and he climaxed.

He lost himself again but this time he had lost himself in Alyssa. When he came back to himself, she was lying down beside him, her hands still tracing random patterns on his chest. He could feel a strange fire seeming to follow across his skin wherever her fingers trailed and as he turned his head to look into her eyes, he also felt the steadying, soothing pulse coming from her.

It's okay, Kyle. You're all right now. You won't feel the need to kill again this day or tonight, your bloodlust is satiated by the killing frenzy tonight. I can help you control your pain and rage. It's okay that you love the kill, the blood—you are an assassin. You will learn to use it, rather than letting it use you. Her words continued to whisper into his brain even as he drifted off into an exhausted, sated slumber. *Sleep, give yourself to me, my love, trust me, I will help you. See, no more pain now. Sleep.*

Kyle was aware of the fire that traced patterns on his skin, the steady dual pulses, one causing pleasure to roll through his body and the other a steady, soothing pulse, calming his mind and body.

He heard whispering voices, one hers, one not.

Please, master, he's not like the others, don't make me do this. There was a pleading note in her mind voice that he hadn't heard before.

Not now, but he will be, unless we help him. You know the risk, child. Now begin, as you were instructed.

The other mind voice was male, firm, cold. Kyle tried to resist them, finding himself drowning under the impulse throbbing through him. The whispering voices continued, oddly echoing each other. The male voice first, then Alyssa's. He could not quite grasp the meaning of the words.

A part of his brain shrieked at him; he tried to struggle, yet the urgency drifted away under the spell of the voices and the fiery pattern that flared across his skin. He had the impression the words were ancient and held power but under her ministrations he gave up and let slumber take him as the fiery net enclosed his mind and body in a web he couldn't break free from. Under the administrations, he was compelled into sleep, into forgetfulness.

Kyle felt awareness flood him again and took a deep breath, feeling calm. Closing his eyes, he sighed. He hadn't felt this good in months. Frowning, he had a vague recollection of leaving the palace to meet Alyssa. He'd lasted for two days then discovered he was burning with the desire to see her again and the need to kill; rage had pulsed through him. Opening his eyes, he found that he stood in the middle of a small home, trembling as the realisation hit him that he was covered in blood and that none of it was his.

There was a man, sprawled on the floor, his head almost hacked from his body. Then Kyle flinched as memory came back to him in a series of flashes. He fell to his knees as if struck by physical blows. He remembered a man calling out from his doorway in anger and threatening him with a sword as he'd gone to walk through their small yard. Killing him had been easy.

The woman, the dead man's wife, he guessed, had thrown herself on him. He'd plucked her off and thrown her against the wall. The power of the veil augmenting his natural strength, she'd hit the wall with such force, he remembered hearing the crack as her head slammed into the wall and she slumped to the ground.

Then the children, they'd been wailing. He had two flashes of memory, he'd run them through with his blade, revelling in the kill, in the blood he was spilling. They hadn't died straight away; their wails became pitiful until they slowly silenced and bled out.

More men had come, guards attracted by the screaming, and he'd butchered them in a rage-fuelled frenzy.

Kyle took a trembling breath. There was a part of him that was horrified by what he'd done. There was another part of him that was calm. The rage, madness, pain—it was gone, and in its place was calm.

Kyle felt her mind, reaching out to him, calling him, and without thought he slammed up his barriers against her. He didn't know how he knew, but somehow he felt the Skulls Assassin was involved.

Kyle shook himself and with one final look around the small home and the family he'd slaughtered, he drew the veil to himself and escaped into the Veiled World, careful to keep his barriers around his mind.

As he moved through the shadow paths, he smiled. At least he'd learned he had mental barriers and that he had to lower them himself to let another gain any kind of control.

His flight stopped, and he realised he was at his father's country estate; it was quiet, not even his brother was in residence. Keeping the shadows pulled around him, he concentrated and appeared in the corner of his own rooms. While he may not have lived in or visited the estate for years, he knew that his Lady Mother kept his wardrobe stocked with suitable clothes that would fit for all occasions.

Assured that there was no one to hear him, Kyle stripped off his bloodied clothes and went to the bathing room. He drew water into the tub, not even bothering to warm it. He plunged beneath the water as soon as it was full. Shuddering as the cold water washed over him, he grabbed a cloth and soap and scrubbed himself clean, trying not to pay attention as the water became tinged with blood.

After several tubs of water, he stepped out and grabbed one of the thick towels from a nearby shelf and dried off, moving back to the main room as he did. Still locking himself down, not allowing himself to think, he moved to his wardrobe and smiled, as he'd been proven right. His mother, or at least one servant, had kept his wardrobe stocked with a selection of clothing, including a set he knew was a recent addition, bearing the crest of the Fourth's Companion. Kyle grabbed a pair of soft black trousers and a dark blue shirt, shying away from his usual brown or black.

After dressing, he gathered his bloodied clothes and walked over to the fireplace, all set waiting to be lit. He lit the fire and, after waiting for it to rise into a nice blaze, sighed as the heat washed over him. Piece by piece, he burnt his ruined clothes.

Kyle shuddered and felt a tear track down his cheek as he slumped against the chair behind him and buried his head in his arms.

"Powers, what have I done? What am I becoming?"

29

COMPANIONS' CONFESSIONS

Kyle woke, startled, half rising from his position curled up on the mat in front of the fire, hand reaching for a blade he wasn't wearing, only to settle back down on hearing a voice almost as familiar as his own.

"It's all right, Kyle, it's just me. I got worried when you didn't come back last night and tracked you here." Jess walked over to the fire and placed more wood into the fireplace before settling next to him.

Kyle swallowed then, shuddering, sank into her shoulder. The movement racked his body as tears trailed down his cheeks. He felt her move, then wrap her arms around him, pulling him to her, making soothing sounds, one hand stroking the side of his head like she was soothing a hurt child. She didn't ask him questions, but he felt her help reinforce the barriers he'd placed around his mind. He sighed as the clamouring at the edge of his awareness, the whispering voice and pulses of rage, faded and were blocked.

He felt her concentration shift and even though he didn't hear her call, he wasn't surprised when Alex appeared, striding into the room, the veil dropping away from him. Kyle heard their conversation but could not bring himself to speak, just closed his eyes as shudders continued to shake his body.

"He's in shock, Alex, and someone has got into his head somehow —it's driving him mad. He was trying to block them but it's like the connection is drilled right into him through his shields. I've imposed a shield around him. Whoever it is isn't happy, I can feel them raging, beating away at my barrier and trying to call to him." Jess continued to hold Kyle, trying to soothe the shuddering body of a man who was closer to her than members of her own family.

Kyle felt Alex settle next to them and felt his friends' hands on his temples, his head turned to look into Alex's eyes and he heard the voice in his mind. *It's all right, my brother, we're here. Let me see.*

A part of Kyle's mind tried to fight, yet he replayed everything that had happened to him. Now he was reliving all of his interactions with Alyssa, he could feel the hooks she'd placed in his own mind.

He could feel his friends' building anger.

"Hold the barrier, Jess, I'll try to break her hold on him."

Alex's eyes drilled into his own and Kyle couldn't draw his own eyes away.

"Hold him. I'm sorry, Kyle, this will hurt."

As Kyle stared into his brother's eyes, he felt as if a knife was slicing into his brain. He screamed in agony, his body bucking. Again and again, he felt that knife entering his head and sawing at those bonds that bound him to Alyssa.

Even in his agony, he knew while Jess held and restrained him, she turned most of her attention and effort into blocking Alyssa from contacting him.

Kyle screamed again and then felt his mind shutting down.

———

Kyle woke once more, although this time he was comfortable so guessed he was in a bed rather than on the floor in front of the fire. His mind was still in an oasis of imposed calm. Unable to help himself, he groaned. Opening his eyes, he found Alex lounging in a large chair next to the bed.

"Shh, Jess is still sleep. We didn't want to leave you unguarded so we've been taking it in shifts." Alex hauled himself up and reached for a small bottle on the dresser near the bed. Kyle then felt himself propped up into a half sitting position with the bottle held to his lips. "Drink, Kyle, it's just a painkiller with a sedative that will help you relax. Sorry, but with what I did to release you from her hold I can feel your pain. Drink, my brother." Kyle complied as Alex tipped the bottle and he swallowed as the liquid slid down his throat. Looking to the other side of the bed, he saw Jess curled up, sound asleep, although she had her weapons close at hand.

Kyle relaxed back into the pillows that Alex had piled up to support him and he felt the pain subside. Despite himself, he relaxed. "Thank you. Alex, what happened?"

"We felt your pain, you called to us then disappeared. Jess tracked you down. You were at your father's country estate. As soon as we'd broken her bonds to you, we moved back to your suite in the Fourth's Compound." Alex reached up and pulled the bell cord near the bed after the door opened and a servant stepped in, bowing.

"Yes, Your Highness?" His voice was hushed, and he was dressed in the livery of the Fourth; he cast a concerned glance at Kyle before looking back at Alex.

"Shane, could you bring me a pot of coffee and a breakfast platter? Also, send an update to William that Kyle is awake but still not ready for visitors." Alex's voice was hushed yet held a note of command he'd never heard in his friend's tone before.

Kyle closed his eyes and contemplated the last few months, what had happened and what he had done. "Powers, Alex, what am I becoming? You saw what I did."

The last was more a statement than a question since he knew Alex had seen the details of the slaughter he'd committed in the small house when he'd searched his memory to find out what was wrong.

Alex looked at him and nodded. "Yes, I saw. That woman, the Skulls Assassin, was driving you to madness. I could see from your own memories you weren't in control."

"I was stupid. You tried to warn me and I didn't listen." Kyle shook his head, wishing he could wipe the memory, what he had of it, of what he'd done out of his mind.

They both fell into silence again as Shane entered with a tray and, at a sign from Alex, set up the coffee table near the blazing fire. He unloaded the contents of his tray before leaving at a wave of dismissal from Alex.

Kyle climbed out of the bed, grabbing Alex's arm to steady himself as he became lightheaded. When his vision cleared, he took a steadying breath and moved over to the table, not shaking off Alex's help. Sitting in one of the large chairs near the coffee table, Kyle accepted the mug of coffee that Alex gave him, taking a sip.

"How long have I been out?" Kyle found Alex had been regarding him, trying to assess his current condition, he guessed.

"It's been two days since we found you at your father's country estate. You had us a little worried." Alex slumped back and drank his own coffee, his concern clear.

Kyle looked at him, shocked. "Two days?"

Alex nodded. "You were in shock when Jess located you and called me. You were battling to block out the rage and anger that the Skulls Assassin was sending to you through those bonds. Kyle, you were close to breaking."

Kyle closed his eyes and tried to assess how he was feeling. "She was trying to call me to her. I–I don't think I'd go to her now." Kyle hated that he heard a trace of uncertainty in his voice.

"Give yourself some time to heal, Kyle. In the meantime, one of us will be with you." Alex raised his hand, cutting off Kyle's objection. "I don't know if she can reconnect those bonds she made in your mind and you are in no state right now to defend yourself if she shows up here." Alex shook his head and smiled. "If it makes you feel better, all three of us are staying put for now."

Kyle opened his mouth to object then closed it again. He took another sip of his coffee and considered. "You're right. I want to track her down and kill her but I can't say right now how I'd react if I saw her again. I didn't even realise the control she had over me."

"I think it might have been her general idea, Kyle. She wouldn't have wanted you to know she was burning bonds into you so she could control you and send you mad."

Alex looked up and smiled as Jess walked over. Climbing over the back of Kyle's chair, she slid in behind him and wrapped her arms around him.

"That bitch is never getting near you again, Kyle. To kill is one thing. To torture another, to turn them to madness, is unforgivable." Jess kissed his temple and pulled his head back to rest on her shoulder.

Kyle sighed, closed his eyes and relaxed back into Jess's embrace, surprising himself with how safe and secure he felt in that moment. He realised that while he'd lusted after Alyssa, he'd never felt safe and after that initial encounter with her when she'd forged that first bond between them, nothing he'd felt or experienced had been his own.

"When did you learn to recognise her bonds, Alex? How did you know how to sever them?" Kyle opened his eyes to see his friend frown.

"I don't know, Kyle. I saw through your own memories what she'd done, although I think I understood it better than you did. I saw how she did it. I could see the bonds she'd burned into you, they were like trails of fire all over your body—thick ropes of power into your brain. I reacted on instinct, I guess." Alex smiled at his friend. "You're clear of her bonds right now, I promise you. Although I think you are still vulnerable to her. At least until you heal."

Kyle closed his eyes again and took a deep, steadying breath. "Thank you. Thank you, both. I've always been the strong one, the dangerous one. I'm not sure how to cope with being the victim." Kyle laughed with an edge of bitterness and shame. "I don't know I'd trust myself if I was face-to-face with her again right now."

Jess hugged him tighter, her lips brushing his temple again. "She got into your head, Kyle. Rest easy, we have your back." Jess looked over Kyle's head to Alex before continuing. "Besides, there was something strange about the traces of her I saw in your memories. I don't know who she is, but she is not a simple thief assassin."

"She spoke in a language I don't understand, but it reeked with power. Whatever she was doing was assisting her in binding you to her will. I agree with Jess. Alyssa is not a simple Skull Assassin." Alex shook his head, considering what he'd learned from Kyle's mind. "She is more powerful than you thought, Kyle. Too much longer and you would have been hers. Heart and soul, you would have belonged to her."

Kyle wanted to object to his friend's assessment but found he could not. Even now when he thought of Alyssa he felt a longing, almost a compulsion to go to her. He shuddered and squeezed his eyes shut, hiding his face against Jess' neck. "If she was in front of me now, I'd go to her. I'm stopping myself from calling out to her. I know she's dangerous, I know I shouldn't, but still there is part of me that wants her. What the hell did she do?"

Alex glanced at Jess, concerned, then rose, moving over and perching himself on the arm of the chair they were sitting on. "Give yourself time, Kyle. The Tainted bonds she bound you with ran deep. It will take time to clear the impulses she set in you, or at least that is what Aaron told me."

30

ASSASSINS PLAY

J ess did her part, dressed to the hilt as the Lady Jessalan, Companion of the Fourth. She mingled, chatted, and was polite to everyone. Now that the full Royal Court was at the Summer Palace, the first of the Summer Balls had been thrown on the arrival of the King and as a celebration of Alex taking a Consort Elect. Well, not quite on his arrival, but a few days after they had arrived and settled in. Still, as pleasant as the ball was and more relaxed than the balls held in the capital, Jess kept her eyes on Kyle. She laughed at Lord Matterling's embellished description of the annual migration of the court and the terrible hardships they'd faced 'on the road', but her eyes tracked across to Kyle.

Jess spotted him over to one side with a veritable gaggle of the court's ladies surrounding him, battling for his attentions. To all outward appearances he seemed calm and in control, back to his old self. He was back to thrashing all of them in the training grounds with his blades. He'd been taking to physical exertion and training with a passion. Nonetheless, there was one area he hadn't bounced back in and that was around women—well, other than her and Elizabeth. Kyle didn't trust his own judgement around women anymore and even though the ladies fighting for his attention did not understand his stress and tension was building, Jess could tell he was almost at breaking point. Jess excused herself from the erstwhile lords who surrounded her and shoved her irritation to one side as most of them trailed after her like a bunch of lost puppies.

Jess saw Kyle turn, his face frozen in shock. She saw the figure approaching behind him and her own eyes widened, her hand reaching for her weapons. She drew in the Taint, yet feared she would be too late with the number of courtiers packed between her and Kyle.

K yle smiled, relaxing, glad that at least this ball wasn't as formal as those that were held in the Winter Court. Still, Kyle wished they'd skipped the night's activities and hit the local pub. Despite that desire, here he was, dressed up; the immaculate picture of 'Lord Kyle Strafford' and, for one of the few occasions in his adult life, so far behaving to the point even his Lady Mother couldn't have been disappointed.

He was getting even better at deflecting the ladies and the constant enquiries as to what had happened. They all knew something had, just not what. Everyone in court was gossiping, although none had guessed what had really happened. That they had all known about the attempted abduction, due to the Kings announcement afterwards, only fuelled the speculation.

Kyle paused as he walked through the garden; suddenly uneasy, he glanced around. Yet nothing he could see seemed out of order. Lamps placed at regular intervals along the length of the garden wall threw out pools of light with a few select trysting spots left for meetings—either business or lovers taking time out. The guards were as always present, both on the walls and standing at regular posts around the well-kept immaculate garden.

Shaking off his uneasiness as a product of his recent run-ins, he continued on his original path winding his way through the garden back toward the ball room. The large floor-to-ceiling doors had been unbarred and pushed back on their rails to the far walls, stacking neatly against each other, opening up the ballroom to the garden. The light spilling from the well-lit ballroom drew him inside.

Glancing around, he spotted Alex, looking relaxed and talking with his brothers. While it wasn't unusual in William's company, it certainly was in Daniel's. Alex and Daniel definitely did not get along; they hadn't as far back as Kyle remembered.

He spied Jess over to one side of the room with her own gaggle of admirers; she looked up as she noted his entrance, a smile on her lips. He had no doubt that was due to the flock of ladies that trailed into the ballroom with him.

Kyle nearly groaned out loud as he felt a hand on his arm and turned, freezing as he stared into familiar brown eyes. His breath caught and part of his brain screamed in panic as he felt her battering, trying to get through his mental barriers. Kyle stumbled back and tripped, falling over as the lady drew her knife. Kyle heard the screaming of the courtiers, sensed that they drew away in panic, hindering the guard trying to press forward. He tried to move, tried to draw one of his own weapons to defend himself but he could just hear her voice in his head.

It's all right, my love, it will be over soon; relax and accept your fate, come with me or die. Alyssa's eyes bore into his own, compelling him to stay, even though part of his brain shrieked at him to move, draw a weapon and defend himself.

Kyle tried to close his eyes as the blade descended, but somehow he couldn't do anything but stare at her. Then a blade intervened, and another mind placed itself between his own and Alyssa's.

A lex laughed along with his brothers, surprising himself that he was even getting on with Daniel, which was a novelty. Generally, William and Elizabeth had spent a great deal of time deflecting some of Daniel's more poisonous pranks and barbs, yet tonight he was like a different man. As the screams tore through the ballroom, the smile dropped from his lips and, without thinking, he drew his blade, spinning around to place himself between his father and brothers and whatever the threat was. Hearing Kyle's mental scream for help, Alex's eyes traced across the ballroom and he saw Kyle stumble back and fall to the ground, staring up at a woman with a blade.

Alex had a moment of instant recognition. The woman was the one from Kyle's memories. The woman was the Skulls Assassin, Alyssa. Motioning to the King's Elite, he barked quick orders.

"Get the King out of here. Now. That is the Skulls Assassin." Alex didn't wait to see if his orders were obeyed but ran forward, leaping over the line of Elite and plunging through the panicking, screaming courtiers, who seemed hell-bent on escaping the confines of the ballroom.

Alex had an agonising moment, wondering if he would make it in time, and heard her whisper to Kyle, *It's all right, my love, it will be over soon; relax and accept your fate, come with me or die.* Seeing her blade plunge down, he put on a burst of speed and lunged, interposing his own blade between hers and Kyle's throat.

As the clash of the blades rang through the ballroom, Alex felt as if the world around him slowed down. He recognised it from

Kyle's descriptions of what it was like for him when he fought, although this was the first time he knew of it himself. His eyes rose to those of the Skulls Assassin and he grinned.

"Let's dance, assassin."

With that, he shoved back, drawing his secondary, shorter blade and the dance of blades began. For the first time in his life, he understood Kyle's passion for the blade and in that instant he felt in tune with the blade in his hand. All the moves he couldn't master over the years seemed to make sense and something clicked in his brain. With everything slowed down around him he could see her telegraph her moves before she made them and was able to counter them.

While most of his brain was concentrating on the fight he was engaged in, he also knew that the ballroom was emptying, leaving himself, the Skulls Assassin, Kyle, Jess and a whole horde of the Elite, almost all with their blades drawn. Alex wasn't aware of how much time had passed while he engaged in his dance with the assassin, although he was aware that Kyle and Jess had joined the fight. If he could have spared the attention, he would have cheered. He only became aware again when time seemed to speed up once more. The Skulls Assassin stumbled back with a blow from his blade, tripping over the corner of a rug and crashing to the ground; she was bleeding from multiple wounds. Before he could end her life, Kyle stepped forward and, with a blank expression, slashed her throat, the spurt of blood showing her artery had been severed. Her hand, which she had raised in a last futile effort to defend herself, fell back, lifeless, to the ground.

In those last moments as the life faded from her eyes, Alex heard and saw a burst of communication from her that caused his own mind to go into shock.

Thank you. You don't understand. Beware the Order, things are not as they seem. Alyssa slumped to the ground, her secrets gone with her.

Alex was almost bewildered that in her last message he felt a burst of emotion—she truly was grateful that she had been released. Alex shook himself and decided he could try to sort out the confusing memories and images she'd sent to him later. With a quick strike, Alex plunged his blade into her heart and withdrew it in a smooth motion, wiping it on a corner of her cloak before he stood and turned, his eyes tracking to Kyle and Jess.

The regular sounds intruded again and he could hear the rhythmic thump of booted feet running as more guards came hurrying into the ballroom. Sobs and screams still rose from the courtiers, who were still pushing and shoving, trying to get out of the room, unaware that the threat had been dealt with. Surprised, he glanced toward the Dias and saw his father's Elite ushering the King, his brothers, sister and Amelia out the royal entrance toward safety.

Alex realised that while to him the battle had seemed to take forever, in reality it had lasted just minutes. Still, it had been long enough that his chest was heaving and he was sucking in air after his exertions. He looked at Kyle, who still knelt next to the lifeless body of the assassin and he realised his friend was descending into shock.

"Kyle, brother. It's ok, she's dead. She can't take you now."

Kyle stared up at him, his eyes wide, before leaning against his shoulder, trying to suppress the shudders. "Powers, Alex. I—" Kyle's words came to a halt as he looked at the blood on himself. Her blood. Alex closed his eyes and drew his free arm around his friend's shoulders, looking over to Jess, who knelt on the other side. He may not have said the rest out loud but they both knew in that moment Kyle wished he hadn't survived the encounter. That was an emotion that Alex was familiar with, having battled with it himself since his mother had died.

Closing his eyes against sudden fatigue, Alex took a deep breath. Noting he was in too awkward a position to place his sword in it's sheath, with a brief glance back he handed his weapons to Marcus, who stood at his back with a ring of Elite. The three of them sat, unable to contemplate moving, as exhaustion fell over them.

Alex laughed and saw the shock on the faces of his friends. He shook his head, explaining. "You think I'd learn to stop drawing every damn bit of power I can when we're threatened. I want to curl up and sleep now."

A lex realised that he'd been awake for some time, just not aware. He snorted as he decided that the concoction the healers had given him after the events in the ballroom must have been a very strong sleeping draught. One benefit of that was that he felt more rested than he could remember having been for a long time. Even that normal dragging weight of exhaustion he'd come to associate with the Veiled World was gone, as if it had left him alone for the night. It may have been because even in sleep he'd had his barriers up. Alex wasn't sure when or how he'd learned that skill but it was handy.

"How is Kyle, Aaron?"

Alex knew without opening his eyes that the healer was sitting in a chair near his bed. He still felt a heavy lassitude he guessed was the drugs. Alex knew he could shake it off if he reached for the power of the veil but was content to rest for the moment. He turned onto his side and opened his eyes to see the healer sitting there as he'd guessed.

Aaron stood and walked over to his patient. "You will have to stop doing this, Alex, it's not good for you to drive yourself to the level of total exhaustion so you collapse. You will rest today. If I find you doing anything strenuous or trying to leave the Fourth's Complex I will have the guards hold you down and then give you a sleeping draught to make sure you rest." Aaron paused, glaring at his patient, who chuckled.

"Okay, Aaron, I will rest today. I was already inclined to anyway in case you hadn't noticed. Now, how is Kyle?" Alex was relieved to see there wasn't much strain or concern in Aaron.

"Recovering, Your Highness. Jocelyn is a proficient mind healer. What that Shadow Assassin did to Lord Kyle is unconscionable. She was very skilled and powerful, a twisted healer's gift. We do our best to strip any power from those who misuse their gifts in that way. Lord Kyle will recover, it will just take time for him to heal—but he will heal. I wish you had called me in the first instance when you discovered what had been done to him." Alex found himself pinned by the physician's glare.

"Sorry, Aaron, Kyle seemed to be on the mend. If that assassin hadn't made a reappearance he would have recovered on his own." Alex smiled at the physician's obvious concern and anger over what had been done.

"Fair enough, Your Highness, he might have. For now, at least, he will remain under Jocelyn's watch until she is certain he is well and truly on the mend. As you discovered, with the state his mind is in, it is easy for another person to take over right now."

While speaking, Aaron had been mixing another of his concoctions and held it out to him, his gaze not shifting until Alex sighed and took the goblet, swallowing the contents in one smooth motion. Satisfied, Aaron took the goblet back off him and placed it on the table by the bed.

"That was just an herbal mix to help you relax and mend. Since you are cooperating there is no need for a sleeping potion."

Alex considered Aaron, wondering how much he could push the subject. "So, healers know more about the veil and those with power in our world than most people guess?"

Aaron sat back down and stared at Alex before nodding. "Yes, Your Highness, we know a great deal. There are many with power in our ranks, like Jocelyn and myself, although all lean toward the healing gifts."

The last was a concession that Aaron had never made, at least not to him. Alex knew the public did not realise that healers used the Taint, even if they used it in a different way to the Tainted.

"I knew you had power, Aaron, I can feel it, see it." Alex was more curious than anything else. The murky Realm of those with power and the stigma attached to anyone found to be wielding more than just a trace of it meant it was a subject that was not discussed all that much. Alex was starting to realise that those with power were more prevalent than he, let alone members of the public, realised.

"Yes, Alex, more than a little. Most of us in the healers' ranks are gifted. It's something we go to great lengths to hide. Oh, most know we have healing gifts, but do not realise it is the same power as that running through those who break, whose minds sunder with the power. We don't quite have as much as those poor souls. So now the subject has come up, how are you, Your Highness?" Aaron once again pinned his patient with his gaze.

Alex almost squirmed. He had the distinct impression that if he lied or tried to play it down, Aaron would know. "I'm all right, but sometimes I get lost and confused. It feels like my brain is about to explode; pain, anger—extreme emotions of any sort just seem to drive me insane." Alex paused and looked at Aaron but saw no sign of shock or horror in the physician's face or demeanour. "I hear voices though the veil, clamouring at me, echoing through my head. It gets confusing; it's hard to know where they end and I begin. I take it there is nothing that your kind can do, otherwise you would have done it already." Alex was astounded that his voice was so matter-of-fact, with so little emotion, given what they were talking about.

"I'm sorry, Your Highness. No, there isn't much we can do except what we have been doing for all three of you. Those with limited gifts, we can sometimes help, but you are all too strong for us, there is too much of the power flowing through all of you." Aaron looked back at him, sincere and earnest. "If we could take this burden from you all we would have by now."

Alex closed his eyes so he couldn't see Aaron's reaction.

"Will I turn into one of the Sundered, Aaron?"

The silence stretched but Alex continued to wait, knowing an answer of some sort was coming and that he wouldn't like the response. Yet, somehow, he still wasn't upset. He was almost relieved to talk to someone outside of the three of them about what was happening to them. He also guessed, given Aaron's 'no nonsense' manner regarding the issue meant that he knew as much, or rather more than, anyone else in the Realm did about the Sundered.

"I'm sorry, Your Highness, I can only go on other subjects I've monitored and the healers' doctrine handed down from master to apprentice. Some become the Sundered. Some seem to disappear. The pain, anger and confusion you describe, the feeling of being overwhelmed, is common to most but is symptomatic of all the Sundered that I have heard about. You know the voices are not your imagination, that they are other Tainted ones, like yourself. You have that advantage over many."

"Thank you for being honest with me, Aaron." Alex smiled a little.

Aaron stood and walked toward the door. "Rest, Your Highness. I'll be back later to check on you."

"Am I at least allowed out of bed, Aaron?" Alex smiled at the physician's stern glare.

"Yes, Your Highness. No swords, or running around. You may remain in rooms or your outer receiving rooms or you may visit Lord Kyle. That is it. Try your best to stay away from the power, at least for today; you've drawn too much of it lately."

Thinking of the assassin's last words, Alex rolled onto his side so he could catch the healer's expression. "Do you know about the Killiam Order?" He was rewarded by a flash of surprise on the healer's face.

Aaron grimaced. "The Killiam Order has been around for a long time, Alex, founded by a man called Gale Killiam; his son was killed by a Sundered. You would do well to avoid them. Their ranks are filled with healers, scholars, aristocrats and even commoners." Aaron walked back across the room as he spoke and sat on the edge of the chair arm. "On the surface they are Lore Keepers, yet their primary mission is to see all those with power are killed. They are the order that has drummed up fear and superstition in the masses for those with power over the generations."

Alex nodded. "Why would Alyssa fear the Order? She was Tainted, powerful."

Aaron snorted at that. "I doubt she was all that powerful as far as the Sundered are concerned. She seemed quite young and I'd say only broke recently." Aaron smiled sadly then continued. "If she grew up where there is a strong chapter of them, knowing she was Tainted, they may have given her cause to fear them. They are fanatical."

Alex frowned. "Why haven't I heard of them before?"

"Your father has never allowed the Order to establish a firm foothold here and will not acknowledge them as a legitimate guild. He didn't want you to be subject to their hatred and fear, Alex." Aaron stood and headed to the door. "Get some rest, Your Highness." He closed the door quietly behind him.

Alex thought about everything he'd been told and contemplated if he wanted to get up. For once, he was happy enough to laze around and even had the physician's injunction to do so. For the first time, Alex did as he was bid and rolled over to sleep a little bit longer.

Tomorrow was soon enough to track down the lair of the Skull Lord.

31

TRACKING THE SKULL

J ess turned, seeing Damien approach, and smiled. She hadn't seen him for some time, although she had to admit she'd been preoccupied with everything that had been going on.

"My Lady Jessalan, it's good to see you again." His smile broadened and he took her fingers and kissed them, causing giggles and whispering from some ladies who were trailing behind her. She'd just broke away from Elizabeth's entourage from an excursion into town yet had seemed to inherit some of the women who'd insisted on wandering after her.

"It's been too long, Baron Harper, but I'll forgive you since the new estates the King conferred on you must consume your time. Come, walk with me, tell me everything that's been going on." Jess played along; she could tell that Damien had something to tell her.

Damien smiled and stepped to her side, presenting his arm to her in a courtly fashion, looking back at the ladies that clustered behind. "If you will excuse us, ladies, I have important things to discuss with Lady Jessalan. I'm sure you understand."

Jess turned and flitted her hands at the ladies in question, who pouted at her but stayed put. She noticed Damien looking at Megan and Callum then back at her.

"I'm afraid the 'go away' hand gesture doesn't work on the Elite, although I can guarantee they are loyal; they will stay out of ear shot if I ask." Jess kept her voice low but knew Megan and Callum heard her anyway, since they dropped back a few more discreet paces.

"It's not that I doubt their integrity, it's just that what I've found out is, well, I don't know how they will react. Or Kyle, let alone His Highness." Damien looked troubled and took a deep breath, keeping his voice low. "Is there somewhere that has an overview of the training yards? Somewhere discreet? This is about the man His Highness asked me to look for—I think I've found him."

Jess felt her eyes widen at the implication. She nodded and guided their way to the upper floors of one of the corner towers, which had large windows overlooking the training yards below. She held her hand up at her guards who acknowledged her order and stayed back near the door, out of earshot if they kept their voices down.

Damien licked his lips then scanned the training yard below, gesturing toward an Elite standing in the far corner.

"He doesn't have the tattoos, although those can be faked; however, he fits the description you gave me. His friends call him Baine; he has the same name and the distinctive scar."

Jess looked down and caught sight of the man in question and felt herself stiffen as she understood Damien's hesitation in bringing this information straight to Kyle or Alex. She watched the man then looked over her shoulder and gestured for Megan to step forward.

"Megan, who is that man?" Jess gestured to the guard down below.

Megan looked at her then down into the training yard, her eyes narrowing.

"That is David Baine, My Lady. He almost got kicked from the Elite years ago but His Highness Prince Daniel likes him. He's assigned to His Highness' protection detail more often than not." Her eyes tracked back to Jess before she asked. "Is there something I should know, My Lady?"

"Not right now, Megan. Thank you." Jess turned back to look at the man below, her face pale. "Thank you, Damien, leave this with me. Do not let Kyle or Alex know. Or anyone else. It amounts to treason."

Damien swallowed and nodded before adding. "There's one more thing. Prince Daniel leaves the palace and attends an old residence in town, some meeting of a group called The Killiam Order. Some offshoot scholars' order. Not much seems to be known about them, but that one, Baine, is the only guard who goes with him. They've been there three times already, every second Tuesday."

Jess frowned at the name given it sounded familiar, yet she couldn't place it. "I'll look into it. Thank you."

Alex found that once he decided, he was more at ease. He'd felt a deep burning anger since he'd seen his friend curled up in shock, shivering in pain. That anger had only grown as he'd seen Kyle's memories of what transpired.

Freeing Kyle of the psychic bonds Alyssa had bound him in had taken hours of painstaking work, wrenching them out one after the other, pulling away the light web of power that seemed to run like spider silk over his body and through his mind. Every time he had broken one of her bonds, the smaller bindings of power had tried to fill the gap and repair what he had cut. It had been a relief when Kyle passed out with the pain.

Yet, in Kyle's memories, he saw her face. He knew every place they'd met up, and that Kyle had made inroads in tracing her and, he suspected, her master's hiding place. Alex had heard the memory of her voice, the whispering words echoing through Kyle's brain, insidious. While Alex couldn't understand the words, he could feel their power and knew Kyle's unconscious brain was following her instructions, even though she was dead; trying, he suspected, to reconnect with Alyssa. Alex was not convinced that he would not fall to another if they came for him.

It was the assassin's brazen attempt to come right into the heart of the Summer Palace, placing them all, including the King, at risk that had prompted his current plan of action. Although Kyle had helped defeat her, it had taken all three of them to kill her. Alex knew Kyle had been in turmoil since. Uncertain if he would have been capable of standing against Alyssa without their help.

While Alex knew that in the long run Kyle would bounce back and the experience would be good for him, right now it was hard to see the uncertainty in his friend. Kyle had always been confident; he remained so with a blade in his hand, but his confidence with women, or rather Alex suspected, his judgement of them, had shaken his confidence.

Although he doubted the rest of the court guessed how shaken he was, Alex knew and so did Jess. Alex also suspected that William had guessed, since he not only knew all the details of what had happened but how close Kyle had come to becoming enslaved to Alyssa. William had intervened with women a few times when they had cornered Kyle in the court.

Alyssa had brought the fight to their home. Alex was determined to take it to hers. It was time for him to track down and pay a visit to the League of Skulls and teach them that declaring war on the crown was not advisable.

At a noise behind him, Alex flicked his eyes toward the door in the mirror and saw William walk in. They stared at each other through the mirror, although Alex didn't turn from his task of getting ready. He placed his secondary weapons in their various sheaths on his body, hidden from view, at least to the untrained eye.

He watched as his brother moved to the side bar and poured himself a glass of liquor. William grabbed a second one and rose it in his direction, his eyebrow raising in enquiry. Alex smiled and shook his head. While alcohol rarely affected him in the same way as it did others, he could burn the effects from his system with the power of the veil if he chose; he felt he was better off waiting until after he got back from the night's planned activities. He finished getting ready then, satisfied, turned and walked over. Smiling, he gestured for William to take a seat before taking his own and just waited.

William spoke. "I take it I won't be able to talk you out of this. You will track the Skulls Lair down."

"No, and yes. I've got a good idea of where they are. This is the second time the League of Skulls has acted against the interests of the crown and before you ask, no, Jess is not coming with me. Where I'm going, to stand a chance of succeeding, I need to go alone. Besides, Jess needs to stay with Kyle in case another of the Skulls' gifted assassins shows up here and goes after him again."

Alex sipped water from the glass that had been sitting on the coffee table and let his brother process what he'd said, smiling as he nodded.

"It took the three of you to kill her, Alex. What if the Skull Lord decides enslaving a prince is better than enslaving a lord?" William took a sip of the liquor he'd poured and smiled in appreciation before looking across the room at him, his concern clear.

"If I have to fight them, I will, but I need to find their lair first and I want to know who the Skull Lord is before I take any action. From Kyle's memories, more of them seem to be able to control the power of the veil to some degree." Alex stood at his brother's nod. "I should be back around daybreak."

Without further pause, Alex pulled the shadows toward himself and slipped into that place between the worlds. He concentrated on where he wanted to go, filling his mind with his destination, and walked, knowing there was no need to rush. Time moved to a different pace, although he still didn't know how this whole process worked. Most of what he did was on pure instinct. He knew he could do it and he would end up where he needed to be.

Alex felt a shift in the shadowed paths and slowed. Letting go of some shadows, he found himself in the rafters of a warehouse. Grimy windows ranged the warehouse just below the roofline. The floor was empty with a pile of forgotten bales of hay and rags in the corner. Alex knew from Kyle's memories that this was where they had first slept together—where Alyssa had inserted her first, insidious bond into Kyle. Off to one side on the floor, Alex spied a dirty brown stain that marked the first kill Kyle and

Alyssa had committed together. The one that Kyle hadn't admitted to when telling the story of his encounter.

Alex rose from his perch in the rafters and jumped off, landing on the floor below, using the power of the veil to slow his descent. He landed in a half crouch. Alex straightened and checked the warehouse, although he doubted he'd find anything of worth.

Satisfied there was nothing in the building except a few rodents, Alex gathered the shadows around him and stepped out into the street. He paused to take stock of his surroundings. The warehouse where Alyssa and Kyle had met up was on the industrial section of Old Town. Between the Old Town and the Docklands were where all Kyle's unsanctioned and uncontrolled kills occurred when he had been overcome. There were some that Alex discovered Kyle wasn't even aware he'd done. All with Alyssa sending wave after wave of anger and rage to him, overwhelming his mind until he was lost.

Alex shook his head and pushed the memory aside; it threatened to overwhelm him with anger, as it had every time he thought about it. Alex walked through the almost deserted streets, to be expected at this hour. As he walked, Alex kept an eye on the rooftops and side streets. He made it to the apothecary, the site were Kyle had first known he was losing control. The shop was boarded up with a sign saying it would reopen soon. Alex had been told it was the man's son who was redesigning the shop. Alex made a mental note to keep tabs on the place once it reopened as it didn't take much of a stretch of the imagination to think the son might have the same connections as the father.

Shaking his head, Alex pushed off the wall he'd been leaning against and walked toward his final destination for the night: the small house where Kyle had slaughtered the entire family. Kyle may not have remembered, but from what Alex had seen of Kyle's memories, he'd been almost driven that night by equal desire to find Alyssa and to kill. If the poor, unfortunate man hadn't come out of his rear door that night and challenged Kyle, it was likely that both he and his entire family would be alive today. Or at least, would not have fallen to Kyle's blade that night.

Alex figured Kyle had been making a straight line from his suite at the palace to where he sensed Alyssa was. That was one thing about the bonds. They may have given Alyssa a great deal of control over Kyle but they also made it easier for Kyle to track her through those same bonds.

Kyle hadn't realised yet that buried deep in his brain he had a good idea where Alyssa and Alex believed the League of Skulls lair was situated. Alex jumped, grasping the top of the fence, and flipped over into the small yard beyond it. The small dwelling sat abandoned and only just showed the signs of its uninhabited state. Alex knew it wouldn't be long before someone took advantage of that to take it over. That an entire family had been slaughtered here would only hold them back for so long.

Looking around, Alex sighed as he walked toward the door, not even pausing at the bloodstain on the rocks that formed the courtyard, and tried the handle. The handle turned, showing that the town guard hadn't even attempted to secure the premises when they'd left. To the left of the doorway, he noticed what looked like a dirty mark down the wall, except Alex knew it was where the wife's head had smashed into the wall. It was blood.

Taking one last breath, Alex walked into the small home and paused just inside the door. It was obvious that even the tragic deaths hadn't prevented people from raiding the home and cleaning out anything of value. The place was almost empty except for a few broken plates and a chair. There was also the blood-stained rug in the centre of the floor. Alex shook his head and wondered if thieves would even take that eventually and attempt to clean or mask the blood stain. Alex paused, closed his eyes and played the awful memory of the slaughter through his mind once more, trying to get his bearings on the direction to Alyssa from Kyle's memories. With one final look around the deserted home, Alex walked out and headed off. Leaping up and over the tall fence, he landed in a yard almost identical to the one he'd been in, these neat little homes in rows that marked the division between the Old Town and the Docklands. Alex knew from Kyle's memories he'd believed he was close to Alyssa's location right before he'd been distracted by the bloodlust.

Now the true search could begin. Alex didn't expect he'd find the lair of the League of Skulls tonight, but he knew he'd made a good start. He'd also been correct in visiting the sights of the kills that Kyle had made with Alyssa and the place of that final slaughter he'd made before slamming his barriers up and running away. They had all helped him piece together the fragmented memories he'd gained from Kyle. Kyle had run away from Alyssa on pure instinct; before that he'd been trying to track her hiding place down.

Alex sat on his perch on the roof of an inn. He glanced at the horizon and grimaced; dawn was not far off. Still, he felt he'd made good headway tonight and had found at least one likely hideout for members of the League of Skulls. He was in an area he knew well since it housed several inns, bars and houses of pleasure—right on the edge of the markets and general business district. Not the worst part of town, but not the best either. The shops his sister would attend, if she was so inclined, were on the other side of the Old Town, in a small section that had been redeveloped and had some exclusive merchants. The area was all the rage amongst the High Lords and Ladies of the court, or at least the ones who could afford it.

Alex grinned in memory. There was also a respectable bar that his father and brother would much rather he frequented instead of his usual establishments here in Docks Row or The Quarter where he ended up when he was at his worst, although he hadn't been back since the abduction attempt. Alex returned his attention to the trio of men.

Nondescript, the type of men you'd be hard pressed to give much of a description of afterwards. Their height, their features, their clothes—all of it was similar to what he was wearing right now. Although despite appearances his own, he suspected, was of much better quality. At odds with their overall appearance, their weapons were of unusual quality and they bore on their person a surprising amount of them. Alex stopped himself from snorting out loud; he was likely bearing more arms right now than they were and than Kyle did when he was out on the hunt.

Still, Alex was certain if he could check them out closer they would bear the Skull tattoos on their bodies. Alex had never worked out why the Skull's mercenaries insisted on branding themselves with the distinctive tattoos that gave away their profession and allegiance to the shadier dealings in the Realm to anyone who spotted them. Still, these three were well covered and Alex couldn't make out if they bore them or not from this distance. Alex grinned as he watched all three walk into a seedy bar called The Brothers Arms; it was a bar he'd been in himself a time or two. Glancing again at the horizon, Alex figured he had just over an hour before dawn hit and the bar would close its doors.

Alex figured they were having drinks before heading to their hideout for the night. Either that, or the entrance to their hideout was accessed from the bar. Deciding what to do, he rose and walked around the side of the inn and dropped into a darkened lane on the other side. Walking forward, he didn't pause but dropped the shadows from himself as he walked from the shadowed lane, across the road and through the doors of The Brothers Arms. Alex kept his hood up, but in this place it wasn't so unusual—half the clientele did. He couldn't risk being recognised, although given everyone knew he was at the Summer Palace with the rest of the Royal Court, they most likely would discount it, even if they thought he looked like the King's youngest son.

Alex was glad he knew the bar well. He paused as he walked through the doors, although his eyes scanned the room and picked up his targets at a table in the far rear corner of the dimly lit, yet spotless bar. Or it would be spotless if it was at the start of the night, rather than the end of it. Still, few in the court would have ever believed the disreputable bar not only was clean but had some of the finest ale in the city.

Alex moved to the corner of the bar and perched on one of the empty stools where he could see both the doors and his targets. He leaned and rested his back against the wooden wall and slumped as if he'd had a long night, which was the truth, only he wasn't exhausted. Taking coins from his pouch, he slid them onto the bar toward the barkeep and was rewarded with a mug of the town's finest brew. Kyle would kill him when he found out Alex had been here without him. Alex took a long swallow of his beer and sighed. He placed the mug on the bar before snagging the hand of the bar wench he knew from his previous visits.

"Ah, Vicki, it's been way too long."

He pulled the unresisting woman into his arms and kissed her, vowing Amelia could never find out or she would kill him. As Vicki drew away from the kiss, her eyes widened in recognition. She leaned into him, her hand trailing up his chest and he heard her breathy voice whispering in his ear.

"Alex, what are you doing here? It's not safe." Vicki drew back and her green eyes stared into his own.

It reminded Alex why he'd spent more than one night in her company. Alex laughed and drew her onto his lap and kissed her again, holding her in place.

"Mmm, I've been busy of late. The men in the far corner, are they regulars?" Turning his mind to business, he glanced briefly to his targets.

Vicki threw back her head and laughed as if he'd said something funny before resting her head on his shoulder.

"Yes. Most nights they come in—before you ask, they always leave just before we close and head toward the back of the Siren, down the street."

With that, Vicki pulled his head down and gave him a lingering kiss that Alex admitted he enjoyed too much. She slipped off his lap with a giggle and he let her go as though unwilling to do so. Alex sat and was rewarded when one of the men pulled off his gloves and he saw the silver Skull ring on his finger. He saw a flash of the trail of Skulls across the back of his hand before it disappeared, hidden by his shirt.

Having the information he wanted for the night, Alex finished his brew and, pushing two more coins across the bar toward Vicki, he nodded to the barkeep and left. Alex looked down the road and spied the Siren but turned and walked down one of the side lanes.

Alex considered his options and the light touching the horizon and swore. He turned and watched the entrance of The Brothers Arms and was rewarded as the three men walked from the bar. They paused just out the entrance and scanned up and down before the three of them turned and, as Vicki said they would, headed toward the Siren. Considering his options, Alex closed his eyes then climbed to the rooftops and made his way to a vantage point where he could just make out the rear yard of the Siren. There was a small, dilapidated building leaning up against the rock wall at the back of the building he'd never noticed. Of course, on the occasions he'd frequented the Siren, he hadn't been inclined to explore the back yard.

A smile touched Alex's lips as he saw his quarry enter the back yard of the Siren and with a final glance around they disappeared into the building.

A lex cursed; he wanted to explore now he knew where his targets had entered. He guessed that the small shack leaning up against what was the old stone wall of the city was the entrance to wherever the League of Skulls called home. Or, at the very least, it was where those men who were Disciples of the Skull called home. If that was the case, he'd only have to follow them—they'd soon head to their master's lair.

Still, Alex knew either way the men were about to bed down for the day. He also knew if he didn't get back to the palace soon that they'd likely send Jess out to look for him. He didn't want that to happen since it would leave Kyle unguarded by anyone who could access the power of the veil. He didn't want to assume that Alyssa was the only one within the ranks of the League of Skulls that had the Taint. She had quite clearly been able to access the palace and get past the normal guards. Although if they did have another as skilled as Alyssa, he doubted they would be able to get past Jess. If Kyle hadn't been so shaken, Alex knew she wouldn't get past him either but Kyle had to learn to trust himself and his own judgement again.

Resisting his desire to investigate, Alex pulled himself onto the shadowed paths and concentrated on his room in the Summer Palace. He found it interesting that it was always quicker heading to somewhere that he knew well, versus a vague memory of a location. Then again, maybe it was faster going back to the palace because he was relying on his own memory, not one he'd gleaned from someone else, as on the way out. Regardless of the reason, he ended up looking at his own room; he found William sitting in one of his chairs, sipping what Alex guessed was coffee, waiting for him.

Taking a steadying breath, Alex left the Shadowed Path and walked into his own room.

William looked up at him, startled. "Damn it, Alex, no matter how many times I see you do that you scare the life out of me every time. It's uncanny."

Alex chuckled, only now realising how tired he was. "Sorry, William, I'm not sure there is any other way for me to do it. I think the servants would be even more startled than you if I left the shadow paths out there instead of in here."

Alex slipped the hood of his cloak off his head and undid the tie, throwing it over the back of a couch. He then stripped off his vest, disposing it on top of the cloak. He walked around and almost collapsed onto the lounge, pulling a pillow under his head.

"I know you're tired, Alex, so I'll let you get some sleep. You can brief me when you wake so I've got something to report to Father. How did it go?" William sat, waiting for Alex to gather his thoughts.

"It was a long night, but I've tracked at least three Skulls Disciples to what I believe is their daytime sleeping place. I won't know if it is just theirs or the entrance to the lair for the League of Skulls itself until I do a little more digging. I'll head back tonight and explore when most of the occupants are off pursuing other interests." Alex turned his head and cracked his eyes open to see if he'd given enough information to satisfy his brother.

William stood and shook his head. "I'm still not sure this is a good idea, Alex, but I understand why you are doing it. Just show common sense and caution. We'll speak again tonight before you go out."

Alex grimaced and sat up, hauling off his boots. "I'm sorry, William, but I have to do this." He rose and placed his hand on his brother's shoulder. "I'll be careful. I promise."

William looked at him with a serious expression on his face before nodding and heading out the door.

Alex shook his head and headed to his bathing room to clean up.

He made short work of his bath before he headed to his bed and collapsed. Groaning, he pulled up the covers, rolling over onto his side. He was asleep almost before he'd completed the action.

32

TREASON

Jess dressed in her comfortable hunting attire, one set without the crest of the Fourth on it, and grimaced. It had taken a few days to decide on the perfect way to follow up on the information that Damien had provided. It was Tuesday night and Alex had gone off on a pursuit of his own. She hoped he wasn't out hunting down Sundered by himself; she should track him down and go with him, but had decided this was more important. Kyle was distracted, with Elizabeth.

That meant she was free to try to follow up on the information she'd gained on Daniel and the guard, Baine. Jess didn't know what to think of the information but hoped it proved to be wrong. If Daniel had been involved, she hated to think of Alex's reaction when he found out. Jess closed her eyes. Worse, if Daniel was involved, what did William, Elizabeth or his father know? She had to know if he'd acted with their knowledge.

She shook her head; it may be nothing. She knew what Damien had reported to her did not prove anything. The guardsman who went by the same name and fit the description of the man who'd organised the kidnapping, well, it could be an unfortunate coincidence. At least that was what she was hoping, despite some things she'd seen and heard. Things she'd dismissed in the past as her imagination pointed in a direction she didn't like at all.

Daniel had always been harsh toward Alex, his pleasant smile dropping when he thought no one would notice. She got the distinct impression he blamed Alex for their mother's death. He almost seemed jealous of Alex's popularity, with the guards, with the courtiers and commoners alike, although Alex courted none of it. Alex was better than his siblings with the blade by a long shot. William and Elizabeth laughed it off, but Daniel had killed himself trying to prove he was better in the last training session he'd attended with them all. He'd failed and had looked like a fool even though Alex had held back—that made it worse. There were times he was almost hostile in his responses. Many small things that by themselves didn't mean much; she'd always discounted it as sibling rivalry.

Jess pulled her wandering thoughts aside and transitioned to the Veiled World, drawing in power from all the different strands she could see. The real world faded, her path stretching where she willed it. She moved down the path but only a short distance, to the small private courtyard off the Royal Wing. She waited, watching. She realised she would be pleased if this Tuesday night, Daniel didn't leave the palace.

The real world was pale, like she was looking at it through a lens or window, almost flickering in and out of focus depending on her concentration and how much power she drew. Jess drew in her breath, shocked despite herself, as the doors opened and Daniel made an appearance with Baine a step behind. Both men mounted the waiting horses and quietly left the palace grounds, heading into town. Jess followed with ease; speed, distance, even how time seemed to function, was different in the Veiled World.

It wasn't long before they arrived in town and Jess tracked them to an old mansion on the river. Jess waited for them to go inside then dropped back into the real world, although she kept the power gathered around her, obscuring her from the casual observer. Jess heard greetings coming from inside the house and walked up to one window with light spilling from it, careful not to make a sound. She cursed that it was problematic to appear inside a premises she hadn't been in before; they'd been warned that if they weren't careful, they could appear halfway through a wall. Jess didn't understand why but she trusted her uncle's assessment to abide by the restrictions.

Jess knew she wasn't as good at this as Kyle, then again, she wasn't all that bad either. She stood shadowed by a large tree with a line of sight into the old mansion. It took no time at all before Daniel made an appearance and greeted the other men and women in the room like they were long-lost friends. Jess frowned and tried to move her position but couldn't quite see the woman's face, only the edge of her skirt. Although her voice sounded familiar, Jess just couldn't place it. Baine stood out of the way by the door. While she couldn't hear all the conversation she could catch enough of it, enough to make her heart sink, for anger to grow, emotion flaring the more she heard.

Daniel had been involved in arranging the kidnap attempt and Baine had helped. They had meant to kill or capture Alex, Kyle and herself, due to the Taint they all bore. Their plans had been thrown into disorder when the rescue occurred. They were planning to try again; this time Daniel was planning to take a more direct action than he did the previous time. She gathered that whatever was in the bottle that Daniel had been given was the same toxin they were dosed with last time. Jess shuddered at the memory of the effect the stuff had on all of them.

Jess withdrew, shaking and pale as the meeting appeared to break

CATHERINE M WALKER

up with no other clear goals she could understand being set. She needed time to think on what she would do, how to react.

Daniel dismounted in the enclosed yard of the old rundown house, looking around uncomfortably. He knew if anyone saw him it would be questioned why he was here. Shaking off the feeling with a snort, he realised it was unlikely that anyone would recognise him here. That was one thing he'd learned from his disgrace of a brother. People wouldn't expect to see him here so would discount his resemblance to 'Prince Daniel'. After all, what would the Prince, of all people, be doing here? Waiting as his man, Baine, dealt with their horses, he looked around once more to be sure he couldn't see anyone then headed up the stairs to the decrepit building, entering without pause when the doors were opened. He walked through without needing a guide. Entering the old study, he smiled, seeing Scholar Clements.

"Scholar Clements, while it's good to see you, the risk is too great. You should not have come." Daniel hugged the old man, his fragility scaring him.

"Nonsense, Daniel, no more than you, should your father or brother learn of your involvement in our cause." Scholar Clements smiled at Daniel as he helped the old man back to his seat before taking one himself.

"I had to come as soon as I learned you were here, although I can't stay long or I risk being missed. After recent events, everything is being reported on." Daniel grimaced. "I know my father will be notified by someone that I have left the palace."

Creswell Vannen stirred in his chair. "You're not the only one here taking risks, Daniel." He stopped, wide-eyed as Baine surged forward and hauled him out of his chair by his shirt front.

374

"Watch your mouth, Vannen, you'll address His Highness as befitting his rank." With a final shake, Baine shoved the now-quivering lord back into his chair. Vannen looked around at the others in the room and realised from their blank expressions he'd get no backup from any of them.

Scholar Clements smiled and raised a hand. "Calm down, everything will work out. We've lost several assets; Alyssa will be missed, yet she laid the ground work. So have you all." He paused, looking around the group, assuring himself that he had their attention. "I believe at least one of our targets, Lord Kyle, has been given enough of the medication and with the grooming that Alyssa has started it won't take much for us to gain control of him. We simply need the opportunity." Clements eyed Daniel.

Daniel stirred in his chair. "What do you need of me?"

"Can you slip him more of the medication?" Clements picked up a bottle that had been sitting on the side table next to him, unnoticed, passing it to Daniel.

"I'm not sure. Not right away; he's under the healers' care right now and either Alex or Jess is with him all the time. I'll do what I can; if the opportunity presents itself, I'll send Baine with word, if I manage it." Daniel looked at the bottle, holding it with care.

"You and Baine have done more than your fair share, Daniel. The amount of work you and Baine put in to arrange the kidnapping, even though it failed, will not be in vain. Your idea to make it seem like the League of Skulls were behind it to throw off the scent was a genius move. We will succeed in taking your brother and his friends under control." It was rare for Kevin to speak up for their gatherings but Daniel knew he was another one of Clements' special people he'd brought with him.

The man made Daniel uncomfortable, yet he didn't quite know why. He trusted Clements, so he should trust the old man's assertions that everyone here was trustworthy. Clements had once been his tutor, long ago, before he left the King's service. His father had dismissed him for trying to teach Daniel about the Order. Daniel had never understood his father on that score and had set out to learn more. As far as he was concerned, the Order were the only ones trying to do something about the upsurge of the Sundered who slaughtered their people.

A third member of their group stirred. "Are we sure this will work? I tried to get my hands on the girl, but your father stopped me." Lady Barraclough glared at Daniel, still smarting at the fact that the King had banished her from court.

Daniel stood and walked across, kissing Lady Barraclough's hand. "I'm sorry for my father's high-handed treatment of you, My Lady. It was a good thought; if you'd managed to get your hands on Jess, both Alex and Kyle would have followed, getting them away from the extra protection the palace affords." Daniel smiled as she preened, yet he thought Lady Barraclough was a simpering fool. Jess would not have complied with her demands even without his father's intervention. Using violence while the King was present had been beyond foolish.

"Enough. Do your best to dose them all again but if no one else, just Lord Kyle. But do not risk yourself, Daniel. You are too important to our cause, placed as you are in the King's Court and council. You should go before you are missed, my boy." Scholar Clements went to stand but Daniel placed a restraining hand on his shoulder.

"No, old man, keep your seat. We'll make our own way out. I will do my best to dose them all and let you know." Daniel turned, walking toward the door before pausing and glancing back, a feral grin on his face, his eyes glittering. "I will try to time it for when they leave the palace for a hunt; there are plenty at this time of the year and those three always go off on their own—that should give the best opportunity."

Scholar Clements laughed. "That would be perfect if you could arrange it that way."

Daniel nodded in satisfaction, leaving the house without a backwards glance, taking the time to secure the precious bottle in the saddle bag before mounting and riding back to the palace.

J ess watched as Daniel left then looked back at the study, indecisive for a moment. Then her desire to find out who the woman was, or at least see her face for future reference won out. The voice was nagging at her, making her wonder if, like Vannen and Daniel, she was a member of the court. If so, she needed to know who the woman was. Given the way Daniel was going and his comments on leaving, it was likely he was heading straight back to the palace. That meant she could afford the time to wait and see the face of the other conspirator. With the decision made, she settled down to wait. As a hunter, one virtue she had in abundance was patience. Looking around, she spotted the carriage sitting out in the street, the doors open with the driver just visible sitting inside waiting.

Jess stirred as before too long a servant appeared at the door; he whistled and waved to attract the attention of the carriage driver. She glanced toward the carriage as the driver climbed out of the dark interior, illuminated in the flare of light from the lamps at the gate. Jess felt her eyes widen; she knew if anyone could see her they would have seen the colour drain from her face in shock. She squeezed her eyes shut, her head shaking in denial.

No, please let this be a mistake.

Jess heard the carriage draw into the courtyard, the distinct sound as the driver jumped down, his booted feet connecting with the cobbles, the creak of the carriage door showing it had been opened. Then the unmistakable sound of the ancient door groaning on its hinges, the rustle of skirts with the dainty clip of court shoes as the woman exited the house.

Jess forced herself to open her eyes and see the face of the woman who had been plotting to harm her and her friends, the woman who had committed treason. Instant recognition slammed into her like a physical blow as the woman turned her head, face visible in the lamplight. Their conversation floating across to her as they walked to the waiting carriage.

"Scholar Clements, you know best but if Daniel ever finds out the Order were responsible for hunting down and killing his mother, he will turn on us all. He idolised her as a child. He still does now."

"Leave handling Daniel to me, Lady Barraclough. The queen was one of the Tainted, our hand in her death has never surfaced, we cleaned up the scene well." The old man paused, his expression firm and commanding. "Her death drove Daniel into our fold, let him have his untarnished memory of her."

Scholar Clements stared at Lady Barraclough until she nodded accent to his will. Satisfied, the scholar walked forward, closing the last of the distance to the carriage. The lady grabbed a handful of her skirts in one hand with the old scholar assisting her into the carriage, kissing her fingers as she withdrew inside, although not before Jess could see the blush that spread up her cheeks as the door closed, hiding her from view.

As the carriage drew away, disappearing out of the guttering pool of light thrown by the lamps, and down the dark street, Jess sank to her knees, in shock. Her own mother's involvement in the plot, her hatred left her bewildered. She pressed a hand to her lips, eyes wide wondering how she would break this news to Alex. That his brother was involved was bad enough. To find out that the Order had also been behind his mother's death, she knew he would react badly. Blood would flow as soon as he found out; being Alex's brother would not save Daniel's life.

33

DECENT

Once again, Alex lay on a rooftop overlooking the backyard of the Siren and the dilapidated shack that the men had disappeared into the previous morning. Alex pulled on the power of the veil, just enough to conceal him if anyone looked in his direction. He grimaced as pain exploded in his head but kept the groan from passing his lips. Alex knew he'd been drawing on more of the power than he should, but circumstances just seemed to transpire of late where it was required.

He winced as his shields slipped, if only for a moment, and the clamouring voices beat through his brain wanting to pull him in different directions. Before they—and Alex believed it was a 'they'—could understand what he was up to, he raised his mental barriers once again with substantial effort and a grimace of pain. Still, he managed it and the voices at least receded but he could still feel them beating at his shields now they had found him. He blocked them.

Alex wondered if it was wise to continue on with his plans for the night given the state his own mind was in, then pushed his doubts aside. He was just going to check out the shack and see if it led to the Skulls' main lair. That was it. The occupants, if it was an entrance to the main lair, would all be out for the night, which is why he was waiting even though he'd seen groups of men leave already.

Alex smiled. He didn't quite know why he persisted in thinking this disreputable shack might just be a shack. He'd seen at least nine men leave already, which seemed way more than could live in such a small place. Still, until he'd investigated, he wouldn't jump to conclusions. He glanced around to see if anyone was looking in his direction and when he was satisfied that no one was paying any attention at all, he pushed his own discomfort aside and slipped from the roof to the courtyard below. Wrapping the surrounding veil to mask his presence, Alex moved across the courtyard to the door of the hut. Using just a little more power, Alex felt around but could not pick up any signs that there was anyone inside the premises.

Taking a breath, Alex eased the door open and went inside, shutting the door when he discovered no one on the other side. Alex inspected the shack; it was rudimentary at best. There was a single rough-looking bed against the far wall with a threadbare blanket that had seen better days thrown over it. A small wooden table and chair in the middle of the room. Off to one side, there was what passed for a kitchen that looked like it hadn't been used for years as it was coated with dust, and a set of shelves against the wall. It was as he thought. There was no way that the nine men he'd seen leaving this place could have all slept here, and they were also not enjoying a meal together.

Moving across the room with care, Alex inspected the shelves first. They didn't contain that much other than some battered-looking, dust-covered pots, chipped plates and some metal goblets. Not a sign of any food or any use at all.

Looking around again, he realised that the old town wall formed the back of the shack so he moved over toward the bed. Alex realised that the bed was a little more solid than it had first appeared, with a firm wooden base. He frowned, looking at the drape hanging on the wall behind the bed, then smiled. Why would there be a drape hanging up on a wall when there could not be a window? Alex stood on top of the bed until he was certain it would hold his weight. Relieved, he let out his breath when he didn't crash through the bed. Alex stepped forward and drew the drapes to one side. He chuckled, seeing the old wooden door behind the drapes. Stepping forward, Alex placed his ear up against the door and tried to listen for any noise while he used his power to search for any presence on the other side.

While he could detect that there were people nearby, he knew they were far enough away that they were not on the opposite side of the door. Taking a deep breath, Alex opened the door and eased inside, closing it gently behind him. Fascinated despite the circumstances, Alex found himself in a corridor that seemed to be within the old wall. He walked down the corridor, using small bursts of power to mask his presence as he went.

It seemed like hours passed as he wound his way through the corridors, ducking into small alcoves when he sensed or heard anyone near him. It surprised him that his eyes got used to the dark cobbled passageways, there were lights placed sporadically along them which he learned not to look directly at since it ruined his night vision. The temperature had grown distinctly cooler, like the vast caverns under the palace that housed, among other things, the wine collection. He'd never realised that a whole world seemed to exist below the city and suspected that its inhabitants had expanded the network of passageways and rooms beneath the city. At one point, he'd been forced to draw his dagger and slit the throat of one man who had stumbled onto him. A part of his brain knew he should be concerned about that —and that he was so calm about killing the man. Yet he wasn't. The other, analytical part of his brain knew the man had been a cutthroat and had the Skull tattoos and weapons to prove it.

Alex also knew he was now passing through winding passages and rooms beneath the city itself. Some rooms bore signs they were lived in, although he'd been correct in his first assumption that most of the residents of these warrens were out and about on their Lord's business tonight.

Alex paused as he made his way through the passageways and tunnels heading toward a presence he could feel. He knew somehow that the presence belonged to the person he was seeking: the Skull Lord. If it wasn't the Skull Lord, then he knew whoever it was wouldn't be far from the person he sought. Alex lost count of the members of the League of Skulls he dispatched on his way through the warren. Beyond ten, he stopped counting as it didn't seem to be important. While Alex could feel the burning anger bubbling inside he didn't think it was the same he recalled from Kyle's memories. Unlike Kyle, Alex wasn't sickened by what he was doing and knew in this place and time he was the one in control and making the conscious choice to kill those who stood in his way.

Kyle only had limited flashback memories of his actions when he'd succumbed to rage and slaughtered people. While at first, he seemed remote from his own actions, he'd then been sickened by what he'd done when he came back to himself. Alex didn't have to come back to himself; he wasn't sickened. He didn't seem to care anything about the people that stood in his way.

A part of his brain recognised that this was not normal. That he should be sickened, he should care. He knew normal people would care. As he moved through the underground lair, a part of his brain continued to puzzle out what had changed and what was wrong.

Alex paused, knowing there was someone coming, and flattened up against the rough, cool rock wall, drawing power to him to conceal his presence, at least until it was too late for the person approaching. Alex could tell that this man also had power but in smaller quantities than what he possessed himself. It was possible he would detect Alex's presence, although somehow Alex doubted it. His experience so far had shown him that while the members of the League of Skulls had access to rudimentary power, they were not proficient at using it.

Alex found he was holding his breath as the man came closer and, with a smile, released his breath and began to breathe again. It wouldn't do if he passed out from lack of oxygen in this place. It would also be a little embarrassing to have to admit later on, as he was sure something like that would come out. The embarrassing stuff always did.

The man was close enough now and Alex could see the Skull ring on his finger and the Skull tattoo across his hand, winding all the way up his arm to disappear under the shoulder of his vest. Looking at him, Alex noted the weapons he carried on his person and smiled. Alex waited until the man passed him with no indication he knew of the presence of another in the tunnel with him. Alex lurched himself forward, grabbing a fistful of the man's hair, pulling his head back with one strong yank while he drew his knife viciously across the man's throat. It was over in moments and Alex let the man drop to the floor.

Alex knelt and wiped his blade on the vest of his fallen adversary and, without knowing why, removed his Skull ring and placed it in the inner pocket of his vest for safe keeping. You never could tell how and when something might come in useful. Still, if he had his way, this was one chapter of the thieves league that would, if it existed at all, be a headless snake and left in a state of disorder after he'd dealt with the Skull Lord. At least for a space of time until someone else rose up to fill the power vacuum his death would create. They might even learn a lesson to leave those who ruled this land in peace. Alex well knew that in the past as long as their excesses were not too bad, it was deemed beneficial to leave them be. After all, that way they knew who to watch.

However, the guild here in the capital had gone through a change of late and grown bolder. Attempts on the life of a high-ranking lord, let alone a Prince of the Realm, even the youngest son, had been unheard of in the past. It was yet another thing that continued to puzzle him. It really didn't fit the League's past behaviour. Alex hopped it was something the mysterious Skull Lord could clear up, before he died.

Alex smiled and continued on his way without a backwards glance at the dead mercenary.

A lex paused, closing his eyes, although it was more out of habit than need at this point. He could feel those of power around him these days without even having to concentrate. They were like bright sparks in his consciousness, although one was much stronger than all the others but seemed to cut in and out, as if the individual was concentrating on something else. Alex paused. His eyes flew open. So his target knew he was coming. His adversary was giving away his location because he was concentrating on tracking his progress through the underground lair.

He paused. The Skull Lord knew he was coming and was tracking his progress—he no longer needed to hide. Alex smiled self-depreciatingly; so much for a surprise attack. Although he kept the shadows pulled around him to mask his presence, he had no illusions. He was expected. He wondered what the Skull Lord had in store for him.

Alex reacted even before he realised what it was he was reacting to, then he saw it, that shadowed movement that triggered his own reaction, and his blade met the other's blade. Alex grinned in anticipation and pulled in more of the veil, concentrating; his opponent was good. Pushing aside the growing ache in his head that seemed to be now spreading throughout his body as well, Alex lost himself in the fight, grateful that his old bumbling real-world self seemed to be banished somewhere. Or perhaps those who had been interfering had given up. Of course, he didn't know who they were, or why, but he couldn't shake the feeling that someone had been interfering. Alex chuckled despite his current activity; perhaps that belief was just a sign of impending madness. No matter the reason, he was grateful. With the increase in power, he saw his opponent's movements and found that he was matching them.

Alex felt a rush of power and had a moment of concern, then grinned when he felt a presence he recognised. *Kyle.*

Alex felt his friend gather his own power and knew what he intended. Alex sparred a moment and sent a shaft of power back down that bond between them.

No, Kyle, brother, you are hurt. It's too late for me. Stay!

Alex didn't have the time to spare for Kyle after that. He knew that Kyle watched still, although he knew he would stay out of this fight at least; right now, his friend needed time to heal. He also gathered his friend would have a few words to say to him on his return to the palace. Pushing that distraction aside, Alex continued with his fight. Grinning, he pulled the surrounding power to him and in that moment his attacker was visible, a shocked expression on his face. Alex raised his main sword and blocked the blade of his enemy, then plunged his long dagger up into the man's heart.

"How—?" The blade slipped from the gifted thug's lifeless hands and he crumpled, lifeless, onto the cold stone floor, his sword clattering next to him.

Alex stood for a moment, looking at the man he had battled, waiting to feel something—anything—as he knew he should. He didn't. Alex was wondering if, despite what they had all thought, it wasn't a deep madness and rage that affected the Sundered. He wondered if it was this *coldness*. This lack of compassion. He idly knew that yes, he was angry, in pain, yet he hadn't killed the men in the Skulls Lair due to that. He'd killed them because they'd been in his way. Unlike what Kyle had suffered, he didn't feel guilty in the slightest and he wasn't suffering from fragmenting control and didn't believe he'd suffer the blackouts either.

Alex shrugged and pushed aside his contemplation of the Sundered. It could wait until tonight was finished.

A lex walked on down the corridor, knowing, sensing, that no one else was coming to confront him, still feeling that malevolent presence although now he knew it was close. He could also tell it didn't fear him. Whoever the person was, they were waiting for him.

Alex found himself at the end of the corridor facing a door. He knew stealth was unnecessary given that whoever was beyond the door knew he was coming and seemed to be waiting for him. Alex was about to open the door when it opened of its own accord. A cloaked figure stood there looking at him.

"Your Highness. My master bid you welcome and asks that you come inside. No one will seek to harm you. You have his word." The man's voice was steady and well spoken, much like the servants in the palace.

Alex took in the palatial hallway with signs of wealth decorating the walls and wondered which of the Lord's town estates he had made his way to. It had to be one of them, he just couldn't fathom which one. Then again it could be one of the wealthy merchant's or even a total unknown; Alex shook his head, he'd find out soon enough who was in charge. Still, if it was one of the lords, it would have to be one of the minor lords since all the major ones had moved along with the court to the Summer Palace. Alex laughed at that, remembering he was at the Summer Palace, yet here he was back in Vallantia, about to walk into the den of a man who had been trying to kidnap himself and his friends.

Alex acknowledged the man as he walked in, sheathing his blades, taking the servant at his master's word. Still, Alex knew he didn't need the sword to kill the servant if it came to that. He paused, allowing the man to close the door and lead the way though the corridor and up a flight of stairs through yet another door into the house. Alex paid little attention to his surroundings, except to note he wasn't even familiar with them, therefore it wasn't the residence of any of his contemporaries. He could feel that Kyle was still following, and that he didn't recognise the place either.

The servant stood at the entryway to what Alex gathered was a meeting room and gestured for him to enter but made no move to follow. Alex paid no mind at all to the door closing behind him—

it wasn't like he needed the door to get out and back to his rooms at the Summer Palace anyhow.

Alex looked up and froze as he recognised the figure sitting, relaxed, on the other side of the room.

"Welcome, little brother. I judge it won't be long before you join our rather select ranks. I was honestly expecting Lord Kyle to be the one who showed up on my doorstep."

34

NOT AS IT SEEMS

A lex shuddered at the man in front of him calling him 'little brother', along with the inference he would join the Sundered ranks soon, the phrase causing his memory to flash back to that time so long ago—his mother's death. He tightened his grip and went to lunge, only to feel himself slam into a barrier that formed between him and the Skull Lord. Alex struggled against the restraint.

"Relax, Alex, I mean you no harm. You are powerful; you will grow, and it's likely your power will outstrip mine in time, but for now you are running on instinct." The Lord gestured to a chair where a goblet of wine sat on a low table next to it. "Please, sit down. I imagine you have questions; you didn't have to kill so many of my men, you know. My name is Simon."

Alex felt sweat bead on his forehead as he struggled against the barrier before he conceded that he would not get through it. He glared at the man in front of him, then nodded. His mind shied away from acknowledging that this man had been a contemporary of his uncle. Or at least he looked just like the man in his dream about his uncle and friends saving the woman with the baby. He even had the same name that his uncle had used to refer to him in the dream. Simon.

Feeling and seeing the barrier dissipate as fast as it had appeared, Alex walked and sat in the chair opposite the Skull Lord. Not hurrying, he glanced at the mug on the table next to him. Shrugging his shoulders, he picked it up and sipped, his eyes never leaving his host as he did so.

Pushing his dreams aside, Alex asked. "Why did you try to kidnap me and my friends?" Alex knew he was being a little blunt, but he didn't have the patience for much else right now.

Simon sighed, his smile fading. "Straight to the point, I see." He paused, picking up his own wine, and sipped. "I didn't try to have you kidnapped, Alex. What need would I have for that?"

Alex shook his head. "I don't know what I want to know. I killed your assassin when she came after Kyle again. It's why I came here."

Simon frowned. "My assassin? I haven't sent an assassin after Lord Kyle. I wouldn't be that stupid. If I wanted Lord Kyle dead, I would have killed him myself."

Alex absorbed Simon's assertion; he wanted to disbelieve the man sitting opposite him, but somehow he didn't.

"Alyssa wasn't sent by you?" Alex flashed back to a memory from the battle with the female assassin in the ballroom at the palace and projected it at Simon, knowing he would see it.

"No, that poor unfortunate soul was not one of mine." Simon considered Alex for a moment before continuing. "There are more Kin around than you know of, Alex; I will see if I can find out any information about her for you. That is how we refer to ourselves, Alex, as Kin. Sundered is a rather derogatory term and misguided."

Alex felt his eyes widen.

"You're Sundered—sorry, Kin—I can feel it and there was your little display earlier. What are you doing here in charge of the League of Skulls?" Alex had relaxed despite himself; if Simon had wanted him dead then he could have done so already.

Simon smiled, picked up the bottle of wine on the side table next to him and walked across to top up Alex's glass before returning to his own chair to refill his own.

"In this era, those who survive the transition to become Kin give up their old lives." Simon raised one eyebrow at him. "People notice that you are not ageing after some time; your old life has to die, after that we tend to move around. For now, I am the Skull Lord, I can help a few of our kind who escape and, if it's not too late, help them through the transition. I was a thief more years ago than I care to think about, so I guess you could say I'm doing what I know. It placed me ideal to keep an eye on you and your friends."

Alex let the silence stretch between them for a moment while he thought through what he'd learned. For his part, Simon wasn't the least bit uncomfortable with Alex's regard.

"I had a dream about my uncle; you were in it." Alex heard the faintly disbelieving tone in his own voice. Despite everything, he was still struggling to believe it all.

Simon smiled. "Yes, Alex, I knew your Uncle Edward, and Cal and Kat."

Alex stared at Simon, struggling with his own disbelief, yet somehow he did believe him and regretfully let go of his initial plan to kill the man. If he was honest with himself, Simon's little display of power when he'd walked in made him doubt that he could kill the self-styled Skull Lord.

K yle sat in a sitting room at the Fourth's Complex, watching as Alex paced, agitated. Still, Kyle knew Alex would tell him what the issue was eventually. Jess, for her part, seemed fine; if it was anyone else, they might even believe it. Kyle could feel the waves of distress coming from her. He tried to block both out of his mind, yet wasn't successful. He found he was more susceptible now after what Alyssa had done to him.

Alex turned, accepting the drink that Miranda handed him. Kyle watched as she moved around the room serving both Jess and himself as well before leaving them all through a side door. Alex sipped his drink, walking to the large windows that led to a private courtyard. He stood watching the garden in the fading light before he spoke. Filling them both in on all he'd discovered, he didn't even hold back on finding the place where Kyle had killed the family. Kyle had closed his eyes, a pang of guilt assailing him, but kept his silence. He knew all of that had been at Alyssa's prompting. Still, it had been his fault she had managed to get through his barriers and into his mind.

He finished recounting his meeting with Simon, the Skull Lord. Kyle shook his head, almost laughing, since while Alex had gone there intending to kill the Skull Lord, he seemed to have left with a good impression. Kyle had followed most of the encounter so wasn't surprised at any of the story but knew Jess had been busy with other pursuits she had been keeping close to her chest, excluding them both. He watched her as Alex detailed what he knew about the Killiam Order from Aaron, and his belief that they were the next place they should look for answers.

Jess jumped at the mention of the Order and paled. He looked at Alex, who had come out of his introspection and noticed how shaken she was.

"Come on, Jess, it's obvious you know something." Kyle watched as she closed her eyes and buried her face in her hands for a moment.

Jess sat back, swallowed, and pulled them both inside the memory of her investigations, starting with her conversation with Damien and finishing up with the woman coming out of the house and the final conversation. In that memory, they could see, hear and feel everything Jess had.

It didn't take long for Kyle to understand why she had been so shaken. He stood and walked to Alex, his hand on the shoulder of his friend.

"Alex?"

They all stood together, watching as the shadows in the empty, overgrown garden lengthened. The guards on watch on lookouts on the wall threw shadows that eerily matched those of the statues who still stood guard around his mother's tomb, still visible in the fading light. The silence stretched between as they each processed what they had learned.

"I don't understand why—why are they doing it?" Jess' voice was soft, the pain clear.

Alex spoke, his face hard. He still didn't turn from his mother's tomb.

"I don't care why. I will deal with him."

Kyle shook his head. "No, Alex, please leave it to us." Kyle stopped, his words freezing in his throat. Alex had shut down; cold, hard anger emanated from him.

"No, Kyle. He is mine. Lord Vannen is guilty of treason, as is Baine. Can you take care of them, Kyle?" Alex turned his gaze to

Kyle, waiting until his friend nodded then his gaze moved onto Jess, assessing her. "Do you want me to—"

"No. I'll handle it, she's mine." Jess turned her mind away from what she needed to do and concentrated on the pulsing flow of the veil, allowing it to calm her.

"What about that scholar?" Kyle asked, turning his gaze back to the garden.

"We'll track him down. I'm guessing that William will know where he is or how to find him, given he was dismissed from Father's service."

They made no further comment. They didn't need to. They stood waiting, watching the garden sink into darkness that was pushed back by the flare of torches from the top of the walls, casting an eerie, flickering light across the garden.

35

ALEX

Daniel rubbed the back of his neck and turned, his eyes widening in shock to see the hooded figure standing there, silent, watching him. Daniel swallowed, his mouth dry, and fear shot through him. His eyes darted to the door, knowing the guards were just on the other side. Still, as close as the person was to him, he doubted he would live long enough for the guards to get to him should the cloaked figure want him dead.

Daniel took a step back, hitting the wall behind him as the cloaked figure walked toward him, closing the distance between them. Fear washed through him, and he felt a sudden, sharp stabbing pain in his chest. Daniel looked down, not understanding as he saw the blade being pulled from his chest. The light died from his eyes as he slumped to the ground, dead.

The figure bent and cleaned the hunting knife on the Prince's cloak then stood, a hand reaching up to push the hood back. Alex stood, the burning anger he'd felt toward Daniel washing away, to be replaced by calmness.

Looking around his brother's room, he spotted the drink counter. He walked across to it, scanning the numerous bottles on the counter. His eyes narrowed as he spotted a nondescript brown bottle at the back of the cabinet. Grabbing it, he held it up to the light, smiling as he recognised it from Jess' memory. The poison they had already used once that his brother had intended to use again.

Alex turned, looking down on the dead body of his brother, knowing he should feel something—anything—at his death, yet somehow he felt empty. His brother had tried to have him and his friends killed or enslaved; he'd been a member of the Killiam Order. The same order that had killed his mother and made his life a living nightmare. A satisfied smile on his lips, he transitioned into the Veiled World, fading from view as he walked the shadow paths, leaving the dead body that had once been his brother to be found by the servants who would check in the morning.

Alex travelled through the Veiled World, the colours flickering around him. The real world he was passing by blurred, giving him his only sign of how fast he was moving. He felt as if his entire world was crushing in on him, his brain running and darting from one subject to another: his mother's death, the Sundered, his brother's broken dead body with the pool of blood spilling out on the floor.

Feeling the draw of the veil, Alex fled into the void, acting on instinct. Driven by anger, by pain, a feeling of abandonment and betrayal, he fled. Seeking another target, an outlet he knew must be out there somewhere. Then he could feel the presence he was looking for, as it flared in the distance, pulsing, dark and hateful.

Not sure what he was doing or how he was doing it, Alex waded through the void between the Veiled World and the real world. Forming a path, the world around him blurred further as his speed continued to increase. He allowed himself to be drawn, summoned to that malignant, mad presence he could feel, that sang to him though the veil.

H e paused in that void between the Realms; the real world settled and became distinct again.

He pulled the veil to him to mask his presence from the one below. A part of Alex's brain realised that this was how Kyle managed some of his kills—the art of the assassin, the veil hiding his presence from humans and, it seemed, Kin alike. Alex watched as the small child played, skipping small pebbles across the pond. Then he gasped as he felt the slight but unmistakable pull of the veil as the child extended the pebble's trajectory, bouncing it clear across the other side of the pond to hit the edge of a pier on the other side. A lot further than one small little boy should be able to skip a pebble. The small boy laughed in delight before turning and searching for another pebble to continue his game. The boy, Alex knew, was Kin, just like him.

Alex waited, knowing the presence that had drawn him here was nearby. Hiding still, just like he was. Then he sensed that small whooshing sound and his gaze shifted to the man who had appeared close to the child. He looked like a man, but Alex knew he was like him. From the feel of the emanations rolling off him, he was of the Sundered, and mad. Alex still waited, watching, feeling the anger build in him as the Sundered's intent became clear and he stalked up to the child who froze, his delight in his new skill leaking from him. The child knew, his eyes widening in fear as the Sundered drew his long, sharp hunting blade from its scabbard. He was holding the child in place using the veil in a way that Alex hadn't known was possible.

Unable to wait any longer, lost in his rage, Alex screamed and appeared in that place, pushing the child aside, his own blade coming up and blocking that of the Sundered. Using his momentum, Alex felt hate flood him and used this and the Sundered's shock to bring his dagger, that he hadn't realised he'd drawn, up through the chest of the Sundered, with a last push piercing the heart.

As the Sundered slumped to the ground, dead, Alex's eyes tracked up and caught the terrified child, who had been trying to edge his way from the clearing but froze again as Alex caught him. Alex felt the rage bubble up, snarling.

"My kill!" Alex screamed his rage out into the veil.

Alex paused, trying to push the pain and confusion of the increased power he suddenly had access to aside. The frozen, terrified child sparked a series of memories to flash into his mind. The images and sounds burned into his brain, one flashing though his mind's eye after the other.

His mother, with her throat slit, blood spurting, crumbling to the ground.

The image of the Sundered he'd stabbed in the clearing, seeing him start healing what should have been a fatal wound.

Then him in the bar on the anniversary of his mother's death, Kyle telling him that his mother had born the Taint.

Simon sitting there saying, "People notice that you are not ageing after some time, your old life has to die, after that we move around..."

His mother's tomb, the five cloaked faceless figures. The one female looking up, her delicate arm and hand reaching up toward where his room was. He knew the figure was female but the hood hid her face in its depths.

Alex, I'm sorry. Forgive me for leaving you. You'll be safer this way.

Then as she turned, a lamp flared, revealing the face in the hood for a brief moment before she disappeared. Into the veil.

Then back in the clearing as the guard picked him up, he caught a flash of his mother's face as the guards covered her broken form. The slash on her neck only going half way across her throat, instead of all the way across. She had begun to heal.

Alex felt anger burn through him. That last image, when combined with the others, he knew. He knew what his nightmares had been trying to tell him. The veil swirled around him, thick strands of power rained down on him, through him, his power to reason and think started to fade. Pain exploded through his body and mind, as he threw his head back and screamed out into the veil.

Mother!

36

KYLE

K yle had dressed impeccably; his target was in the court tonight. He could still feel the connection, that bond with his friends, their pain echoing through and multiplying his own. He heard in his mind voice the moment a part of Alex broke, heard him scream in anger and pain. Saw him kill in his mind's eye, like he was looking through a window but couldn't intervene. Kyle paused, his eyes closing, pain flashing across his face.

Ah, my brother, I wish I could take your place. Stay safe. Kyle sent his own mind voice out, but given how lost he knew Alex was, he doubted that he heard.

Kyle walked into the court, noting the various lords' and ladies' shocked expressions as they backed away, clearing a path for him. He spared them no attention, just stalked across the ballroom, even ignoring the looks from the King and William, their eyes widening as he grabbed a now-shaking Lord Vannen and threw him across the floor. Kyle stalked up to him like he was stalking prey.

"You are guilty of treason, Vannen. You are a member of the Killiam Order. The same order that tried to kill Prince Alexander, Lady Jessalan and me." Kyle didn't even bother to pull his weapon out; he knew he didn't need it. He grabbed the sobbing lord on either side of his head. Hauling him upright, he ignored the man's babbling and begging for forgiveness. "The same order behind the death of the Queen." With that final piece of information, he glanced up at the King and William; both nodded, their faces blank.

"Do it, Kyle, his life is forfeit for treason." The King's voice was cold.

Kyle snapped the quivering man's neck, not having to look to see the King's face had gone pale with anger. William tried to shield Elizabeth and Amelia.

There was a moment of silence in the court, then the shrieking and sobbing began as if someone had thrown a switch. Kyle turned and followed his own path back out of the ballroom, back toward the Complex of the Fourth.

No one moved to stop him as he transitioned between one step and the next to the Veiled World.

Kyle strode down the shadowed paths, not even trying to push down the bloodlust that had reared its ugly head. He let it roll through him, knowing he had a job to do. It didn't take him long to track down Baine. He'd done his homework and found out that the guard was on a day off and making his way into town with a full purse, likely to drink it all before returning to the palace. Kyle spotted his target close to the palace on a side trail, making his way into town. His eyes narrowed as Baine rode down the path toward town without a concern at all. That was about to end.

Kyle snarled. Drawing in the power, he slammed it into Baine as he'd learned to do, fighting the Sundered. At least the Sundered had a reason for what they did—they couldn't help the madness they had been driven to. This monster had had a choice in everything he'd done. Kyle dropped out of the Veiled World as his target went flying off his horse and slammed into a nearby tree. He paid his horse no attention as it reared and went running down the road. Kyle stalked over to the groaning man, yanking his head up by his hair and had the pleasure of seeing his eyes widen in fear, his hands raised to deflect the blade, his scream cut short as the sharp blade sliced through his neck.

Kyle dropped his head, stood looking down at what had once been a man who had caused him and his friends a great deal of pain. Ignoring the blood that was splattered all over him, dripping from his own face, he wiped his blade and disappeared once more into the veil.

K yle walked the veiled paths, the goal clear in his mind. While Alyssa was out of his mind and dead, the negative impulses she'd forced on him had persisted. Not that he'd confessed that secret to Alex or Jess; both had their own issues and problems right now. He knew even though they hadn't confided in him either that they too were struggling with the Taint, being Sundered, or worse than they'd dreamed.

Kyle paused, waiting in that place between worlds near the room that was his target, shaking off the sorrow and fear that threatened to swallow him. He stepped through, appearing in the room.

"Welcome, Kyle, I wasn't sure if you would come." The Skull Lord lounged in his chair, not showing the slightest concern that Kyle had appeared in his quarters. It almost looked as if he had been expecting Kyle to come to him.

Kyle licked his lips, nervous about what he would do, yet he knew there was no other way forward. "I heard what you said to Alex about being able to help those going through transition if it wasn't too late. Can you stop me from killing my friends?"

Kyle expected harsh laughter, triumph, scorn, yet he saw none of that. He stood his ground, stopping his first impulse to grab a weapon as the Skull Lord stood and approached him.

"With your permission, Kyle?" The Skull Lord's eyes maintained contact with his own, waiting.

Kyle took a shuddering breath and nodded. "Yes, My Lord."

A smile touched the Skull Lord's lips. He placed his hands on Kyle's temples.

Relax, Kyle, let me see the damage that has been done. The Skull Lord's tone was gentle, which surprised Kyle.

Taking a shuddering breath, Kyle tried to calm himself and lowered his barriers even though every instinct in him screamed against allowing the Skull Lord entry to his head. Kyle wasn't sure if the almost delicate probing of his mind took hours or minutes, only that it seemed to take an eternity. Much to his astonishment, the Skull Lord withdrew and stepped back, regarding him.

"Yes, Kyle I can help you. I can stop you from killing your friends." Kyle felt himself slump with relief, falling to his knees as emotion hit him. He bowed his head, groaning as he felt an assault of overwhelming emotions crash over him in one wave after another, as he had since he was drugged. Since he'd met Alyssa.

He shuddered, wondering what he was about to become, what the life of a Sundered Assassin would be like.

37

JESS

J ess travelled via the shadowed paths to a place she knew well yet hadn't paid a visit to for a long time. She was calm. Too calm. She contemplated as she walked, pausing at the home of her target. Knowing the house, Jess appeared in the Solar since she knew it wouldn't be used at this hour. She smiled bitterly, looking around the room that appeared like it had never changed.

Jess paused as she first heard Alex's cry, his pain, yet she remained calm even as she could hear Kyle. Her instinct was to go to him, to help and try to drag him back to sanity, yet she had her own job to do; he hadn't flinched from his. She wouldn't either. She waited a moment, knowing Kyle was next. She felt and saw it as he stalked up to Lord Vannen. She didn't even flinch when Kyle snapped the man's neck, even remaining calm as he transitioned into the veil. She followed him as he stalked the man Baine and killed him with brutal efficiency.

The location he went to next gave her a brief pause and cracked her composure a little.

Kyle, what are you doing? No!

That last was screamed at her friend as it became clear what he would do, yet it was too late. He paid her no mind and then that spark that was Kyle disappeared from her own mind.

Jess walked out of the solar, allowing the veil to flow through her as she walked, not even trying to hide her presence in the house at this point. She knew there was no one near, not even a servant at this point. Her target would be in the sitting room, waiting for the appropriate time to appear for dinner. Even at home, everything had to run according to propriety. Pausing outside the door, she looked with her mind's eye, seeing only the one glowing pulse she knew signified a heartbeat inside the room. Glancing around her, she smiled, satisfied. As she had thought, the others in the house were getting ready for dinner. Jess walked into the room, closing the door, marvelling at how calm she still was. The occupant of the room gasped in shock, not expecting company at this hour, standing, a hand raised to her mouth.

"Why, Mother?"

Lady Barraclough's eyes widened. "I don't know what you mean. Jessalan, what ..."

Jess walked forward, disgusted, as her mother stumbled back from her approach, afraid. Jess cut her mother off as her back hit the wall behind her.

"Why were you involved with the Killiam Order?"

Her mother looked around as if she expected someone else to appear to save her, yet she'd trained her servants too well. She was alone in this room, as she always liked to be. Then her expression turned ugly as she spat her answer out.

"You're a monster, you and your friends—don't think we don't know the truth about you all. The Order will take all of you. You won't be so high and mighty then!" Lady Barraclough's voice had risen to a screech, her voice harsh, face screwed up into an ugly hate-filled mask.

Jess drew her blade, stepping in, and plunged it up through her mother's abdomen, watching as the tip of the blade pierced her heart. Her eyes dead, Jess shoved her mother back with one hand, watching as she crumpled to the floor.

"Goodbye, Mother." Jess dissipated into the Veiled World, leaving the crumpled, lifeless body of the woman who had been her mother on the floor in an expanding pool of her own blood.

Jess felt the anger she expected to feel rolling through her, consuming her, and considered the emotion. It was different. She was different in multiple ways, hard to put a finger on.

As she contemplated what had changed, the surrounding veil transformed into a forest. She wasn't thinking about it or willing it to occur. It was just happening. The change sweeping out from where she stood in a rolling wave changed the place she stood in. Trees, rocks, flowers, vines and a tranquil pool of water were being fed by a small stream. Calming.

Jess moved to one side and sat on a fallen log, overgrown with moss. It looked like it was from the deepest jungle where few humans had encroached, yet she knew it hadn't been there moments before until she'd sat.

Jess turned her thoughts inwards and examined herself. She could feel the anger she had felt moments before on discovering the deception her uncle and the others had been playing on her. If she thought about it too much, that anger threatened to rise once more and consume her. She could kill, she'd been trained to be a very effective killer her whole existence. Yet she could push it aside, ignore it. After a moment more in consideration, she did just that. It would be easy to let the rage consume her and just kill without thought, but perhaps things were not productive that way.

Her mind flitted onto Kyle, her brother, and sadness almost threatened to overwhelm her. He had sunk, succumbed to the lure of killing that Alyssa had instilled in him. She knew he would have been capable of pushing aside that desire, just as she was. Jess' eyes widened, startled at the thought that had occurred to her.

He'd chosen not to. Kyle had chosen to put himself on the path he was on. Her mind was unsettled by the thought and ran in circles, waves of sadness and anger washed through her.

Jess screamed as the rage, sadness, pain and loss consumed her. Once more, the whispering across the veil paused, almost like they were waiting to see which way she would go.

Jess forced down the emotions that threatened to overwhelm her and settled once more. She found that she was standing in the middle of the clearing, her blades in hand, raised, ready to kill. Shaken, since she didn't remember standing or drawing her blades or what she had intended to kill, Jess sheathed her blades, allowing the calmness to wash over her. Another part of her brain analysed the effect. It wasn't just calmness. She was dispassionate, calculating. She could kill or not kill as she chose.

Jess threw her head back and laughter erupted, ringing through the small haven she'd created for herself. Alex, this is what Alex had done. The path through the madness he had taken. That he'd chosen to take. Once again, Jess didn't know why or how he'd come to that moment. In one way she could see why, it was easier than dealing with all the new and raw, overpowering emotions. Yet Jess knew from what she had been going through that it was possible to exert control, to tread that path between, courting madness. Then there were those that were of the Sundered. The mad ones didn't choose a path. It was likely they didn't have enough knowledge to know there were options. They had likely just been overwhelmed with the power crashing over and through them, their minds breaking under the strain.

That was one problem with transition: it was a gradual change. At first you thought you were on top of it, that you could control it. Then you woke, and the world was crashing in on you.

Jess thought about where she belonged now. While it was a difficult decision to come to, she knew she could not go back to the palace at this point. She was too dangerous to all around her. At least until she learned control, and after her interactions with Damien, she knew she would. A path crystallised in her mind.

Kyle was keeping close to the world of the Sundered Lord, learning everything he could about them, she was certain of that now. There was more to Simon, he had the Taint, and yet Alex's memories from meeting him showed he was not mad not like the Sundered they had met and killed.

Alex was following the path of the broken, tracking and going after the Sundered ones. To kill them, she felt certain, but also to help them if he could, to discover why they were breaking in such numbers. Those poor souls who had been left to themselves with no training or understanding of who and what they were. Those who had sunk to madness. Those who had been deserted by their own kind and left to die or live as luck and chance would have it.

Jess considered her own path and concluded that with her brothers grasping the end of one path in this new world and seeking to unravel its inner workings, it was up to her to follow the only other path left. The Elder. They existed. And as she contemplated everything that had occurred she believed she knew where to start. Damien, there was more to him than she'd realised, of that she was now certain. If Damien wasn't one of the Elder, she was certain he knew where to find them. Those that controlled and had far more influence on the human world, which went on, oblivious that the other world existed.

Jess smiled cynically. Except the King. Jess knew the King and William must know much more about the world within their world than they had let on. Jess felt her mind settle as she came to her own decision. She stood and walked the path between the worlds, the glade in the forest she had created dissipating as she disappeared into the grey fog, obscuring her from any casual observers. Then she paused, her eyes narrowing as another thought occurred to her; sudden anger washed over her, only this time she didn't stop it.

Damn it, Uncle! You're not dead. You're not some otherworldly trainer from the veil. None of you are. You are all Kin.

Jess screamed her words out into the veil. She felt the veil quieten in response, the ever-present whispering pause as others like her and those further along their paths listened and took note before continuing with their various pursuits.

38

AMELIA

melia walked through the hallways of the Summer Palace, making her way to the Complex of the Fourth. Her dress trailed behind her, along with assorted guards and ladies who seemed to have become a permanent fixture since she'd been made the Consort Elect of the Fourth. She paid them no mind at all. She hadn't since Alex had disappeared. The ladies chatted; Amelia knew of that if only peripherally, though she didn't care enough to listen.

She was always watched, never truly alone. Her mind went back to the warning Kyle had given her about there being a price to pay for being in the inner circle of the Royal Family. She smiled a little bitterly as she realised that while at the time she hadn't understood the warning, now she did. It was a beautiful cage she lived in, gilded with gold and all the trappings, but it was still a cage. A part of her wished she'd listened to Kyle. The other part of her heart cried out. He was gone and she was lost, locked in a cage of her own devising.

The only solace she had was that at least in the Complex of the

Fourth she had some refuge from the rest of the court. She had to get there.

Breathing a sigh of relief, she raised her hand as she entered the Complex of the Fourth. The guards stepped into the path of the gaggle of ladies that had been following her, blocking their entry into the complex that had become her home. She could hear the disappointment as she left them behind, yet again. The doors closed behind her with a thump.

Amelia walked the familiar hallways into the garden, her pace measured. Turning her head, she murmured thanks and waved her hand at the guards. They stopped at the entrance as she bid them to. It was not like anyone could get to her here. It was a garden in the middle of the compound that few had access to. The garden was wild; Alex had liked it that way and ordered that it remain as it had been since he was a small boy. The trees were old; vines ran up the walls, garden beds were overgrown. Yet still, despite it all, she found it soothing. She could block out the guards on the walls and the entrance. All of them looking at her, watching her, looking for anyone else that might be after her. Their only goal was to keep her safe.

Amelia's careful, measured pace faltered as she came to the mausoleum at the centre of the garden. Four guards were standing to attention at each corner, facing outward, swords drawn, grasped in a double-handed grip, raised with the hilt across their faces, the tip planted in the ground.

Die, I deserve to die.

What have I done?

I'm damned, evil.

The sobs Amelia had been holding at bay escaped her as she

collapsed, skirts billowing around her, face in her hands as the insistent whispering voices filled her head.

Made in the USA
Middletown, DE
28 April 2021